Things We Need To Say

ALSO BY LINDA MIDDLETON

Things They Never Said
First Impressions
Things We Need To Say

Linda Middleton

things
we
need
to
say

Choc Lit
A JOFFE BOOKS COMPANY

Choc Lit, London
A Joffe Books company
www.choc-lit.com

First published in Great Britain in 2025

© Linda Middleton

Cover art by Jarmila Takač

ISBN: 978-1781899045

It's two years since Choc Lit published my first novel Things They Never Said *and I want to thank them for taking a chance on me. You have helped me to achieve a life's ambition.*

Thank you too, so much, to everyone who has read both my novels, and I hope you enjoy this third book just as much. If you have taken the time to write a review, I especially want to thank you as the reviews are so important in helping to make a book a success. It means so much to know that the words I have written have brought others enjoyment.

I also need to thank my family, who are so supportive, especially when I ignore them in favour of the people who live rent free in my head!

CHAPTER ONE

Jay finished arranging the devilled eggs on a silver platter so they could be taken out to the waiting guests. It felt strange to be back at Weatherton Grange, the home of Lord Henry Weatherton. He had last cooked here for the engagement party for Henry's daughter, Lucinda. Now they were celebrating the christening of her first child. But the place was locked in Jay's memory for other reasons. It had been the first event where he and Emma, who had then been a part-timer with the company, had worked together as a couple. The heady memory of that first flush of love filled him with longing. Eighteen months later, their affection had only grown, but their relationship had settled into something of a routine. They both had demanding jobs with unsocial hours, so time was definitely not their friend.

As though his thoughts had conjured her up, Emma walked through the kitchen door. Although she now worked as a trainee manager at a prestigious West End hotel, today she had offered to help out on her day off, as this was such an important event to Jay and Liz. As he watched her, Jay thought that her slim figure suited the black pencil skirt and fitted white shirt she wore, and, with her dark brown hair tied neatly at the nape of her neck, she was the epitome of efficiency. She might be dressed conservatively, but he still thought she looked hot. Emma never failed on that score.

Jay gestured towards the platter of eggs. 'These are ready to go out.' He tried and failed to focus on the food rather than the lurid thoughts about his girlfriend.

'Great,' she said. Instead of picking it up, she placed a hand gently on his arm. 'It takes me back, being here again.'

'I was just thinking the same.'

Emma grinned. 'When we first got together and couldn't keep our hands off each other?'

'Umm . . .' His face flushed, and not from the heat of the kitchen.

'We should try to make some more time to spend together and date like we used to.'

Jay leaned down to kiss her. 'We should. But between your shifts and my functions, it's not always easy.'

'I know.' She nodded. 'But promise me we'll try?'

'I promise.'

'Better get these out then.'

She looked at him lovingly, but something in her tone worried him. Did she not believe him? His last relationship had failed because he'd been too busy with work. He didn't want the same thing to happen with Emma. This time it wasn't just him who worked long hours, though. But then again, she was just starting out in her career and didn't have any control over the shifts she worked.

Not that he had much control over his time either. As a partner in an increasingly successful catering business, he was busy too. Jay loved working with his friend Liz, and enjoyed the variety of the work, but it wasn't his ultimate dream. He always hoped he'd be running his own restaurant with his name above the door by the age of thirty. He was turning twenty-nine on his next birthday and time was running out to reach that goal.

Jay shook his head as he began to assemble more hors d'oeuvres. All this wanting was getting him nowhere. He and Emma loved each other and they would be fine. He knew it.

* * *

Emma pinned a smile to her face as she handed out the platter of devilled eggs. Her cheeks ached with the constant effort. She'd always loved working in the hospitality industry, loved the sense of fulfilment from making someone's event perfect, of making them feel special. She'd worked hard on her degree, coming out with top grades, and had immediately secured a management position at the Rosemont Hotel. And that was where she had got stuck.

Of course she realised that advancement in her career would take time, but what she hadn't expected was her line manager, Heather. A woman who, for some unknown reason, seemed intent on making her working life a misery.

Emma shuddered as she remembered the humiliation she'd suffered the previous day in front of several members of staff. She was at a loss to know what she had done to deserve such treatment and she didn't know how much longer she could carry on like this. Every day she dreaded going into work, not knowing what would greet her when she got there. At least she had Jay, she thought, trying to console herself. They might be in a bit of a rut at the moment, which would take a lot of time and effort to get out of, but they would get through this. She knew they would.

* * *

'Liz! How lovely to see you again!' Lord Weatherton said, giving Liz a kiss on each cheek.

'It's always a pleasure to see you too,' she replied. She liked Lord Weatherton. For all his wealth and status, he was so down to earth and she loved his enthusiasm for both life and her food. She'd met him when she'd been catering at an open evening for a block of apartments that her now-husband, Alex, and his business partner, Tia McIntyre, had refurbished and were hoping to sell. From there, Lord Weatherton had asked her to cater for his daughter Lucinda's engagement party on his estate in Hampshire, which had been a huge success.

Lord Weatherton interrupted her thoughts. 'The food is as exquisite as usual.'

'I'm glad you're enjoying it.'

'How could I not? I'm not going to be able to eat for a week after today.'

Liz laughed. 'That's how it should be. And it's good to see Lucinda looking so happy.' She remembered the first time she'd met Lord Weatherton's daughter. To her surprise, Lucinda had had very little to do with the actual planning of her own engagement party — she'd left the details to her father's personal assistant, and on the day of the event itself she'd seemed rather aloof. But motherhood had changed her and today she'd greeted Liz like a long-lost friend, eager to show off her baby son, who was ensconced in a confection of vintage lace, a family heirloom. As Liz had gazed down on the chubby-cheeked, blue-eyed boy, she'd thought Lucinda had every reason to be proud. Her hand had involuntarily hovered on her own stomach, with a feeling of hope.

She hadn't told anyone yet, not even Alex, but she suspected she was pregnant. In the days leading up to the christening party she'd been run off her feet, and she wanted to keep her suspicions to herself until she knew for certain. She would do a test and, if it was positive, she'd share the news with Alex. She couldn't tell him before because she didn't want to build up his hopes. She needed to handle the situation sensitively.

Alex had lost his first wife to sepsis when she'd been carrying their baby. He'd always longed for another child, but because Liz had been severely anorexic as a teenager she'd been told it might be difficult for her to conceive. She needed to make sure her body wasn't playing tricks on her before she voiced her suspicions. Since her recovery, her periods had always been erratic, so, when she had missed her first and then her second, she hadn't paid it much attention. But recently she'd started to feel different and that had given her hope.

Tomorrow she had a day off. She would do a test and hopefully, by the evening, she and Alex would be celebrating.

As Lord Weatherton moved off to socialise, someone else approached. Someone Liz was much less willing to see. Susie, Jay's ex-girlfriend. The sight of her conjured up memories of the last time she'd been here. Memories she had pushed to the back of her mind. As much as she had tried to like Susie, they'd never got on. When Susie had been seeing Jay, she had always been suspicious of Liz and Jay's close friendship, unable to believe it was purely platonic. To make matters worse she was also friends with Nikki, a woman Alex had been seeing before he and Liz had got together. It had been here, at the engagement party, that Susie had gleefully told her that Nikki and Alex were getting back together and Nikki was pregnant. Of course it had all been lies, but Liz hadn't known that then. It had been enough to split her and Alex up, as she hadn't wanted to stand in the way of him becoming a father, especially when she might not be able to have a child herself.

Liz pinned a smile on her face. Susie might be the last person she wanted to speak to, but Liz was here as a professional.

'Liz! How lovely to see you!' To her surprise, Susie wrapped her arms around her in a hug. Liz remained stiff in shock and was glad that the embrace only lasted for a second until Susie stepped back, looking at her intently.

'How are you? You look well.'

'I'm fine, thanks, and you?'

'Oh, yes. Just wonderful. I'm getting so many commissions at the moment I'm even having to turn them down.'

'Well, that's good.'

'Yes. And Nikki's in the same boat. She's got such a successful career over in New York.'

So that was the reason for this effusive welcome — Susie wanted to rub Nikki in her face. Again. Only it wasn't going to work. By rights Liz should hate Nikki, but, when Nikki had eventually confessed to her lie, she'd realised that her behaviour had come from a place of severe insecurity. Both Susie and Nikki were models and, after the truth had been revealed, Nikki had moved to New York, where her career had really taken off. Liz was genuinely pleased that she had found happiness and even more pleased she was living on another continent.

'Yes, I'd heard. I'm very happy for her.'

'Are you?' Susie frowned.

'Of course I am. I don't like what she did to Alex and me, or tried to do, but she was very unhappy and I'm glad that life is going well for her now.'

'Oh, right, okay.' Susie's frown deepened as though she couldn't understand.

'Well, Susie, it's lovely to see you, but . . .'

'Actually, I was wondering . . .' Susie paused. 'Are you and Jay still working together?'

'He's my business partner, yes.'

'And is he here today?'

'Yes, working hard in the kitchen.'

'Perhaps I could go and see him?'

Liz stayed Susie with a hand on her arm. 'I don't think that's a good idea. You can see how many people we're catering for and you know what a perfectionist Jay is, so I think it would be better not to disturb him.'

'Yes, I can see that but—'

'Tell you what.' Liz interrupted her. 'Why don't I let him know you're here and then if he has a moment he can come and see you?'

'Oh, yes, that would be good.'

* * *

Emma watched as Susie approached Liz and flung her arms around her as though they were long-lost friends. Her stomach

6

churned at the sight of Susie and she moved a little closer so that she was in hearing distance of their conversation. She'd always been nervous of the woman. And even though Susie had been the one to end her and Jay's relationship, Emma still saw her as a danger as she had witnessed how heartbroken Jay had been when Susie had cheated and dumped him. He had been so in love with her and who could blame him? Susie was perfect. Tall, exquisite bone structure and long dark hair that hung down her back like a shining curtain.

As much as Emma wanted to get away and not listen in, she couldn't help herself. She had to know what Susie wanted. She gasped as she heard the other woman mention Jay and that she wanted to see him. How would Jay react to that? As a five-foot-four Plain Jane, Emma knew she was no competition for the glamorous model, and that was without the fact that she'd always wondered, deep down, if she was Jay's rebound relationship. Yes, they had been going out for eighteen months now and he told her he loved her, but, if Susie offered herself to Jay on a plate, Emma genuinely didn't know who he would choose. The last thing she felt she could cope with right now was losing Jay.

* * *

As Liz broke away from Susie, she spotted Emma handing out the canapés. Although Emma was smiling, Liz could tell worry lurked beneath. Had she seen Susie? And worse, had she overheard their conversation? Liz headed over to her, took the nearly empty silver platter and handed it to another passing server.

'Can you take this back to the kitchen, please?'

Emma looked startled. 'Liz? Is everything okay?'

'That's what I was about to ask you.'

'Everything's fine,' Emma said. But Liz could see that she was blinking back tears.

'Did you see Susie?'

Emma nodded.

'And did you hear what she said?'

'Yes,' Emma whispered.

'Let's go somewhere a little quieter.' Liz led Emma out of the main ballroom and into the study, where Lord Weatherton had let them store their belongings. When they'd catered for Lucinda's engagement party, it had been summer and the theme had been an Edwardian garden-party. But as it was now the middle of February, they'd been given the run of the ground floor for the event, and Liz was glad there was somewhere quiet they could go. Emma sat down on one of the comfortable Chesterfield sofas.

'Just because Susie wants to see Jay doesn't mean he'd be interested in her.'

'Why not? She's gorgeous.'

'So are you.'

Emma laughed, but it lacked warmth. 'Not compared to a model.'

'I used to think that when Nikki was around. But it's not all about looks. It's how you are together. Susie always wanted to have things her way, just like Nikki, but that's not how successful relationships work. That's not how you and Jay work.'

'He was in love with her once.'

'He was infatuated with her. But they weren't compatible — not like you and him. He can see that now. He'd never go back to her.'

'Wouldn't he?'

'No! Of course he wouldn't. Susie's a fake and you're the genuine article.'

'You said you'd tell him she was here.'

'I only said that to stop her from going into the kitchen. There's no way I'm telling him.'

'Why not?' Emma asked.

'Why would I? He doesn't need Susie in his life again.'

'But surely that's his decision to make? And if he does choose her, at least I'll know one way or another.'

'Oh, Em. He's not going to choose her.'

'Then there's no harm in telling him, is there?'

'If that's what you want.'

Emma nodded. 'I do.'

'Okay, I will. If only to prove to you that it's *you* he wants. But, Emma, I have to ask. Is everything okay between you two? It's not like you to have these doubts.'

Emma sighed. 'Oh, I don't know. My head's a mess. We are in a rut — we're both so busy that we barely see each other. But I think we can work it out. Or at least we could if there's no one else to put a spanner in the works.'

'We have been really busy. Maybe he's been working too hard.' Liz felt a pang of guilt. 'Perhaps I'll suggest he takes some holiday. Would that help?'

'That would be lovely, but I've no chance of getting any time off work.'

'How is the job going?' Liz asked.

'That's the other problem. Work is just awful.' And to Liz's surprise, Emma burst into tears.

CHAPTER TWO

Instinctively Liz put her arms around her friend and hugged her.
'Tell me what's the matter.' She reached for the tissue box
on the ornate coffee table and handed it to Emma.

'It's my line manager. She's making my life hell. Nothing
I ever do is right and she's constantly pulling me up in front
of everyone. Yesterday she asked me to go and see Chef about
an amendment to a function tomorrow, but when I got to the
kitchen he'd nipped out. One of the other chefs told me he'd
only be a minute so I decided to wait. We were chatting away
when Heather barged into the kitchen. She gave me a dress-
ing-down in front of all the other staff, shouting that I was
useless and incompetent. She literally snatched the paperwork
out of my hands and stomped off to find Chef herself. I was
so embarrassed!'

'I can imagine.' Liz sympathised. She was familiar with
workplace bullying. Both she and Jay had been bullied by the
same chef, Louis Garcia, when they'd worked at the Michelin-
starred restaurant La Emporium. 'And what do the other staff
say about it?'

'I don't really know the other staff. Certainly not enough
to talk to them about this.'

10

Liz remembered all too vividly how Louis had made her feel. How anxious she'd become, questioning everything she did so that her confidence had quickly diminished and she'd started making real mistakes he could pick on. It had frightened her so much she had feared she'd relapse into anorexia.

'I do understand how you feel, but you can't let it go on. You'll make yourself ill. You either have to go over her head and make a complaint, or get to the root cause of the bullying.'

Emma frowned. 'I daren't go over her head. You know what the industry is like. It'd probably make things even worse.'

'You might be right there. I do think things are slowly changing and management have a responsibility to take any allegations seriously, but you still have to work with the woman. She has to be held accountable for what's she's doing, though, and, if you don't feel that you can make a complaint, the only other way is to find out why she's picking on you.'

'I don't understand.'

'Bullies are often people who feel insecure about something, that's why they lash out. If you can get to the root of her problem, maybe you can make her to face up to it.' When Emma still looked confused, Liz continued. 'Look, I realise that the onus shouldn't be on you to find out what's wrong with her, but if you can't call her out, this might be the only way to make it stop. Kill her with kindness and get her to confide in you. Then she'll see you as her ally and not her enemy.'

Emma nodded slowly. 'I have no idea how I'd do that. She's about as friendly as a rattlesnake. But it's worth a try, I suppose. Things can't get any worse than they already are.' She scrubbed at her eyes. 'I must look a state and we've been gone for ages. We should get back.'

Liz looked at her watch and gasped. It was nearly time to get everyone sitting down. 'Yes, we should. There's a cloakroom just down the hall if you want to wash your face. I'll go and see Jay.'

'Thanks, Liz. Not an ideal time for me to have a meltdown, I know.'

11

'There's never a good time, but I'm always here to listen.'

'You're a good friend. But how are you? Working here must bring back memories.'

Liz thought back to the engagement party, which had ended with a phone call from her sister telling her that their father had been in a terrible car crash in Cheshire. Sadly, after weeks in a coma, he had died.

Liz nodded and fought back her own tears. 'It has brought back memories, but I'm trying not to dwell on them. I have so much in my life to be grateful for, even though I still miss him and think about him every day.'

'I'm sure you do.' Emma gave her friend a big hug before going to repair her face.

* * *

Jay wondered where Liz had got to. He was conscious that time was slipping by and they needed to get the starters out. The last of the canapés were being taken out of the kitchen when Lord Weatherton ambled in. Jay groaned inwardly. As much as he liked the man, he didn't have the time to talk to him right now. But Lord Weatherton was the client, so Jay pinned a smile on his face. 'Lord Weatherton, how nice to see you. I hope everything is to your satisfaction so far?'

Lord Weatherton beamed and his chubby face lit up. 'Indeed it is — the food is excellent as usual. I was just coming to see how things were going.'

'All good,' Jay replied. 'The last of the canapés are just going out and then we'll be ready for everyone to take their seats.'

Lord Weatherton looked around the kitchen. 'That's good, that's good.'

Jay suspected he'd come in here looking for any titbits. Liz had warned him that Henry liked to sample the food personally. He quickly called one of the servers back. 'While you're here, Lord Weatherton, would you like to sample some of these aigrettes? They haven't been out before, so you won't have tasted them.'

'Oh, yes, delightful. And, please, call me Henry. Lord Weatherton is such a mouthful.' His eyes roved over the silver platter as it was put down in front of him. 'They look a bit like profiteroles.'

'They do. They're made from a savoury choux pastry with cheese, which is deep-fried, and inside they are filled with a variety of fillings. We have hummus, tzatziki and taramasalata.'

'Oh, delicious,' Lord Weatherton said between mouthfuls. 'What a clever idea. Liz's dishes are always so creative — and of course she employs the perfect chefs to execute her ideas.'

Jay cleared his throat. This was what he was met with all the time — just being seen as one of Liz's members of staff.

'Actually, Lord Weatherton, Henry, I'm not her chef. I'm her business partner.'

Lord Weatherton's eyes widened. 'Oh, really, I didn't know. I thought Liz always flew solo.'

'She did.' Jay smiled. 'Until your daughter's engagement party, which really put her on the map. So much so that she asked me to come into partnership with her. We'd been friends for years before that and we work really well together. In fact, the aigrettes were my idea.'

'Excellent choice,' Lord Weatherton said. 'And I'm very pleased for you both. This little business seems to be going from strength to strength. I always feel at ease when I attend any event that Liz is involved with — it's guaranteed that the food will be out of this world.'

'Well, thank you,' Jay replied. 'That's good to hear.'

The door to the kitchen swung open and Liz came bustling in, much to Jay's relief. If they didn't get a move on soon, the main course would be spoiled.

'Henry, this is where I find you. Skulking in the kitchen again!' Liz said as she approached them.

Lord Weatherton chuckled. 'Ah, my dear Liz, yes, guilty as charged. I just can't help myself.'

Liz smiled. 'Oh, Henry, you really are a delight, but we need to get everyone settled down in the ballroom. Then you'll get to taste some more.'

'Excellent,' Lord Weatherton replied. 'Let's get this show on the road then.'

As Liz ushered Lord Weatherton out of the kitchen, she turned to look at Jay. He mouthed, 'Five minutes'. She nodded and he went to get the trays of smoked-salmon terrine and sea-trout mousse from the fridge, relieved to be able to get back on track.

* * *

Jay was just cleaning down after sending the dessert out — a trio of chocolate tartlets, panna cotta and cheesecake, which was a staple on their function menu — when the door to the kitchen was pushed open. Expecting to see either Liz, Emma or one of the servers, he gasped in surprise as Susie, his ex-girlfriend, walked into the kitchen. For a moment he was speechless. What on earth was she doing here? Whenever he'd seen her in the past he had often felt a jolt of electricity as she'd walked into a room, but today he was pleasantly surprised to feel nothing except wariness as she came towards him.

'What's up, Jay? Cat got your tongue?' Susie said, with a sultry smile that had always won him round in the past.

'Just surprised, that's all,' he said, finding his voice. 'What are you doing here?'

'I'm one of Lucinda's friends. Of course I'd be invited to the christening of her first child.'

'No, I mean, what are you doing in my kitchen?'

'I think you'll find it's Lord Weatherton's kitchen.'

'You know what I mean.'

'Of course I do.' She came closer, close enough that he could smell her perfume. Something heavy and pungent that

14

he took an instant dislike to. Emma's perfume was light and floral, and, he realised, was much more appealing. 'I heard you were working today, so I thought I'd come to say hello.' She put a hand on his arm, her long red fingernails in sharp contrast to his white chef's jacket. He fought the urge to tear his arm away. That would look like she was having an effect on him. That he was still emotionally engaged.

'Well, it's nice to see you, but I am rather busy and I don't really think we have anything to say to each other, do you?'

'Oh, Jay, don't be like that.' She leaned in closer. 'I've been thinking a lot about us recently. About how good we used to be together.'

'We were a disaster, Susie, or at least that's the way I remember it.'

'Oh, you're being too harsh. But, yes, I admit, we did get things wrong then. But we've both moved on and I was wondering if things might be better second time around?'

He laughed. 'I don't think so, Susie. But you are right about one thing. We have moved on. Or at least I have. I'm with Emma now and nothing would tempt me to come back to you.'

'What, your plain little waitress? You're telling me you prefer her over me?'

'Yes, I am,' he said, finally pulling his arm away from her. 'So if you don't mind, I'd like it if you'd leave my — this kitchen.'

'Well, if that's your attitude then I'm better off without you,' she said as she stalked back across the kitchen.

Jay breathed a sigh of relief as he went back to clearing up the kitchen. To see Susie and feel nothing had finally laid a ghost to rest. And she was wrong. It was he who was better off without her.

* * *

That evening, Jay and Emma lay next to each other on the sofa with the remains of a Chinese takeaway on the table in front of

15

them and some mindless television on in the background. All night Emma had been trying to put thoughts of Susie and Jay together to the back of her mind. After the desserts had been served, she'd gone back to the kitchen, to make the coffee for the final stage of the event. She'd just opened the door when she'd seen Susie in the kitchen, standing so close to Jay, her hand on his arm. Assuming that Liz had told Jay Susie wanted to see him, and he'd agreed, Emma fled. Later, when she'd plucked up the courage to go back, Jay was alone. He hadn't mentioned Susie's visit, and had been silent about it all night. Emma hadn't the courage to ask him either, imagining that if she did he'd tell he was going back to his ex-girlfriend.

'You're quiet tonight,' Jay said after they had sat in silence for a while.

'I'm just tired,' she replied.

'I know what you mean. Finally we get an evening off together and look what we're doing with it — slouching on the sofa. Back in the day, an evening off would involve drinking and dancing, not behaving like two old fogies.'

'I think we deserve to put our feet up after the day we've had,' Emma said. 'And besides, I'd rather be snuggling on the sofa with you than in some noisy club.'

Jay put his arm around her and squeezed her gently. 'Would you?'

'Of course I would. Why do you ask?'

'I just worry sometimes. You're only twenty-two, you should be out enjoying yourself. I know I was when I was your age, and I fear that I'm holding you back because I'm over that now. These days I prefer a quieter life, but is that enough for you? You said yourself we're in a bit of rut.'

Emma had never been a party girl — she too had always preferred a quieter life and she thought Jay knew that. What she'd tried to explain earlier was that they didn't see each other often enough. Now, though, his words made her wonder if this was his exit speech. Was he going to try to convince her that she didn't want to be with him, rather than the other way around?

Jay continued when she didn't answer. 'I'm right, aren't I?'

She decided to bite the bullet. 'No. Actually I was thinking about something else. I saw Susie at the christening today. Did you know she was there?' She wondered if he would confess about being with her in the kitchen.

'Yes, Liz told me. And then Susie herself came to see me.'

'Did you tell Liz you wanted to see her?'

'I didn't but she came into the kitchen anyway. So typical of Susie, only ever thinking about what she wants.'

'And what does she want? To get back with you?'

'Yes. She said it would be better second time around.'

'And your reply was?' Emma held her breath.

'I told her we were in the past.' Emma let out her breath in relief. He didn't want Susie after all. She waited for him to say it was her he wanted to be with, but instead he continued. 'Susie and I were a definite train-wreck and nothing would convince me to go back there.'

'Well, that's good to hear,' she said. But once again she felt that tears weren't very far away. What was wrong with her today? She was an emotional wreck. She should be pleased that Jay hadn't wanted to get back with Susie, whatever the reason.

'Going back to what we were talking about,' he said, pushing the Susie issue aside as though it wasn't important. 'What are we going to do to make our life more exciting?'

Emma's head was spinning at the sudden change in conversation. She wanted to delve deeper into why Jay didn't want Susie, but he'd obviously closed down that conversation. She decided to follow his lead.

'I know it's often difficult to get time off together, but, when we do, maybe we should plan to make the most of it?'

'What? Like date nights?'

'Yes, something like that.'

He grinned. 'I like the sound of that.' He paused. 'As long as that's not too staid for you?'

'Of course it's not. You know I've never been much of a party girl. And I really don't see our age difference as a problem. Its only eight years.'

'Um maybe.'

'You don't sound convinced. Is it my age that bothers you more than yours? Am I too young for you?'

'No!' He sat up suddenly on the sofa and gathered her in his arms, kissing her gently. When he pulled away he said, 'It's my age that bothers me. I'm nearly thirty and I don't feel like I've achieved half of what I wanted to by this age.'

'You're a partner in a successful business — I'd say that's quite an achievement.'

'It still feels more like Liz's business than mine, though. Well, let's face it, it *is* her business, whatever my contribution.'

'But it wouldn't be as successful without you.'

'Yes, I know that but . . .' He paused. 'Take today for instance. Lord Weatherton came into the kitchen and assumed I was Liz's chef. An employee. It really gets to me. I want to develop my own reputation.'

'Have you told Liz that?'

'No. I don't know how to approach her about it. Or what she could even do if I did.'

Emma was surprised by the look of sadness on his face. 'If I know Liz, she'd want you to be upfront with her. She can't deal with something she doesn't know anything about and she wouldn't want you to be unhappy. You're friends as well as business partners.'

Jay sighed. 'That's what I'm worried about. I don't want to lose our friendship.'

'You're more likely to do that if you keep things from her. So what are you saying? Do you want to wind up the partnership?'

'Not exactly, no. Not yet, at least.' He paused. 'You know I've always wanted to own my own restaurant.'

'Yes, you used to talk about that a lot.'

'It just seems so unattainable so I've stopped talking about it.'

'Because you haven't got the money for it yet?'

'Exactly!'

'So you still need to work with Liz.'

'I do. And I love working with her. I just need to be able to do something for myself too.'

'Like what?'

'I don't know. I was thinking about entering some competitions.'

'What, like *MasterChef*?' Emma said with a laugh. She remembered Jay's old obsession with the television programme.

'No! I don't think I'm brave enough for that. Not sure I would want to be filmed either. But maybe get some experience in some smaller competitions?'

'I think it's a great idea,' Emma said, cuddling up to him again.

'You do? I'm worried I'll need to take time out of the business and that Liz will have to take everything on herself. And what about us? It would mean spending even less time together.'

'But if you're happier, then maybe we will be too. And I'm sure you can work it out with Liz. If you do well, it will be a great advertisement for the business.'

'I hadn't thought about it like that.'

'Then you should. We only have one chance at life. Speak to Liz and see what she says. You never know, she might even be able to help.'

'I will. But what about you? You haven't seemed very happy recently either. If it's not us, what is it?'

Emma sighed. 'It's work too.'

'Is Heather still giving you a hard time?'

She nodded and blinked back the tears as she remembered once again the humiliation of the day before. 'It's getting worse and I'm not sure how much longer I can carry on working with her. I dread going into work wondering what she's going to do next.' She told him about what Heather had done yesterday and how it had made her feel. Jay hugged her closer.

'No one deserves to be treated like that. I think you should make a complaint about her.'

'I know, but I'm worried it'll make it worse. I've only been there for five minutes. She's been there for years. I don't want to be seen as a troublemaker.'

'You have witnesses, though. That must count for something.'

'Maybe. But you know what this industry is like. You're expected to tough it out.'

He sighed. 'Yes, I do know what you mean. If you don't feel like you can make a complaint about her now, why don't you keep a diary?'

'A diary?'

'Yes. Write down every time she bullies you. That way, if she carries on and you feel you do need to make a complaint, you have the facts to back it up.'

'That's a good idea. Thanks, Jay. I always feel better when we share our problems.'

'Me too. Trouble is, we don't get enough time together usually to actually talk.'

'No, we don't. So let's see what we can do next week and plan our date night.'

'Sounds good.'

Jay yawned. 'I don't know about you, but I'm shattered. Fancy an early night?'

By the tone of his voice, Emma knew that he wasn't talking about just sleeping. She kissed him softly, glad that their relationship seemed to be back on track.

'Sounds good to me.'

CHAPTER THREE

'I'd like you to work in the restaurant today,' Heather said when Emma walked into their shared office the next morning. Emma hated the office. It was tiny, so their desks were practically on top of one another, which was hardly ideal when the woman opposite was intent on making her life a misery. 'We're two servers down so you need to fill the gap.'

'Of course,' Emma said. She tried to keep a smile on her face. She didn't want to rile Heather, even though a large part of her would like to confront her about the way she had spoken to her in front of the rest of the kitchen staff, and how Heather consistently used her to fill staff shortages without any attempt to give her any managerial training. But on the plus side, working in the restaurant meant that she wouldn't have to be in this office today.

'Did you enjoy your day off?' Heather asked, as though they were the best of friends. Heather might not like Emma, but she was always keen to find out what was going on in her private life. Despite her resolve to be nice to her line manager or, to use Liz's phrase, kill her with kindness, Emma couldn't resist the opportunity to put Heather's nose out of joint.

'Well, it wasn't really a day off. I was helping my boyfriend and his business partner out in Hampshire.'

'Hampshire? That sounds posh.'

'Yes, it was at Lord Weatherton's estate, actually. His grandson's christening.'

'You were moonlighting?' Heather asked, looking grim.

'Not moonlighting, no.' Emma panicked, wondering if the hotel frowned upon staff working elsewhere on their days off. She wished she'd kept her mouth shut. 'I was just helping Jay out.'

'I see,' Heather said. 'And it was a big event, was it?'

'About a hundred,' Emma replied. 'Just close friends and family. But they fitted easily into the ballroom.' She tried to sound as though this was a normal experience for her.

Heather's mouth twisted disapprovingly. 'Must be an impressive place.'

'Oh, it is. Before I graduated, we did Lucinda's engagement party — it was in *Hello!* magazine. It was in August, so we themed it on an Edwardian garden-party and held it outside. Now that really was out of this world.' Emma smiled inwardly at the look on Heather's face, which was nothing short of pure envy. 'Obviously that wasn't possible in February, but the ballroom itself is incredibly beautiful.'

'It must be nice to have such important contacts.'

'It's nice to see how the other half live, I must admit,' Emma said smoothly. 'But it's just as satisfying working at the Rosemont, so I'd better report for duty.'

* * *

The restaurant was fully booked over lunchtime and Emma was rushed off her feet. She got on well with the restaurant manager, Paul, though, and it was a relief to be working with someone who appreciated her.

'It was good of you to offer to fill in while I'm short-staffed,' Paul said, during a lull in service.

'I didn't exactly offer,' Emma said. 'Heather told me this was where I would be working today, but at least I enjoy it better than some of the other jobs she gives me.'

'Really?'

Emma nodded. 'Last week I was cleaning rooms, and the week before that I was an honorary kitchen porter.'

'And there was me thinking you were on the management trainee programme.'

Emma shrugged and tried to look as though she didn't mind. 'At least I'm learning from the ground up. And they say a good manager should never ask someone to do something they wouldn't be prepared to do themselves.'

'So what does that make Heather then?' he asked. 'She'd never lower herself enough to wash dishes or clean rooms.'

'I couldn't say.' Emma didn't want to get sucked into bad-mouthing Heather. Paul seemed lovely, but she knew he was a bit of a gossip and she didn't want a stray comment to get her in more trouble.

'If you ask me, she's jealous,' Paul said after a pause.

'What has she got to be jealous of?'

'You. You're young, intelligent and you're certainly a hard worker. You have your whole career in front of you. But Heather, well, she's in her forties, she's been in her current position for ages now, and I can't ever see her getting any further. There's a lot for her to be jealous about. And she has form. She's always hardest on the young female trainee managers who are sent her way.'

That piqued Emma's curiosity. 'Have there been a few, then?'

'Several. None of them lasted more than six months, so you're in good company.'

'Well, I'm not thinking about leaving,' Emma said.

'That's good to hear. And although I don't think you should be serving in the restaurant, I'm very glad for your help. You do a cracking job.'

23

'I'm glad you think so.' Emma smiled at Paul before she went to clear a table.

* * *

When Emma returned to the office at the end of service, Heather was at her desk, seemingly engrossed in paperwork. Emma thought about what Paul had said. Heather certainly wasn't the kind of manager who led from the front — the management style she so admired in Liz. Thinking of her friend's words from yesterday, Emma cleared her throat and said, 'Heather, what time do you finish your shift?'

Heather turned to her and frowned. 'In about half an hour. Why?'

Emma steeled herself. 'I was just wondering if you fancied going for a drink when we finish. I should be done by then too.'

'A drink?' Heather asked sharply. 'With you?'

'Yes. Why not?' Emma tried hard to ignore her boss's horrified expression. 'I thought it might be nice for us to get to know each other a bit better. Away from the hotel.' When Heather continued to stare at her, Emma hastily added, 'But I should've realised it'd be far too short notice for you. I'm sure you have a busy life and much better things to do than go for a drink with me.'

Heather stood up. 'Well, yes, I do have plans. I've got a few things to finish off, but I've done the management rotas for next week. Can you send them out on the WhatsApp group?'

'Of course.'

When Heather had left, Emma sat down at her desk feeling deflated. She should have realised it would take more than a simple offer of a drink to warm the Arctic ice in Heather's veins. But she'd made a start. She'd just have to carry on with a dripping-tap campaign. Emma opened up her laptop and clicked into the rotas folder. When she looked at her own name, she saw that Heather had put her on five lates and two overnights in the hotel for the next week. She sighed. She'd just have to hope that Jay was free during the day sometimes or she'd never get to see him. There was some light in the shade, though, she thought, as she looked at the rest of the rota. At least Heather had put herself down for days so, despite an overlap in the middle, Emma wouldn't have to see her that much. It would give her time to work on a better plan than just asking her to go out for a drink.

* * *

Liz's hands shook as she removed the packaging from the pregnancy test. She held it in front of her and stared at it for a few moments. What this little plastic stick would tell her could alter her life for ever. *Was she ready for this? Ready to grow a life inside her, and then care for and nurture it for the rest of her own life?* She shook her head at her silly questions. If she was pregnant there'd be no choice. Best just to get on and do the test.

As she waited for the result, she wondered how she would feel if it was negative. Sad was the answer. For both her and Alex. The thought of holding a baby in her arms filled her heart with joy. She just hoped she was up to the job. Steeling herself, she looked back to the test. Two blue lines. She was pregnant.

Liz grinned, contemplating how she would break the news to Alex. She was sure he'd be overjoyed, but she suspected it would also stir up past emotions in him. She paced the flat, unable to sit still. She was constantly getting to her feet to tidy things that didn't need tidying. When she was stressed her normal coping mechanism was to go for a run, but she didn't feel like doing that today. Rationally she knew it wouldn't harm the baby — in fact it would probably do them both good. It just didn't feel like the right thing to do.

She forced herself to sit down, switch on her laptop and look at the bookings they had coming up over the next few weeks. She'd told herself she wasn't going to do this today, that she was going to have a complete day off from work, but, apart from running, work was the other thing that settled her mind. But even that didn't help. Instead she opened up a browser and clicked on the Rightmove website. She and Alex had been talking about moving from their city apartment, which used to be just his before she'd moved in, and buying a house of their own. Their current apartment overlooked the River Thames and was as luxurious as anything could possibly be, but it had never really felt like home. Tia McIntyre, Alex's business partner who was an interior designer, had been responsible for its decoration, and, while it was exquisite, to Liz it felt like living in a hotel. A new house, which they could decorate and furnish together, was just what they needed. But she was getting ahead of herself. They hadn't even found a suitable property yet and there had been no alerts from the website recently, so she knew that there was nothing new on the market. Now she was pregnant, though, the timescale of finding somewhere felt more pressing. She wanted to be in and settled before the baby was born. Liz started a fresh search, wondering if her criteria had changed since she'd done the test. One thing was for sure — having a garden was non-negotiable now.

Liz was so lost in her search that she jumped when Alex came through the front door. She hastily closed down the screen of the laptop.

He smiled at her. 'What's up? Caught you looking at your property porn again?'

'Guilty as charged.' She laughed nervously. Liz's desire to move was stronger than his, but she was sure he'd change his mind when she told him the news.

He put his briefcase down, strode over to her and pulled her into his arms. 'I've told you, you don't need to stress about it. We'll find the right place eventually.'

She gently pulled away from him and said softly, 'I think you'll find that we have a tighter timescale than eventually.'

He frowned. 'Why?'

She put her hand to his face and looked into his eyes. 'I know it wasn't planned, but I'm pregnant, Alex.'

He pulled away from her and stood back abruptly. Confusion was written all over his face. 'But I thought you couldn't . . .'

'The doctors told me it was unlikely. But they were obviously wrong.' She reached across the coffee table to where she'd placed the test and handed it to him. 'See.'

He looked incredulously at it and then back at her. 'Oh, Liz! I can't believe it. But are you sure? Have you done more than one test?'

'I don't need to,' she said, smiling at him. 'I've been feeling different for a while now, but the test has confirmed it.'

'But why didn't you say anything? Why didn't you tell me?'

'I didn't want to build your hopes up before it was definite.'

'Liz, this is amazing!' He plonked himself down on the sofa and drew her to him.

'I wasn't sure how to tell you. I realise this is going to bring back a lot of memories for you and I want you to know that I'm here for you, if you ever need to talk.'

'Yes, it does bring back memories,' he said softly. Then his face brightened. 'But this is our time now. I'll never forget the past, but I won't let it get in the way of our future.'

She put her arms around him. She was grateful that he was so strong. Liz knew he would have fears that this would all go wrong as it had last time, and that they'd both have to work hard to overcome them. But they could do it. Together.

'So have you been to the doctor yet?'

She laughed. 'Give me a chance — I only did the test today. But I'll make an appointment tomorrow morning.'

'Good,' he said. 'And how far along do you think you are?'

'About seven weeks, I think.'

He stared at her as though he had never seen her before. 'Wow! It hasn't sunk in yet.'

'It takes some getting used to. I've been jittery since I did the test.'

'You're going to have to start taking it a lot easier from now on.'

'Alex . . .' She put her hand on his arm to warn him not to get too carried away. 'I'm pregnant, not ill. I know you want the best for me, and why, but you have to let me decide for myself what that is. In return, I promise you, I'll do everything I can to protect this baby.'

He nodded. 'All right. But you know I *am* going to be overprotective, so you have to cut me some slack.'

She laughed. 'Yes, I will, but I'll tell you if you're being too much, okay?'

Alex grinned. 'Okay,' he replied. 'When do we tell people?'

'I'd rather keep it just between us until I'm a bit further along if that's all right with you?'

'Yes. Very sensible.' And then he added quietly, 'Just in case.'

She squeezed his hand and whispered, 'Just in case.'

CHAPTER FOUR

'You look troubled,' Liz said when she met Jay in the function room of Diva's the next day. Eighteen months ago, Alex, Tia McIntyre and chef Roberto Bianchi, who already owned La Emporium, a Michelin-starred restaurant, had gone into business to purchase and run the three-storey Diva's. The ground floor was a dedicated restaurant, with a bar and seating area on the middle floor. Liz and Jay currently catered for functions on the third floor, in addition to any other private functions that they carried out in people's homes.

Jay ran a hand through his curly hair — a sure sign he was stressed. 'There's something I want to talk to you about.'

Liz made them both a drink and they sat down at the small table used for their planning sessions. When Jay didn't say anything, she offered up.

'Well, this obviously isn't going to be good news, so you might as well just come straight out with it.'

Jay cleared his throat. 'The thing is, Liz, you know how I love working with you . . . .'

'I'm sensing a but.'

He nodded. 'This has nothing to do with you, or the way we work together, but it still feels very much like *your* business. *Your* reputation and everything.'

'Oh! Jay, you know I don't think of it like that. You bring so much to the business and some of your dishes are inspired. I'd never have thought of putting them on the menu.'

'I know that, and, like I say, this is nothing to do with you or the way we work together, but I feel like I need to build my own reputation. Independent from you.'

She gasped. 'Oh.' This was the last thing she'd wanted to hear today. She'd woken up overjoyed at her secret and had come into work trying not to smile too much in case she gave herself away. 'You want to dissolve our partnership?'

'No!' It was Jay's turn to look shocked. 'No, I didn't mean it like that. Oh! I'm not explaining myself very well, am I?'

She shook her head. 'No, you're not. Just tell me straight.'

Jay sighed. 'You know it's always been my dream to own my own restaurant?'

'Of course. I thought that was a long way off, though.'

'It is. But when I am in the position to go ahead, I also want to have built up a reputation, so that people will invest in me.'

'So what are you saying?'

'I want to start entering competitions.'

'Competitions? Is that all?' Liz breathed a huge sigh of relief.

'It might not sound much to you, but I need to start somewhere.'

'No, don't get me wrong, I didn't mean to denigrate it, not by any means. I just thought you wanted out and it's a relief to know that you don't. I presume you're asking for a bit of time off as and when you're tied up elsewhere?'

'That's about the size of it, yes.'

'That sounds fair enough. I'm presuming you'll get some advance notice of when competitions start so that we can plan our bookings? And if there's any clashes, we can always employ more agency chefs.'

'Really? You're okay with it?'

'Of course I am. This is our business, Jay, so we need to make it work for both of us.'

'Oh, thank you, Liz. I was so worried about telling you. If it wasn't for Emma, I might have bottled it completely.'

'Oh, Jay! You daft thing!' She leaned over and gave him a hug. 'I know we're in business together, but, first and foremost, we're friends. You should be able to tell me anything. Besides, I might need you to return the favour soon so we can work things around each other.'

'Really? How come you might need time off?'

Liz took a sip of her drink, stalling. She'd nearly let the news about her pregnancy slip when it had been her idea to keep it quiet in the first place. 'Alex and I are thinking of moving. We haven't found anything yet, but we're looking at houses, so I might be a bit tied up with that in the future.'

'Oh, congratulations,' Jay replied. 'I know you've wanted to get a new place that you can put your own stamp on for a while now.' He paused and then asked, 'But will that mean you'll be selling our flat?'

Jay had taken over Liz's old flat when she'd moved in with Alex, and later Emma had moved in too. At the mention of buying a house, Jay looked so stricken that Liz felt the need to reassure him. 'Don't worry about that. I'm not looking at selling the flat — your home is safe.'

'Thank goodness for that.' Jay's smile returned to his face. 'I thought for a minute we were going to be homeless.'

'I wouldn't do that to you.'

'But don't you need the money to put into the new house?'

She shook her head. 'When Dad died, he left me and Mel quite a significant inheritance from when he sold the farm. It seems fitting to invest that money in the house, so that Dad can become part of my future.'

'That's a nice idea.'

Liz changed the subject; she always began to well up when she spoke about her dad. 'So, competitions. Do you have anything in mind?'

'Nothing so far. I wanted to clear it with you first.'

'Okay. As long as we give each other plenty of notice I'm sure we can work things out.'

'Thanks, Liz.'

'No problem.' She paused. 'I don't suppose you're thinking of entering *MasterChef*, then?'

Jay laughed. 'No, not yet anyway. That's what Emma asked. But I've never done a competition before, so I thought I might start smaller.'

'That does sound sensible. Although I'd say you'd be more than a match for most of the chefs I've seen on that programme.'

He blushed. 'Thanks Liz.'

'I'm imagining you'll need to start on building your repertoire. Let's have a look at the bookings we've got coming up and see if you can incorporate any of your ideas into the menus.'

* * *

Jay left Diva's feeling so much lighter than when he had walked in only a few hours earlier. The thought of telling Liz had been weighing on his mind, but Emma had been right — Liz had readily accepted his ambitions. He should have trusted in both of them before now, then he wouldn't have had to suffer so many sleepless nights. He whistled as he walked towards Tottenham Court Road Tube station. Liz had made a valid point, though — he did need to work on his repertoire. For years he'd worked at La Emporium cooking dishes inspired by Roberto and, although he had more creative input working for Liz, a lot of the dishes were designed according to either their clients' requirements or whether the dishes were suitable for mass catering. For the first time in a long time, he'd be creating the dishes he wanted to cook. The ability to experiment filled him with joy. He would have to go through all the classic techniques and make sure he'd know what to do in any given situation. Jay stepped up his pace. He couldn't wait to get home and start planning his future.

* * *

'He wants to do what?' Alex asked later that night.

'He wants to start entering competitions to build up his own reputation,' Liz replied calmly.

'That's going to take a lot of time and effort.'

'It will, but it's far better than I was expecting. At first, I thought he wanted to dissolve our partnership.'

'It's a shame about the timing, though. This is the last thing you need right now.'

Liz handed Alex a glass of wine and poured herself an apple juice.

'It's not great timing, and for a moment I was really tempted to tell Jay about the pregnancy.'

Alex looked horrified. 'But you didn't?'

'No, I didn't. We agreed not to say anything. Besides, it might make him feel guilty for wanting time off.'

'But how are you going to manage it?'

'We'll just take fewer bookings when he's not around. And for the time off I might need. Don't worry, we'll work it out between us. And it'll be a lot easier in a few weeks when I can tell him about the pregnancy.'

'As long as you don't overdo it by trying to do everything. I know what you're like.'

She kissed him on the lips. 'Don't worry, Alex, I have every intention of keeping this baby safe and that's more important than any function.'

Alex smiled. 'Things really are going to change for us, aren't they?'

'They certainly are.'

CHAPTER FIVE

Jay finished preparing the pigeon for the starter, then placed it on a baking sheet and slid it into the chiller. The tables had already been set out in preparation for the small function that evening and, later on, two of Liz's regular staff would come in to set everything up. He thought fondly of the time when Emma had still been a student and had been one of them. He remembered how excited he'd felt waiting for her to come into work. But now that she was qualified, he understood her need to gain more experience. He just wished she was working somewhere she was appreciated.

As tonight's function was for twenty people, Jay would be cooking with another part-timer to help out. Sometimes he missed the camaraderie of the restaurant kitchen and the thrill of a busy service. On a whim he decided to go downstairs to seek some company. Service would just about be over and, as some of the chefs had moved across from La Emporium when Diva's had opened, there was bound to be someone he could have a chat with.

To his surprise, Roberto the owner-chef was in the kitchen. It was rare to see him there these days — he usually left the day-to-day running to his new executive chef, Tom. Life had changed for Roberto when he'd had his first child, who was now sixteen months old, and he'd become determined to create a better work-life balance so that he didn't miss too much of his daughter growing up. Jay was a little envious. He'd love to buy a house, set up home and have a family himself, but that was way in the future. Right now, his career had to come first.

Roberto greeted him enthusiastically as he hovered by the entrance to the kitchen. 'Jay, how are you? Long time no see.' Roberto walked over and hugged him, giving him a hefty clap on the back.

'I'm good. And how about you? Is that daughter of yours keeping you in line?'

Roberto laughed. 'Oh, she certainly is. She definitely knows who's boss and it's not me or her mother.' He paused and then added, 'But I can scarcely remember a time when we didn't have her. It feels like she's been with us for ever.'

'I'm so happy for you, for you both.'

Since Jay had left La Emporium, he'd formed a relationship with his former boss that he'd never had before. When Jay had been Roberto's employee, Louis had been in charge and hadn't liked anyone other than himself getting too friendly with the chef. But Jay respected Roberto both as a man and as a chef, and was always ready to take any advice he had to give.

'And how are the functions going? I see you have a small party in tonight.'

'Yes, they're good. Steady. We've had a few big ones in recently.'

'Not as big as the christening you did the other day, though?'

Jay laughed. 'Nothing gets past you, does it, Roberto?'

'I might not be around as much as I used to be, but I like to keep my fingers in the pies — just to check they are hot enough.'

'You're a wise man, although Tom seems to have things under control.'

'Yes, he does.' Roberto glanced towards his executive chef, who was supervising the clean-down after the lunch-time service. Soon all the chefs would get something to eat, before starting on the prep for the evening service. Life in the kitchen was certainly busy. 'And La Emp is doing well too, so I'm a very happy man. I do like to pop in when they're least expecting it, just to keep them on their toes.'

'And I bet you send your spies in incognito from time to time too.'

Roberto chuckled. 'Ah, you know me too well. Have you got time for a coffee?'

'I do,' Jay replied. 'Everything is prepped for tonight and it would be good to have a catch-up.'

'Let me get you one, then, and we can go through to the restaurant.'

When they were seated at one of the empty tables, Roberto turned to him. 'So, are you still enjoying working with Liz?'

'I am, yes. It's different every day.'

'Don't miss the restaurant life, then?'

Jay decided to be honest. 'I do a bit. I like having more creative control, but I'd still like to have my own restaurant one day.'

'Most chefs do.' Roberto nodded. 'Sadly, most don't make it or make a hash of it when they do. But you . . .' Roberto narrowed his eyes as he scrutinised Jay's face. 'Yes, you, I can see making a success of it. I'll have to watch my back.'

Jay laughed. 'That's a long way off yet.'

'What's stopping you? Money?'

Jay nodded.

'Have you thought about getting yourself a financial backer?'

'Thought about it, yes. But if I did, it would have to be a silent partner. There's no point having your own restaurant if you've got someone interfering all the time.'

'And if people invest in a restaurant, they usually have an ulterior motive,' Roberto said. 'Either they fancy having a go at it themselves, but don't have the experience, or they want to show off to their friends.'

'Exactly. So I was thinking that I could start small, maybe renting somewhere, and build it up. I need to save a lot more money before I can do that, though. No point doing it without having a financial buffer.'

'Too true. And in the meantime, you're using your creativity to develop a potential future menu?'

'In some ways, yes. It's not the same, though, creating individual dishes or ones for mass catering. I'd like to go a bit further than I'm doing at the moment.'

'How so?'

'I was thinking of trying my hand at competitions.' Jay felt nervous — it was a big thing to admit it to a chef he looked up to and he hoped Roberto wouldn't laugh at him.

But Roberto didn't laugh. Instead he said, 'And have you found any you want to enter?'

'Not yet, no, I've only just started thinking about it.'

'In that case, I might be able to help you.' Roberto sipped his coffee.

'Really?'

'Yes, there's a new competition being set up to celebrate the food of London and the south-east. Chefs will be selected to have their own dish on the menu at a banquet later in the year.'

'What? You mean like *Great British Menu*?'

'Yes, but it's only celebrating food from this region and it won't be televised. It might be a good place to cut your teeth on competitions and at least it's local.'

'Sounds exciting.' Jay took out his phone to find it online.

'It does. You'll have to get your skates on if you want to apply, though. The closing date isn't far away.'

'I'll definitely look into it,' Jay said. 'How did you find out about it?'

'They asked me to be a judge.'

'You're a judge?' Jay asked, panicked that it would rule him out from entering.

'No, I turned it down. I don't have the time for anything like that at the moment, much as I would have enjoyed it.'

'Well, it sounds perfect for me. Thank you, Roberto, you've made my day.'

CHAPTER SIX

As they reached the exit of Bethnal Green Tube station, Jay took Emma's hand in his.

'Are you nervous?' he asked.

'Very.' Although they'd been going out with each other for over eighteen months now, this was the first time she was going to meet any of his family. When Jay had come home on Friday night and said that his nan had invited them both for Sunday lunch and he'd like her to go, she'd been more than a little surprised, if not shocked. Jay had always been very private about his family. His dad had died when Jay was a teenager, and his mum had later remarried and had two more children — Jay's half-brothers, twins who were now nine years old. Jay hadn't got on with his stepfather and this had created a rift in the family. A rift that hadn't healed. The only family member he did get on with — apart from his nan — was his older sister, Hannah, who lived in Australia.

Jay had gone to live with his nan when he was seventeen and was still very close to her, but, even so, whenever Emma had asked about meeting her, he'd always said it wasn't the right time and had swiftly changed the subject.

'Don't be nervous,' he said now. 'You and Nan will get on like a house on fire.'

'Will we?'

'Of course. Nan's salt of the earth — a good old-fashioned East Ender. Be nice to her and she'll be nice to you.'

'Okay.' As they walked down a street of red-brick terraced houses, Emma asked, 'But why now, all of a sudden, am I allowed to meet her?'

Jay shrugged, once again in defensive mode. 'It's just the right time.'

'Eighteen months is a long time not to meet any of your family. I can understand your mum and step-dad, but not your nan. Are you ashamed of me?'

'No, of course not!' He put his arm around her shoulders and hugged her to him. 'It's just complicated, that's all.'

'Did she ever meet Susie?' Emma asked, determined not to be fobbed off yet again.

'Once. They hated each other on sight.'

'That doesn't bode well, then.' She was even more nervous now.

'No, it's fine. They didn't get on because Susie looked down her nose at Nan, and Nan wasn't having any of it.'

'So did that put you off introducing me to her?'

'Sort of. Not really. I can't explain. Let's just see how today goes, shall we?'

Emma sighed inwardly, realising she wasn't going to get any more out of him. This whole family thing was so frustrating.

Jay interrupted the silence. 'It's not as though I've met any of your family, is it?'

'That's different. They live in Portugal.'

Emma had to admit he did have a point. She could have arranged a trip for Jay to meet her parents if she'd wanted to. But they showed precious little interest in meeting up with her, let alone her boyfriend. Maybe she and Jay were both as bad as each other where their families were concerned. She changed the subject.

'So, as long as I mind my p's and q's I'll be all right then?'

'Of course you will. Just be yourself and Nan will love you.' He leaned across and gave her a reassuring peck on the cheek. 'How could she not?'

Emma smiled hesitantly and hoped he was right.

They turned into a small pedestrianised courtyard with a patch of lawn and a cherry tree facing three terraced houses. Jay stopped in front of the middle one and said, 'This is it.'

The black door was immaculately painted, the windows sparkling in the afternoon sunlight and draped with bright white net curtains. Emma could tell by the look of it that Jay's nan was house-proud.

Jay walked down the immaculate, weed-free path and rang the doorbell.

'Door's on the latch,' a voice shouted from within. 'Don't stand on ceremony.'

'Nan, how many times do I have to say it? You shouldn't leave the door on the latch, you never know who might walk in.'

Jay led Emma down a narrow corridor to a large kitchen at the back, where a small, plump woman with white hair scraped back into a messy bun stood. 'Nonsense. Everyone knows me round here.'

'No, Nan, they don't. Times have changed. You need to be more careful.'

Jay's nan turned towards Emma. 'He's only stepped through the door and already he's on at me. What kind of a hello is that? You must be Emma. Pleased to meet you, seeing as my grandson hasn't had the decency to introduce you.'

'You've barely given me a chance, Nan. Getting a word in edgeways might be nice.'

His nan tutted and Emma smiled nervously back at her. 'Pleased to meet you, Mrs Green.'

'Never mind this Mrs malarky. Call me Betty.' Her pale blue eyes, the same colour as her grandson's, twinkled at Emma.

'Pleased to meet you, Betty.' Emma handed her the bunch of flowers she'd been clutching nervously.

'Oh, tulips, my favourite,' Betty said appreciatively. 'I'll just put them in water. Take a seat.' She gestured to the scrubbed wooden table surrounded by four chairs. Before either of them had the chance to respond, she continued. 'I should really show you to the best room, but I prefer it in here. It's nice and cosy.'

'It certainly is,' Emma said. 'And lunch smells glorious. It's making my mouth water.'

Betty smiled and bustled off to find a vase for the flowers. Emma looked around the immaculately clean kitchen. Against one wall was a dresser crammed full of plates, photos and bits and bobs. In another corner was a worn but comfortable-looking armchair nestled by a side table, and at the other end was the compact kitchen area. A rather large ginger cat lay asleep on the chair. At the sound of their voices he opened his eyes, stared at Emma, yawned and then went back to sleep. Emma was tempted to stroke him, but didn't want to disturb him.

'What a lovely cat,' she said instead.

Jay laughed. 'That's Roland. Does nothing but sleep and eat.'

'Don't you be making fun of my Roland,' Betty replied defensively. 'He's getting on in years and needs his sleep. Do you like cats, Emma?'

Emma chose her words carefully. 'I do, although we never had any pets when I was growing up and I wouldn't want to have one where we live. It's far too busy.'

'Yes, I can understand that. But round here is perfect for Roland and he still likes to go hunting at night-time. During the day, he keeps me company. I wouldn't be without him.'

'Sounds like the perfect companion for you,' Emma replied. 'Can I help you with anything?'

'You most certainly cannot. You're my guest,' Betty replied gruffly. 'Jay, get the girl a drink. She'd die of thirst if it was up to you.'

41

Jay raised his eyebrows despairingly at Emma and she just managed to stifle a giggle. His nan certainly was a character.

'What have you got, Nan?'

'Whatever you want. Look in the fridge. There's wine, beer, cider, orange juice.' She frowned as she looked at Emma. 'You don't want a soft drink, do you? Not with a Sunday roast?'

Emma had been about to suggest just that as she wanted to keep a clear head, but judging by Betty's tone she thought it best to change her mind. 'I'll have a small glass of white wine, please, Jay.'

'Good choice.' Betty nodded happily. 'And you can pour me a glass of cider.' She pushed some of the photos aside and squeezed the vase of flowers onto the dresser, then said, 'Now, I'll crack on with the dinner.'

'Are you sure . . .'

Jay interrupted her. 'Nan has her own way of doing things and doesn't like anyone interfering,' he said quietly.

'The boy's right,' Betty said. She didn't miss a trick. 'You just chat among yourselves and dinner will be on the table in a jiffy.'

Jay smiled. 'We'll be lucky to get a chance to talk with you going on like you do.'

Betty swiped him with her tea towel. 'Don't be so cheeky.'

Emma watched as Betty dextrously reached into the oven for a large roasting pan, which she put on a chopping board on one of the worktops. She spooned the fat over the meat and sniffed appreciatively. 'Ah, nothing smells quite so good as roast beef.'

'It smells delicious,' Emma said.

Betty scooped it out of the pan and put it on a plate to rest. 'You can carve that for me in a bit, Jay.' She went on to make gravy from the meat juices, while keeping up a constant flow of conversation. Emma watched her in awe. Betty might be in her late seventies, but there was certainly nothing slowing her down. She felt an enormous amount of respect for the lady and had a feeling that Jay was right. They were going to get on like a house on fire.

Dinner was just as delicious as the smell of it had promised and Emma ate with enthusiasm, much to Betty's approval.

'So, Jay tells me you're in the hospitality business too?'

'Yes. I've not long finished my degree and I'm working as a trainee manager at the Rosemont Hotel in the West End,' she answered between mouthfuls.

'Um, very posh.'

'Not so much behind the scenes.'

'And are you enjoying it?'

Emma paused before answering. 'I'm still finding my feet and it's very much a junior role.'

'So you get all the rubbish jobs?' Betty replied knowingly.

'A lot of the time, yes, but it's the best way to learn.'

'Well, that's certainly a good attitude.' Betty nodded. 'But it won't be long before you're moving up the ladder, bright young thing like you.'

Emma blushed. 'Thank you.'

'And Emma still helps out me and Liz,' Jay said.

'Ah, Liz. How is she?'

'She's good, Nan.'

'And how did you get on at the big fancy do you were at the other week?' Even though Betty was keeping up continual conversation, Emma noted that food was still rapidly disappearing from her plate.

'At Lord Weatherton's?' Jay replied. 'It went really well.'

'To think, a grandson of mine hobnobbing with the great and the good.'

'He may be a lord, Nan, but he's very down to earth.'

Betty huffed. 'Still got a fancy-pants estate and Lord before his name.'

'He wasn't supposed to inherit, he was only a distant relative, but the heir died young and he found himself the next in line. The previous lord had gambling debts and when Henry inherited the place was practically falling down. But he turned it round and now he's in the top rich list.'

'Good for him.' Betty nodded approvingly and smiled. 'Tell me then? Is he single?'

'Nan!' They all laughed at Jay's exclamation.

'Now, who's for treacle sponge and custard?'

Although she felt full to the brim, Emma couldn't resist the temptation of a home-cooked pudding.

'I meant to tell you, Nan,' Jay said, when they were scraping their dishes clean. 'I'm applying to enter a cooking competition.'

'What would you be wanting to do that for?' she asked.

'So that I can better my reputation.'

'Don't you have a good enough reputation already with your business?'

'I might be a partner, but sometimes I still feel it's more Liz's business.'

Betty got up to clear the dishes. 'Yes, I can see your point.'

Emma jumped to her feet. 'Here let me help.' She still felt awkward about letting the older woman do everything.

'Just rinse them and pop them in the dishwasher,' Betty said. 'The rest can be done later. I want to hear more about this competition. Jay, get us all another drink, there's a love.'

Once Jay had poured the drinks, he said, 'The competition is to celebrate the food of London. The winners will get to cook their dishes at a big banquet being held later in the year.'

She nodded. 'Sounds promising. And your cockney heritage should stand you in good stead.'

'Well, I had a good teacher.' Jay grinned at her.

Betty got up from the table and opened a drawer in the dresser. She picked up a large leather-bound book and held it in her hands for a moment before passing it over to him.

'No, I did. This will help.'

Jay looked at the book reverently. 'Is that what I think it is?'

'Yes,' Betty said. 'It's my mother's recipe book.'

* * *

Jay couldn't believe she was actually giving him the book. It was her prized possession. He'd always wanted to have a look

44

at it, but had never been allowed so much as to touch it. Now he smoothed his hand over the leather exterior.

'But, Nan, you can't give me this.'

'Why not? I know every single recipe in it off by heart, so I've no further need of it. My mother wanted it to be passed to the daughter of each generation, but there's no point giving it to your mother. Mary can burn water. But you, I think you can make good use of it, and it might help you to win that competition. There's a lot of history in that book.'

'Oh, Nan! Are you sure?' Jay asked, scarcely able to believe his good fortune.

'I certainly am. You've wanted that book for years. Mother said it had to be passed on at the right time, and now is the right time.'

Jay gently opened the book and admired the neat, inked handwriting of his great-grandmother. The spatters on the pages showed that the recipes had been well used. It was such a precious gift.

The front door banged open and a voice called out, 'Hi, Mum, only me!'

Jay's head shot up, startled.

'What . . . ?' He trailed off.

Betty looked shifty. 'Mary said she might pop round. Didn't think it would be this early though.'

'Hi . . . Oh! Um, hello, Jay.'

'Mum,' Jay muttered under his breath and looked away.

'I'm sorry, I didn't realise you'd be here,' Mary said quietly. 'Maybe I should go. I can always come back later.'

'Don't be ridiculous,' Betty said. 'Sit down.'

'Jay, pour your mother a glass of wine — looks like she needs one. Emma, shall we take our drinks through to the other room, leave these two in peace? They need to talk. This thing has gone on quite long enough.'

* * *

As Emma got up from the table, Jay looked across to her. The poor girl looked petrified, so he nodded to her to let her know he was okay with her leaving him alone with his mother. He poured the wine and set it down in front of Mary. For a moment they didn't say anything, then he plucked up his courage and said, 'Looks like we've been set up.'

'Yes, it does.' Mary took a sip of her wine. 'To be honest, I'm surprised she hasn't done it before now.'

'I thought it odd that she suddenly invited both me and Emma for dinner. Should have guessed.'

'Emma? Was that your girlfriend?'

'Yes.'

'She looks nice. Pretty, too.'

'Yes, she's lovely.'

'I'm pleased for you, love.'

Not knowing how to reply, Jay lapsed once more into silence.

'Maybe your nan's right,' Mary said. 'Maybe this has gone on long enough.'

'Maybe, but I can't forget what he did or that you backed him up.'

'Steve bitterly regrets what happened that day. And so do I.'

'Really? You stood by him over your son, though.'

'I didn't stand by him. Not as such. I didn't really know what had happened at the time and then I was caught between the pair of you.'

'He hit me, Mum.'

'I know and, like I said, he still regrets it. He shouldn't have done it, Jay, but you weren't entirely innocent in all of it.'

'Oh, so you're still taking his side, then?'

Mary protested. 'No! I don't want to take sides at all. But it wasn't as straightforward as you make out. You were a very angry young man and you did some terrible things too.'

'Because my dad had died and then *he* came in riding roughshod over Dad's memories and over us all.'

Mary sighed deeply. 'I'll never stop loving your dad, but after he died, Steve, well, he helped me get through the grief. It was a difficult time for us all.'

Jay shook his head. 'I'm sorry, Mum, I just can't forgive him.'

'I'm not asking you to,' she said in almost a whisper. 'And neither is he. We're both very sorry for what happened and I'd like to be able to move on from that. Being cut off from you all these years has hurt more than I can say and I'd like to have some part in your life, even if it's just the odd text or phone call.'

Jay sighed. 'Maybe. I'll think about it.'

'Thank you.' She leaned across the table and squeezed his hand. Jay didn't know whether he wanted to pull away from her or lean in for a hug. Instead he did nothing and remained still, not daring to move either way.

'Well, I've said my bit. I'll leave you to it,' she said as she got up to go.

* * *

Jay and Emma left soon after that too. Jay didn't know what to say to her. Emma's first meeting with his nan had been going so well and he'd loved how the two women had got on together. He'd even imagined regular Sunday lunches and toyed with the idea of inviting his nan to their flat so that he could cook for her for a change. Not that she'd enjoy it — she was far too much of a control freak. When she'd given him the recipe book, he'd thought his heart would burst. Then his mother had walked through the door and ruined everything.

'Cup of tea?' Emma asked quietly when they got back to the flat.

'I'd prefer a beer. There's some in the fridge.' Jay sat down on the sofa. He knew his silence was hard on Emma and she didn't deserve that. She'd been pulled into the firing line and he felt he owed her an explanation. He'd never told her exactly what had caused the rift between him and his mum. Never opened up to her. And whenever she'd questioned him about his family, he'd changed the subject. But if he loved her, surely he'd be able to tell her anything? As he listened to her moving around in the kitchen, he thought about their relationship. Was he being unfair on her? Because he was afraid she'd think less of him if she knew? But was it worth the risk? To try to be free of it all. Maybe it was time to bite the bullet.

Emma handed him a beer, and put down a cup of tea for herself on the coffee table. Then she sat down on the opposite sofa.

'What? Don't you want to sit next to me?'

'I wasn't sure you'd want me to,' she said hesitantly.

'I'm not surprised. I'm such a moody sod, aren't I?'

'I wouldn't say that. It's been a difficult day for you.'

He looked at her, lost for words that she was so understanding. 'I just wasn't expecting it. Nan truly dropped me in it.'

'She was just trying to make things right.'

'See, I told you you'd get on well with her. You're already taking her side.' But he said it with a smile to try to lighten the mood.

'You don't have to talk about it if you don't want to.'

'I don't want to, but I think it's important that I do. I'm sorry. Sorry that you had to get involved in that. And, if I'm honest, I'm sorry I didn't introduce you to Nan earlier.' *And that was because I didn't want you to know what I'd done*, he added silently.

'Well, I'm sorry too. No offence to you, but that woman cooks like a dream.'

Jay grinned. 'She does. I learned from the best.'

'And she gave you her mother's recipe book.'

'She did.' He was itching to pore over the pages of the recipe book and he would, once he'd got this out of the way. He knew that he'd uncover countless treasures in the pages. 'I'm not proud of what has gone on in my family.' He paused and, when she didn't speak, he continued. 'As you know, my dad died in an accident at work. He was a railway man.

Someone didn't secure some rolling stock properly and he was knocked over. Hit his head and died in hospital.' He paused again and still Emma didn't interrupt. 'I was fifteen at the time. I idolised that man and it felt as though my whole world had been taken away from me.'

'I bet it did. Such a terrible age to lose your dad.'

'So from then on it was just me, Mum and my sister.'

'And you became the man of the house.'

'I thought I did, but I was still a child. A child trying to be a man and not making a good job of it.' He paused. 'Dad hadn't been gone even a year when Mum introduced Steve.'

'I can see why that would hurt.'

'More than you'd know. I couldn't bear another man taking Dad's place, especially not one who acted as though Dad never existed and he owned the place. Or at least that's how I saw it then.'

'And now?' she asked quietly.

'I've been thinking about that all afternoon. Today, Mum said I'd done some pretty bad things myself, and that's something I've not been able to admit before. Steve had been around for about a year when it all blew up. I was seventeen. Thought I knew everything and saw everything in black and white. He tried to lay down the rules, but I ignored them. Why should I listen to him? He wasn't my dad. We fought constantly. It was usually my fault because I went out of my way to provoke him. Then one night I got blind drunk and, when I got home, he was there having a go at me. We got into a row and I was up in his face, goading him. He got so angry with me, he hit me.'

Emma gasped. 'He shouldn't have done that. In reality you were still only a child.'

'A child who was acting the big man,' Jay replied. 'It wasn't that which hurt me though. It was Mum. She took his side.'

'I can see why that would hurt.'

'I think I was acting up because I wanted her to see how much she was hurting me. I wanted her to put me first, not him. But she didn't, not even then. So I walked out and went to stay with my nan.'

'And you haven't spoken since?'

'The odd text here and there when one of us was feeling guilty or lonely, but, no. I did go and see her when my brothers were born and I've visited them a few times, but mostly I've shut them out of my life because I wanted to punish her. That's why I haven't been able to talk about it. Because deep down, it's myself I'm ashamed of.'

Emma moved to sit next to him and put her arms around him. 'You were a teenager, you were grieving. There probably wasn't a right or wrong way for any of you to behave. You were all just trying to work it out as you went along, so you shouldn't blame yourself.'

'Maybe not for that. But I do blame myself for carrying it on. It's just that the longer it went on, the harder it was to find a way to stop it. Nan was right in pushing us together today. The only problem is, I don't know what happens next.'

'How did you leave it with your mum?'

'She said she'd like it if we could keep in touch. Even if it's just the odd text or phone call.'

'So text her.'

'What, now?'

'Yes. Tell her it was good to talk. Tell her you want to find a way to move forward too, but you need to do it slowly.'

'Just like that?'

'Yes. Do it now.'

Jay frowned. 'And what if she doesn't reply?'

Emma smiled and handed him his phone. 'I have a feeling she will.'

CHAPTER SEVEN

Emma woke up late the next morning, and had to jump in the shower and dress hurriedly to make it into work on time. She'd slept fitfully during the night and had fallen into a deep sleep when she should've been getting up. Jay had gone out early. He'd left a mug of tea on her bedside table, but it was already cold and she didn't have time to make a fresh one. She took a mouthful of it, grimaced and headed out of the door. She didn't want to be late, didn't need to give Heather an excuse to have a go at her.

As she sat on the Tube, she contemplated all that had happened the previous day. It had certainly been eventful. As she'd predicted, Mary had texted Jay back straight away, and that had been followed by a flurry of messages. Leaving them alone, Emma had run a bath and then had gone to bed, but she'd still been awake when Jay had come in. They'd made love, slowly and tenderly.

She felt as though something had shifted in their relationship, as though an invisible barrier had been removed. She'd loved meeting his nan and hoped there would be many more get-togethers. Maybe in time she would even get to know the rest of the family. That was something she longed for. To be part of a family.

Her mum and dad had had her later in life and there had been no more children. She didn't know why and they'd never discussed it with her. Both her parents were only children, so there were no aunties, uncles or cousins. Even her grandparents had passed away by the time she was a toddler. Her parents both had good careers, her father a doctor and her mum a solicitor, and they'd taught her to be hardworking at school and self-sufficient. There'd been little outward show of affection. For the most part she didn't miss it — how could she miss something she'd never had? But as she'd grown older and had seen how other families lived and loved, she'd yearned for her parents to show her affection.

In an attempt to earn their approval she'd worked hard at school, but no matter how hard she'd tried it just hadn't seemed good enough. They valued academia, but she wasn't naturally academic. She preferred the practical side of things and working with people. They'd visibly shown their disapproval when she'd decided to study hospitality management and, while she was at university, they had retired and bought a property in Portugal. They didn't come home and, during the rare times Emma had visited them, she'd felt that she was an inconvenience, getting in the way of their busy social life.

The thought that maybe one day she could be part of a proper family, one that, if Jay's nan was anything to go by, took life by the horns, filled her with hope. The only thing she had to do now was to fight the fatigue of a broken night's sleep and get through her shift without falling foul of the hateful Heather.

* * *

'You're late!' Heather threw the accusation at her the moment she walked through the door. Emma looked at her watch. Five minutes. She was five minutes late. Tired and on a short fuse, she bit her lip and forced herself to apologise.

'I'm sorry.' Emma turned to her desk and groaned quietly at the huge stack of paperwork sitting on it.

Heather continued, oblivious to her apology. 'Timing is crucial in this industry. You may think you're only five minutes late, but your five minutes delays everyone else as well.'

Emma could see her point if she was talking about service, but not when the only one who was waiting for her was Heather, who had probably spent the time devising ways to torture her for the rest of the day.

'Yes, of course, you're right. And I'll make the time up at the end of my shift. What's this?' She gestured towards the paperwork.

'Health-and-safety documents. They need to be uploaded onto the system today.'

'Right.' Emma tried not to groan again. She knew that keeping everything up to date was important, but today she'd rather be cleaning rooms than processing this lot in the same office as Heather.

'I'll just grab a quick coffee and then I'll crack on. Do you want one?'

'No, and don't think you can waste any more time chatting in the staffroom. As I said, that lot needs to be finished today, ready for the management meeting tomorrow. And when you've input it all, I want a list of anything that might be outstanding so that it can be booked in to be done. You won't be going home until it's all finished, so don't think it's an excuse to faff around.'

'Okay,' Emma said. She hung her coat up, sat down at her desk and prayed that by the end of the day she wasn't falling asleep over her computer.

'Right, well, I've got a meeting to go to. I'll see you in about an hour.' Heather grabbed some papers and sailed out of the office, trying to look as though she had somewhere important to go to, while Emma did her best to resist making rude gestures behind her back.

Emma spent the next half an hour shifting through the paperwork and trying to get some sense of order out of it. She badly needed caffeine to help her focus, so while Heather was out of the way she decided to run to the staffroom to grab a coffee.

A man she'd often seen working behind the bar was lounging in a chair as he sipped his drink. He was incredibly good-looking, tall and tanned, even in the depths of winter, with dark hair and deep-brown eyes. He'd always been friendly towards her and said hello, although like most of her colleagues they hadn't had a chance to get to know each other properly yet.

'Hiya, Emma, isn't it?' he asked as she filled the kettle and searched for a mug.

'That's right, and you're . . .'

'Nick.'

'Hi, Nick.'

She spooned coffee into the mug and drummed her fingers on the worktop, waiting impatiently for the kettle to boil.

'You look like a woman in a hurry.'

'I've got a pile of health-and-safety paperwork needing urgent attention.'

Nick groaned. 'The dreaded health and safety.'

'Yes, but it's got to be done, although it goes back months.'

'And tomorrow is the management meeting,' Nick said. 'And your lovely line manager, Heather, needs to catch up, but can't be arsed doing it herself.'

'Not for me to comment,' Emma replied, trying to be diplomatic. She poured the water into her mug and splashed in some milk. 'Anyway, nice to meet you, Nick, but I've got to go. Health and safety waits for no one.'

* * *

The coffee helped her focus and once she had everything in order, by room and date, it was easy enough to input it into the database. An idea came to her to set up a spreadsheet by room and type of document, with dates for when everything needed to be renewed. Rather than writing a list, she could send the spreadsheet to Heather. She knew Heather would pass it off as her own at the meeting, but at least Emma would have a copy she could update so Heather wouldn't be able to spring any last-minute surprises on her in the future.

As she worked, Emma thought about what Liz had said. How was she going to get inside Heather's head, to find out what was really going on? She decided she'd try again to invite her out for a drink again or for a coffee. If she kept on, surely even Heather would run out of excuses.

* * *

In the office at Diva's, Jay was planning the functions for the next few weeks. If he could get ahead, he'd finally be able to have a look at the recipe book, which was burning a hole in his bag. Although he anticipated that the recipes would be rustic, providing proper working-class East End food, he hoped they'd give him the basic principles to work on and finesse for the competition.

He was putting together a food order when Liz walked into the office. For a moment he was startled by her appearance. There were dark smudges under her eyes and she was even paler than usual.

'Are you okay?' he asked as she sat down at the desk next to him.

'Yes, I'm fine. Think I must have a touch of food poisoning.'

'That's not good!'

'Oh, not from anything we've cooked! Must have had some dodgy shellfish. We went for a trip to the coast yesterday. You know how I can't resist.'

He frowned at her. Liz was gushing. She never gushed and he knew a cover-up when he heard it.

'Are you sure?'

'Yes, of course I'm sure,' she said sharply.

Liz didn't snap at him either. Something was definitely wrong and he hoped it wasn't what he was thinking. She'd worked hard to overcome the anorexia she'd been hospitalised for when she was seventeen, but he knew that it could be triggered at any time. Something bad must be going on because, even when her father had died and there had been all that trouble with Nikki and Alex, she hadn't allowed it to affect her recovery. So what on earth could it be?

'If you're ill, maybe you'd be better off tucked up in bed,' he replied gently.

She brushed him off. 'No, I'm fine. I'm sure the worst is over. And we need to get on with the plans for the week.'

'I'm ahead of you there. I've been working on them already.'

She smiled wanly at him. 'That's good, then.'

'Can I get you anything to drink? Tea? Coffee?'

She paled even more, if that was possible, at his words,. 'No, I'm fine, thanks.' She reached in her bag and pulled out a bottle of water. 'Probably better to stick to this for the moment. It seems to be the only thing I can keep down. So come on, tell me where you're up to.'

They spent the next hour focusing on the week ahead, making sure they had enough staff booked in and detailing who would be in charge of each event. Then they put plans in place for bookings further ahead, so that they could get staff on board. When they'd finished Liz sank back in her chair, looking exhausted.

'And now I insist that you go home.'

She nodded. 'I will. Now that I know we have everything covered, I should be able to get some sleep.'

'Yes, that's the best thing.' He paused and decided to ask the question regardless of her reaction. 'Look, you can tell me to mind my own business and I suspect you probably will, but is it really just food poisoning? I'm worried in case you've . . .' He trailed off, not knowing how to voice his fears.

'You're worried in case I've lapsed.' She finished his sentence for him.

'Well, yes, I'm sorry but . . .'

'There's no need to be sorry. I can see why it would look like that, but I promise you that isn't happening. I never want to go back to that place again.'

'Okay, I believe you.' He studied her face and saw the telltale crease that appeared across her forehead whenever she was thinking about something that troubled her. 'But you know I'm here if ever you need to talk. Not just as your business partner, but as your friend.'

'Yes, I know.' She smiled. 'And I'm grateful for it.' She sighed and sank back into her chair. 'You're right, it's not food poisoning . . .'

'You know anything you tell me won't go any further.'

She groaned. 'Alex will kill me if he finds out I've told you. We promised that we wouldn't say anything.'

'He won't find out from me but now you've got me really worried.'

'There's nothing to be worried about,' she said. 'The thing is, I'm pregnant.'

'Oh, Liz!' A rush of elation gushed through him and he flung his arms around her. Then he hastily retreated in case his sudden movement made her feel even more nauseous. 'That's wonderful news.'

She smiled again. 'It is. Although when I insisted to Alex that we should keep it a secret until after the twelve-week scan, I didn't know I'd feel this bad.'

'How far gone are you? If you don't mind me asking.'

'Eight weeks. I was hoping I'd sail through the early weeks, but, seeing as that isn't happening, I can hardly keep it from you when food is the last thing I want to see right now.'

'I can imagine. Is it just confined to the mornings? Do you start to feel better as you get through the day?'

'Mostly. By mid-afternoon, I'm usually back to my normal self. Although I have to admit, it's taking it out of me and I'm exhausted in the evenings too.'

Jay refreshed the screen on his laptop. 'We're going to have to rethink these rotas. No lunchtime functions for you for the foreseeable, and late functions are out too.'

'That doesn't leave much, does it, though?' The telltale frown had returned to her face.

'No, but your health is more important. I can cover whatever I can and we'll just have to hire in more agency chefs.'

'That's not going to look good on the profit margins.'

'Maybe not, but we just need to keep going until we can work out a better long-term solution. Hopefully it won't be too long before you're feeling better.'

'I can still do a lot of the prep for the evenings. That might ease the pressure.'

'And maybe take on more of the paperwork? Find some better deals with our food suppliers to take some of the sting away from higher staffing bills.'

'Yes, I can do that.' She paused. 'I'm sorry, Jay.'

'What are you sorry for? It's brilliant news and I couldn't be happier for you both.' Jay knew how important having children was to both Alex and Liz, and now they had this chance they all had to do whatever they could to protect it.

'I'm glad you feel like that. But I can't help thinking I'm scuppering your own plans after what you told me the other day.'

'I'm sure we'll find a way to work it out.'

'Yes, we will. I don't want this to get in the way of what you want to do too. But actually, I'm glad I've told you, and I'm going to tell Alex you know. We decided to keep it private in case anything went wrong. I don't think either of us could bear everyone's sympathy if we suffered that loss, especially Alex. But you're not everyone, Jay, and I realise now that I need your support, especially as far as the business is concerned. But can we keep this between ourselves?'

'Of course we can. I won't tell a soul.' He paused. 'And as it's time to come clean, I need to make a confession too. I've applied to enter a regional competition.'

'But that's great, tell me all about it.'

Jay outlined the nature of the competition and then added, 'I might not even get through to the heats.'

'I'm sure you will. When do they take place?'

'Towards the end of March.'

She smiled. 'Well, that's okay, then. I should be feeling better and I can pick up the slack. And when we know for sure, we can always take fewer bookings during that period to give us both some breathing space.'

'That's a good idea. Maybe cut back on our own bookings and concentrate on Diva's, so we can fulfil our contract with them.'

'It will mean tightening our belts, though. Are you okay with that?'

'Yes,' he replied determinedly. 'If it means we both get what we want in the end, it will be worth it. And in the meantime, you have to promise to be honest with me, and don't try to battle on if you're not feeling up to it.'

'I will.' She put her hand on her stomach, protectively.

He grinned at her. 'Then we'll work it out together.'

* * *

After Liz left, Jay made himself another cup of coffee and pulled his great-grandmother's recipe book and a notebook out of his bag. For a moment he smoothed his hand over the leather covering. He'd been itching to look at it properly, but now the time had come he hesitated at turning over the pages. He wanted to savour his first read.

The handwriting at the front was larger and more rounded than in the later pages. Not only that, but it was part recipe book, part diary. Fascinated, Jay took a sip of his coffee and began to read.

> *Today Mummy showed me how to make a Victoria sponge cake. The trick is to use the freshest eggs possible and beat them really hard into the butter and sugar. It's the only way to create a really fluffy sponge.*
>
> *When it was baked, we filled it with Mummy's home-made strawberry jam and lots of cream.*

As Jay read, he realised his great-grandmother, Annie, had started to write the recipe book when she was eleven years old in 1939 — just before the start of World War Two. Things would have been about to change for the innocent girl his great-grandmother had been, baking alongside her own mother, using recipes already handed down the generations. Life was about to get a lot tougher with not just the introduction of food rationing, but also the threat of Hitler's bombs raining down on them.

Jay read on, learning how in September 1939 there were bumper crops of berries wherever there were hedgerows, and the women and children had all joined together for fruit-picking and jam-making sessions. The results would see them through the months ahead when the taste of something sweet would be a welcome treat. Annie wrote about helping her brothers turn the garden into an allotment to grow vegetables while her father was already doing his basic training before being sent to France. The pages were full of enthusiasm as they turned their small garden into something that would reward them with a largely vegetarian diet when meat became scarce. Jay scribbled down notes about dishes that might be suitable to showcase regional food of London and the south-east. When he finished his read-through, he looked up, and was surprised to see that the winter sky was already darkening into night. He yawned and stretched, knowing that he had some promising ideas for what he could cook in the initial heats of the competition. All he had to do now was to add a twist to the dishes so he could turn them into fine dining.

CHAPTER EIGHT

Emma was having the day from hell. She was supervising a luncheon where far more guests had turned up than had been confirmed, so they had nearly run out of food. She'd had to cajole the chef to put on extra and then she'd checked the portion control just to make sure everyone had got enough to eat. And despite the fact that the problem hadn't been the hotel's fault, the company who'd organised the event had made a complaint to the general manager. To top it all off, one of the servers had just spilled a tray of drinks over two of the guests. After calming them down, Emma had no choice but to offer to pay for their dry-cleaning.

When the event was over, she returned to the office.

'Well, that was a complete and utter disaster, wasn't it?' Heather launched into a tirade as soon as Emma stepped through the door. 'You keep telling me that you're ready for more responsibility, but the moment I give it to you, you make a complete and utter cock-up of it. I thought you had experience in this area, or was that you just bigging yourself up?'

Emma attempted to explain, but Heather didn't let her get a word in. 'I've already had a call from the general manager about the customer's complaint, so not only have you made a fool of yourself, but you've also made a fool of me. This just shows that you are not ready for a managerial role yet. You're not competent enough.'

Again, Emma tried to explain. 'But it wasn't my fault. There were at least twenty extra guests.'

'Then you should have checked the function sheet before-hand, so you would have been aware that the numbers had changed.'

'I did check the sheet,' Emma replied, trying to keep her voice calm. 'The numbers hadn't changed. The organisers swore blind they'd let us know, but there was nothing in the notes.'

'Well, they can't have done then, can they? And you should be able to deal with all eventualities,' Heather told her. 'Part of being a successful manager is being able to think on your feet.'

'I did,' Emma said. 'As soon as I realised we were likely to run out of food, I got the chef to improvise.'

'And the couple who were drowned in white wine? That's likely to be a hefty dry-cleaning bill.'

'Accidents happen,' Emma said between gritted teeth. 'There was nothing I could do about that, apart from pacify them after the event.'

'That's not good enough. The Rosemont prides itself on excellent customer service and what you provided today was way off that. It will be a long time before I can trust you again.'

Emma nodded, knowing that if she said anything now she'd probably live to regret it. Heather obviously wasn't in the mood for being reasoned with, so there was no point in trying. As it was the end of her shift, she put on her coat and walked out of the office, not even bothering to say goodbye. She headed through the lobby and out of the hotel, wondering how much longer she could cope with working with Heather. Soon she'd either have to make a complaint against her line manager or move on herself.

'Jay!' She stopped in her tracks as she saw him waiting in front of the hotel for her. It was such a surprise as they hadn't arranged to meet. In fact, they'd barely seen each other in the last few weeks as they'd both been so busy at work. He pulled her into his arms as she stepped out onto the pavement and she relished the feel of his arms around her. She had never been so pleased to see him as she was right now.

Emma eventually pulled herself away from him. 'What are you doing here?'

'I thought I'd surprise you,' he replied with a smile.

'You've certainly done that. And I couldn't be happier — I've had a pig of a day.'

'Then I'm glad I came to meet you. Now, why don't we have a few drinks in a little wine bar I know, followed by dinner at Luigi's?'

'Sounds perfect,' Emma said. She would have preferred to have gone home first to change out of her suit and her shoes, which were cramping her feet, but she wasn't about to look this gift horse in the mouth. Especially when it meant spending an evening with Jay. It was just what she needed after that confrontation with Heather.

'So what's been happening at work, then?' he asked once they each had a drink in front of them.

When she told him, he covered her hand with his and gave it a squeeze. 'That does sound like a bitch of a day. Heather's a piece of work. But from what you've said, pinning anything on her will be difficult.'

'I know, but I don't even want to think about that tonight. We've got a rare evening together so let's not waste it.'

'I'm sorry. It's not been easy recently, with me covering for Liz.'

'What's wrong with her? She said it was a virus, but it seems to be lingering. I keep meaning to phone her to see how she is, but I haven't got round to it. I'm such a rubbish friend.'

'No, you're not, you're just busy. Liz is finding it hard to shake off, but she is starting to feel a bit better so hopefully she'll be back to normal soon.' Jay looked away and she wasn't convinced he was telling her the truth, but she wasn't about to push him on the subject. She didn't want to ruin the evening. Tomorrow she would definitely make that phone call.

'Hopefully. You must be knackered, though.'

'I am, but it won't be long until she's covering for me.'

'She will?' Emma asked. Then the penny dropped. 'Have you heard back?'

Jay grinned, a smile so wide it split his face. 'I've got through to the first heats. They start on the twenty-fourth.'

'Of this month?'

He nodded.

'That doesn't give you much time. Especially not with the hours you're working at the moment.'

'I know, but I've got the menu planned out, so now all I need to do is practise the dishes.'

'What are they?' Emma asked eagerly.

'Well, I've got to do a main course and a dessert. I want to do something that is traditional East End fare, so I've settled on pie and mash, and treacle tart.'

'Really? Are you sure that will be enough? It's difficult to make pie and mash look elegant.'

Jay smiled. 'I know what you mean, but I have a few tricks up my sleeve.'

'If anyone can do it, you can, Jay. But I'm glad we're eating Italian tonight.'

'Why's that, then?'

'Because I have a feeling I'm going to be eating a lot of pie and mash in the next few weeks.'

He laughed. 'You're right there. But I'll try to make it a pleasant experience.'

'I'm sure you will,' Emma said. 'All this talk of food is making me hungry. Shall we go to the restaurant?'

'Yes, let's.'

CHAPTER NINE

Jay was faffing. He knew he was faffing, checking and double-checking everything he needed for the day ahead, but he couldn't help himself. He'd barely slept all night and, when he did finally fall into a fitful slumber, he'd dreamed about turning up without a vital ingredient and everything going wrong. For about the hundredth time he wished he'd never entered this competition. Just what did he need to prove anyway?

'Do you want me to come with you?' Emma asked quietly.

'No. I need to do this on my own.' The moment the words were out of his mouth, he regretted them. She'd been nothing but supportive in recent weeks, dealing with his moods swinging from elation when things had gone right to downright despair when they hadn't. 'I'm sorry. I know you're only trying to help and I do appreciate it, but I'm no company and I'd rather be on my own.'

'I understand,' she replied good-naturedly. 'But I'm not in work today, so if you need to ring me, at any time I'm here for you.'

Jay reached out to give her a hug. He had to admire how calm she always was with him. He wasn't sure he would have handled it so well if it had been the other way around.

He sighed. 'This whole competition seems to have taken over our lives.'

'It's important to you and I understand that. At least you know you've got the dishes down to perfection. You could cook them in your sleep.'

'Hopefully.' He secretly thought to himself that he was so wound up with nerves, he didn't think he'd remember his own name later, let alone how to cook.

'No hoping about it. And the dishes are wonderful — I can testify to that.'

'You should do, you've eaten them enough times.' He'd barely cooked anything at home other than his entries for the competition recently and she'd always been a willing guinea pig for his trials.

'True, and they are delicious, but I must admit that I won't miss them after today. Although, taking in spare treacle tart to work has made me very popular. Even Heather seems to have thawed a little.'

'Wonders will never cease.'

'And if it was down to a public vote, you'd definitely have the Rosemont Hotel voting for you.'

'Good to know,' he said. His mind wandered again, as he wondered if he'd forgotten anything.

'Give me your list,' Emma said.

'What?'

'Give me your list of everything you need to take and I'll tick it off as you put it in the van. That way you'll know you haven't forgotten anything.'

He smiled and wondered what he would do without her. 'Thanks, Em.'

'Nothing to thank me for.'

'Yes, there is — you've been brilliant.'

'And you're going to smash it. And in anticipation of that, shall I book us a table somewhere tonight and we can eat out for a change?'

'I might not feel up to it.'

'Okay, well, I'll cook for you, then. I'll get a bottle of wine in and we can have a relaxing evening at home together.'

'Perfect,' he replied as they loaded up the van.

On the journey to Greenwich, where the heats were taking place, Jay thought more about Emma and how grateful he was that she was in his life. If he'd still been with Susie, there'd have been nothing but arguments, tantrums and complaints about being neglected. Instead, Emma had taken it in her stride, especially while he was still working crazy hours as Liz's morning sickness continued. He knew Emma was suspicious and had taken to calling Liz most days to see how she was. He hated lying to her and on more than one occasion had been tempted to come clean. But it wasn't his secret to tell and he had promised Liz. Thankfully she was going for her twelve-week scan today, so soon the secrecy would be over.

The satnav announced he'd arrived at his destination and he looked up at the large warehouse where the heats would be taking place. He pulled up beside a man wearing a high-vis jacket and wound down the window.

'Are you a competitor?' the man asked.

Jay's throat was dry with nerves. 'I am.'

'Go down that road there, take the first left, then right, and you'll be in the car park at the back. Go through the door and register, and then you'll be able to bring your stuff in.'

'Thanks,' Jay replied. He contemplated driving straight on and not bothering with the competition after all. But deep down he knew he couldn't do that.

He parked up and walked towards the entrance, where a metal door was propped open. Inside, a young woman was seated at a circular table with a clipboard and a box of name tags in front of her.

'Are you a competitor?' she asked.

'Yes, Jay Williams.'

She looked down her list and then ticked him off. Another young woman in a white shirt and black skirt with her hair tied back into a neat ponytail appeared from further down the corridor.

'Leanne will show you where your workbench and the changing rooms are, and then you can bring your ingredients in and start familiarising yourself with the equipment. After that you can get changed, and the heats will begin at eleven o'clock. Okay?'

'Yes, that's fine,' Jay said. His legs trembled as he allowed himself to be led down the corridor. *Treat this like a normal function*, he told himself as he resisted the urge to ask where the nearest toilets were so he could be sick.

Leanne led him into a room containing eight large workstations, surrounded by cookers, fridges and equipment, with a long table and three stools at the front. His stomach churned again as he imagined the stools occupied by the three judges, watching the competitors' every move as they cooked. *Get a grip*, he told himself as he remembered Emma's words about being able to cook these dishes in his sleep. He certainly hoped she was right and that once the competition started his muscle memory would kick in. For the time being, he would concentrate on getting himself organised and try not to think about what lay ahead.

Jay managed to distract himself for the next half an hour and then changed into his chef's whites, tying his traditional navy-and-white headscarf around his auburn curls to keep them in check and to stop him running his fingers anxiously through his hair. So far he'd managed to avoid talking to the other competitors. He was afraid that would make him even more nervous, so had merely nodded at them politely. But as they all gathered in the small lounge off the changing area, conversation was unavoidable. There were eight of them in total — six men and two women. Two of the men he judged to be in their early thirties. One of them, Ben, had worked briefly at La Emporium. He had short dark hair and a neatly clipped beard, and wore chef's whites that looked brand new. Jay recalled that he'd been quite fastidious by nature, but lacked creative flair. He also remembered Ben as being cock-sure, but that his skills weren't as good as he gave himself credit for.

The other man of a similar age was in complete contrast to Ben. As he'd shaken Jay's hand he'd said his name was Demetri. He looked scruffier than Ben, with long hair tied back in a ponytail. His whites were older and bore the marks of food stains that hadn't quite come out in the wash. He wore his sleeves rolled up, and his arms and hands were heavily tattooed. The two younger men looked to be in their early twenties, both with traces of acne still on their skin. One, Andrew, was tall and thin with pale hair, freckles and a Scottish accent, the other more thickset man, was Dan, but they both seemed nervous and could barely look anyone in the eye. There was one Asian man who had shyly introduced himself as Rav. He had a few streaks of grey in his thick, dark hair, which was swept back from his forehead, and Jay guessed he was in his forties. He smiled a lot and Jay wondered if it was from nerves. Of the women, Lucy was perhaps in her mid-thirties. She was short and thin, with mousey blonde hair in a scruffy bun, while Sarah was in her fifties, tall with short silver hair in a neat crop.

'Well, there's no going back now,' Andrew said. He jiggled his leg nervously from his position on the sofa

'No,' Sarah replied. 'I did this because I thought I needed a challenge, but now I'm beginning to wonder what I'm putting myself through.'

Jay agreed readily. 'Me too.'

'Life is boring if you don't challenge yourself,' Ben said in his overly confident manner.

Jay remembered something his mum used to say to him before an exam. 'Just do your best — you can't do any better than that.' He nodded to himself as he thought of her. Although they were still at a tentative stage it was good to have her back in his life. He hadn't met up with his stepfather yet, but he knew that would have to come eventually. In the meantime, he was happy enough to head into the competition with his mother's wise words in his ears.

Leanne appeared at the door and said, 'If you'd all like to come through, the judges are ready for you.'

Jay felt his stomach lurch again as he stood up. They all muttered hesitant wishes of good luck before following Leanne into the kitchen.

Jay positioned himself behind his workbench at the back of the room. He was glad he wouldn't be in full view of the judges as they were seated at the table, although he knew that they'd be going around the room and speaking to each competitor, so he wouldn't be entirely out of their gaze.

He clasped his hands behind his back as they waited for the judges to enter, mainly to stop anyone else from seeing how much they were shaking. After a few minutes, three judges filed in and there was a collective gasp as everyone realised who they were. There were two men and one woman. The woman was Angela Markham, Chef Patron of a two-Michelin-starred, modern British restaurant in Surrey. She was a chef Jay had admired for many years and the thought of being in the same room as her, let alone being judged by her, terrified him.

The second judge was Philip Saunders. Now in his sixties, he was well known not only for the three restaurants he owned, but also for his commitment to sustainability and using local produce. But it was the third judge who made Jay's stomach almost drop through the floor. Louis Garcia, his former head chef and the man who had bullied both him and Liz at La Emporium. The man who had lost his job because of what Jay had told Roberto. How had Louis managed to turn things around so that he was now a judge in this competition? And would he want to use this competition to exact his revenge?

Around him, he sensed movement. The competition had started and everyone was busy at their workstations, but he couldn't move. His eyes were firmly fixed on Louis, who was talking to Angela. But then Louis suddenly looked up and locked his eyes on Jay. Louis smirked and Jay felt as though he'd been punched in the stomach. Fury rose within him. What was it about people like Louis who, no matter what they did, always came up smelling of roses? And then he realised what he had to do. He couldn't let the man get the better of him. He'd have to show him that he wouldn't be cowed, just like last time. There were three judges in the competition, not one. He'd have to go all out to impress the other two and then whatever opinion Louis had would be outweighed. As he gathered his ingredients together in front of him, he wondered if he could really do it. Well, he'd just have to give it his best shot like his mother had taught him. Jay took a deep breath. First things first — he needed to make the broth for the sauce.

In an ideal situation he'd simmer the broth for several hours to get the depth of flavour he needed, but he only had two hours and within that time he also had to cook the pie, so he'd experimented using a pressure cooker to reduce the cooking time and was pleased with the results. He also placed a roasting tin containing bones with marrow in the oven. The bone marrow would add flavour and the all-important umami flavour to the gravy inside the pie. Once the stock was on, Jay started work on the shortcrust pastry. He had considered using flaky pastry to elevate the dish, but he wanted to make the pastry from scratch and that would put him under too much time pressure. He'd perfected his shortcrust so that it was buttery and crumbly, but also strong enough to hold the filling without anything leaking out.

Once the pastry was resting in the fridge, Jay started on the pie filling. Reaching for the onions, he spotted the judges heading towards him and tried not to let them see that his hands had started to shake again. He took a few surreptitious deep breaths to calm himself down.

'Hi, Jay. How's it going?' Angela asked.

'Good, thanks.' Jay pinned a smile on his face in the hope that it would make him appear confident.

'And what are you making for us today?' Philip asked.

'Well, I was born in Bethnal Green and, as this is a regional competition, I wanted to stick to my roots and the food I grew up with. Us East Enders love our pie and mash, so that's what I'm making for you today.'

'Pie and mash?' Louis asked with his telltale smirk of disdain. 'How on earth are you going to turn that into fine dining?'

Jay kept the smile on his face. 'Traditionally, the pie was made from the cheapest cuts, minced beef usually, bulked out by whatever was available to the cook. But today I'm using the finest fillet of beef. Again, going back to tradition, oysters were commonly eaten in Victorian London, before the Thames was silted up with animal waste and they became more of a coastal food. But today I'm adding oysters to give the feeling of extra sumptuousness. You can see I'm making the broth in a pressure cooker, to give it the depth of flavour it needs in the short time it has, and I'm also going to add roasted bone marrow. Instead of a traditional pie dish I've sourced these springform moulds, so that the pie will stand alone and provide better presentation.'

Louis scoffed. 'Let's hope you can get the pies out of the moulds in one piece then, or you won't have a dish.'

'I've practised it many times and, as long as I grease the inside of the moulds sufficiently, there shouldn't be a problem.'

'And how are you going to present the mash?' Philip asked.

'Well, that's where I'm cheating a bit. Instead of mash, I'm actually making pommes Anna as it's easier to present on the plate.'

'Lovely. And will we be expected to eat the eels?' Angela asked, pointing to a bowl on his workbench and pulling a face.

'I will be cooking them,' Jay replied. 'But I know they're not to everyone's taste so I'm just using them to flavour the liquor, so that it's authentic.'

Angela smiled at him. 'Sounds like you have it all worked out. I'm looking forward to tasting that. And what are you doing for your dessert?'

'Again, I'm sticking with tradition and I'm making treacle tart. It was a favourite dish in my nan's house when I was growing up.'

'So, you're making two dishes with shortcrust pastry as their base? That's not particularly well thought out, is it?' Louis smirked.

'Yes, well, I did have a bit of dilemma in choosing this dish. In working-class homes, the abundance of carbohydrates was a good thing because everyone used up so much energy through manual labour. But for the competition, I've developed a cheesecake-base mixture, which will also incorporate a hint of ginger. And instead of custard I'll be serving it with vanilla-and-rhubarb ice cream, a brandy-snap toile and stem-ginger syrup.'

'Delicious. I can't wait to try that,' Angela said.

'Well, Jay, it sounds like you've got a lot to do, so we'll leave you to get on with it,' Philip added before they moved away.

Jay let out a sigh of relief. He felt he'd deflected Louis' objections well and he hoped he'd impressed the other judges too. Now he just had to make sure that everything was ready on time.

With the first few processes underway and the judges' questions successfully answered, Jay's nerves calmed and the muscle memory he had been counting on took over. So far everything was going like clockwork. He was glad he'd spent so much time practising because he'd ironed out the things that could go wrong before going in front of the judges. To his surprise, he even found he was enjoying himself. It was good to be able to focus on just the one thing without other distractions. But all too soon the judges were announcing that there was only half an hour left. Jay consulted his list of things he had left to do. The pie and the pommes Anna, along with the treacle tart, were in the oven. The liquor was simmering nicely and the ice cream was churning. It was just the finishing touches he had to do now and, if he carried on with the same focus he'd had all morning, he might just finish on time. He'd hate it if he didn't get everything on the plate. That would feel like he'd failed before he'd even got to the judging stage.

Around him he could sense rising panic as the other chefs realised what little time they had left and tried to step up a gear. Then suddenly there was a loud crash.

'Oh, sugar!'

Jay looked up. Rav had dropped a pan and there was sauce everywhere. Rav now stood mesmerised, unable to move. Jay raced over, grabbed the pan and scooped up the sauce that had spilled onto the worktop, and not on the floor, back into the pan.

'Here you go, mate — probably not as much as you'd like, but not a complete disaster and at least the judges will have something to taste.'

Rav snapped out of his stupor. 'Oh, thank you, you are a life saver.'

'Not a problem. I'll give you a hand clearing this up — don't want any more accidents.'

'Thank you, thank you.' Rav grabbed a cloth and started to clean up.

Back at his own workbench, Jay tried to refocus. He'd lost some valuable minutes but he'd been glad to help, even if Rav was the competition. Now he just needed to catch up.

All too soon Louis called out, 'Time's up. Put your dishes at the end of your benches.'

Jay breathed a sigh of relief. He was ready, on time, and everything had gone according to plan. He'd done it. Now the judges just had to like it. If they didn't . . . well, he'd done his best.

Around him, some of the other contestants were still trying to put the finishing touches to their dishes, but Louis wasn't having any of it.

'Stop what you're doing and put your dishes to the end of your benches,' he said. Jay caught his eye and suppressed a smile. It wouldn't do to antagonise the man, but at least today he had shown he wasn't scared of him. He couldn't wait to tell Liz.

As he waited to be called up, he wondered how she was getting on with her scan. He really hoped that everything was all right with the baby. He knew how desperate she was for this scan to go well, for both her and Alex's sake. As much as it was joyous that Liz was pregnant, Jay recognised it must be bringing back some very painful memories for Alex.

The first four chefs received mixed reviews from the judges and Jay felt a sense of trepidation. These judges didn't miss a trick and they certainly weren't easily impressed. He wished they'd call him up so that he could get the verdict over and done with, whatever the result. Then it was Rav's turn.

'Oh, this is just divine,' Angela said as she tasted his dish. 'What's this called again? It's got a unique flavour.'

'It's called shatkora. It comes from the Sylhet region of Bangladesh. Shatkora is a citrus fruit native to the area.'

'It's got such a delicate build-up of spice, not surprising as you had so many ingredients on your bench, and it's tangy and exotic all at the same time. An excellent dish.'

'Well, I'm grateful to Jay that the sauce was saved, otherwise you wouldn't have had any to taste,' Rav replied.

'Yes, well done, Jay,' Philip said. 'I know this is a competition, but if you get to the banquet stage you'll all have to help each other, and it's nice to see some great team spirit at this early stage.'

Jay felt the colour rise in his face. He'd acted out of instinct rather than any need for praise, but it was nice to see that his efforts were appreciated.

'And would you say this is a traditional dish for the southeast of London?' Louis asked.

'I would, yes,' Rav said, his voice controlled. 'From the 1950s, as part of the Commonwealth countries, many Bangladeshi people migrated to London to help rebuild the city after World War Two. We also came to the East End as a response to the Bangladesh Liberation War in the early seventies.'

'Exactly,' Angela added. 'You have to remember, Louis, that London was a hotspot for immigration, which is why today we have so many types and flavours of food in our cuisine.'

Louis looked away as a hush descended on the room. Jay couldn't believe that he'd made such a rookie mistake and wondered if he'd said the first thing that had come into his head to distract from the praise Philip had given Jay. If that was the reason, it had backfired. Louis had completely discredited himself.

'And your pudding?' Philip said. 'This looks interesting.'

'It's *narkel er payesh*. It's a Bengali coconut rice pudding, cooked with Bengali kalijeera rice, in grated coconut, coconut milk and cardamom powder. It's topped with coconut flakes, dried rose and cornflower petals, and crushed pistachios.'

'Beautifully creamy, yet sweet and spicy at the same time,' Philip said.

'And the rice is cooked to perfection,' Angela added. 'Well done, Rav.'

Then Jay heard his name being called. He took a deep breath as he placed his dishes on the judging table.

One by one they tasted Jay's food. Again he held his hands behind his back to stop them from shaking. His mouth felt dry, his stomach churned.

'Oh, wow, this is amazing,' Angela said. 'The depth of flavour in that sauce is incredible.'

Philip nodded. 'And the pastry is so crumbly, it just melts in the mouth. Yet it's strong enough to hold the filling. There's not an ounce of leakage.'

Louis frowned. 'I find the liquor a bit too salty.'

'That's the flavour from the eels,' Angela countered him. 'And I think you'll find that is how it is supposed to be traditionally. Perhaps it could be adapted to use a little less salt to cater for today's palate, but on the whole I think it's a very clever and enjoyable dish.'

Jay let out a breath. The first hurdle was over and he was glad he'd managed to win over the other two judges. He couldn't believe just how much they were going against Louis, but perhaps they too sensed that his judging wasn't exactly honest.

'Now for the treacle tart.' Angela delved into it and added a dollop of ice cream on her spoon. 'Oh, yes,' she said after a few moments of silence. 'The rhubarb in the ice cream provides the perfect tartness to balance the sweetness of the treacle. That's inspired.'

Jay waited as the other two judges tasted the dessert.

'Perfection,' Philip said.

Louis replied, 'Yes, very nice.'

Jay felt like doing a fist pump in the air, not just because he'd received such good comments but because Louis had found little to complain about. He resisted the urge.

The competitors filed back into the lounge while the judges deliberated on who was going to go through to the next round. Only four of the eight would go through and then they'd have to wait for the other heats to take place before they could get to the next stage. Despite the positive comments he'd received, Jay's stomach quivered at the thought. He really wanted to get through. No, he corrected himself. What he really wanted to do was to get all the way to the banquet, but he couldn't get ahead of himself just yet.

As they all sat down, Jay was surprised to find how friendly everyone was now that the competition was over.

'Well, I don't think I stand a chance,' Sarah said. 'I made a complete mess of both my dishes. You, on the other hand, Jay, are a shoo-in.'

Jay blushed. 'Oh, I wouldn't say that.' He hoped it was true, though.

'Well, I would,' Rav said. He buttoned up a fresh chef's jacket that he had collected from his locker, as the one he had been working on had been heavily splashed with the sauce from his dish. 'And you deserve it too. I wouldn't stand a chance if you hadn't been so quick-thinking and saved my sauce. I really can't thank you enough.'

'It was nothing,' Jay said. 'But I'm glad they got to taste it. It would've been devastating if you'd lost the lot.'

Rav nodded. 'It would.'

'Louis is being a bit of an arse, though.' Ben said. Then he turned to explain to the group. 'Jay and I used to work at

La Emporium. Jay worked there a lot longer than me — mine was only a brief stint — but even so I couldn't stand the man.'

'Neither could I,' Jay said. 'And if anyone is going to mark me down, then it'll be him.'

Ben continued. 'I always thought he was a bit of a bully.'

Jay's neck prickled uncomfortably. While he'd been the one to blow the whistle on Louis, he didn't want it to be common knowledge, especially among these chefs.

'I would say his management style leaves a lot to be desired,' Jay said diplomatically.

'I can't say I took to him at all,' Lucy said, as she tried to refasten her escaping hair back into its bun. 'There's something about him that gave me the creeps.'

'I don't think the other two like him very much either,' Sarah said.

They all nodded in agreement.

'Do you think you should declare your previous acquaintance with him to the other judges?' Sarah asked.

Jay looked to Ben. He hadn't thought about that.

'Perhaps we should,' he said. 'Although my pre-acquaintance with the man certainly won't do me any favours.'

'But for the sake of clarity,' Ben agreed. 'We probably should speak to the judges.'

The door opened and they were asked to return to the kitchen.

The eight chefs stood in a row, all anxiously waiting to hear their fate.

'Right, well, I know how nervous you all are,' Angela said. 'So I won't keep you waiting too long. What I do want to say, though, is congratulations to you all. The standard was incredibly high and you made our decision very difficult. But the chefs going through to the next heat are . . .' She paused. 'Jay, Rav, Lucy and Ben.'

'Commiserations to you other four,' Philip added. 'But please don't think of it as a reflection on your cooking. You are all very talented chefs and will go far in your careers.'

Jay stood in disbelief as the other chefs clapped him on the back and he realised he'd done it. He was through to the next heat.

As the other chefs filed out, Jay nodded to Ben and hesitantly they approached the judges' table.

'Gentlemen,' Angela said. 'Congratulations.'

'Thank you,' they said in unison.

'Is there something we can help with?' Philip asked.

'Yes well,' Jay said, taking the lead. 'We thought that, in order to be transparent, Ben and I should let you know that we used to work with Louis at La Emporium.'

'I didn't work there for very long,' Ben added. 'But all the same.'

'Quite,' Philip said and turned to Louis. 'Did you not think to mention this during the selection process?'

Louis shrugged. 'I didn't think it was important.'

'Well, it obviously is,' Angela said. 'We'll have to declare this to the sponsors and seek their guidance, going forward. But thank you, gentlemen, for bringing this to our attention.'

'But we will still be going through to the next round, won't we?' Ben asked.

'Yes, you will,' Philip said. 'The marks you were awarded by both Angela and me guarantee that.'

'Well, that's a relief,' Jay said but couldn't help noticing the way Louis was glaring at him.

CHAPTER TEN

Liz squeezed her legs together. 'I wish they'd hurry up. I'm desperate for the loo.' She and Alex were sitting in the waiting room and it was half an hour past the appointment time for her twelve-week scan. She didn't think she could hold all the water she'd drunk this morning much longer.

'I told you I was happy to go private. We wouldn't have been kept waiting then.'

'I'd rather do this through my own doctor and local hospital.' Liz was unable to shake off her working-class roots, even though they could easily afford to go private. 'I just wish they'd hurry up.'

If she was honest, her irritation was partly fear. What if they found something wrong with the baby? And she couldn't help thinking it must be so much worse for Alex.

A nurse called out. 'Elizabeth Sinclaire.' Liz got up with a sigh of relief and they both followed her down a corridor and into an examination room.

'I'm sorry to keep you waiting. I know how difficult it can be when you have a full bladder.'

'I wasn't sure how much longer I'd be able to wait,' Liz said.

'Let's get this done as quickly as possible and then you can go to the loo. If you'd like to pop onto the bed and pull your top up. Dad, if you'd like to take a seat over here, so you'll be able to see the screen when little one makes an appearance.'

Liz shared a smile with Alex at him being called Dad.

'I'm going to put some gel on your tummy. I'll try to warm it up, but I'm afraid it's going to feel a bit cold.'

'That's fine,' Liz said. 'I'm sure there's a lot worse to come.'

The sonographer spread the gel over her stomach and then picked up the scanner. 'Now, I might have to press quite hard to get a good image, so I apologise in advance if it pushes on your bladder. If it's too much, give me a shout. Let's see if little one is camera shy.'

Both Liz and Alex pinned their gazes on the screen above, anxious to get a first look at their baby.

'Ah, here they are,' the sonographer said after a few moments.

Liz and Alex exclaimed at the same time. 'They?'

'No, don't worry. Just the one so far. I say they to avoid saying he or she. We can't tell at the moment anyway, if you wanted to know the gender.'

'No, we've decided to wait until the birth,' Liz said. Alex nodded in agreement. Although it might be nice to know the gender of their baby, they'd decided that they'd prefer a surprise.

'Well, here we are. There's the head, body, arms and legs.'

'And is everything all right?' Alex said anxiously.

'Looks fine to me, all present and correct. I'll just take a few measurements to confirm, but the heartbeat is strong.'

Alex clasped Liz's hand as a goofy grin spread across his face. 'Oh, that's good.'

'Now, I'll just clean you up and then you're done. You can go to the loo and then order your pics to take home with you.'

Liz smiled back at Alex, feeling as though a huge weight had been lifted from her shoulders. 'Fantastic!'

* * *

In the car on the way home, Alex sighed contentedly. 'I can't tell you how relieved I am. I know this is only the first step, but it's good to know that everything's okay so far.'

'It certainly is,' Liz said. 'And I'll be so relieved to be able to tell everyone. It's been really hard keeping it secret, especially at work, and especially because I've been feeling so ill.'

'I can imagine, but at least you seem to be improving.'

'I am, and I'm looking forward to feeling a bit more like my old self.'

'Let's hope so,' Alex said. Despite everything, Liz thought, he sounded sad.

'I know this must be hard for you, bringing back all sorts of memories.'

'It is,' Alex said. 'It's bittersweet in a way. But the good far outweighs the bad, and we have so much to look forward to.'

Liz gave his arm a squeeze. 'Whatever happens, we'll deal with it together.'

'Yes, and, talking of the future, I've got something to show you.' He turned off from their normal route home and headed away from the city.

'What? Where are we going?'

'Well,' he said slowly. 'I put my ear to the ground and I think I've found the perfect house for us.'

'*You have*? Where is it?'

'Holland Park,' he replied.

'Holland Park? Isn't that where all the celebrities live?'

He shrugged. 'I believe so. But it's a great area to bring a family up in. It's still not too far from central London, but has a village feel. There are lots of cafés and restaurants, and with the park on the doorstep I think it's just perfect.'

In the years when she'd first set up her business and had scrimped and saved to make ends meet, she'd never imagined she'd even consider living somewhere like Holland Park.

'But can we afford it?'

'We can. Business is going well and with the sale of my apartment and your contribution from your inheritance we'll be okay. We'll still need to make sure we get it for the right price, though. From the photos, it looks as though it belonged to an older person. It needs a bit of work, which will bring the asking price down. And although it's going to be a family home, it could also be an investment.'

Liz smiled. Trust Alex to be thinking of it with his business head on.

'Wow,' she eventually managed to say. She hardly dared hope that this would be the perfect house and she would end up living in Holland Park. Today was turning out to be a remarkable day and she didn't want the bubble to burst.

CHAPTER ELEVEN

'Right, you're on paperwork duties again today,' Heather said as soon as Emma walked into their shared office. Her heart sank. What tedious last-minute job did Heather have in store for her today? As she took off her coat, she looked across to the towering pile of paper dumped on her desk.

She gingerly picked up a piece of paper from the top of the pile. 'What do you want me to do?'

'Customer feedback,' Heather said with a satisfied smile. 'It all needs to be collated into a spreadsheet. Management wants to see how we're doing.'

'Okay,' Emma said. There was no point arguing with Heather. She was sure the woman had been storing this up for ages and like the health-and-safety documents had sprung it on her at the last minute, no doubt hoping that she wouldn't finish it in time. She knew the spreadsheet she had designed had gone down well with the management team, but she was certain Heather would have claimed it as her own. It didn't seem fair, but she'd just have to grin and bear it, and hope that eventually someone noticed the office was being run a lot more efficiently now that she was in it. And somehow, subtly, without putting Heather's nose out of joint, maybe she could make them see that it was actually herself who was responsible for the changes. For now, though, she'd just have to get on with the task in hand.

'You can grab yourself a coffee before you start if you like,' Heather said. 'Can't have you deprived of your caffeine now, can we? And you can get me one while you're at it.'

Emma smiled to herself. Of course. She might have known her boss was too lazy to get her own coffee.

'So how did your chef get on yesterday?' Heather asked when Emma returned with the coffees.

Emma stifled her surprise at the question. 'He did really well. He's got through to the next round.'

'Ah, that's good,' Heather said. 'So what are we going to be tasting next?'

'I don't know. He hasn't had the brief yet. Although I'll be glad not to eat pie and mash for a while, as lovely as it was.'

'I'm sure you will. If he gets much further, he'll really be going up in the world.'

'I suppose so.'

'You'll have to watch yourself.'

Emma twisted in her chair to face her boss. 'Why?'

'Stands to reason, doesn't it? With his success he might not want to know the likes of a trainee junior hotel manager.'

'I'm sure our relationship is stronger than that.' Emma turned back to her desk so that Heather couldn't see the tears she was struggling to blink back. Because whether she knew it or not, Heather had struck right to the very heart of Emma's own fears.

On the night she'd met Jay's mum and nan, she'd thought they'd grown closer and their relationship was stronger, especially when he'd opened up to her about his family's relationship. But since then, he'd become distant again. She knew this competition meant so much to him, and he was putting every ounce of effort into making sure he was successful, but it was all he seemed to think about.

Yesterday had been a huge achievement. She was so happy for him, and she'd assumed they'd celebrate his success together. Instead he'd gone to the pub with some of his fellow competitors while the meal she'd cooked for him had congealed in the oven. And when he had come home, it had been to give her a blow-by-blow account of the day and the praise he'd received from the judges for his food, not even stopping to ask how her day had been. She'd put it down to him being high on adrenaline. She knew she'd have to be patient with him while the competition was all-consuming, but Heather's comment had struck a nerve, even if it had been said to taunt her. Emma shook her thoughts away and focused on inputting customer feedback onto the screen.

Several hours later, when Emma felt as though she was going cross-eyed, Heather got up from her desk and announced she was going to a meeting and would be back in an hour. When she was sure she was gone, Emma leaned back in her chair with a sigh, glad that she had the office to herself for an hour. As she'd been going through the feedback, she'd been developing ideas on how things could be improved in the hotel. Now that Heather's beady eyes were off her, she opened up a new document on her laptop and began to type them up before they slipped from her mind. Perhaps she could find a way to bypass Heather and send her ideas through to higher management herself. It was the only way she could think of to get herself noticed.

Five minutes later, there was a knock at the door and Nick popped his head round.

'Room service.' He produced a cup of coffee and a sandwich. 'I've just seen the wicked witch gossiping with Sandy from the spa and thought you'd be hard at it.'

Emma laughed, and took the mug and plate from him gratefully.

'Thank you, Nick, that's very kind of you.' For the second time that day she felt tears welling in her eyes. What on earth was wrong with her?

'My pleasure. I do have an ulterior motive, though. How did Jay get on yesterday?'

She smiled. 'Great. He got through to the next round.'

'That's brilliant news!'

'Yes, it is, isn't it?'

'Isn't it?' He sat down in Heather's chair. 'You don't sound so sure.'

'Oh, don't listen to me.' Emma waved her hand towards him. 'Of course I'm pleased for him. I'm just being silly.'

Nick frowned. 'In what way? If you don't mind me asking?'

Emma paused. She wasn't sure she should confide in someone she hardly knew, but she couldn't speak to Jay about it and Liz had her own problems at the moment.

'Oh, I'm just feeling a bit pushed out, that's all. Like I said, silly. And I really do want him to succeed.'

'Of course you do. And I don't suppose it helps having to work with her ladyship.'

'She doesn't make things easy, that's for sure,' Emma said with a sigh.

'Tell you what, there's a bunch of us from here going for drinks tomorrow night. Why don't you join us?'

'Yes, I'd love to,' Emma said. She was on a day shift tomorrow and a night out could be just what she needed. Jay was working, so she'd only end up sitting in the flat on her own. Again. And it would be good for her to get to know some of the other staff, too.

'Great, I'll let you know the details, then.' Nick stood back up and put his hand on her arm. She looked up. He was staring down at her intently. She'd never really noticed before how green his eyes were, but the way he was looking at her made her feel uncomfortable.

* * *

The morning after the competition, Liz came into the kitchen, where Jay was already working. 'So come on then, tell me all about it.'

'No, you first,' Jay said. 'How did you get on yesterday?' He watched as the smile spread across her face, and felt a wave of relief.

'It was wonderful. Do you want to see a pic?'

'Of course I do,' he said. She reached into her bag and pulled out an envelope containing a black-and-white photograph.

Jay made out the shape of the baby and grinned at her. 'So everything's okay, then, is it?'

'Couldn't be better.'

'I'm so pleased for you.'

'There's still a long way to go, and I am a bit worried about Alex, but it is a relief to know that there are no problems so far. Now, enough about us — tell me all about yesterday.'

Jay launched into everything that had happened the day before and heard her gasp when he told her about Louis being a judge.

'How on earth has he managed that?'

'I don't know, but it does feel as though the other judges don't like him very much. They did contradict him quite a lot yesterday. And they weren't very impressed when Ben and I declared our history with him, especially as he hadn't said a word himself.'

'I bet they weren't. Are they going to do anything about it?'

'Yes, they're going to inform the sponsors. With any luck they'll kick him off the judging panel.'

'That will certainly make life easier for you. What did you think when he walked into the room?'

'That I wanted to run away. But I'm glad I managed to calm myself down and I think I impressed the other judges.'

'Too right. Who were they?'

Jay watched Liz's mouth drop open as he told her.

'Oh, Angela Markham has always been an idol of mine.'

'Me too. And she's so nice, but I am a little bit in awe of her.'

'I bet you are. I've always thought that Philip Saunders was a bit of a silver fox. Is he as good-looking in the flesh?'

Jay grinned. 'Oh, I should say so.'

'So what's next, then?'

'Well, the rest of the heats need to take place until sixteen people have been selected. And then we'll all go into more intensive heats to get down to eight and then the final four. But that won't be for a while yet.'

'Sounds like tough competition.'

'It is. Who knows if I'll get through, but it won't be for want of trying.'

'I'm sure it won't,' Liz said. 'And I'm backing you all the way.'

'Thanks, Liz. Looks like we're both starting on a journey.'

CHAPTER TWELVE

After work, Liz returned home to cook a dinner of seabass, oregano new potatoes and Mediterranean vegetables. When Alex arrived he immediately pulled her into his arms and kissed her. 'So what have you been doing today?' he said smiling down at her.

'I had a lie-in this morning and later I went to help Jay for a few hours. And don't worry, I haven't overdone it.' She sat down at the table.

Alex frowned. 'I didn't mean it like that. I'm interested in your day, that's all.'

'Sorry.' She knew she was being touchy, but she hated it when he tried to wrap her in cotton wool.

'I just know how much of a perfectionist you are. Maybe you should let Jay do more? He's going to have to take control when you're on maternity leave.'

'Jay is doing more than his fair share of the physical work. As a compromise I've taken over more of the paperwork. Besides which, I'm pregnant, not brain dead.'

'Yes, I know.' He sounded contrite. 'I'm sorry, I just worry.'

'I know you do,' she said, more softly. 'And I understand why. I promise to be careful, but you have to let me be the judge of what I can and can't do. Come on, let's eat before our dinner gets cold,' she added getting up again to dish up their meal.

'Of course.'

They were quiet for a while — the only sound was the scraping of cutlery against plates. When they'd finished, Liz spoke. 'Shall I tell you what else I've been doing today?

'Go on.'

'I've been looking at the house, online.'

His face lit up. 'So tell me. What do you think?'

When they'd been to visit the house yesterday, she'd really liked it. It was a three-storey white-fronted building in the middle of a terrace. With four bedrooms, two en suites and one family bathroom, it more than suited their needs. It also had four reception rooms, two on the ground floor and two in the basement, one of which led straight out into a two-tiered garden. Although it had everything they needed on paper, it was such an important decision that she'd needed some time to think about it. This would be their first proper home together, where they would raise their family, and she wanted them to make the right choice. But as she'd looked at the rooms again online she remembered how they'd looked and how she'd felt there. She'd quickly realised that she had just been procrastinating.

'I think it's perfect,' she said.

'You do?'

'Yes. It's got everything on our tick list. But more than that, it has a good atmosphere and I think we could be happy there.'

'So do I.' He got up from the table and walked over to the coffee table, where he'd left his phone.

'What are you doing?'

'I'm going to phone the estate agent.'

'But it's half past seven. There'll be no one there now.'

He shrugged. 'There might be. And if not, I'll leave a message so they get it first thing in the morning. These kinds of properties get snapped up really quickly. It might be gone already.'

Liz's stomach lurched at the thought. What if someone else had put an offer in while she'd been dithering? She held her breath as the phone rang out and then to her surprise was answered. She listened to the one-sided conversation as Alex offered twenty thousand pounds below the asking price. She sucked in her breath when he said it, because if houses like that were in such demand there was no way the seller was going to accept that.

'Well?' she asked when he put the phone down.

'He's going to speak to the vendor tomorrow. So we'll just have to wait and see.'

'Don't you think your offer was a bit low? I doubt they'll go for that.'

'I doubt they will. They'll know we're interested, but not a pushover. I'll go to the asking price if I have to, but there's no point offering it straight away. Whatever we save will go on fixtures and fittings.'

After they'd cleared away the dinner plates and tidied the kitchen, they sat down together on the sofa. Liz's head was buzzing with thoughts of what they would do to the house if they got it. Now that they had put an offer in, she was desperate to hear that it would become theirs.

'If we do get the house, we'll have to go back straight away and go round each room to see what we want to do with them.'

'Can't wait,' Alex said. 'Although you're only going to be doing the planning. We'll get people in to do the actual work.'

'Of course we will.'

She was a bit disappointed at that. She'd had a romantic image of them shrugging on work clothes and painting the house together. But deep down she had known that would never happen. Alex always got work done by professionals — he wasn't into DIY. Besides, she knew he'd never let her do anything physical. Just in case. She smothered a sigh. This pregnancy wasn't turning out to be the joy she'd hoped it would be. It was so confining. But she was pregnant and that was a blessing in itself. She hoped that as the pregnancy progressed Alex would become a little less insecure about something going wrong, which would take the pressure off. In the meantime, they had a new home to plan. Even if they didn't get this house, she was now determined to find something just as good. And perhaps Alex was right about getting professionals in. She wanted to be in their new home by the time their baby was born.

'It's going to be great buying a new place together.' Alex interrupted her thoughts. 'I've loved living in this apartment, but it's always been more of a bachelor pad than a family home.'

'I agree. And I can't wait to put our own stamp on it.'

'Yes. It's going to be a lot of work, though. Are you sure you don't want me to ask Tia? We can tell her the look we want and make sure she sticks to it.'

'No,' Liz said, sitting up abruptly. 'You know what Tia's like. Whatever we say, she'll push her own ideas on us. I want this house to look like a home, not a show house. And I want it to be *our* home.'

'Fair enough. But if it gets too much . . .'

'It won't. Once we get a feel for what we want, we can source most things online. That way it won't be too taxing. I'm really not budging on this.'

'No, I can see you're not. You always were stubborn.' He kissed her lightly on her nose.

CHAPTER THIRTEEN

The wine bar was already noisy by the time Emma and her colleagues arrived. Emma ordered a glass of white wine before joining Nick and four others at the last empty table. Nick introduced them all — Jenny from HR, Mike, who was one of the chefs, Louise from Reception and, finally, Toby, a server in the restaurant whom she'd previously met when she'd helped out when they'd been short-staffed. Emma had never socialised with them before. She'd kept to herself after the bumpy start she'd had with Heather, but now she realised she'd been missing out. She slipped easily into their banter and felt at home with them almost immediately. It might be nice to have friends outside of her and Jay's life, and could go some way to making work more enjoyable.

After her third glass of wine, Emma was feeling quite tipsy and easily joined in with the laughter around the table.

'I suggest we raise a glass to Emma,' Nick said suddenly.

'Me? Why?' Emma asked, surprised.

'Because you've lasted longer than any of the other train-ees under the wicked witch's supervision.'

'Wicked witch. You called her that yesterday.'

'Well, she is, isn't she?'

Emma laughed. 'She is to me.'

'Well, there you go then. She goes through trainee managers like most people go through socks.'

'How does she get away with it?' Emma asked.

'Who knows? But somehow she manages to persuade management to believe her rather than them. I certainly wouldn't trust her, though. She's always sneaking around listening in on people's conversations when they least suspect it.'

'So what's her background?' Emma asked. She'd given up on getting to know Heather after she'd continually rebuffed her invitations to socialise, but maybe this was a way to find out more about her.

Nick shrugged. 'She doesn't let on about her own life.'

'And she's not interested in coming out with us,' Jenny added. 'I've asked her several times, but by the look on her face you'd have thought I'd asked her to do something horrible.'

'She obviously considers herself above us, so we don't bother with her anymore,' Louise said.

'Which is no hardship,' Nick added. 'She's really not a nice person.'

'We're well out of it, if you ask me,' Toby said. 'At least with each other we can relax and have a good time. You couldn't do that if she was around.'

They all agreed and changed the subject, but, despite how horrible Heather had always been to her, Emma couldn't help feeling just a little bit sorry for her, and she wondered if Heather was lonely.

One by one everyone left, leaving just Emma and Nick. Throughout the evening he'd sat next to her and, because of the limited space around the table, Emma had been aware of the closeness of his leg next to hers. Now that it was just them, there was more room, but still he didn't move away from her. Once again she began to feel uncomfortable.

She edged away from him. 'I think I'd better get going as well.'

'I'll see you home.' He picked up his jacket.

'No, there's no need. It's only a couple of stops on the Northern Line.'

'All the same, you've had a few drinks and I'd never forgive myself if anything happened to you. You live in Kennington, don't you?'

'Yes.' Emma wondered how he knew where she lived. She certainly hadn't told him.

'I don't live too far away from you so I'm going that way anyway.'

'Okay then.' She decided that she'd just have to keep him at a distance.

But she needn't have worried. Nick was the perfect gentleman all the way back.

'Well, this is me,' Emma said when they arrived outside her flat.

'Nice area,' Nick said.

'It's not bad.'

He stepped towards her, staring intently into her eyes, and for one crazy moment she thought he was about to try to kiss her.

'Thanks for seeing me home.' She moved backwards to create some distance between them.

'My pleasure.'

'Well, goodnight then.'

'Goodnight.' He turned to go and then swung back round, standing far too close to her. 'Emma, I—'

He was interrupted by a van pulling up at the pavement next to them. Emma looked at it in shock and again moved away as she realised it was Jay.

Jay got out of the van and headed towards them. 'Emma, what are you doing?'

'Oh, I . . . um, I just went out for a drink after work. Nick wanted to make sure I got home safely.'

Jay looked at Nick. His whole body looked rigid. 'That's very kind of you.' He put his arm protectively around her and she bristled at his action.

'Well, now that you're back, I'll leave you to it,' Nick said, all smiles. 'Nice to meet you, Jay. Glad to hear you're through to the next stage in the competition.'

'Thanks,' Jay said. 'I'm really pleased.' Emma thought he sounded anything but.

Jay turned to her when they were safely inside their apartment. 'So what was that all about?'

'Like I said, I went for a drink after work with some colleagues and Nick wanted to make sure I got home okay.'

'It looked to me as though I turned up just at the right time.'

'What do you mean by that?'

'I mean, it's not very nice to come home from work to find my girlfriend alone with another man, looking like she's about to be kissed by him.'

'Now you're being ridiculous!' She was angry at the implication that she'd wanted to be kissed by Nick, even if she suspected that was exactly what Nick had wanted to do. 'He was walking me home. He was saying goodbye when you pulled up.'

'I bet he was.'

'Oh, that's enough, Jay.'

'Well, that's what it looked like.'

'So? Even if he did want to kiss me, do you think I would have let him?'

'No, of course not.'

'Don't you trust me, Jay?'

'It's not *you* I don't trust. It's him.'

'And I don't have any say in the matter? For your information, the only man I want to be with is you. It's just a pity you don't believe me.'

She kicked off her shoes and headed towards the bedroom, furious with him. She hadn't questioned who he'd been with the other night, even though he'd known she'd been waiting for him, so what right did he have to question her now?

'Emma, I'm sorry, I didn't mean . . .'

'I know exactly what you meant, Jay. I think I'll sleep in the spare room tonight.'

* * *

Emma woke suddenly and felt the darkness engulf her. She checked the time on her phone. Three o'clock. Her head was throbbing as though it had its own heartbeat and her mouth was parched. She reached out for Jay and, finding only emptiness beside her, remembered flouncing off to sleep in the spare bedroom.

Lying as still as she could, she recalled the evening. It had started out so well, the comfortable feeling of togetherness in the pub that she hadn't experienced since she'd left uni. But she'd drunk too much and Nick had offered to walk her home. She remembered the shiver of unease as Nick had stood too close to her on the pavement outside, and then Jay had turned up. She could see how it had looked, but what had made her really angry was that Jay thought if some other man wanted to kiss her she'd let him. She loved Jay and wasn't the type to be unfaithful, not like Susie. If she really felt as though their relationship had no future, she'd end it before starting to see someone else. The thought of Susie reminded her of the woman's hand on Jay's arm on the day of the christening. And even though she had felt very insecure about Susie's presence, she hadn't gone off on Jay, the way he had with her last night. She groaned as she remembered how she'd stormed off. She felt she had every right to be angry, but maybe she had overreacted, just a little. Emotions had been running high on both sides, and they needed to sit down and talk calmly. But not when she had a hangover. She was working a late shift later today, so there was no need for her to get up early. She'd stay in bed and avoid any kind of confrontation until she was feeling much more like herself.

* * *

Jay too was lying awake, wondering what was going on with Emma. When he'd first seen the two people standing on the pavement as he'd pulled up in his van, they'd looked as though they were about to go in for a kiss. But when the woman stepped back, the light of the street lamp caught her face and he'd realised with shock that it was Emma. He'd jumped out of the van to find out what was going on, but stopped himself from rushing at them. Going in all guns blazing would do more harm than good. So he'd pretended to be polite, even though inside he was raging. Of course they'd made out it was all above board, but Jay knew what he'd seen. And Nick was too smooth and too good-looking. He came across as a person who was used to getting what he wanted. Just like Susie. He wondered what Emma would have thought if she'd seen Susie with him in the kitchen on the day of the christening. But that was different. Susie only put her hand on his arm — she hadn't attempted to kiss him.

Jay trusted Emma, of course he did, but the way she'd flown off the handle later was definitely out of character. He wondered if there was something else that was bothering her. She hadn't been pleased when he'd missed their meal after the competition, but he'd been high on adrenaline and, when someone had suggested going for a drink, he'd jumped at the chance to wind down with people with whom he had a shared experience. But now that he thought about it, perhaps that wasn't very fair on Emma. She'd been a rock in the weeks leading up to the first heats of the competition and he felt a stab of guilt at the thought that he'd been neglecting her. Perhaps that was why he had overreacted when he'd seen the two of them together. Because deep down he wondered if she deserved something better, someone better. Someone who wasn't obsessed with his career to the point of neglecting his girlfriend?

Jay turned over and thumped his pillow in frustration. He certainly didn't want to lose Emma and knew he'd have to find some way of making her feel more appreciated, while also not losing sight of his career plans. Somehow he would have to find a way to fit it all in and keep everyone happy.

CHAPTER FOURTEEN

When Emma was sure that Jay had left the flat, she got out of bed and had a shower, which made her feel a little less hungover. As she made coffee she took some paracetamol, hoping to dispel the headache, which was still lingering. Then she made herself some toast, knowing that she had to eat something even though she didn't feel like it.

As she was buttering the toast, a text message came in. It was Jay saying sorry for last night and asking if she wanted to go out for dinner later. She frowned at the message. Although she was glad for the apology, she was a little disappointed that he didn't know she was working. She always wrote her shifts down on the calendar in the kitchen, so he obviously hadn't taken the time to find out what she was doing. Then again, perhaps she was just being over-sensitive. She texted him back to say she was sorry too, but she was working tonight so they'd have to go out another time.

When her phone rang a few minutes later, her first thought was that it was Jay. She really didn't feel like a conversation with him, so she was relieved to see Liz's name flash up on the screen.

'Liz, hi. How are you? Are you feeling better?'

'Much,' Liz said to her relief. 'In fact I've got some good news to tell you.'

'You have? What's that?' Emma had been beginning to think Liz had something seriously wrong with her, so she was pleased that the news was good.

'I'm pregnant.'

'You're pregnant?' Emma repeated, stunned. Then the penny dropped. 'So that's why you've been feeling so rotten recently. It wasn't a virus?'

'No it wasn't, and, Em, I really sorry I lied to you. Alex and I didn't want anyone to know until I was past the twelve-week mark and we knew everything was progressing normally.'

'Yes, I can understand that. Liz, I'm really happy for you both,' Emma said, although part of her felt a little hurt that her friend hadn't confided in her, and had, in fact, deliberately gone out of her way to deceive her.

'I'm so glad, Em. You wouldn't believe what a relief it is to be able to tell you. I've hated all the deceit. And I'm really sorry that I asked Jay to keep it from you too. I had to tell him because of work, but I've been really sensitive about anyone else knowing.'

'Of course you had to tell him. You work so closely together, and it would have been difficult to keep it from him as you were feeling so poorly,' Emma said. She might feel hurt, but she was still determined to be a good friend. At least that explained why Jay had been so secretive recently.

As she walked into the hotel a few hours later, Emma's headache was still lingering. She was dreading work today. She hated it when her boss was on an earlier shift, and wondered if she spent the time working out new ways to torture her. Those afternoons were always the worst and Emma wasn't sure she could cope with the mind games today. They had a big function on later that afternoon for a seventieth birthday party. Heather was supposed to be running it, but Emma anticipated that, as was often the case, her boss would have left it for her to do the donkey work in setting it up. After that they had an awards evening for over a hundred people. It was going to be a busy day. But it was her own fault. She should never have gone out last night. She also hoped she wouldn't bump into Nick as the thought of seeing him again made her feel uneasy. As she reached the office door, she pinned a smile to her face, and walked in.

The smile faded as Heather looked up from her desk and glared at her. What had she done now?

'Oh, so you're here, are you?' Heather looked pointedly at her watch.

'I'm not due in until two. It's only quarter to,' Emma replied, her hangover making her less patient than normal.

'And yet you know how busy we are.'

'Just tell me what you want me to do and I'll get on with it,' Emma snapped. 'Just like I always do.'

'There's no need to take that attitude. I'm your line manager and I deserve some respect. I've a good mind to report you to the senior management team.'

'Report me for what? Being fifteen minutes early for work?'

'No, for your general attitude towards someone who is trying to teach you to be a good manager. You've come in fresh from a few years at college and think you know everything. Well, I'm not going to put up with your abusive behaviour.'

'*My* abusive behaviour?' Emma asked, shocked at the accusation.

'*You* might try to pass things off as banter, but it goes much deeper than that. What's banter to you is really hurtful to others.'

Emma frowned. 'I don't know what you're talking about.' Had Heather finally lost the plot?

'Does the name "wicked witch" mean anything to you?'

'Wicked witch?' And then the penny dropped. The name that had been bandied about in the pub. And while she had laughed with the others, she hadn't brought it up in the first place. Was it her fault Heather made herself so disagreeable to everyone that they retaliated?

102

'Ah, yes, so it's true. I can tell by the look on your face. You know exactly what I'm talking about.'

'Yes, but it wasn't me who—'

'Don't try and wriggle out of it,' Heather interrupted her. 'I heard it straight from the horse's mouth. Your friends were laughing about it in the staffroom. They didn't know I was outside. And I know it was you who called me it.'

'I . . . I . . .' Emma didn't know what to say. Should she drop the others in it by telling Heather that was what they all called her? She couldn't do that even though, right at this moment, she was absolutely furious with them.

'You see, you can't deny it, can you?' Heather continued, her rage mounting. She pointed her finger at Emma. 'You're nothing but a bully in the making.'

Me? Emma was incredulous. *'I'm* the bully?' Something inside her snapped. 'Well, I suppose you should know what a bully looks like, because you're the biggest bully I've ever met.' She reached into her handbag and pulled out her notebook. 'And I have the evidence to prove it.' She waved the book at Heather. 'In here is a detailed list of every time you've bullied or belittled me since you've been my line manager. Believe me, it covers quite a few pages.'

Heather tried to snatch it off her, but Emma was too quick and pulled it back.

'Oh, no, you don't. Because I've had enough and it's me who's going to report you. I've put up with it for so long because I was hoping that one day I'd finally impress you and you'd back off. But now I can see that's never going to happen.'

She strode towards the door.

'Where are you going?'

Emma stopped and turned back to face her. 'I'm going to the general manager's office. And we'll see what he has to say about bullies.'

Before Heather could protest, Emma strode out of the office and down the corridor. After her outburst she was literally shaking, and knew she needed to calm down if she was going to put a rational case forward to senior management. She made a U-turn and headed towards the staffroom. They had so much to do this afternoon that she didn't really have the time to waste, but she was so hyped up she didn't think she could work in the state she was in. She switched the kettle on and as it rose to the boil she thought about what had just happened. How dare that woman accuse her of being a bully after all she had put Emma through. Yes, she had been complicit in calling her a witch, but she hadn't actually said it out loud before last night and she hadn't come up with the nickname. But she had condoned it and maybe that made her as bad as the rest.

Emma spooned coffee into a mug and poured the boiling water over it. As she put the kettle down, a noise behind her made her turn. It was Nick. She really didn't want to see him right now.

'Feeling rough?' he asked.

She reached for the milk. 'Not the best.'

'It was a good night though.'

She nodded her head. The actual evening had been good, but she wished she'd left the pub on her own and definitely wished she hadn't drunk so much. She wouldn't be doing that again in a hurry.

'But the after-effects maybe not so much?' he asked.

She didn't want him to think that it was just a hangover that was affecting her. 'No, especially when I've just got it in the neck from Heather for calling her names.'

'What?' He looked confused, but she wasn't going to let him off the hook. Nick had been the first one to call Heather the name and she wondered if he'd been involved in the gossip that morning.

'She overheard a group of you talking about her. Calling her the wicked witch. Somehow she got the impression it had come from me.'

'Oh, shit! Sorry. Yes, we were talking, and we did mention your name, but only because you're the one she picks on the most.'

'Well, she definitely heard my name because she's holding me responsible for calling her that. She even said I was a bully.'

Nick laughed. 'That's rich. Coming from her.'

'That's what I thought, which is why I told her that I was going to report her to the general manager.'

Nick's eyes widened. 'Shit! You said that?'

'I did.'

'And are you really going to do it?'

'I think so,' Emma said slowly. 'But not today. I need to think it through properly before I do. Rehearse what I'm going to say first.'

'Well, I wish you luck with that,' Nick said. 'Only don't be surprised if you don't get the outcome you want.'

'What do you mean?'

'It's happened before and it didn't turn out well for the person who accused her.'

'In what way?'

'Let's just say that, after she made the complaint, Heather made her life even more of a misery. In the end she couldn't take it and left.'

Emma nodded. 'If that happens, it happens. But I need to stand up for myself. I've let her get away with it for far too long.'

'You're right, of course. And it's good that you're thinking it through and not rushing into it. And it would be even nicer if you stayed.' His tone had softened and Emma felt as though they were heading back into dangerous territory. She took a sip of her coffee and was about to head out of the room when he moved closer.

'I really enjoyed last night. Especially when it was just the two of us. Might be nice to do it again sometime?'

'I enjoyed going out with *everyone*. It's nice to have work friends.'

'So this is where you are!' Faye Greenwood, one of the senior managers, bustled into the staffroom. 'I've been looking for you. Might have known you'd be slacking in here. Come on, you've got work to do. The afternoon-tea function isn't going to manage itself.'

For a second Emma wondered why Faye thought she was a slacker, as though this happened all the time. But then she latched on to what Faye had said about running the function.

'I thought Heather was in charge of that.'

'Heather has gone home sick. Migraine apparently. Brought on by stress. So you'd better get yourself down to the Orchid Suite and make sure it's set up in time. The guests will be arriving in an hour.'

'Yes, of course.' Emma put her coffee down and went to leave, but Faye wasn't finished.

'And you'll be in charge of the running of the function as I'll be setting up for the awards event in the Clover Suite. I'll need you to help me with that when you've finished. It's all hands to the pump today, Emma, and I expect you to pull your weight.

'Yes, of course. I'll get on it straight away.'

* * *

Emma dashed straight back to the office and picked up the clipboard with all the information for the afternoon's function. She quickly glanced through it. Then she put her notebook back into her bag and locked it in her desk drawer, slipping the key into her pocket. Heather might have done a runner following her threat, but she didn't really trust anyone at the moment and she didn't want the book getting into the wrong hands. She straightened her hair back into her ponytail and took a deep breath as she prepared to step into the fray. With Heather out of sight for the evening and Emma being under Faye's scrutiny, she would show Faye she was a hard worker and could be a good manager if she was given half a chance. This was her opportunity and she was determined to make the most of it.

* * *

The Orchid Suite was one of the hotel's more intimate function suites, with French doors that led out to the small but immaculate garden at the back of the hotel. Today it had been decorated with *Happy Birthday* banners and balloons with *70* on them, but that was where the preparations ended.

Emma took one look at the chaos of the rest of the room and went into battle. The serving staff had been working at a snail's pace with no one to supervise them, and they were nowhere near ready. Only half the tables were set and there was more chatter going on than polishing the silver and glasses.

'Hi, everyone.' She spoke in her loudest voice while also forcing a smile. 'The guests will be arriving in an hour, so I think we need to step up the pace to make sure we're ready.'

'Where's Heather?' Sally, a waitress whom Emma had always found sullen and uncooperative, asked.

'She's gone home sick. So you'll have to put up with me. Now let's get organised. Sally and Joanne, you're on silver. Quick as you can so we can get the tables laid up. Eric, John, same with the glasses. Amy, how are you at folding napkins into fans?'

Amy smiled. 'Yes, I like doing that.'

'Good, and, if you haven't finished when the tables are set, we'll all join in to help. Now, I'll go and get the centrepieces, and when I'm done I'll start laying up the tables, so make sure you have plenty for me to work with.'

'You're going to lay the tables?' Sally asked in surprise.

'Yes.'

'Heather usually leaves us to it.'

'Well, I'm not Heather and we don't have much time left. It's teamwork we need now and that means everyone. Got it?'

Sally nodded and, as Emma turned her back on her, she smiled to herself. She'd show them. She'd show them all.

* * *

It was all going well, Emma thought, standing at the edge of the reception room as the servers poured drinks for the fifty guests. After her little pep talk, the team had pulled together and Emma had quickly realised that showing them she was capable of doing whatever she asked them to do was a wise move. Even Sally had seemed to thaw a little. The room had been ready on time, and now the champagne was flowing and the kitchen was ready to serve the afternoon tea. Emma was just about to ask the guests to find their places when the woman whose birthday it was came rushing towards her, looking panic-stricken.

Emma instantly went to her side. 'Is everything all right?'

'No, I'm afraid not,' the woman said breathlessly. 'It's my granddaughter.' She pointed out a teenage girl dressed like a goth. 'Last week she was vegetarian, which is down on the menu choices, but in the last five minutes she's told me that she's now vegan, so what I've ordered for her isn't suitable. I'm sorry it's such short notice.'

'Well, I'm sure we can accommodate that,' Emma said. She hoped the kitchen could back her up. 'Let me just go and have a word with Chef.'

As Emma was about to leave the room, Sally came over.

'Is anything wrong?' she asked.

'Just a last-minute dietary requirement. I need to go and see Chef. Can you keep the drinks flowing in my absence?'

'Will do.' Sally smiled and Emma was amazed at the change in her from earlier that afternoon.

The heat from the kitchen hit her as she walked through the swing door, while a cacophony of busyness assaulted her ears.

Chef was standing in the middle of the kitchen directing operations. As Emma walked towards him, he turned round. He was a stickler for precision and ruled his kitchen with a rod of iron. He was also known for having a grudge against any front-of-house staff member who didn't do exactly as he asked them, the moment he asked them to do it.

'Ah, Miss Taylor, the afternoon-tea trays are just about ready to go. Do you want to send your staff in to collect them?'

'Not quite,' Emma said, her voice quavering. 'I have a slight problem. I've just been told one of the vegetarian dishes now needs to be vegan. I know it's last minute, but I'd really appreciate it if you could accommodate that.'

'Right, well we do have vegan options on the restaurant menu, so we'll just have to find something we can switch. . . .'

'If you could, I would really appreciate it. This is only the second function I've managed on my own and I need it to go well.'

'Where's Heather?'

'Sick, apparently.'

'And left you in the lurch?'

'Something like that.'

'Okay, so we've got vegan cheese tartlets on the menu and I could rustle up some bean wraps, and then there's vegan chocolate cake. If you can give me ten minutes, I'll have it sorted for you.'

'That will be perfect. Thank you so much.'

'My pleasure. Especially when you've asked so nicely, rather than come in here demanding.'

Emma rushed back to the function room with a sigh of relief, knowing that disaster had been averted. Sally looked up as she came through the door and she nodded towards her with a smile before going to speak to the guest of honour.

'Oh, thank you so much,' the lady said, beaming at her, when Emma told her it had all been arranged. 'I've been planning this party for months and want everyone to enjoy it. I'm very grateful.'

'It's our pleasure,' Emma replied. 'Give me five minutes, and I'll start to ask everyone to find their seats.'

'Excellent. Thank you again.'

Emma smiled. It was good to be appreciated.

* * *

'Thank you again for a wonderful afternoon.' The guest of honour came over to Emma as the last of the tea cups were being cleared away.

Emma sensed a presence by her side and turned to see that Faye Greenwood had entered the room.

'I hope everything was to your satisfaction?' Faye asked before Emma could reply.

'It was far more than satisfactory. The food was excellent, the service ran like clockwork and this young lady went out of her way to make a last-minute adjustment. Carly loved her meal, by the way — she had everyone wanting to try her vegan cheese tartlets.'

'I'm only glad we could accommodate her,' Emma replied. 'And, most importantly of all, that you've had a lovely birthday.'

'Oh, I have! And so many of my friends have said it's the best afternoon tea they've ever tasted.'

'That's lovely to hear. Is there anything else I can do for you?'

'No, thank you, dear, I just have to say my goodbyes to everyone and then we'll be on our way.'

Emma smiled as the woman went to join her friends.

'Well, that obviously went well,' Faye said. 'Looks like you did a good job.'

Emma blushed slightly at the praise. 'It all went according to plan and the guests seemed happy.'

'And that's the main thing. But now, there's no rest for the wicked. The function in the Clover Suite is about to start and I need you and two of your servers.'

'Sure,' Emma said. She spotted Sally and beckoned her over.

'There's another function about to start and they're short on servers. Would you and Amy be able to help out?'

Sally smiled. 'Of course, I'll go and grab her. Where is it?'

'Clover Suite,' Emma replied. She turned back to Faye, to find her frowning. 'Is anything the matter?'

'No, not really,' Faye replied. 'I'm just a bit surprised, that's all. I don't think I've ever seen Sally smile before. At least not when you ask her to do something. How did you manage that?'

Emma blushed, but tried to sound nonchalant. 'She's a really good worker when you get on the right side of her.'

'Well, you certainly seem to have managed that.'

CHAPTER FIFTEEN

By the time the second function was over, Emma felt like a wrung-out dishrag. Her legs and back were aching and all she wanted to do was to go home, take off her shoes, get into her pyjamas and drink a very large mug of hot chocolate before going to bed. But when everything was cleared away, Faye asked, 'Fancy a drink in the bar before heading home?'

Emma nodded reluctantly. That was the last thing she wanted, but she didn't feel as though she should turn the invitation down.

'That would be nice.'

The lounge bar was relatively quiet and Emma sat down at a corner table as Faye brought over two large glasses of white wine. The smell turned her stomach and Emma immediately wished she'd asked for a soft drink, but after the first few sips she began to feel a little better.

'You did well, today,' Faye said after a few moments.

'Thank you.'

'You seem to have a natural flair for running functions.'

'I don't know about that,' Emma replied with a chuckle. 'But I've had plenty of practice.'

'Have you?' Faye raised an eyebrow in surprise. 'Not here though?'

'No, I've only done one function here on my own before today.' Emma decided to take a risk 'I don't think Heather trusts me enough to do anything other than the most menial of tasks.'

Faye frowned. 'I see. But you have previous experience?'

'Yes. While I was at college I worked part-time for a private chef, Liz Sinclaire, or Cartwright as she was then. For the bigger functions, I'd organise the front of house while she prepared the food.'

'Does Heather know this?'

'Oh, yes. A few weeks ago, we did the christening for Lord Weatherton's grandson. Heather was keen to hear all about it.'

'You did that?'

'Yes, we originally catered for his daughter's engagement party, so he asked us back.'

Faye raised her eyebrows. 'That was in *Hello!* magazine, wasn't it? Very posh do.'

'It was and it put Liz on the map. She and my boyfriend, who's also a chef, went into partnership and they combine private catering with the functions at Diva's restaurant in Fitzroy Square.'

'Isn't that run by Roberto Bianchi?'

'He's a partner in it, yes, along with Liz's husband, Alex Sinclaire, and Tia McIntyre, the interior designer.'

Faye drank the rest of the wine in her glass and got up from the table. 'Do you want another?' she asked. Emma shook her head. She'd only drunk half of hers and didn't want any more.

When Faye came back from the bar, she asked, 'So if you have all these connections in the catering industry, why did you choose to work at the Rosemont?'

'I don't just want to do functions, I want to learn about all the aspects of hotel management. I suppose I could have done that at Alex's hotel. In fact, he did offer, but I wanted to do something on my own merit, not through my connections.'

'Well, that's good. And what have you learned so far?'

Emma paused, and thought carefully before answering. 'Some of the paperwork has been quite interesting.'

Faye frowned as though she was trying to remember something.

'Tell me, the health-and-safety database. Whose idea was that?'

Emma hesitated again and Faye answered for her. 'By your silence I can only assume it was yours?'

Emma nodded.

'And the recommendations following the collation of the customer-feedback questionnaires?'

Emma nodded again.

'And did you know that Heather passed them off as her own?'

Emma tried again to formulate a diplomatic answer. 'I suspected she might have done.'

'I probably shouldn't be saying this, but she's done you a great disservice. She's had us all believing that you are lazy and difficult to work with.'

Shocked that Heather had been bad-mouthing her so much, Emma took a large gulp of her wine and decided that it was now or never.

'I don't know what I've done to turn her so against me, and I don't like to speak ill of people when they're not around to defend themselves, but she's the one who's been difficult to work with. I've been unhappy for a while, so I've kept a notebook of all the things she's said and done that have made me feel uncomfortable.'

'You should have said something.'

'I didn't like to and I was hoping that, if I worked hard, things would get easier. But ironically, today she accused me of being a bully, so I decided to do something about it. I told her I was going to take the book to the general manager.'

'But you didn't?'

'No. I needed to calm down first, so I went to the staffroom and that's where you found me.'

'And Heather suddenly developed a migraine.'

'I suppose so, yes.'

'It's all beginning to make sense now,' Faye said. 'Thank you, Emma.'

'What for?'

'First of all, your professionalism tonight under what must be difficult circumstances. But also for your honesty. You may not have felt comfortable speaking against your line manager, but these things needed to be said.'

Emma didn't know how to answer that, but Faye finished her wine and patted her on her arm. 'Come on, it's late and you must be shattered. Let's get you a taxi home on account. It's far too late for you to be getting on the Tube on your own. And just for the record, I suspect things are going to be very different for you from now on.'

* * *

As she sat back in the taxi, Emma contemplated the day. It had certainly been a day of challenges and surprises, but it had been good to stretch herself and to earn respect from other staff, particularly Faye. But for now, she was more than ready for her bed.

When she walked into the apartment, a light was shining from under the living-room door and she could hear the rumbling of the television. Although she was tempted to go straight to bed, she opened the door and went in.

Jay sprang up from the sofa. 'Emma, at last! I thought you were never coming back!'

'The function I was working dragged on,' she said, not wanting to mention the drink she'd had afterwards. He'd probably jump to the wrong conclusion.

'Oh, I see. Well, I've been waiting for you because I wanted to say I'm sorry for last night and I'd really like us to talk.'

She sighed. 'I'm sorry too, Jay, and don't take this the wrong way, but right now all I want to do is go to bed.'

114

'Oh.'

'I know we need to talk, but I just can't do it now. I'm dog-tired.'

'Okay.'

He looked so crestfallen, she tried to reassure him. 'Look, let's forget about last night. Maybe we both overreacted. Let's put it in the past and concentrate on the future.'

'So you still want us to have a future?'

She crossed the room to him and gave him a hug. He hugged her back tightly. 'Of course I do. We just need to work out how we can manage it around everything else we have going on in our lives. Right now, though, I just need to sleep.'

'All right. I understand. But you're sleeping in our bed, right?'

'Of course.'

'Good. I really missed you last night.'

'I missed you too.'

CHAPTER SIXTEEN

Jay pushed down the handle on his nan's front door and it yielded, just as he'd known it would.

'Hello, Nan!'

'In the kitchen.'

He walked down the hallway to where Betty spent most of her time when she was at home. She pulled a tray of freshly baked scones out of the oven.

'They smell wonderful.'

'Then you've timed it just right,' she said with a broad grin.

'I certainly have.'

He didn't dare tell her that he'd just eaten a huge breakfast and wasn't hungry — he knew better than to refuse any food his nan offered him. Emma was on a late shift again so, determined they should spend some time together, he'd made her favourite brunch dish — shakshuka.

'This is nice,' Emma had said, yawning as she'd walked into the kitchen.

'I didn't think you'd have had much of a chance to eat last night.'

'You're right, I didn't. And I'm absolutely starving.'

He placed the pan containing eggs cooked in tomato sauce and spices in the middle of the table, and added freshly baked bread.

Emma sat down and ate hungrily. When they were both finished, Jay turned to her. 'I'm sorry if I've been neglecting you recently. I haven't meant to. You mean the world to me, but I've had a lot on my mind.'

'I know that and I understand. All I want to do is to support you, but I can't do that if you shut me out.'

'I get that and I'll try to include you in the future.'

'That's all I'm asking. Being shut out makes me feel insecure. I suppose it stems from my childhood. I never really felt like I was part of Mum and Dad's life, so maybe that explains why I have a tendency to overreact if it happens to me now I'm an adult.'

He felt another wave of guilt at her explanation. She'd never really spoken much about her parents, other than saying that they weren't close, but this explained a lot. When they had more time together, he decided he would ask her more about what her life had been like growing up, so that he could understand her even better.

'I forgot to mention it last night, but Liz phoned me yesterday,' she said, startling him out of his plans.

His stomach lurched. 'Oh?'

'Yes, she told me her good news. I'm thrilled for them both.'

'Yes, me too. She never thought it would happen.'

'She told me you already knew.'

'Yes, I did.' He paused. 'Look, I'm really sorry I kept it from you but I made her a promise.'

'I understand. It wasn't your secret to tell,' she said.

'I don't think she would have even told me if she hadn't been suffering from terrible morning sickness.'

'Well, at least it now all makes sense. The virus excuse certainly didn't.'

'Yes.' He sighed, glad that it was finally all out in the open.

'I knew you were keeping something from me, so it's a relief to know that's what it was.'

'Again, I'm sorry. No more secrets from now on.'

She smiled then. 'Good, I'm glad we've got that all sorted.'

* * *

'Jam and cream?' Betty asked, interrupting Jay's thoughts.

'Of course.' He groaned inwardly as she handed him a huge plateful of her baking. 'Nan, I wish you'd keep your front door locked.'

'I know. You keep telling me.'

'If you'd just put your key in the lock when you come in, then you'd always know where your key was.'

'I always do know where it is. It's on the dresser. See. Here.' She picked up the key and waved it under his nose. 'Besides, if the door was locked, I'd have had to come and open it for you just now and my scones might have burned.'

'Nan! Anyone could walk in. I worry about you.'

'Oh, okay, I give in.' Betty stomped down the hallway and he heard the key turn. 'There! Happy now?' she said as she came back into the kitchen.

'Very.'

'Good, now eat up. Do you want a cuppa?'

'Please.'

'So,' she said while she waited for the kettle to boil. 'Tell me what you've been up to.'

'Working mainly. I didn't tell you when we spoke on the phone, but Liz and Alex are expecting a baby.'

'Oh, that's wonderful news!' She clapped her hands. 'I'll have to get my knitting needles out. I love having a baby to knit for.'

Jay smiled. Knowing Alex, he suspected all Baby Sinclaire's clothes would be designer. 'That's lovely, Nan. The thing is, Liz has been suffering from terrible morning sickness and the last thing she needs is to work with food, so I've been trying to pick up the slack for her.'

'That can't have been easy alongside the competition. Is she feeling any better?'

'Starting to, yes, which is good timing because I've just got the brief through for the next stage.'

She moved towards her armchair and scooped Roland up into her arms. 'Come on you, time to let the humans have a seat.' She put him gently down on the floor and he looked up at her. *If cats could scowl*, Jay thought, *that one was definitely making his feelings known*. 'Go on, go outside.' Betty nudged him gently with her foot. Roland twined himself around her ankles, jumped onto a kitchen chair and plonked himself down again. 'Oh, well, have it your own way.' Betty turned to Jay. 'So what have you got to do this time?'

'Well, it's the same brief as last time, but now it's a starter and a fish course.'

'And do you know what you want to cook?'

'Not really, no. I've been looking through the recipe book, though, and it has given me some ideas, but I'm not sure if they're too simple.'

'What are you thinking? I might be able to help you there.'

Jay was surprised. 'Help me create a banquet-worthy dish?'

'Don't mock. I've been watching *MasterChef* and I figure I've learned a bit about fancy-pants cooking.'

Jay stifled a chuckle. He could see she was being sincere and, if she thought he was laughing at her, she'd be deeply offended. He could always run it past Liz later.

'Well, a lot of the recipes were written during the war, so many of them are vegetarian due to rationing.'

'That's right,' Betty replied. 'Meat was in such short supply, even after the war ended as the rationing continued. Everyone had turned to their gardens into vegetable patches and were practically vegetarian.'

'And with plant-based foods being so popular now, I thought I might try to make a version of a vegetable soup.'

'Vegetable soup?' Horror was written all over Betty's face. 'Are you off your trolley?'

'Don't worry, it won't be a chunky, stick-to-your-ribs kind of soup.'

'The kind I make, you mean?'

'The kind you need on a cold winter's day to warm your cockles.' He was rewarded with a smile. 'No, I'd treat the veg very delicately and use edible flowers. But the soup itself would be a vegetable consommé. There's an enormous amount of skill in making that properly.'

'There is,' Betty replied knowingly. 'But consommé doesn't sound very English.'

'I suppose it doesn't,' Jay said, realising she had a point. 'The ingredients are English though. Maybe I could call it a vegetable broth?'

'That sounds better. And you can serve it in one of those glass teapots they like so much. And put the vegetables and flowers at the bottom of a wide dish so that they look like a garden.'

Jay stared at his nan, dumbfounded. 'You *have* learned a lot on *MasterChef*.'

She grinned at him. 'Told you so.'

'Maybe I could call it, "Garden on a Plate"?'

'Oh, yes, I like that idea. So what are your ideas for the fish course?'

'Fish and chips?'

'Hmm, yes, a good old staple, but how can we posh that up? What fish were you thinking of using?'

'Traditional cod or maybe seabass. Either way, a delicate white fish.'

'And instead of doing chips, you could do those spirally things and deep fry them.'

'Now that is a good idea,' Jay replied, once again impressed.

'Will you be having mushy peas?'

Jay pulled a face. He'd never been a lover of mushy peas. 'No, samphire, maybe, and I'd serve it with a champagne-and-cockle sauce.'

Betty frowned and Jay asked. 'Don't you like champagne?'

120

'Can't say I'm overly fond. But it's French again. Why don't you use sparkling English wine? They make that in Kent, don't they?'

Jay gave her a hug. 'You know what, Nan? You're a genius.'

'There's wisdom in this old head of mine, and don't you forget it.'

'I won't,' Jay said. He was keen to get back to the kitchen to crack on with turning their ideas into winning dishes.

'Now, before you get too carried away.' Betty stopped him in his tracks. 'How are you getting on with your mother?'

'Nan! You know I wasn't impressed with that little stunt you pulled the other week.'

'I know you weren't and your mother said the same. But someone needed to do something to bang your heads together. The question is, did it work?'

'Well, we're texting each other more often.'

'But you haven't met up yet?'

'No. I've been too busy and I'm not sure my head is in the right space at the moment. I've got too many other things going on.'

'Yes, I can see that. But don't keep putting it off for the sake of it.'

'I won't, Nan, I promise. Maybe when this competition is over we can meet up, and then take it from there.'

'Good. Make sure you do. And now, you'd better get off. I can see you want to be back in your own kitchen.'

Jay reached out and gave her another hug. 'You know, Nan, sometimes I think you know me better than I know myself.'

'You might well be right there, son, you might well be right.'

* * *

Emma was nervous as she walked into the hotel, worried that Heather would have recovered from her migraine and be back

121

at work. She was still furious with her line manager for giving her a bad reputation among the others, and wondered whether she'd be able to keep a lid on it if she had to deal with Heather face to face.

One of the receptionists called out to her as she passed by the desk.

'Emma, Faye asked you to go to her office when you came in.'

'Okay, thanks,' Emma replied. A flurry of nerves somersaulted in her stomach. She hoped this wasn't going to be bad news. When she reached the office, she tapped lightly on the open door. Faye looked up and smiled.

'Emma, come in and take a seat.'

Emma sat gingerly on the chair opposite Faye's desk and waited for her to speak. 'Heather phoned in sick this morning and informed us that she is likely to be off for at least the next two weeks.'

Immediately Emma felt a surge of relief. She wouldn't have to see her for a whole fortnight. Despite her jubilance, she kept her face nonchalant.

'Two weeks. That sounds serious. I thought it was just a migraine.'

'Yes, so did I, but it appears she is suffering from severe stress.'

'Stress?' Emma was shocked. 'Did she say what has caused the stress? She's not blaming me, is she?'

'No, you don't need to worry about that. I'm just advising you that I'll be taking over as your line manager in Heather's absence.'

'You will?' Emma once again felt a surge of relief.

'Yes, so if you can let me know where you're up to in your training programme?'

'Training programme?'

'Yes, your four-week rota covering each department from the top to the bottom. Which departments have you covered so far?'

'Well, um . . .' Even though it wasn't her fault that Heather had never actually told her about the plan, Emma felt the heat rise in her face. 'I haven't done any of them. Not really. Most of the time I've just been filling in wherever I've been needed most. So I've been a server in the restaurant, room cleaning, the bar and whatever admin she has needed me to do.'

Faye pursed her lips. 'So, no formal training plan, then?'

'No, I'm sorry. I wasn't even aware there was one.'

'No need for you to apologise.' Faye put down the pen she'd been fiddling with. 'In fact, I'm sorry. We should have kept a closer eye on what was going on. There's a lesson for us all in this and I can assure you that it will be investigated.'

'Oh, okay.' Emma thought to herself that, if Heather thought she was stressed now, she'd be under even more pressure when she did return to work.

'So, we established last night that you're experienced in functions. Where would you say you have the least knowledge?'

'Well, I've never worked on Reception or had anything to do with room allocation.'

'Right, well then, I suggest you take the weekend as your days off and from Monday you'll start a four-week stint on Reception, followed by housekeeping, where you can learn how to run the department, not just clean rooms, then twelve weeks in the office, four doing general admin, four in finance and a further four in HR, and, after that, twelve weeks in food and beverage. How does that sound?'

'That sounds fantastic.'

Emma was stunned. She had never imagined today would turn out like this. Finally, she was going to get the all-round training she'd been hoping for when she'd first taken the job.

'Good. You might want to finish up any paperwork in your office for the rest of today so the decks are cleared, and I'll liaise with Reception to sort out a new rota for the next four weeks. Is that okay?'

'That's wonderful, Faye. I can't thank you enough for this.'

'There's no need to thank me. This should have been implemented from the start of your employment.'

Emma rose from her seat. 'I'll get straight to it.'

'Good.' As Emma was about to leave the office, Faye added, 'Oh, sorry, just one more thing. Could you go through the paperwork on Heather's desk and let me know if there's anything that needs to be dealt with?'

'Will do,' Emma said. She was barely able to keep the smile off her face as she stopped off at the staffroom to make a quick cup of coffee. She couldn't wait to get stuck into the outstanding paperwork so that she could start afresh on Monday, learning the ropes of Reception.

* * *

When she had cleared her own desk later that afternoon, Emma sat herself down in Heather's chair. It felt weird to be there and occasionally she looked over her shoulder in case she was caught in the act of doing something she shouldn't. But Faye had asked her to do this, so she was only following instructions. The desktop and in-trays were clear, so Emma opened the top drawer of the desk just to make sure she hadn't missed anything. But as she struggled with the drawer, she found she had to push down the contents before she could pull it open. Inside was a huge mass of paperwork. Emma pulled it out and piled it up in the centre of the desk. The other drawers revealed similar rafts of paperwork, which Emma piled up with the others. It formed quite an impressive tower.

Emma eyed the paper. 'So this is where you've been hiding it.' She'd often wondered how Heather always managed to look so efficient, with the top of her desk clear. Now she knew the answer — she'd been hiding it all away.

As Emma began to work her way through the pile, a knot of anxiety grew in her stomach. There was so much outstanding. Changes to future function bookings, personnel requests that needed to be followed up with HR, reports to be compiled for management meetings. As much as Emma didn't get on with Heather, and was unhappy about the way the woman had treated her, she didn't feel comfortable reporting her to management. It was such a mess. She began to work through it all, dealing with what she could but knowing she would have to pass a lot of it on to Faye.

Emma gasped as she read an email that had been printed out. She blinked and re-read it, not sure if she was seeing things. Her thoughts slipped back to the first function she'd overseen for Heather, when twenty guests had unexpectedly turned up. She remembered the roasting Heather had given her for not checking the paperwork, accusing her of incompetence, yet here was an email dated five days before the function advising them of the change in guest numbers. And Heather had obviously seen it because she'd printed it.

She let out the breath she'd been holding. Had this been an oversight? Had Heather printed this off and forgotten about it, or had she planned that Emma would be in charge of the function and had deliberately withheld the information to drop her in it on the day? What Emma did know was that the complaint was still being investigated and she had no choice but to pass this on to Faye. It wasn't even a matter of conscience. She put the email to one side and continued to sort the rest of the papers into type of action and order of urgency. When she'd finished, she placed the most incriminating email on the top and went to find Faye.

Faye was at her desk, her eyes focused on her computer screen. She looked up and smiled when Emma tapped gently on the door.

'Ah, Emma, what can I do for you?'

Emma walked into the office, aware that Faye's smile wasn't going to last for very long. She put the folder she was carrying down on her manager's desk and said simply, 'You asked me to go through Heather's paperwork and bring to you anything that needed to be dealt with.'

Faye's eyes widened. 'And all this needs to be dealt with, does it?'

'I'm afraid so. I've done whatever I could, but this is what is left.'

'Where did you find this? Heather's desk looked pretty clear to me.'

'It was. I found these in the drawers. I've sorted them into department and urgency.'

Faye nodded and pulled the pile towards her. As she picked up the piece of paper on top, Emma explained what it was.

'So, we did receive the revised numbers after all?' Faye asked when Emma had finished explaining.

'Heather must have known because she printed it off, but she categorically denied it.' She paused. 'I really didn't want to drop her in it, but I felt it was important.'

Faye nodded. 'You've done the right thing. Not having this information would have made us look very foolish when reporting back to the client. And don't worry about dropping Heather in it. She certainly didn't have any qualms about doing the same to you.' She paused and passed over another piece of paper to Emma.

'Here you are — your shifts for the next four weeks. I've put you on earlies for the first week so you can get to grips with what happens from the beginning of the day. You'll be shadowing Inga — she's one of our most experienced receptionists and she enjoys training up the newbies, so you'll be in good hands.'

'Thank you,' Emma said. She couldn't believe how relieved she felt to be working for a manager who had her best interests at heart. She knew she would have to make the most of the next few weeks because there would be hell to pay when Heather came back to work.'

Faye looked at her watch. 'It's almost the end of your shift. Why don't you get off and enjoy your weekend?'

'Thank you. I will do.' Emma paused at the doorway. 'I really do appreciate this, you know.'

126

Faye smiled and nodded. 'There's absolutely no need for you to thank me. From now on, you'll be getting the training you deserve, and I can only apologise for what you've suffered so far. I can assure you, it will be properly investigated, and it will be my mission to make sure it never happens again.'

Emma resisted the temptation to say thank you again. Instead she nodded and got up to leave, a smile spreading across her face.

CHAPTER SEVENTEEN

As soon as Emma left the hotel, she called Jay to see if he had any plans for the evening.

'Just a quiet night in,' he replied. 'I was thinking of ordering a takeaway. I don't feel like cooking tonight.'

'How about we eat out instead?'

'Sounds wonderful, if you're not too tired.'

'Definitely not. I've got the whole weekend and I'm in the mood to celebrate.'

'Wonderful!' Jay said. Emma was relieved that he seemed keen and hadn't made excuses to stay in. 'Is it just the time off you're celebrating?'

'Nope, much more than that.'

'What, then?'

She chuckled. 'I'll tell you later. I'll be home soon, have a quick change of clothes and we can go somewhere to eat.'

'Sounds perfect. Do you want me to book Luigi's?'

'Yes, let's, and then afterwards why don't we go to Winston's and dance the night away.'

'Winston's? We haven't been there for ages. You are in the mood to celebrate.'

'Oh, I certainly am.'

* * *

When they were seated at a corner table in their favourite restaurant, Jay asked, 'So come on then, tell me what we're celebrating?'

She told him and Jay immediately raised his glass to clink with hers. 'Oh, Em, I can't tell you how happy I am to hear that. I know what you've been going through and at last that Heather woman is going to get what she deserves. But more than that, I'm glad that now, finally, you have the chance to prove to everyone just how good you are.'

'Let's just hope I can do it.'

'Oh, you can. I know that for a fact.'

'I must admit, it does feel like a great weight has been lifted from my shoulders. Which is why I feel like dancing.'

'Then dance we will. Till the early hours. And I've got nothing on tomorrow, so we can have a lie-in and a lazy Saturday together.'

'Sounds wonderful. It's been ages since we've had the time to do that.'

'And we're going to make the most of it,' he said, leaning across the table to kiss her.

* * *

Winston's was crowded when Emma and Jay arrived. They ordered drinks and were lucky enough to find a spare table as a couple got up to leave. The music was loud yet mellow, and they drank and danced and laughed for the next few hours. Emma couldn't remember the last time she had felt so carefree. She vowed that she would make the time so that Jay and she could do this more often. She was so happy she didn't notice Susie walk into the bar until she was standing over their table.

'Hello, Jay,' Susie said, smiling, then turned to Emma. 'Hello . . . Um, sorry, I can't remember your name.'

'Emma,' she replied through gritted teeth. She hoped that Jay wouldn't let Susie spoil their evening.

'Oh, yes, Emma.' She turned back to Jay. 'Haven't seen you in here for a while, Jay, darling. Thought you'd got too serious to party.'

'Never too serious to party,' Jay replied. 'But life has moved on for me. As I told you at the christening.'

'The christening, yes. So you haven't had a change of heart after our conversation?' She smiled at him in what Emma suspected she thought was a seductive pout, but Jay didn't react.

'No, Susie, I haven't. Emma and I are very much together, but I wouldn't want to be with you even if I was single.' As the music slowed, he turned to Emma. 'Fancy a dance, Em? The air around this table has gone suddenly toxic.'

He pulled her into his arms on the dancefloor and she snuggled into him, her heart pounding. Jay sending Susie away like that was the perfect end to what had been an amazing day.

* * *

Emma didn't feel quite so amazing when she woke up the next day, with the sun streaming through the bedroom window, dazzling her.

'Oh no.' She groaned and quickly shut her eyes. 'It's far too bright.'

Jay smiled. 'That's what happens when you refuse to drink water before you go to bed after a night on the booze.'

'Okay, you're right, I should have listened to you. But if you're feeling fine, could you get me a glass of water and some paracetamol?'

Jay chuckled. 'I'd be happy to. And after that, you can go back to sleep for a while and I'll put together a picnic.'

'A picnic? What for?'

'I think we need some fresh air in our lungs. So I prescribe a walk on Hampstead Heath, and after our lunch we can come back here and, if you're still feeling rough, we can snuggle on the sofa and binge-watch a box set.'

'Sounds just about perfect,' she said. 'As long as you hurry up with the water and painkillers.'

* * *

Although the journey on the Tube made her feel queasy, Emma felt herself returning to something resembling a human being once they were walking across the heath. As they sat down on a bench on Parliament Hill, Jay opened the bag he had been carrying and spread out the picnic on the seat between them. Emma immediately picked up one of the homemade sausage rolls he'd prepared while she had been sleeping off her hangover and bit into it ravenously.

'Oh, Jay, this is divine. If only we could spend more time together like this.'

'I know. We really do need to make more of an effort. And I need to stop being so focused on what I want to achieve and make more time for you.'

'I'm not asking you to do that. I know how ambitious you are and that's part of who you are, so I wouldn't ask you to change. All I want to feel is included.'

'Yes, I get that. You know, you said something the other day about your childhood and how your parents pushed you away. We've been together a while now, but we don't really speak to each other about the important stuff.'

'It's not something I like to talk about.'

'I'm guilty of that too,' Jay said. 'But maybe these are the things we do need to talk about.'

Emma sighed. 'Okay. What do you want to know?'

'I want to know everything about you,' he said.

'There's not a great deal to know. I'm an only child and both my parents were only children too. They had me later in life and there was no other family. They were very academic and career-orientated, and, growing up, I wondered why they had bothered to have me at all. They certainly didn't seem that interested in me. And there was very little in the way of hugs or love.'

'Oh, Em, I'm so sorry.'

'The other day, when I saw the relationship you have with your nan, I realised that's what I've always been missing.'

'My own family situation hasn't been that great, as you well know.'

'Yes, I understand that, but maybe that can be good again if you work on it.'

He nodded. 'Maybe.'

'But what you have with your nan is so easy.'

He grinned. 'It is. She's always been my idol.'

'I always felt as though I had to fight for Mum and Dad's approval, and, no matter how hard I worked, I never quite lived up to their expectations.'

'That's really sad.'

'It is. You should have seen them when I said I was going into the hospitality industry. It was as if I'd told them that I'd murdered someone. At first they tried to get me to change my mind, but I think they both knew I wasn't cut out for what they wanted me to do. After that it felt as though they gave up on me. I went to uni and they moved to Portugal. And they've held me at arm's length ever since. So, that's the reason I hate it when I feel like you're pushing me away.'

Jay leaned over the remains of the picnic and pulled her towards him. 'I'm so sorry, Em. I shouldn't have made you feel that way. At least now I understand.'

'I'm so glad we've had the opportunity to talk. Just know that I'll support you in whatever you want to do, but don't shut me out.'

'I won't.'

CHAPTER EIGHTEEN

Jay was puzzling over the sauce for his fish dish in the function kitchen at Diva's on Monday afternoon. He was meeting Liz here later so had decided to do a practice run before she arrived. Maybe she could shed some light on the problem. He looked up as the door opened, expecting it to be her. Instead, he watched Tia enter the room. His heart sank. He wasn't in the mood for a wrangle with her this afternoon.

When they'd first taken on the contract and Liz had been having difficulties with Tia, Jay had confidently told her he would be the front for the function catering at Diva's. He had thought then that Tia would be a pussycat underneath her hard-nosed business persona. Now he knew differently. If she were any kind of cat, she would be more like a jaguar than the average domestic moggy. And she was very much a lady who needed to be in control. Of everything. He didn't know how Alex and Roberto put up with her being their business partner. They must have the patience of saints.

'Tia, how nice to see you.'

'I didn't know anyone would be up here. There aren't any functions on tonight, are there?'

'No, not tonight, no, but—'

'So what are you cooking there?'

'I was . . .' Jay stalled for time as he chose his words carefully. 'Trying out a new idea for the function menu.'

'I see.' She pursed her lips. 'And you're doing that in our kitchen?'

'Well, yes. That's not a problem, is it?'

The door opened and Liz breezed in. She looked from Tia to Jay. 'Is everything all right?'

Jay waited for Tia to reply. He wasn't at all certain why she was being so frosty.

'Jay was just telling me he was testing out a new dish for the menu.'

'Oh, are you?' Liz's face brightened. 'What is it?'

'What it is, is irrelevant.' Tia cut in before Jay could reply. 'It's the fact that you seem to be using this kitchen for your personal business purposes and not just for carrying out Diva's own functions.'

'Well, we do use the area for forward planning. And it makes more sense for us to do the ordering here as we can see what stocks and equipment we have on site. Testing out new dishes in the kitchen they will eventually be cooked in is also useful. And we do need to keep the menu fresh. Lots of your clients have guests within the same social circles, so it wouldn't look good if we served up the same dishes time after time.'

'No, it wouldn't,' Tia said. 'But are you using those dishes on your own private menu as well?'

'We do try to keep them separate, but if someone asks for something similar it makes sense to provide what they want.' Liz paused. 'Tia, I really don't understand what all this interrogation is about.'

Tia sighed and rolled her eyes. 'Because, Liz, if you're using Diva's as your main business premises, then by rights we should be charging you rent.'

'But we're not!' Liz said in protest. 'We have our own kitchen for our private work.'

'It doesn't look that way to me. Take today for instance. There are no functions and yet you're both here.'

'To put the orders through for the functions next week,' Liz said. 'As I have explained.'

'Be that as it may, but I've discussed it with the others. Perhaps it's time we do start to charge you rent.'

Liz was quick to reply. 'That's not in our contract.'

'No, but your contract is due for renewal in a few months, so perhaps we'll need to take this into account when we renegotiate terms.'

Before either of them could reply, Tia turned on her heel and swished out of the room.

Liz stared at Jay, dumbfounded. 'What was that all about?'

Jay pulled out a chair and sat down. 'I have absolutely no idea. It came out of nowhere.'

'She's got a real bee in her bonnet about something and I don't think it's just about a little bit of rent.'

Liz sat down opposite Jay.

'Neither do I,' Jay said. 'In fact, now I think about it, she's been prickly for the last few weeks. I just put it down to her usual control freakery, but she has got worse.'

Liz tried to think what could have caused it. 'She usually behaves like that when she's not getting her own way about something, but I have no idea what that might be.'

'And Alex hasn't said anything?'

'Not a thing. He's more intent on me and the baby. Fussing around me like I don't know what.'

'Getting on your nerves, is he?'

'Just a bit.' Liz sighed. 'I know I shouldn't complain that he's so concerned, especially as the morning sickness has been horrendous and considering what happened to him before, but he's acting like I don't have a mind of my own.'

'You'll just have to humour him until he gets used to the idea.'

'I suppose I will.' Liz was silent for a moment. 'Just clarify something for me, Jay. Tia did say she'd discussed it with the others, didn't she? I didn't mishear that?'

'She definitely did.'

'So why hasn't Alex told me, then?'

'As you say, he's probably trying to protect you. Maybe he thought it was just another of Tia's passing fixations and it would all blow over.'

'Maybe,' Liz said, getting up from her chair. 'All the same, it would have been good to have been forewarned about that little ambush. I'll have to have a word with him tonight. Try to find out what this is really all about. I'm going to make a cup of tea. Do you want one?'

'Please.' As Liz put the kettle on, Jay went over to the hob and lit the gas to reheat the sauce. As he did so, Liz turned to face him. 'So what's this new dish you're planning for our menu?'

Jay blushed. 'Ah. When I told Tia it was for the function menu, I wasn't exactly telling the truth. It's a dish I'm experimenting with for the competition.'

Liz burst out laughing. 'It's a good job you managed to think on your feet. If you'd told her what you were really doing, she'd have blown a gasket.'

Liz noticed that Jay had started to look around the room nervously. 'What's the matter?'

Jay frowned. 'You'll probably think I'm letting my imagination run away with me, but I'm starting to wonder if she's planted hidden cameras or had us bugged. Maybe she's sat in her office listening to every word we're saying.'

'I hate to say it, Jay, but that's not actually as daft as it sounds.'

'You're not mad at me, then?'

'Of course I'm not. I do think we need to take this seriously, though. But first things first — what is this dish you're creating?'

'Well, the brief is a fish dish so I'm working on a poshed-up version of fish and chips. But not fish in batter. So I'm going to do pan-fried white fish of some variety. I thought about doing a champagne velouté sauce with it, but Nan suggested a sparkling white wine from Kent to make it more of a regional dish.'

'Good old Nan. How is she?'

'She's great. As usual. I hope you don't mind, but I told her about the baby and she said to give you her congratulations. I will warn you, though, she's getting her knitting needles out.'

'Oh, how lovely.' Liz added a splash of milk to the tea. 'I do like hand-knitted baby clothes.'

'Do you? I thought you'd be more into designer these days.'

'Jay! You forget that I come from good old-fashioned farming stock. Mind you, I can't imagine Mum knitting anything, but Ruth, my stepmum, is a dab hand with the knitting needles, so you'd better warn your nan she'll have competition.'

Jay chuckled. 'I will. That will really spur her on.'

'So is that the sauce, then?' Liz nodded to the pan Jay was stirring.

'It is. There's something missing from it, but I can't quite put my finger on what it is.'

'Let me have a taste.'

Jay picked up a clean teaspoon, dipped it in the sauce and handed it to her. When she tasted it, she frowned. 'Yes, I see what you mean. It's got quite a good depth of flavour, but I think it's missing a little bit of acidity to cut through it. Would a splash of lemon juice help?'

Jay immediately cut a fresh lemon in half, squeezed some into the sauce, stirred and re-tasted. 'Bloody hell, Liz, you're a genius. Why didn't I think of that?'

Liz smiled and said, 'Let me try it again.'

He handed her another spoon and she nodded as she let it roll around her tongue. 'Yes, much better. But I was also wondering what fish stock you used?'

'Just the standard one we often use.'

'Could you make it fresh? That way you might be able to create even more depth of flavour.'

'Mm, probably not in the time allowed.'

'And you couldn't make it yourself beforehand and take it in with you as a pre-prepared stock?'

137

'I don't know. I'd have to check, but it would be good if I could. Thanks for your help, Liz. I really do appreciate it.'

'Not a problem. We want you to win this after all.'

'Well, I'm going to do my best.'

'I'm sure you will.' She paused. 'So what do we do about Tia, then?'

'I don't know.' Jay turned the heat off the sauce and poured it into a plastic container. 'Stay out of her way as much as possible, I suppose.'

'Good plan. We'll have to start using the kitchen below your flat more, though it is rather small so it's not ideal.'

'But best not to give her any ammunition, at least until after the contract renewal.'

'Agreed. The timing's not great, though. If she does get her way and they charge us rent, it will come right at the beginning of my maternity leave.'

'And we'll already be out of pocket because we'll be employing staff to cover you.'

Liz took a sip of tea. 'How would you feel if we didn't renew our contract at the end of the term?'

Jay sat down with a bump. 'Gosh, I don't know. I've never really thought about it.'

'If we just had our own business to concentrate on, we'd have more control over our workload. Less profit admittedly, but less expense too.'

'And we wouldn't have to kowtow to Tia.'

Liz laughed. 'Now, that would be a bonus.'

'How do you think Alex would feel about us ending our contract?'

'Not sure. But if it means I'll be working less, he'll probably be all for it as I'll be less stressed. What does worry me, though, is can we earn enough with just our own private catering?'

'I don't know. We've been doing pretty well here at Diva's so we haven't really been pushing our own business that much. If we concentrated on that, maybe we could make it work. At least then we wouldn't be splitting ourselves in two.'

'I'll have a look at the accounts and see what we've already got booked in, and then we can have a meeting early next week to see if the figures pan out.'

'Yes, that works for me.'

'And we can also discuss staffing levels. I definitely think we need to take on a temporary chef and I was wondering about front of house too. If we had someone solid out front, it would certainly make things run more smoothly.'

'Perhaps. Did you have anyone in mind?'

'The other week I was wondering about Emma. I know she said she wanted to learn the ropes of managing a hotel and stand on her own two feet, but she seems so unhappy in her job at the Rosemont. Do you think she would be up for it?'

'I really don't know,' Jay said. 'The situation with her line manager came to a head last week and Heather's gone off sick. Another manager has taken over as Emma's manager and she's set her on a proper training programme. In fact, she started on Reception this morning. And best of all, Heather's conduct is going to be investigated.'

'Well, that is good news. I'm so happy for Emma, she didn't deserve to be treated like that.'

'I completely agree. It's like a huge weight has been lifted from her.'

Jay got back up to tidy up the kitchen.

'So you don't think she'd be interested then?'

'It won't do any harm to ask her, but, like I said, she's much happier now.'

'Do you want to speak to her or shall I?'

'I'll do it, but I think we might have to have a Plan B.'

'Fair enough. Are you two getting on better now? Managing to find more time for each other?'

'It's not easy but we're working on it. We had a brilliant weekend. We went to Winston's on Friday night and then for a walk on the Heath with a picnic on Saturday.'

'Ah, Winston's. I remember those days well. Seems like a distant memory.'

'You have other things to keep you entertained now.'

'I will do soon,' Liz replied, resting a hand on her stomach.

'Susie was there,' Jay said casually.

Liz raised her eyebrows. 'Was she now? Did she make her presence felt?'

'Tried to, but I told her again I wasn't interested.'

'Good for you.'

'I know. Even though we'd split up, at first whenever I used to see her my heart would start to beat that little bit faster, but the last few times I've felt nothing.'

'That's good, Jay. Have you told Emma that?'

'What?'

'That you don't feel anything when you see Susie.'

Jay frowned. 'No, but she knows I don't want Susie back.'

'Tell her, Jay. Put her mind at rest.'

'Why is she worried about Susie?'

'Because Susie's a model. Us normal beings tend to feel a little inferior when our boyfriend's ex is a model.'

'That's daft.'

'But it's also true. So tell her.'

Jay nodded. 'Yeah, okay, if you say so.'

'I do. I think you and Emma are perfect for each other, so I'm sure you'll be all right, but you just need to make more time for each other and make sure that you tell each other how you're feeling. And ask her about the job, and in the meantime I'll think about an alternative if she turns us down. We can have a catch-up next week.'

'Good idea,' Jay said. 'Now, let's get out of here before we incur the wrath of Tia again.'

* * *

To Liz's surprise, Alex was already at home when she arrived and there was a delicious smell wafting towards her.

She walked into the gleaming white kitchen. Of all the rooms in what she thought of as a show apartment, this was the one where she was most at home, which was hardly surprising, considering her occupation. She pulled out a bar stool and sat down at the kitchen island.

'That smells wonderful. What are you cooking?'

He shrugged. 'Just a chicken casserole, nothing to your standard.'

'I'm sure it will taste lovely. Especially as I haven't cooked it myself. You're home early.'

'Yes. There wasn't much I was needed for at the hotel today.'

'All running smoothly, then?'

'Yes. I suppose I should be glad but I do feel a bit in limbo at the moment. I'd like a fresh challenge, but I don't want to take anything on that's too involved just before the baby. Do you want a cup of tea?'

'No thanks. I had tea with Jay earlier. I'll just have some water if you don't mind getting it for me?'

'You look tired. You're not overdoing it, are you?' Alex reached for a glass and removed a jug of filtered water from the fridge.

'No, of course I'm not. I do have some decisions to make though.'

Alex handed her the glass of water, then took the saucepan off the heat and turned off the gas. 'About?'

'About the business and what happens when I go on maternity leave.'

'Can't Jay run it and you can get in some extra staff on temporary contracts?' He opened the fridge and reached for a carton of milk.

'Well, that was the plan but I'm not sure it's going to work out that way.'

'How come?' He pulled out a bar stool and sat down opposite her.

'I went to Diva's today to see Jay.'

'Oh? There wasn't a function on, was there?'

His answer was so reminiscent of Tia's that she wondered whether he did know about Tia's threat of charging rent.

'No, there wasn't.' She decided not to mention that Jay had been there experimenting — she wanted to get a genuine reaction from him, not one that was clouded by other issues. 'When I got there, Tia was talking to Jay. She was . . .' Liz paused, searching for the right word.

'Agitated?'

'Yes, she seems to think that that Jay and I are spending too much time at Diva's, and we're using it as a base for our whole business and not just for the Diva's functions.'

'And are you?'

'No. We can't just turn up there on the day of a function. We hold stock in the kitchens, so it makes sense to compile our orders there so we're not buying in things we don't need.'

Alex nodded. 'Yes, I can see why that makes sense.'

'And sometimes planning for Diva's overlaps in planning for the private catering.'

'And Tia isn't happy with that?'

Liz looked him straight in the eye. 'I think you know the answer to that.'

He held her gaze for a moment and then looked away. 'Yes, I must admit Tia does seem to have a problem with it. She's mentioned it a couple of times.'

'Mentioned it? She gave me the impression that she's taken it a lot further than that. She says she's spoken to both of you about charging us rent.'

Alex spluttered. 'What? That's the first I've heard of it. I just thought she was having one of her gripes and it would all blow over. That's why I didn't tell you. She started going on about it when you were first pregnant, when you were feeling so ill. I didn't want you to be worrying about Tia when I didn't think it would come to anything.'

Liz nodded. She would probably have done the same in his position. And his reaction about the rent seemed genuine enough. It definitely looked like a case of Tia throwing her weight around.

'She also reminded us that our contract is due for renewal in a few months and it's an ideal opportunity for her to renegotiate the terms.'

Alex sighed. 'Sometimes Tia forgets she has two other partners. I'll have a word with her. There's no need for her to create obstacles where there aren't any. You and Jay are doing a brilliant job with the Diva's functions and I don't understand why Tia is trying to rock the boat.'

'Don't have a word with her, Alex, not on my account anyway.'

Alex frowned. 'Why not?'

'The contract is up for renewal just when I'm about to go on maternity leave. Jay has entered this competition and, if he does really well, I don't know what opportunities might open up for him afterwards. But if he's having to run both sides of the business, he won't be able to take up any of the opportunities that might come his way.'

'But you've worked hard to build up your business.'

'I have, but I've always said to Jay that the business shouldn't get in the way of our friendship. So in all honesty, if he wants to pursue other ambitions, I don't want to be the one to stand in his way.'

'You're too nice for your own good. Jay has earned a bloody good living since you made him a partner.'

'And he's earned every penny.' Liz took a sip of her water. 'It's not just about Jay, though. My life is about to change massively when our baby is born and I'm wondering if it would be simpler if we just concentrate on the private side of the business, especially if Tia is going to be so difficult.' She paused. 'I know she's your business partner, Alex, but she's not mine and I haven't got the energy to have to deal with her mind games.'

'She can be difficult and I can see how life would be easier if you just had one business to deal with, especially while you're on maternity leave. I certainly don't want you to be any more stressed than you have to be, but will that earn enough income for both of you?'

'I don't know, but Jay and I have time to work it out and generate enough bookings. Whatever we decide, I promise you we'll give you plenty of notice to find a replacement if we decide not to renew the Diva's contract.' Liz thought privately that it was a lot more than Tia actually deserved after the way she had spoken to them today, but she was determined to keep the peace for Alex's sake.

Alex came over and gave her a hug. 'I do appreciate that. But I'm going to have a word with Roberto. I think Tia needs a gentle reminder that Diva's is a partnership, not her solo project.'

'I think Roberto might agree with you,' Liz said.

'The restaurant is running well, as are the hotels. Maybe I'm not the only one who wants a new challenge. Maybe Tia needs one too, something that stops her sticking her nose in where it's not needed.'

Liz smiled. 'That's a good idea. And in the meantime Jay and I are going to do our very best just to keep out of her way.'

'I don't blame you,' Alex replied. 'Now enough about work. This should be ready.' He took the casserole dish out of the oven. 'I hope you're hungry. I've made loads.'

'I'm starving,' Liz said, thinking how good it was to finally have her appetite back.

CHAPTER NINETEEN

Two weeks later, Jay's stomach felt as though it had turned to liquid as he changed into his chef's whites in the changing room at the Greenwich warehouse. He knew the dishes he was about to cook inside out, but he still couldn't contain his nerves and wondered if he'd ever get over his anxiety. Rav entered the room and the two men greeted each other with a clap on the back.

'Good to see you, Jay,' Rav said.

'And you!' Jay replied. 'Are you as nervous as I am?'

'Oh, I should say so.'

'Glad it's not just me, then.'

'Nope. My hands are literally shaking. Let's just hope I don't knock my sauce over. Although if I do, you're welcome to save it again.'

'I'm sure that won't be necessary but I'm here for you mate.'

A woman who looked to be in her twenties, with a dark plait that fell down her back, a black biker jacket, and clumpy boots on her feet, entered the room.

'Hi,' she said hesitantly. 'I'm Chloe.'

'I'm Jay and this is Rav.'

'Pleased to meet you both.' She flashed them a smile, which showed incredibly white teeth. Her smile lit up her intensely green eyes and Jay found himself mesmerised by them. 'Now, I'd better get ready or you'll be starting without me.'

She moved past them and Jay watched as the dark plait bounced jauntily as she walked.

'Well, that's three of us.' Rav broke the silence. 'Just need to see who else turns up.'

One by one, five more fellow chefs entered the room. It started to feel stuffy and the butterflies in Jay's stomach returned.

Leanne, the assistant from the previous heat, opened the door and conversation ground to a halt. 'Good. You're all here,' she said. 'Would you like to come through?' They stood behind their workstations, nervously anticipating the arrival of the judges. The door opened and the three of them filed in. Jay was disappointed that Louis was still part of the judging panel and could only assume that the sponsors weren't worried about their previous working relationship. He'd just have to make sure he impressed Angela and Philip as he'd tried to do all along.

Angela was first, her long blonde hair piled on top of her head and her chef's whites pristine. As she stopped by the table at the top she smiled and looked to each of them. 'Hello, everyone, and welcome back. You are all well-deserved winners of the first set of heats and have earned your place in this round of the competition.' She paused and Philip took over in what was obviously a rehearsed narrative.

'Although there are only eight of you here today, sixteen contestants in total have made it through to this stage of the competition. You will cook your starters and fish courses today, then the other eight will cook tomorrow. After that, two contestants from each group will leave the competition.'

Jay's stomach twisted at the thought of that, and he hoped he wouldn't get knocked out.

'The next round will be another eliminator, leaving eight contestants in total', Philip continued. He paused to allow

Angela to take over and Jay noted that Louis wasn't being given a chance to address them. The irony wasn't lost on him. He knew how much Louis liked the sound of his own voice.

'The remaining eight will then cook as part of a group. This will help us to identify how well you work together. The aim of this competition is to cook at a banquet to celebrate food that is prevalent in London and the south-east, whether that be purely British food, or international cuisine that has been adopted by our region. At the banquet you will all need to help each other out, so the ability to work as a team will be critical. Following on, there will be head-to-heads to determine who will cook each course at the banquet.

'I know that's a lot of information to take in,' Angela continued. 'We just want you all to get a general idea of what is going to happen over the coming weeks. Now, has anyone got any questions?'

Everyone shook their heads.

'Good. So let's get on with the cooking, shall we?' Philip said with a smile. 'You have one hour to complete your starters.'

Jay concentrated on the ingredients in front of him. One hour wasn't much time to create the dish he was hoping to achieve but he had practised it many times and he knew that, if he focused properly, he could get it all done in time. Just. Jay began by preparing the mushroom stock for the dish he had named 'Garden on a Plate'.

Half an hour later he was lost in the process when he felt, rather than heard, the judges approach his workstation.

'Jay.' Philip smiled at him. 'Can you tell us what dish you are cooking today?'

'Yes.' Jay took a deep breath and began the explanation he'd practised. 'As more people are moving towards a plant-based diet, for both health reasons and the sustainability of the planet, I've decided on a vegetarian starter, which I have designed to tantalise the taste buds.'

'Okay, that sounds good,' Angela said. So, what does your dish consist of?'

147

'The base is a mushroom stock,' Jay said. 'I've used different varieties of mushrooms, including portobello, to give it a meaty flavour, along with fresh and dried shiitake and dried porcini mushrooms for extra taste. The main part of the dish is going to be composed of garden vegetables — hence the name. The dish is inspired by my great-grandmother. She was a brilliant cook and wrote all her recipes in a leather-bound journal, which has been handed down through the generations and came into my possession just as I was applying for the competition. My great-grandmother lived through World War Two, so you can imagine she developed a lot of vegetarian dishes due to rationing. My grandfather was also a keen gardener and had an allotment, so there were plenty of veggies in our diet growing up.' Jay finished in a rush, wondering whether he was talking too much, but was relieved when Angela smiled at him.

'That's what I like to see — dishes that come from the heart, created from childhood memories. Good luck, Jay. I'm looking forward to trying your dish. It sounds as though it's going to be made with love.'

As the judges moved away, Jay found he couldn't stop grinning at the praise from a chef he had always admired. Then, realising how little time there was left, he shook himself out of his reverie and once again forced himself to focus. The rest of the hour seemed to flash past in what felt like a matter of moments, but Jay made sure that he left enough time to allow himself to plate up with precision. The presentation of the dish was extremely intricate and it was important to him to do it justice. Finally, just as Louis announced that their time was up, Jay placed the last edible flower on the dish and stepped back with relief.

* * *

By the end of the day, Jay was exhausted. Both his dishes had been well received and he was delighted that he and Rav had got through to the next round. Rav had cooked a Bengali starter similar to samosas, but made from a lighter and flakier pastry, and a fish dish made of flat herring called hilsa in a spicy mustard gravy with turmeric and chillies. Ben and Lucy from the first round had been sent home, but Jay was happy that Chloe would be staying in the competition. From their conversation in the lounge area earlier, he had learned that she was originally from the north-west, but had trained in France and was now based in London. She seemed to be a cool and competent chef, and he looked forward to seeing her in the next round.

Now, it was just a case of planning the main course and dessert for the next stage of the competition. He had a good idea for the dessert, but he would just have to go back to the drawing board for the main course. And he'd have to do it quickly, because he had a busy working week ahead of him and little spare time to design and practise both dishes.

* * *

The following week, Jay found himself back in the kitchen at Greenwich, once more riddled with nerves. Of all the heats, this was the one he'd been most dreading and the one he was least prepared for. After further consultation of his great-grandmother's recipe book, he had settled on pork tenderloin with masala sauce, bubble and squeak cut into small discs and stacked, and pea purée. The idea had come from her journal entry about the pig club that local neighbours had formulated during World War Two, when they had all joined forces to supplement meat rations.

As the competition began, Jay tried to shake off his nerves and put all his focus on creating the best dishes he could. Channelling his skills and concentration paid off — by the time he brought his dishes in front of the judges he was fairly pleased with results. It was the dessert that had proved to be most tricky. He'd wanted it to be a real showstopper, so he'd had some moulds made in the shape of an apple, which he'd

149

lined with white chocolate. The inside was filled with layers of apple mousse, biscuit crumble and raspberry ice cream, and, when the two halves had set, he'd moulded them together and sprayed them green to look like an actual apple, which he'd served with a toffee sauce. The result hadn't been as perfect as he would have liked, but he knew the flavours were good. If he got through to the next round, he'd definitely be concentrating on perfecting that dish.

A wave of relief washed over him as the chefs filed out of the kitchen. That was it. He had cooked all four of his dishes and there was nothing more he could do now. It was all in the hands of the judges. He looked up from packing up his belongings towards the judges' table. Only two of them were there — Angela and Philip. They were deep in conversation, their heads bent closely together.

Louis had obviously sloped off somewhere. He'd tried not to let the chef put him off through the competition, although it had been difficult at times. He decided to pack up his van before getting changed. There would probably be a crush in the changing rooms at the moment.

As Jay was finishing loading up his van he saw Rav, still in his chef's whites, doing the same. They walked back into the building together and Jay clapped him on the shoulder. 'So, how do you think it went today?'

'I'm not sure. I made a few silly mistakes that I wouldn't normally make, so I can only hope I've done enough,' Rav said. 'I cooked a dish that is often served as a celebration dish, particularly at weddings, called kacchi biriyani. I've cooked it many times, but I think my nerves got the better of me today. And compared to your apples, my attempt at gulab jamun, which is a popular dessert within my cuisine, just couldn't compete.'

'You had some good comments from the judges, though, so maybe you're being too hard on yourself.'

'Well, I hope so, because I'd like to go through to the group challenge. That will all be about working together and I think we'd make a pretty good team.'

Jay laughed. 'That *would* be good, but there's no guarantee I'll get through either.'

'You've definitely got a good chance. Were you listening to what they said today? I reckon your apple dessert was the dish of the day.'

'Thank you, Rav, that is high praise coming from you. I just wish they'd let us know the results today, as they have done in the previous rounds, rather than make us wait until next week.'

'I imagine it will be a difficult decision at this stage in the competition,' Rav said, 'so they are going to want to take their time.'

'I suppose so. I'm just being impatient. Come on, let's get changed.'

They moved towards the changing rooms, but just outside the lounge area they heard a cry that sounded like someone in pain. After a quick glance at each other, Jay pushed through the door with Rav hot on his heels. As Jay stopped short in shock, Rav bumped into him. To his surprise, Louis was lying on the floor clutching his groin in agony. Standing above him with her hair escaping from her plait and her face bright red was Chloe.

'Are you okay?' Jay asked her, even though Louis was the one on the ground.

'I am now,' she said defiantly and then looked down at Louis. 'But if you try anything like that again, a knee in the groin will be the least of your worries.' With that she stepped around them all and stormed out of the room.

Jay and Rav looked at each other in astonishment.

'Did you see what she did? You're my witnesses,' Louis gasped from the floor.

'I didn't see anything.' Jay turned around to follow Chloe out of the room.

She was sitting on a chair in Reception. All her defiance had gone and she was trembling as she held her head in her hands.

Jay crouched down before her, but far enough away so that she didn't feel he was invading her space.

'Are you okay?'

She nodded numbly.

'Want to talk about it?'

She held her head up and he could see that she was close to tears.

'He caught me alone in the room, came on to me, and told me that if I was nice to him he'd make sure I got through to the next round.'

'That's disgusting,' Jay said, appalled at Louis' behaviour.

'Isn't it? And when I said no, he tried to take what he wanted anyway. But his loafers were no defence for my boots. And once I'd caught him off guard, I gave him a good knee in the nuts, which is when you came in.'

'That must have been really scary.'

'For a few minutes it was,' Chloe said. 'But I've trained in some of the toughest restaurants and there are a lot of chefs who behave like him, so over the years I've learned to defend myself.'

'You shouldn't have to though.'

At the sound of footsteps, they both looked up, to see Louis with his bag and his coat. He cast a brief, worried glance at them and scuttled out of the door.

Rav joined them. 'Well, at least he's gone now.'

'Are you going to report him?' Jay asked.

Chloe nodded her head. 'Oh yes. I'm not going to let him get away with this.'

'If you want some moral support while you speak to the judges, I'd be happy to come with you.'

'That will be wonderful, thanks.'

'And I'll come too,' Rav agreed. 'We may not have seen the actual assault but we'd trust you over Louis any day.'

'Thanks guys, I really do appreciate it.'

* * *

The three of them walked back into the kitchen area, where Angela and Philip were still huddled over their notebooks, obviously discussing the outcome of the day.

Chloe cleared her throat.

'Hi, I'm sorry to interrupt, but I was wondering if I can have a word?'

Angela looked up and smiled at her. 'Of course you can.' She shuffled her papers together and covered them with her notebook. 'What can we do for you?'

'It's about Louis,' Chloe said and Jay noticed her voice had a slight wobble. She looked up. Jay smiled at her and she continued. 'He assaulted me in the changing area.'

'What?' Angela exclaimed. 'Please, tell us what happened.'

'When I came out of the changing room area, Louis was in the lounge,' Chloe said. 'He told me he found me attractive and that he'd like to take me out sometime.' Jay noticed that Philip was frowning, but didn't actually look surprised. 'When I said I wasn't interested and it wouldn't be good to fraternise with a judge, he said it could be our secret and that it would be to my advantage for the competition if I did.' She took a deep breath. 'I said no again, that I wasn't interested, and I picked up my bag and started to walk towards the door.'

'What happened next?' Angela asked.

'He grabbed hold of me and tried to kiss me.' She closed her eyes as she remembered. 'I turned my head away and then I stamped on his foot. He was startled and while he was off balance I kneed him in the groin.' She said the words in a rush.

'That's when Rav and I came into the room, to see Louis on the floor,' Jay said.

'So you didn't see what happened?' Philip asked.

'No, but—'

Philip held his hand up to stop Jay. 'I'm not saying that because I don't believe Chloe — I do. It's Louis I don't trust, and I can imagine he'll deny it and say it's his word against Chloe's.'

'It's a good job I've got proof then. Well, at least I hope I have,' Chloe said. 'I've always been wary of Louis and the

153

way he stood just a little bit too close to me. I'd just sent a text when he came into the room, so I switched on a recording app on my phone. I haven't listened to it yet, but I hope it's recorded okay.'

'Well, that's good,' Angela said. 'I'm sorry you had to go through that. You won't have to see him again in the kitchen. We'll report this straight away and get him thrown off the judging panel. Philip and I had our doubts about him from the beginning. We reported the fact that he knew Jay from previous employment to the sponsors when Jay told us on the first day of the competition. By rights Louis should have been the one to tell us, but he didn't. We thought the sponsors would replace him, but, for reasons we can't go into to, they wanted to keep him. I can't imagine they'll be able to now though.' Turning to Chloe, she said, 'What you've described is certainly assault, so I'm wondering if you are thinking of reporting him to the police? You'll have our full support if you do.'

'I don't know. I hadn't really thought that far ahead,' Chloe said. 'But maybe I should. I'm not afraid to hold him accountable for his actions.'

'It's entirely your decision.' Angela squeezed her arm. 'It's not an easy thing to do, but if you do decide to report him there's a station just round the corner.'

Chloe nodded. 'Yes, I will. It is the right thing to do.'

'Want some company?' Jay asked.

Chloe nodded. 'I'd appreciate that.'

'And I'll come too, if I may?' Rav said.

The three of them smiled at each other.

CHAPTER TWENTY

'Thanks for helping out tonight.' Liz sat down and eased her shoes off her feet. 'I don't know what I'd have done without you.'

'No problem,' Emma replied. 'It wasn't as though I was doing anything else.' She finished making a cup of coffee for herself and a fruit tea for Liz, brought them over to the table and sat down next to her friend. 'How are you, by the way? I haven't had chance to ask. If you don't mind me saying, you look shattered.'

'I am a bit,' Liz said. 'It's been a busy few weeks, especially as Jay has been tied up with the competition.'

'Hm, not exactly great timing for you, is it?'

'Not really,' Liz said. 'But it can't be helped. And to be honest, I didn't think pregnancy would be as tiring as it's turning out to be.' She paused. 'Emma, I want to say sorry again about pretending I had a virus.'

'It's okay. I understand why you wanted to keep it a secret, especially with Alex's history. How is he?'

'He was worried at first, naturally, and very protective of me, but I'm hoping that will start to ease now that I'm a bit further down the line.'

'I'm sure it will, but try not to overdo it in the meantime. And if you need any help, give me a shout. I'll be there for you if I can.'

'That's kind of you.'

'Jay spoke to me about your offer of the front-of-house role when you go on maternity leave. I do appreciate you thinking of me and a few weeks earlier I might have jumped at the chance. But I really want to learn about the hotel business, and now that I've got a new line manager I'm going to get the training I need.'

'I completely understand. When I spoke to Jay about it, I didn't realise how much things had changed. You would always be my first choice, but you have to decide what's best for you. How's it going, anyway?'

Emma smiled. 'It's intense and, after everything thing that's happened with Heather, I do feel like I'm being scrutinised. But I love it. I'm learning so much, so, yes, it's going well.'

'I'm really pleased,' Liz said. 'I know what it's like to be bullied and it puts such a strain on you.'

'It did, yes, but hopefully that's all in the past now.'

'And how is Jay? I've barely seen him. How did he get on yesterday?'

Emma shrugged. 'I don't know.'

'Sorry?'

'Last night, I was waiting for him to phone me when the competition was over, but I didn't hear from him. He didn't come in until I was asleep and then I was out first thing this morning.'

'And you haven't been in touch today?'

'Nope. I suppose I could have phoned him in my break, but, if I'm honest, I'm a little bit disappointed in him, so I'm waiting for him to make the first move.' She sighed. 'I could be in for a long wait, though.'

'Oh, Em, I'm sorry. I thought the pair of you were getting on much better now.'

'We were. But this competition and the people he's met there are all-consuming. It's not so bad in between the rounds — in fact, we had a lovely weekend the other week — but when he's in the throes of it, it's like I don't exist.'

'It must be very difficult. For both of you.'

'I know. I'm trying to be supportive and I really want him to do well, but, even though we've spoken about it, it just feels like he's shutting me out.'

'I don't know what to say, Em, except try to be patient. Maybe when he's not in full-on competition mode, explain to him how you feel.'

'I will. And in the meantime I'm just trying to concentrate on work.'

'That's a good plan. I'm sure everything will change when the competition's over and then you'll get the old Jay back.'

'I hope so,' Emma said.

When she got home, Jay was sitting on the sofa with a beer in his hand and his feet up on the coffee table. Strewn all around him were recipe books.

'Hiya,' he said as she walked through the door. 'Where've you been? I thought it was your night off tonight.'

'It was. I texted you to say that Liz had asked me to serve at a function as one of the girls had let her down.'

'Oh, right.' He frowned. 'I don't think I got that message.' He leaned over to the table and picked up his phone. 'Oh, yes, here it is. I've had a really busy day, I've been trying to come up with some ideas for some new dishes in case I get through to the next round.'

'Do you think you will? How did you get on yesterday? You didn't bother to let me know.'

A moment of guilt flashed across his face. 'Ah, yes, well, after the competition finished—'

'Don't tell me, you went for a drink with your fellow competitors.'

'We did, later, yes, but it's more complicated than that.'

'Go on then, tell me.'

'One of the other chefs, Chloe, well, she was attacked by Louis in the changing room. Rav and I were around just after it happened, so we stayed with her while she reported it to the judges and then to the police.'

Emma dropped her hands from her hips, immediately contrite.

'Oh! How horrible for her. Is she okay?'

'Yes, Louis was no match for her. She kneed him in the nuts.'

'Well, I'm glad that she was able to defend herself and that she reported it straight away. And I'm sorry for being angry with you, but I didn't know. You didn't tell me.'

He got up and gave her a hug. 'I'm the one who's sorry, I should have phoned you to let you know what was going on, I just got caught in everything. This competition seems to be taking over my life.'

'Our lives.' Emma felt whatever energy she had left drain from her. 'Look, Jay, I'm shattered. I've done a full shift at the hotel today, as well as Liz's function, and I'm on early tomorrow. I think I'll just head to bed.'

'Sure.' He kissed her gently on the lips. 'I'll be in in a bit.'

Emma drifted into sleep long before Jay came to join her.

* * *

Jay trembled as he stood with the other chefs, waiting to find out which of them would proceed to the next stage. He prayed he wouldn't be among the ones going home. His fingers were crossed so tightly behind his back that he wondered if he'd ever be able to uncross them.

Angela and Philip walked into the room. Rav, who was standing next to Jay, nudged him. 'Here we go, buddy. Good luck,' he whispered.

'And to you,' Jay replied.

'Good morning, ladies and gentlemen,' Angela said. 'Today is a big day for you all as we announce who is going through to the next stage of the competition.'

'But before we go any further,' Philip said, 'We have another announcement to make. Unfortunately, Louis can no longer be here as he . . .' Philip paused. 'Has other commitments.'

Jay, Rav and Chloe glanced at each other knowingly. Earlier Chloe had told him that Louis had been charged with assault. At first Louis had tried to deny it and claimed that it had been Chloe who had assaulted him, but the evidence on Chloe's phone had proved that he was the aggressor, so in the end he'd pleaded guilty.

'So from now on, you'll have to put up with just Angela and myself.'

The competitors laughed nervously before Angela took over. 'I'm afraid only eight of you will be lucky enough to go through to the next stage. It's been a really tough decision and you certainly haven't made it easy for us — you are all excellent chefs.'

'Now, to those of you we have selected,' Philip said. Jay listened anxiously as both Rav and Chloe's names were called out. He smiled at them, pleased that they were on the list, but an anxious knot formed in his stomach as he realised he might not be joining them. And then he heard his name and his breath rushed out in a whoosh of relief. Rav clapped him on the back and Chloe grinned at him. The three of them were going to stay together for the time being and Jay couldn't have been more delighted. They watched sympathetically as the four people who hadn't been selected shuffled out of the kitchen, their disappointment plain for all to see.

'Congratulations to all of you,' Angela said. 'But now the hard work really starts. Next week there will be a series of tests across the week. You'll be split into two groups of four. The first task is to demonstrate your ability for mass catering — providing lunch for the staff at the National Maritime Museum in Greenwich. After that you'll be going head-to-head with the starters and fish dishes you have already cooked for us, and finally it will be the same with mains and desserts. You will be scored on each task and the chefs with the highest points for each course will be going through to the banquet.'

Philip smiled. 'I know that's a lot of information to take in again. But we are striving for perfection here. Now, I'm going to let you know who you are going to be in groups with and after that you'll have one hour to decide on a menu for the first task. We'll give you the remit and the number of dishes we want for each course. Then you'll need to put together a list of ingredients for us to put your orders through. Make sure you don't miss anything off the list because what isn't ordered today won't be available to cook with on the day. Right, now, here are the groups.'

Jay was relieved to hear that both Chloe and Rav were on his team, along with a young Chinese chef, Chen, who fused his Chinese heritage with modern British cooking. He knew they'd work well together and that would make things much easier in the long run.

The two groups sat either side of the kitchen as they planned what they would cook.

'I think I'd like to have a go at the fish course,' Chloe said. 'With my training I can add a classic French twist to regional ingredients.' They all agreed and settled on Chen doing the starter, Rav the main and Jay the dessert. Each of them then went through the ingredients for each dish, checking with each other to make sure that nothing was missing from the list. It was going to be a long week, but, after that, they'd all know who'd be cooking at the banquet. The ultimate winner wouldn't be decided until the day of the banquet, but after the heats were over it would be a relief to get back to work and concentrate on real life until the big day. If he got through, that was.

CHAPTER TWENTY-ONE

Emma came home to find Jay in the living room. He'd sent her a brief text to say he'd got through to the next round, but that was all she'd heard from him. 'Congratulations on getting through.' He looked up from his laptop.

'Thanks.

'You must be really pleased.'

'I am.'

'You don't sound it.'

'There's still a lot of work to be done. Where have you been?'

'I went for a drink with people from work.'

'Was *he* there?'

She bristled at his tone. She didn't feel as though he had any right to question who she was with when he was often so distant. 'Who?'

'Him. The one that walked you home the other week.'

'Nick? Yes, he was there. Among others.'

'And did he walk you home again?'

'No. He didn't. I got the Tube. Let's not go through this again, Jay. You know you can trust me whoever I'm with. And for information, I was out with a group of colleagues to

161

celebrate me finishing my four-week stint on Reception — in case you're interested.'

'Em, don't be like that. Of course I'm interested.'

'You've got a funny way of showing it.'

He shook his head. 'I'm sorry. I've been caught up in—'

'The competition.' She cut him off. 'And I also know how important it is to you, which is why I haven't complained about the fact that I often feel like we're just sharing a place to live, not in a relationship. Once this competition is over, Jay, we need to sit down and have a long, honest conversation about where our relationship is going. But until then, I think we should just try to get on with each other. Which means that I won't complain about your infatuation with this competition and you don't complain if I occasionally go for a drink after work with my colleagues.'

'Fair enough,' Jay said softly. 'But just so you know, Em, I do love you and I do want this relationship to work.'

'Sure.' She left him to whatever he was doing.

* * *

As she lay in bed, Emma tried not to think about their conversation. She'd told Jay that they needed to get through the competition before they made any decisions. For now, she just wanted to push everything to the back of her mind. She was drifting off to sleep, a combination of early starts and a couple of glasses of wine lulling her into slumber, when Jay came into the room.

As he changed and climbed into bed, she slowed her breathing so that he would think she was asleep. But she need not have worried. Jay turned so that he was facing away from her, and kept himself to his side of the bed. Immediately she wanted to reach out and hug him, to make everything all right between them. But everything was not all right and she didn't know how they were going to change that. And even though Jay was lying in bed beside her, she couldn't have felt more lonely.

* * *

162

Jay couldn't sleep as he listened to the sound of Emma breathing. He didn't know what he was doing anymore. This competition had become all-encompassing and he was neglecting every other aspect of his life: his business, his relationship with Emma and even his family. He felt guilty that he hadn't been to see his nan for weeks now. And as for his mum, well, they'd exchanged a few texts, but he hadn't had the time or headspace to meet up with her and talk properly. A conversation that he knew was long overdue. Why was he neglecting everything that was important to him? So that he could massage his ego in a competition he could get kicked out of at any moment.

Initially he'd been overjoyed when his name had been called out and he'd realised that he'd got through to the next round. Then he had felt a little bit daunted when he'd realised what it would entail. But he knew that, with his experience of mass catering, he was better equipped than most to deal with it. And he'd been delighted when he'd realised who his team members would be, as he knew they would work well together. He was confident that the dishes they had chosen were good ones and that they'd be able to deliver them on time. Once next week was over, he told himself, he would start concentrating on his real life and everyone around him who deserved better from him.

CHAPTER TWENTY-TWO

Emma felt groggy as she made her way into work the next morning. She'd slept badly and wasn't firing on all cylinders. It was her first day working properly in housekeeping, along-side the head of department, so this was the last thing she wanted. She'd need her wits about her if she was going to make a good first impression. When she'd filled in cleaning rooms previously, Mrs Henderson, the head housekeeper, had been on holiday, so she hadn't met her yet, but Emma knew she was a stickler for detail and didn't suffer fools gladly. In an attempt to wake herself up earlier, Emma had turned the shower to as cold as she could bear it, and now she was sipping a takeaway espresso.

She'd enjoyed her time on Reception and felt she'd learned a great deal, but she was keen to see how things worked on the other side. Although Heather's two weeks off had long passed, her former line manager had still not returned to work, much to Emma's relief. Faye was turning out to be the perfect line manager and had given her good feedback on her time on Reception. Now she just had to do the same in housekeeping.

Her nerves were jittering as she took the lift up to the housekeeping department. Not all department heads liked having management trainees shadowing them — not only did it take up their time, but they weren't keen on the scrutiny. Mrs Henderson in particular liked to run things her own way and Emma knew she'd have to be diplomatic to get her on side. She took a deep breath as she knocked on the open door to the manager's office.

Mrs Henderson barely looked up from the paperwork she was frowning over. 'Take a seat, Miss Taylor.'

'Emma, please.'

'Emma,' Mrs Henderson said. Emma noticed that she didn't offer her own first name in return. 'I understand you're going to be with us for four weeks, shadowing every aspect of the department.'

'That's correct, yes.'

'Okay, so, every morning, Reception sends over a spreadsheet of all the guests who are leaving and whether the rooms have been reallocated.'

'Yes, I'm familiar with that. I've just finished four weeks on Reception.'

'Right.' Mrs Henderson pursed her lips. It seemed that Emma might be wise not to interrupt her new boss in the future.

'I usually print them off and then allocate them to my housekeeping staff. Ideally each member of staff will be able to do a full turnaround of ten rooms per shift, but when we're short-staffed we have to allocate more. It's certainly not ideal and is, in fact, our biggest challenge. And I'm afraid that's the case this morning. I'm just about to do a briefing and my staff are not going to be happy bunnies.'

'Is there anything I can do to help?' Emma asked.

'With the briefing?'

'No, with the rooms.'

'You're offering to clean rooms?'

'Well, yes.' Emma wondered why the head housekeeper looked so perplexed.

'You're management.'

'But surely the best way to learn everything you need to manage is to start at the bottom and learn from the ground up.'

'Well, there is that, but I don't really have the spare staff to train you up today.'

'I did do some stand-in days a few months ago.'

'Really? Must have been when I was away. That's not how I run things.'

'Maybe you can put me with an experienced staff member and we can work the rooms together. That way we can get through the work quicker, especially if we make the beds together.'

'That might work. You could help Adejo. But your clothes?' Mrs Henderson pointed to Emma's best work suit.

She had a point. It would be difficult to work in this suit, especially as the skirt was narrowly fitted. Then she remembered her spare clothes. 'I've got my gym kit in my locker. I was going to do a work-out when I finished, but, after a day in housekeeping, I guess I won't need to. If you can lend me a tabard, I'll fit in with everyone else.'

For the first time since she'd entered the office, Mrs Henderson smiled.

'Do you know, Emma, I think we're going to get on just fine. I'm Jane, by the way.'

* * *

Emma was delighted that she seemed to have won over Mrs Henderson. But judging by the look on Adejo's face when she learned that Emma was going to be working with her, she knew she had another hurdle to climb.

'Follow me,' Adejo said when the briefing was over. She walked away and left no room for Emma to make conversation. Adejo pushed the trolley with the fresh linen while Emma steered one containing everything else that was necessary to replenish the rooms. While they waited for the lift, Emma smiled at her colleague.

'Have you worked here long, Adejo?'

'About ten years.'

'That's a long time. You must like it here.'

Adejo glanced at her. 'I do it for the money.'

Emma nodded. She was afraid to make another comment and say the wrong thing. Adejo was obviously not the kind of person to be won over by mere conversation. She would just have to prove that she was capable of hard work. It was probably the only way to gain her respect.

The silence in the lift was tense and Emma was glad when they reached the first bedroom. Adejo swiped her card to open the door.

'What would you like me to do first?' Emma asked.

Adejo shrugged. 'You're the boss.'

'Not today I'm not. I'm here to work for you and lighten your load.'

Adejo frowned as if the concept was unfamiliar.

'Okay,' she said slowly. 'First thing is to strip the bedding and put it in the basket in the trolley outside. Then all the surfaces need to be cleaned and polished. The teas, coffees, milk and sugar need replacing. There's a list on the trolley. I'll make a start on the bathroom.'

Emma nodded and got down to work. She was already sweating by the time she'd stripped the bed. It was so large she could see how difficult it would be for one person to remake it.

She was just about finished when Adejo came out from the bathroom to collect the towels. She looked around the bedroom and gave a nod of approval. Emma sighed with relief at the thought that she had done a good job.

While Adejo was putting the towels in the bathroom, Emma collected the linen, ready to make the bed. When Adejo came back, Emma had spread the bottom sheet across the bed. Adejo took one side of the bed while Emma took the other and together it was an easier job. When it was done, Adejo looked at the bed, and then at Emma, and nodded in satisfaction.

'That was easier with two of us. Now you hoover in here and lock the door afterwards. I'll make a start on six-one-eight. Meet me in there.'

When Emma had finished, she took out her phone and noted down the time it had taken for the two of them to complete the room. Then she made her way to the next room.

Adejo had just finished stripping the bed when Emma joined her.

'Do you want me to do the bathroom this time?' she asked.

Adejo frowned again. 'I like to do it a certain way.'

'Okay, well, shall we do it together? You can show me how you do it and I can do it the same way as you?'

Adejo nodded and Emma made sure she mirrored everything Adejo did. When the room was complete, she got out her phone and noted the time it had taken them.

'You got somewhere else to go?' Adejo asked.

'No,' Emma said. 'I was just checking how long it takes to do each room.'

'Are you timing me?'

'Not you, no.' The frown had reappeared on Adejo's face and Emma realised that she needed to tread carefully. 'I was just wondering how much quicker it is with two people work-ing on each room together.'

'What? So you can report it back to management?'

'It's just an idea I had—' Emma was about to explain when Adejo interrupted her.

'I do a good job here and I don't like being spied on.'

'I'm not spying on you, I just . . .' But Adejo had stomped off to the next room.

They cleaned the next two rooms in a strained silence. Emma was wondering how she could explain when Adejo abruptly spoke.

'Tea break. Let's go.'

Emma followed Adejo to the staffroom. When they both had drinks and had sat down at a table in the far corner of the room, Adejo turned to her. 'I have a saying — "If it ain't broke, don't fix it."'

Emma nodded. 'I'm not saying anything is broken.' She sighed. 'You think I'm a newbie, straight out of college, wanting to change things I don't know anything about.'

Adejo nodded. 'Something like that. I've been doing this job for ten years and I think by now I should know what I'm doing.'

'You do, and you do your job really well. I don't think Mrs Henderson would've asked me to work with you if she didn't value you.'

'Thank you,' Adejo said. 'So why the criticism?'

'I'm not criticising you. You're right. I am a newbie and when I was stripping that first bed I wondered how on earth anyone could manage that on their own, room after room. It must kill your back.'

'Yes, it does. Sometimes it aches so badly the first thing I have to do when I go home is to put a hot water bottle on it. And lots of people call in sick with back problems.'

'And you said yourself that it was much easier with two.'

'I did and it was.'

Thinking she was making some headway, Emma rushed on. 'So I thought that if it was easier working in pairs, and I could prove it saved time as well, then I could do something that would make life easier for you all.'

Adejo nodded. 'You're right about the beds, but that's not the whole picture.'

'Then tell me. I'm not here to see things from a management perspective. I want to hear from the people who do the job, day in, day out. You're the ones who know what you're talking about, certainly more than someone who sits at a desk.'

Adejo looked surprised for a moment and then searched Emma's face, as if deciding whether or not she could trust her. Eventually she spoke. 'I'm a single mum with four kids. A day doesn't go by when I don't have a problem to sort out with one or other of them. I come here not just to earn money, but to get some peace. I like working on my own, I like the solitude and the routine. I like the fact that while I'm here I have something I can control. I wouldn't have that if I worked with someone else.'

'I see.' Emma suddenly felt deflated.

'It wouldn't be so bad if I worked with someone like you,' Adejo said as though sensing her disappointment. 'You get on with the job and work hard. But others are lazy and I know I'd end up doing their job for them or having to say something. That's why it wouldn't work for me.'

'Yes, I can see your point,' Emma said. 'Thank you for sharing that with me.'

'It's good that you listen. It's not very often that someone does. Now, if you've finished your coffee, it's time to get back.'

* * *

Early on Wednesday morning, Jay was in the kitchen beneath his flat, preparing for a dinner party for ten people that evening. He planned to serve dishes he had prepared often, so he was allowing his mind to wander as he worked. On Monday, after they had put their orders in for the mass-catering challenge, the judges had called them all together.

'You've all done really well to get to this stage of the competition. But now we as judges would like to get to know you better, to find out how you tick and what your goals are.'

'We also think that it's good for you to get to know each other better too,' Philip added. 'If you get through to the banquet, it will help you work as a team.'

They all nodded but no one spoke.

'Rav, would you like to go first?'

Rav looked stunned at being the first to speak, and began slowly. 'As you know, I have Bangladeshi origins. My family came to England in the early 1970s as a response to the Bangladesh Liberation War. At first they were met with a lot of prejudice, but they knew they had to make a success of their lives here because they had left everything behind in India. My grandfather was willing to work at anything he could, but many English people wouldn't give the Bangladeshi people a chance, so they kept together and formed their own community. My grandfather became friendly with a local shopkeeper. He was getting on in years and needed the strength of a young man to do the heavy lifting. He did it to help at first, but soon the man rewarded him with paid employment.' Rav paused. 'Forgive me if I'm talking too much.'

'No, no,' Angela said. 'Please continue, I'm fascinated.' They all murmured their agreement.

'Most of the women clung together, stuck to their traditions and their language. But my grandmother had spirit and an inquisitive nature, and, as my grandfather learned to speak English, she asked him to teach her everything he knew. She soaked it all up and even went to night school so she could read and write in English, as well as speak it. My grandmother was an excellent cook. Soon she started selling some of her food in the shop and it was a great success. Even English people, cautious at first, started to buy it.

'When the owner of the shop died, he left it to my grandparents as he had no family of his own. Eventually they concentrated more on the food side, developing a takeaway and then opening up their first restaurant. Our family now have four restaurants in total and I run one of them. My inspiration is Attar Islam from Birmingham, who has brought fine dining to our Indian heritage. I entered this competition because I hoped it might develop my skills, and already I've learned so much from the people around me.'

Philip nodded. 'That's an amazing story, Rav. And I have no doubt you'll achieve your ambitions.'

'Thank you,' Rav replied. He bowed his head, a gesture, Jay realised, he made whenever he was embarrassed.

Angela filled the silence. 'And Chloe? What about you? What's your background?'

'Well, originally I'm from Manchester. Unlike you, Rav, I don't have family heritage driving my food influences. I come from a working-class background and, while bringing up three children, my mother had to work as many hours as she could to make ends meet. For us, food was fuel, something she'd get out of the freezer and bung in the oven or the microwave. But when I first started food-tech classes at school, something inside me changed and I realised food could be a magical thing, not just something to be shoved in your mouth while watching television.'

Everyone laughed at that and Chloe continued. 'My food-tech teacher was my inspiration and she encouraged me all the way. She even let me stay behind after school and taught me more than I ever could have learned in a class full of pupils, most of whom didn't even want to be there. I left school at sixteen and went on to catering college. I was fascinated by French cookery and Raymond Blanc in particular. I decided I wanted to learn French cookery in its country of origin, so I taught myself French and got a job in a restaurant in Paris.' She pulled a face. 'God, it was dire! The other chefs hated me being in their kitchen. They gave me all the rubbish jobs and constantly made fun of me, not just behind my back but to my face. They thought I didn't understand the language, but I understood perfectly. While they didn't want me in their kitchen, they weren't opposed to me in other areas. That's where I learned my skills in self-defence.' She laughed nervously.

Angela put a hand on her arm. 'Kitchens can be deeply misogynistic workplaces and I know where you're coming from on that. But I'm glad you didn't let your experience put you off. We need women in the kitchen as there are still more male chefs than female, as you have seen by the entrants to this competition. Don't get me wrong though, I wouldn't promote a woman over a man if they didn't have the skills, but I firmly believe that nothing should be a barrier to advancement if you have the talent and the work ethic. None of the chefs in my kitchen would ever get away with any form of misogynistic — or racist, for that matter — behaviour.'

Chloe smiled. 'I like the sound of that.'

'So where do you see your future?' Angela asked.

Chloe paused. 'I'm not sure, to be honest. I'm excited about the next stage of the competition and to cater for large numbers of people.' She looked shyly towards Jay. 'And we're lucky to have someone in the group who has experience in that kind of catering. I'm sure I'm going to learn a lot.'

'I'm sure you are,' Angela said. Jay recalled his conversation with Liz when they were discussing the need to hire a new chef. Chloe would fit in perfectly for the duration of Liz's maternity leave, especially if she was interested in catering for large numbers.

'And what about you, Jay? What are your goals?' The sound of Angela's voice brought Jay back to the conversation.

'I'd like to own my own restaurant one day,' he said simply.

'With Michelin stars, I presume?'

He grinned. 'That would be lovely, of course, but I'd settle for it being successful and profitable.'

'And you run your own business currently?'

'I'm a partner in a business, yes. But it originated with my business partner, so I wouldn't say it was mine. That's why I want to do well in this competition. I want to develop my own reputation.'

'And before that you worked at La Emporium as a sous chef,' Philip said.

'Yes, as I mentioned the other week, Louis was the head chef when I worked there.'

Philip pursed his lips, a look of distaste on his face at the mention of the disgraced judge.

'If you don't mind me giving you some advice?' Angela asked.

'Not at all,' Jay replied. 'Advice from you would be most welcome.'

'The success of a restaurant isn't all about the food. That has to be excellent, of course, but it's also about numbers, and I don't just mean bums on seats. It's about profit and loss, managing your overheads, as well as your staff. You're already an excellent chef, and I have no doubt that people would love your food, but I suspect that managing a whole concern, alone, will be where you might need to gain some experience.'

Jay nodded and thanked Angela for her advice.

* * *

Two days later, Jay was still contemplating Angela's words as he cooked. What she had said was spot on. At La Emporium, his focus had been solely on the food. Even though he did more menu design and costing of dishes with Liz, she was the one who hired staff and did the accounts and most of the marketing. And while she was still going to be involved during her maternity leave, Jay wanted to do whatever he could to lighten her load, especially during the early days of motherhood, which he understood could be overwhelming. And it would be win-win if it gave him the opportunity to gain some much-needed experience. As soon as the competition was over, he would speak to Liz, and use the time to learn as much as he could from her before the baby was born.

Liz burst through the kitchen door and interrupted his thoughts.

'Hello, you,' he said. 'I wasn't expecting to see you today.'

'I thought that we could have a catch-up as you're not at the competition.'

'Good idea,' Jay said. 'Can I get you a coffee?'

'No, thanks,' Liz replied. 'Even the thought of coffee makes me want to heave.'

'Still feeling rough, then?'

'Not too bad. It's just certain things that set me off.' She reached for a glass and turned on the water tap. 'I'll just stick to the hard stuff.'

Jay laughed. 'I've nearly finished the prep for tonight, then I'm all yours.'

'I'll give you a hand.' Liz took off her jacket and lifted an apron from the hook on the wall. 'What can I do?'

'Coriander needs chopping and the ginger needs grating. Those smells don't get to you, do they?'

'No, that's fine.' She reached for a large Sabatier knife and began chopping the coriander. 'I didn't realise just how debilitating being pregnant would be. I naively assumed I would sail through to the last month when I was too big to work comfortably.'

'You've had a rough time of it,' Jay said. 'But hopefully you're entering an easier stage now.'

'Here's hoping. I'm just sorry it's put more pressure on everyone else.'

'It hasn't helped that I've been tied up with the competition either,' Jay said. 'Are you going to be okay next week? I'm afraid I'm going to be away for most of it.'

'Yes, I've got it covered. We haven't got a great deal on, just a couple of functions at Diva's.'

'And talking of Diva's, how's Tia?'

'Not too bad. She seems to have calmed down a bit since we've been using this kitchen more, but I still think something's niggling her, so I tend to mostly keep out of her way.'

'I don't blame you. And what about Alex? Did he know anything about a charge for rent?'

'No. He knew she was obsessing about us using the kitchen, but he wasn't aware of her threat to charge us rent. He wasn't happy about that and I gather Roberto isn't either. They've decided they want to have a meeting with her to discuss a strategy for the future, but she's being elusive.'

Jay took the chicken that was marinating for tonight's main course out of the fridge, gave it a good stir, re-covered it and placed it back in the fridge. 'I find that really strange. Maybe she needed them to help set things up, but now that everything's running smoothly she wants to be in complete control. She always was a bit of a control freak.'

'I agree, but I still think there's something more. I just can't put my finger on what.'

'Hm, well, I guess we'll just have to let Alex and Roberto sort it out and see what happens when the contract comes up for renewal.'

'You know, the more I think about it, the more tempted I am not to renew the contract at Diva's. Once the baby is born, I'm not sure it will work being at Tia's beck and call, especially if I don't have a business partner to lean on.'

'What do you mean?' Jay shut the fridge with a thump.

Liz stopped chopping and looked him in the eye. 'What I mean is that we have to face facts. Both of us. You're doing really well in this competition. In fact, I'll suspect you'll go all the way.'

He blushed. 'Thanks.'

'And if you do, you'll have all sorts of offers. I wouldn't want to hold you back. It's always been your dream to open your own restaurant and I wouldn't want your loyalty to me to get in the way.'

'I've been thinking about that, actually.' Jay began to pack up the utensils he would need for that evening into large plastic boxes. 'In fact, I was talking to Angela about it the other day.'

'I still can't believe Angela Markham is one of the judges. I've always thought she was a brilliant chef.'

'She is and she's a really nice person too.'

'I envy you.'

'She said she thinks I'm a really good chef, but that I need more experience in the business side of things.'

'Okay.'

'I mean, there would be no point in rushing into owning my own restaurant, getting the numbers wrong and quickly going bust, would there?'

'That's very true.'

'And when you have your baby, you'll have your hands full, especially at first.'

'Yes, I can imagine I will.'

176

'So once the competition is over, could you show me what I have to do and I'll take as much as I can?'

'Okay, yes, I can see that working. But what about the functions, Jay? You can't do everything.'

'No. We'll need get some extra staff. And I think I might have found a chef for us. I haven't spoken to her about it, so it might just be pie in the sky, but she's said she wants some experience working for larger numbers, so she might well be interested.'

'And who is this chef, then?'

'Her name's Chloe — she's one of my fellow competitors. She's got talent and we get on well. She's the one who saw off Louis.'

'I see.' Liz raised her eyebrows. 'Well, she's obviously got your approval, so you'd better sound her out and, if she's interested, then we can fix a date for me to meet her.'

Jay grinned. 'Great.' His phone started to ring and, as he looked at the screen, the smile slipped from his face. He answered it. 'Mum?'

'Sorry to bother you, Jay. I know how busy you are.'

He frowned even more at the sound of her voice. 'That's okay. Is everything all right? You sound—'

'Not it's not. It's your nan. She's been taken into hospital. They think she's had a heart attack.'

'Which hospital?' Jay asked immediately.

'The Royal London.'

'Are you there with her?'

'Yes.'

'Then I'll be there as soon as I can.' He put the phone back in his pocket and turned to Liz. 'I've got to go. Nan's in hospital. They think it's a heart attack.'

Liz gasped. 'Of course you must go. I'll finish up here. And I can do the function tonight too.'

'Would you? That would be great. Sorry, I'm not much use to you at the moment.'

'Don't be daft, Jay. Family comes first. Especially your nan.'

CHAPTER TWENTY-THREE

The journey to the hospital was excruciatingly slow and all Jay could think about was how little time he'd spent with his nan recently. He prayed that she'd be okay and make a full recovery. He vowed he'd visit her more often. And he'd have to make more time for his mum as well. It had shaken him to hear how upset she'd sounded and was grateful that she'd let him know about Betty. After he parked the car and made his way to the main entrance, he phoned Mary so she could let him know where they were.

Betty had been given a bed in A&E and, when he'd been allowed through, the sight of his usually robust grandmother sitting in bed with an oxygen mask over an unusually grey face frightened him. She looked at least ten years older than when he'd last seen her and it suddenly dawned on him that she was an old lady. She'd always been such a powerhouse, he'd never thought of her as old, but he did now. He was struck with the horrible realisation that she wouldn't be around for ever. When things had fallen apart with his mum, she'd been there for him. She was the one who had given him a stable and loving family life, the wings to find his way in the world and the support that encouraged him to achieve his ambitions. He didn't know what he'd do without her and hoped he wouldn't have to find out just yet. But he pinned a smile on his face and in a jovial voice said, 'So what's all this, Nan? Scaring us to keep us on our toes?'

She pulled down her oxygen mask. 'It's all a fuss about nothing. A sit-down in my favourite chair with a nice cup of tea and I'd have been as right as rain.'

'Now, Mum . . .' Mary put her hand over her mother's. 'The paramedics didn't think that or they wouldn't have brought you here. And while you are, it's best to get you checked out.'

'I suppose so, but it's a waste of time if you ask me.'

A nurse carrying a plastic bowl containing needles and syringes opened the curtains around the bed.

'Now, Mrs Green, we'd like to take some blood if that's all right and then do an ECG so we can find out what's going on with your ticker.'

'All right, love, you just get on with what you need to do.'

'We'll sit outside and give you some privacy.' Mary led Jay away.

'Do you want me to get you a cup of coffee?' his mum asked in the waiting room. 'You almost look as grey as your nan.'

'No, thanks. I don't think I could stomach it. It's been a bit of a shock, but I'm glad you phoned me.'

'I didn't know whether to or not, to be honest. I didn't want to upset you in the middle of your competition, but I figured that if you were cooking you wouldn't be able to answer your phone anyway. Besides, I didn't think you'd forgive me if I didn't tell you. You and Mum have always been so close. I'm glad you're here, though.'

Her words came out in a rush and for a moment Jay couldn't reply — there was a large lump in his throat. He swallowed a few times before speaking. 'Naively, I always thought she'd be around for ever. Today has made me realise I shouldn't have taken her for granted.'

'Me too. She's so independent, but maybe now's the time we start taking more care of her.'

Jay laughed. 'She won't like that.'

'No, she won't, but perhaps she'll get used to it. Over time.'

'I'll try to visit her more often. Although it's not too easy at the moment.'

'Mum says you're doing really well in the competition. You seem to be smashing it.'

'I keep getting through, that's the main thing.' He paused. 'It shouldn't be Nan telling you, though.'

'She was only trying to keep me up to date.' His mum looked anguished.

He quickly tried to explain. 'What I meant was it should be me telling you, not Nan. I'm sorry, Mum, I seem to have wasted so much time. And all over a silly feud.'

'You were hurt, love.' She patted his arm. 'And I can see why. I should have supported you more. I should never have let you go.'

'The way I remember it, you couldn't have stopped me,' Jay said wryly. 'But I was a child. I only saw things in black and white. Now that I'm older I can see the world in shades of grey.'

'Life isn't always straightforward,' she said. 'Can we put it all behind us and start again?'

'I'd like that.' He leaned in to hug her, realising it was the first time in twelve years that he'd felt his mother's arms around him and smelled her familiar perfume. All of a sudden he was a child again, being comforted by her after grazing his knee or waking up from a bad dream. He blinked back his tears, afraid that if he let them fall now he'd never be able to stop. He leaned backwards and looked away to give him time to compose himself.

To his surprise, he heard her gentle laugh. He turned to her, puzzled.

'Looks like your nan has finally got her wish. She's been conspiring to get us back together for long enough.'

And suddenly the tears were gone and laughter bubbled out of his mouth.

The nurse who'd been tending to Betty approached them. 'You can go back and sit with her now. Although I have to tell you, she's not happy about being here.'

'Oh, I know that,' Mary said. 'She'll just have to get used to it, though, because she's not going anywhere until we find out what's wrong with her. Can I take her a cup of tea?'

The nurse shook her head. 'Best not. Just in case we need to do any procedures. She's better off nil by mouth for now.'

'Oh! Do you think she'll need an operation?' Mary asked.

'It's just a precaution,' the nurse said. 'Once the consultant has finished his ward rounds, he'll review her tests and come and see you. Hopefully it won't be too long.'

'Thanks.' Mary got up. 'Well, we'd best go and break the news to her. But she's not going to like it. Betty without a constant supply of tea is not going to be pleasant.'

'We're just going to have to try to distract her, then,' Jay said.

The nurse laughed. 'Good luck with that. I'll see if we can get you some answers as soon as possible.'

* * *

'Well, Doctor. What's the news? Am I going to live?'

The doctor smiled at Betty. 'You are indeed. I've been through your test results and I can safely say that it wasn't a heart attack.'

'Told you so.' Betty beamed at them all. 'Lot of fuss about nothing. Can I go home, then? I'm gagging for a decent cuppa.'

'I'm afraid not, Mrs Green. While it wasn't a heart attack, you had a severe angina attack.'

'What's that, then?'

'Simply put, it's chest pain caused by reduced blood flow to the heart muscles. Tell me, Mrs Green, what were you doing directly before the attack?'

'I was hoovering. I like to keep my house looking nice.'

'I'm sure you do. Angina can be brought on by a trigger, for instance, exercise, so you may need to take things a bit easier in the future. The good news is that you appear to have the most common type of angina, which is called stable angina and can be treated with medication. We'll prescribe some beta-blockers to make your heart beat slower and with less force. They should help prevent future episodes.'

Betty pulled a face. 'Can't say I'm too happy about that. I've never taken pills before and I don't like the idea of taking them now.'

'You've been lucky, then, but I'm afraid they are necessary.'

'And how long will I need to take them for?'

'For ever, I'm afraid. I'll also prescribe you a mouth spray, which will help you if you do have any further episodes. If you do, the first thing you must do is rest. Then take the spray. Wait for five minutes and, if the spray hasn't worked, try it again. If that doesn't work, you'll need to call for an ambulance, but the spray — it's called glyceryl trinitrate — is very effective, so try not to worry about it.'

Betty nodded.

'Now, is there anyone at home who can take care of you?'

'I live on my own, Doctor, and I intend to carry on doing so for a long time yet. But I have family who will look in on me.'

'Yes, we will, Doctor,' Mary said. 'As often as we need.'

'Not too often,' Betty gently scolded her daughter.

The doctor smiled. 'Well, that's okay, then. I'd like you to stay in hospital just for tonight so we can keep an eye on you and start you on your medication.'

'Is that really necessary?'

'I'm afraid it is, Mrs Green. Hopefully it will only be for one night.'

'But I haven't got anything with me.'

'Don't worry, Nan,' Jay said. 'As soon as you're on a ward, Mum and I will go and get your things.'

'But what about Roland?' she said.

'Who's Roland?' the doctor asked.

'My cat. He likes his routine and he won't be happy about all this.'

'Don't worry about Roland,' Jay said reassuringly. 'I'll feed him when we're picking up your things and give him a cuddle. I'll go round first thing in the morning to give him his breakfast, too.'

Betty harrumphed. 'I suppose that will have to do. Thank you, Doctor.'

'My pleasure, Mrs Green. And on my way out I'll ask one of the nurses to get you that cup of tea.'

When the doctor had left, Betty looked from Jay to Mary before speaking. 'It looks like you two are finally getting on together. Shame it took a near heart attack to do it.' But even as she spoke, she was smiling.

'Yes, well, we thought we'd better make amends,' Mary said dryly. 'Just in case you croaked it.'

'You can't get rid of me that easily, so don't be thinking that you can.'

* * *

After collecting the essentials for his nan and feeding Roland — who had been meowing loudly at being left on his own — Jay returned to the hospital with Mary to drop them off.

'I won't stay if you don't mind,' he told his mum and nan. 'If I get my skates on, I'll be able to help Liz out. She said she'd cover for me, but she's being doing a lot of that recently and I don't want her overdoing it.' He turned towards his mother. 'Give me a ring in the morning and, if Nan's going to be discharged, I'll give you a lift to pick her up and take her home.'

'Thanks, Jay.' His mum leaned in for another hug. Once more he breathed in her familiar smell and a wash of guilt overwhelmed him. What a fool he had been all these years.

183

'I'm not sure I'd have got through today without you,' Mary said quietly.

'You'd have done just fine, Mum. All the same, I'm glad I was here too.' His voice cracked with emotion.

* * *

Everything ached by the time Emma finished work that evening. Jay was working, so she'd have the flat to herself. She couldn't wait to have a good long soak in the bath. Working in housekeeping was a hard job and she really admired people like Adejo who'd been doing it for years. She supposed you got used to it, but then she also thought people in Adejo's situation didn't have much choice either. She had a family to take care of on her own.

After her bath, Emma poured herself a glass of wine and heated up some soup, which was all she felt like eating. When she'd eaten, she got out her laptop. Although Adejo hadn't been too keen on her idea of cleaners working in pairs, they had continued to work well together. Now Emma was brimming with ideas on how to improve things and was itching to get them down in black and white. Not that she'd talk to anyone about them just yet. She would bide her time until she wasn't such a newbie and by then her ideas might be taken seriously.

* * *

The sound of the door opening jolted Emma awake. After switching off her laptop she'd settled down to watch some television, but she'd struggled to keep her eyes open and had fallen asleep on the sofa.

She pulled herself upright as Jay walked into the living room.

'Emma, I didn't expect you still to be up.'

'Um, I fell asleep. Long day.'

Jay yawned. 'Me too. The longest. I think I need a drink. Want one?'

She shook her head, aware that another arduous day lay ahead. 'No, thanks. I'll sit with you for a while, though, if you like?'

'That'd be nice,' Jay replied. 'I've got a lot to tell you.'

He went into the kitchen to get a cold bottle of beer, then came back and sat down next to her.

'What's up?' she asked.

'Nan's been taken to hospital.'

'*What?*' She hadn't expected that.

'It's nothing too bad, although they're keeping her in overnight. They thought she'd had a heart attack, but it turned out to be angina, so at least it's treatable. She's not best pleased, though.'

'I bet she's not. Will she be able to go home tomorrow?'

'We hope so. Mum's going to give me a ring and I've said I'll take her over to pick up Nan if they're going to let her out.'

Emma was surprised. 'You've been with your mum?'

Jay smiled. 'Yes, she rang me to let me know Nan had been taken in and I went straight over. If nothing else, it gave us the opportunity to talk. I think Nan being ill has made us both realise life's too short to bear grudges.'

'Oh, Jay!' Overcome with emotion, Emma put her arms around him.

'I'm so glad you've finally managed to sort things out.'

'Me too. Mum and I have both agreed, though, that Nan's going to need more looking after. Whether she likes it or not.'

'Not, I suspect.'

'I agree. I'm not sure how I'm going to fit it all in. But we'll manage it somehow.'

'I'll help out if you like?'

'Really?' He looked at her. 'You'd do that?'

'Of course. I know I've only met her the once, but I really liked her and I'd be glad to help.'

He kissed her tenderly and she relished the feel of his lips on hers, which she'd been missing recently. When he pulled away, he said, 'Actually I was thinking of cooking Sunday dinner for her.'

'Here or at hers?'

'It'd have to be at hers, I think. Maybe in time we can prise her away from her home, but I doubt she'd be ready for that just yet.'

'I'm not working on Sunday. I can give you a hand with the cooking if you like.'

'I'd appreciate your help, but keeping Nan away from the kitchen will be the biggest job.'

Emma smiled. 'Oh, make my life easy why don't you? But I'll do my best.'

'Come on.' He took hold of her hand. 'Let's go to bed. It's been one hell of a day.'

After they had undressed and got into bed, Jay reached out for her. She moved into his arms and, as tired as she was, felt her passion for him mounting. Afterwards, satisfied and ready for sleep, Emma turned on her side. As she waited for sleep to claim her, she suddenly realised that in all their conversation she hadn't had a chance to tell him about her own day.

CHAPTER TWENTY-FOUR

It was Sunday and the smell of roasting beef filled the air in Betty's kitchen. Betty and Emma were seated at the kitchen table. Every so often Betty would try to get up to 'help' Jay, but Emma would put a hand on her arm.

'Let Jay do it.'

Betty grumbled. 'I'm not an invalid.'

'Of course you're not, but Jay needs all the practice he can get, especially with that fancy pudding. It could mean the difference between him making it to the banquet or being kicked out of the competition,' Emma replied tactfully.

Jay was glad to have Emma's support. With all the interruptions this week, he hadn't had much time to practise. The dessert he'd be making on Friday was the apple dish he'd produced in one of the earlier rounds. He'd been quite pleased with it then, but he knew it needed some more work to make it a contender for the banquet.

'Tell me again what you're making,' Betty asked Jay. She was sitting in her armchair, with Roland fast asleep on her knee.

'It's an apple, Nan,' he replied.

'An apple?'

'Yes, it's a white chocolate casing of two halves, which when put together forms the shape of an apple. Inside are layers of apple mousse, a biscuit crumble and a raspberry ice cream. And it's served with a toffee sauce.'

'Flavours of toffee apple, then?' Nan said. 'Although far more fancy-schmancy.'

'I'm out to impress, Nan.'

'I'm sure you will. I'm just wondering what our lot will make of it.'

'Well, they're going to be my biggest critics, so if anything needs changing I'll know in advance.'

When he'd offered to cook Sunday dinner, he'd thought it would just be the three of them, so he'd been taken aback when Betty had told him she'd also invited his mum, stepfather and twin half-brothers, who, to Jay's shame, he'd rarely met. He wasn't sure how much time he'd get to spend with them today either, with everything he'd set himself up to do. Not really auspicious timing for their first meeting in such a long time, and it was definitely going to be awkward. He was beginning to regret that he'd chosen to practise his competition dish on them.

They'd decided that it would be too much of a squeeze in his nan's kitchen, so that morning he and Emma had set up the table Betty had used to host Christmas dinners in years gone by in the front room, using all Betty's best crockery.

'It'll be great to have all the family back together again,' Betty said. 'Just a pity Hannah can't make it, but then it's a bit far for her to come for just Sunday dinner. Why she had to move to Australia, I really don't know.'

Jay had a pretty good idea. Hannah hadn't got on with their stepfather either and, when her then-fiancé had been offered a transfer over to Australia with the company he'd worked for, she'd leaped at the chance. Jay still kept in touch with her and his two nephews through video calls, but he hoped one day he'd be able to take a trip out there to spend some proper time with them.

He checked on the apple mousse, which was firm to the touch in the fridge. The raspberry ice cream was also churning nicely in the ice-cream maker he'd brought over with him. Finally, he checked on the chocolate casing, which looked as though it was setting nicely. If he could make this dish in his nan's cramped kitchen, it would stand him in good stead for the competition. But although everything was going according to plan, he was still nervous about what his family would think and didn't want to give them any cause for criticism. He just needed to make sure his nerves didn't get the better of him.

* * *

Emma looked across the kitchen to where Jay was prising the chocolate shells out of their silicone casing. She knew better than to interrupt him — whenever she'd offered to help during the morning he'd quickly rebuffed her. She'd thought that helping out today might bring them closer together, but, aside from when they had set the table together, he'd barely spoken to her. She knew he was stressed at the thought of seeing his family again, but if it hadn't been for Betty she might as well have not been here at all.

'Do you want another cup of tea, Betty?' Emma asked.

Betty smiled. 'Don't mind if I do.'

When the family finally did arrive, the noise levels soared. Emma was relieved that it wasn't just the three of them anymore. Mary hugged her enthusiastically and chatted away happily, whereas her husband, Steve, was silent and sullen, as though he was only here under duress, which he probably was.

Betty did her best to fill the awkward silences with her cheerful nattering, but the boys looked awkward and concentrated on their phones rather than engaging in conversation, studiously ignoring Jay and Emma, despite their attempts to chat to them. When Jay served the dinner Mary and Betty complimented it, even though his nan still looked miffed that it wasn't her doing the cooking. Steve, on the other hand, complained that the beef was underdone and he didn't like the rosemary and garlic that the potatoes had been roasted in.

The apple dessert was magnificent — it had such a variety of flavours, all contained in a perfect apple shape — but Steve commented that it was too cheffy and he preferred good old-fashioned apple pie.

Emma watched as Jay smarted at his comments. His jaw clenched with tension. She could see he wanted to defend himself, but he held back, probably not wanting to upset either his mum or his nan.

'Well, I'm never doing that again,' Jay said once they were in the van on the way home.

Emma tried to lift his spirits. 'The food was lovely. Especially the dessert.'

'Steve didn't think so.' Jay nearly spat his name out.

'I don't think Steve's your target audience. I thought the balance of flavours was just right and the judges are bound to see that too.'

Jay turned into their street. 'Thanks, Em. You've been a great help today. I'm sorry I wasn't much support to you, meeting my family for the first time. It was just so stressful.'

'Yes, I could see that.'

'But Mum really liked you. She told me just before we left.'

'I really liked her too,' Emma said. But she couldn't get rid of the heavy weight in her chest, which had been present all day.

CHAPTER TWENTY-FIVE

It was the biggest week of the competition and, after the events of the previous week, Jay couldn't have felt less prepared. Today the rest of the team were looking to him to lead them. He'd had every intention of working out a time plan for them all, but he'd been too overwhelmed with everything else. Now it was all he could do to remind them of the dishes they'd elected to cook and let them get on with it.

'Are you okay?' Chloe startled him out of his reverie.

'Yes, I'm just . . .' He faltered, not sure how much he should reveal to her. 'I've just had a busy few days and I'm not as prepared as I'd like to be.'

'Well, we're all in this together today. So let's just focus on our own dishes first and then we can all help each other out later.'

Her words were comforting and just what he needed right now. He smiled down at her, glad that she was in this competition with him. And although they were competitors, he did feel as though he was in a team with her.

'Thanks, Chloe.'

'What for?'

'For being so supportive.'

She squeezed his arm again. 'It works both ways, Jay.'

The judges came in and Chloe went back to her workstation. He watched her for a moment as she calmly set things straight on her workbench and wondered what it would be like to work with her outside of the competition. Then he shook his head in frustration. He was getting away with himself. *Come on, Jay. Focus.*

Time was limited and he had a lot of prep to do before he would be able to help anyone else. He needed to concentrate on his own dish first. He'd chosen to make almond shortbread with balsamic strawberries, lavender cream and strawberry coulis. If all went well, he would garnish it with frosted basil leaves. It was a simpler dessert than the ones he'd previously made, but, with the reduced time and the numbers they were catering for, he felt that a simpler, well-executed dish would score more points than something over-complicated. The downside was that he would have nowhere to hide. He began by making the almond shortbread so that it would have time to rest in the fridge before rolling out and baking it. The strawberries worked well together with the lavender, and both were staples that his grandfather had grown on his allotment.

With the shortbread resting in the fridge, he concentrated on making the strawberries and balsamic filling so that too could chill before he had to plate the dish up. Then he made the coulis and prepared the basil leaves.

As he placed the strawberry mixture in the fridge, he looked around the team to see where everyone was up to. Rav was still prepping the vegetables for the Bengali chicken curry he was making for the main. He looked worried, so Jay went to join him. 'You okay?'

'Bit behind, to be honest.'

'I've got some time. What can I do?'

'All those sweet potatoes need peeling and chopping ready to go into the stuffed parathas.'

'Pass them over, then.'

'Thank you, Jay.'

'No problem.' Jay clapped him on the back. 'We're here as a team.'

He took the tray of sweet potatoes back to his workstation and began preparing them. The judges soon wandered over.

'How's the blue team doing?' Philip asked.

'Okay so far,' Jay replied. 'I've prepped the main elements for my dish and I'm just helping Rav with the filling for the parathas. Then I'll roll out the shortbread and get it in the oven, and make my lavender cream before checking if the others need any help.'

'Good work,' Angela said. 'Nice to see you working as a team. And that you have it all under control.'

Jay smiled as they moved across the kitchen to speak to the red team, who didn't seem to be faring quite so well. Judging by the sounds of banging and crashing from their side of the kitchen, Jay could only assume they were starting to panic. The judges lingered to ask more questions and Jay heard Philip say, 'Well, you need to crack on — you've got a lot of catching up to do.'

Jay knew the key to this task was to remain focused and work efficiently, and that was exactly what he intended to do. He took the sweet potatoes back to Rav, who thanked him and tipped them into a large pan of water that was coming up to boil. Jay then began to roll out his shortbread. He tried to make it as thin as possible so that, when he plated it up, he'd have a round of shortbread on both the top and the bottom of the dish, with the filling in between.

Time sped by and Jay looked up to see Chloe waving at him. He rushed over to her side.

'My sauce has split for the fish and I can't get it right no matter what I do.'

'Here, let me,' Jay said calmly. 'Can you whip up some cream for me?'

She looked relieved. 'That I can do.'

Jay focused on making the sauce and he soon had a shiny, thick sauce that coated his spoon. He set it aside to be reheated before they served the fish, then went over to Chen, who was making the starter.

'You okay?' he asked.

Chen seemed calm and collected. 'All on track. The dim sum I've made are all ready to be batch-steamed, and all three fillings worked, so there should be a good variety for everyone. The dipping sauces are done and now I've just got to put the prawn crackers in the oil so they puff up.'

'Good man. I've just got my lavender cream to finish and I need to keep an eye on my shortbread, then I think we can all give you a hand plating up.'

Jay looked across to the red team, who still seemed to be working chaotically. The race wasn't won yet, but he hoped they would at least earn points for being the most collected. They'd just have to hope that the staff at the maritime museum preferred their team's dishes.

CHAPTER TWENTY-SIX

Jay was finally close to finding out if he was going to make it to the banquet. It was the last day of the head-to-head part of the competition where he was cooking the pork and apple dishes he'd presented in the earlier heats. Today was the day when everything he'd done would either pay off or be for nothing. His hands were shaking and he knew he'd have to get them under control if he was going to stand any chance of not messing up the intricate work that was needed for the perfect presentation of his dessert. This morning had gone well with his pork dish, but there was so much that could go wrong with the intricate apple dessert that his stepfather had disapproved of.

Jay took a few deep breaths. It was incredibly hot in the kitchen today, which would affect the outcome if he wasn't careful. He would just have to keep his nerve, not make any silly mistakes through panic, and pray. Scaling it up for the number of guests at the banquet would be a completely different matter, but he couldn't begin to think that far ahead. If things didn't go right today, he wouldn't even get that far.

And then they were cooking. Jay tried to fix his focus purely on the food, doing his best to ignore the distracting thoughts in his head. He needed to get the chocolate tempered and into the moulds to set before moving on to the mousse and the ice cream.

But at his first attempt, the chocolate split in the heat so he had to start again. As he told himself not to panic, the second attempt turned out much better and it was a relief to get the moulds into the blast chiller. Not wanting to push his luck, he had made more moulds than he needed, just in case any cracked when he tried to get them out. But now he was behind with the mousse and, in an effort to claw back some time, he added the cream too quickly. When he tasted it, he realised it was too grainy and not something he could use. Before he started to make a fresh batch, he set it to chill anyway — as a last resort if he needed it.

He powered through the second batch and then concentrated on making the raspberry ice cream followed by the biscuit layer. Then came the tricky task of releasing the chocolate from the moulds. His hands were shaking so much that the first two cracked. He had to force himself to calm down and start again. Eventually, with the required number of moulds, he filled and sealed them and put them back into the chiller. Then with ten minutes left, and the cases still to be sprayed apple green, he remembered that he hadn't yet prepared the toffee sauce. He measured the ingredients out as quickly as possible, then placed the cream, butter and sugar in a pan and gently brought it up to the right temperature. Thankfully it didn't burn and his first attempt produced a lovely sticky and shiny sauce. Next, he grabbed the apple moulds from the chiller and began spraying them. His hands were shaking so much, his first couple of attempts weren't as neat as he would have liked, but he carried on, hoping he would have time to give them another coat at the end. He pushed on and managed to have everything plated up just as time was up. Jay leaned against the bench. He was shaking from head to foot. *That was close.* There was nothing left but the judging now and, if it wasn't enough to get through, at least he knew he'd done his best. If anything it was a relief just to get to the end.

The competitors moved back to the waiting area.

Chloe sat next to him. 'How did you find that?' she whispered. She was so close to him that his first instinct was to reach out and hug her. He stopped himself just in time. That would not be appropriate, but he felt like he'd known her for much longer than he actually had. He supposed that was because their experience in this competition had been so intense.

'Terrifying. I didn't think I was going to finish and I made so many mistakes.'

'Me too.' She sighed. 'Ah, well, what's done is done.'

Chen sat on the other side of Jay. He looked as though he was about to burst into tears.

'You okay?' Jay asked gently.

Chen shook his head. 'No, I really messed up. I've never made that dish so badly. There's no way I'm getting through.'

'You just have to hope it's not as bad as you think. Any of us could be knocked out at this stage.' But Chen was usually so calm and collected that Jay feared for him.

'I'll be devastated if I go out at this stage. I'd really hoped that this was going to be a stepping stone to something better.'

'I remember you told the judges you're working in a restaurant in Chinatown.'

'Yes, cooking the same old dishes day after day. The food we cook isn't even authentically Chinese.'

'You've got a lot of talent,' Jay tried to reassure him. 'You wouldn't have got this far in the competition if you hadn't.'

'Yes, I suppose so,' Chen agreed, but he didn't look as though he believed him.

'Even if you don't go through, there's nothing stopping you from looking for a better job. You just need to believe in yourself.'

Chen nodded. 'Yes, that's what's being in this competition was about. I've always lacked confidence.'

'You should be proud of yourself.'

Chen smiled. 'Thanks, Jay. Those are wise words and I'll remember them.'

Finally they were called back to the kitchen. Jay's stomach was churning like a washing machine, and his mouth was so dry he could barely swallow.

'Once again,' Angela said, 'You've all made our job very difficult.'

'If it was down to us, then all eight of you would be cooking at the banquet,' Philip continued.

'But unfortunately we can only put four of you through,' Angela said. 'So let us put you out of your misery.'

'Cooking the starter will be Alan from the red team.' Philip paused.

'Cooking the fish course will be . . . Chloe.'

Chloe gasped with joy and Jay grinned at her. He was delighted that she had made it and at least one member of the blue team was through to the banquet.

'Cooking the main is . . .' Philip looked at them all. 'Rav.'

Rav bowed his head solemnly, but again Jay was thrilled for him. But now came the scary bit. Would he too be going through to the banquet or would he be going home?'

'And cooking the final dish of the banquet . . .' Angela paused dramatically until Jay thought he couldn't bear it any longer. 'Will be Jay!'

Jay gasped. In the last few moments, he had convinced himself he'd be going home. If it wasn't for Rav clapping him on the back he'd have thought he'd misheard Angela. He glanced over to Chen and his heart sank. He looked as though he was about to burst into tears as he realised he was out of the competition. Jay wanted to commiserate with him, but there wasn't time.

'Our sincerest commiserations to all of you who haven't made it through to the banquet, but please go away with the knowledge that you are all very talented chefs.'

The four unlucky chefs wished them all luck and trooped out of the kitchen. Jay tried to give Chen a reassuring smile, and hoped he would see him later. But if not, he would definitely keep in touch with him. Then there was just the four of them and the judges. He wasn't sure who had made the first move, but suddenly all four chefs were huddled together in a group hug.

'I think this calls for champagne.' Angela produced a tray of glasses and a bottle, which Philip opened. Jay was shaking with relief. He'd actually made it through to the banquet. And he was going to be cooking for one hundred people, showcasing the food of the region. He couldn't remember the last time he'd felt this happy. When the champagne was finished, they made their way to the changing rooms. Jay retrieved his phone from his locker to let everyone know his good news. Emma picked up his call on the third ring.

'I wasn't sure whether to phone you at work.'

'No, it's fine. I've been so nervous waiting to hear. So, tell me then, did you . . . ?'

'Yes, I got through. I'm actually cooking at the banquet.'

'Oh, Jay! I'm so delighted for you. Which dish will you be cooking?'

'Dessert.'

Emma laughed. 'I told you that dish was a winner.'

'You did, so thank you for having faith in both it and me!'

'I'll have finished work in an hour. Shall we go out and celebrate?'

'Actually, I've already had a couple of glasses of champagne. As you can imagine, everyone is thrilled. Both Chloe and Rav got through as well, so we were thinking of leaving our cars here overnight and going for a proper drink.'

'Oh, right . . . Well, yes, I can see why you'd want to do that. Do you want me to cook something for us later?'

'No, don't worry. We'll probably eat out. Me and you can celebrate tomorrow.'

'I'm on an early shift tomorrow and then I'm working for Liz in the evening.'

'Oh, yes, I'd forgotten about that. Maybe the day after, then?'

'Sure. Have a nice evening.'

Jay frowned as the call ended suddenly. Thinking it was poor reception, he went off to get changed.

* * *

Emma's hand was trembling as she ended the call and put her phone down on her desk.

'Are you all right?' Jane asked. 'You've gone very pale.'

Emma looked up. 'Yes, I'm fine, thanks. That was my boy-friend, Jay.'

'The one that's in the competition?'

'Yes, that's right. Sorry to take a personal call, but he was phoning to let me know that he's made it through to the banquet.'

'That's wonderful news. So why are you looking so disappointed?'

Emma shook her head. 'It's nothing. I'm just being silly.'

Jane came across and sat on the edge of her desk. 'I doubt you are. You're a very bright young woman.'

Emma shrugged. 'No, I am being silly. I was hoping he'd want to celebrate with me tonight, but he'd rather go out with his new friends from the competition. He didn't even ask if I'd like to join them.'

'Um, I can see your point. But I imagine people form bonds very quickly in that kind of situation. All that adren-aline. I suppose you'll just have to be patient and see what happens.'

'I suppose I will.' But in her heart, she wasn't convinced.

She was walking through Reception at the end of her shift when Nick called her name.

'Hi, Nick,' she said. She'd been doing her best to avoid him recently, not wanting to encourage his attention, but after speaking to Jay she was just happy to see someone who actu-ally looked pleased to see her.

'A bunch of us are going for a drink in the Lord Nelson. Care to join us?'

Emma thought back to the times she had gone out with them before. How much she'd enjoyed their camaraderie. What did she have to lose? The alternative was going home to pizza, an empty flat and a box set.

'Yes, why not? What time are you going over?'

'Some of the crowd are already in there. I've just got to get changed and then I'll be good to go.'

'I'll meet you over there, then,' she said. She didn't particularly want to walk there with him. People might begin to talk. But her evening was starting to look up and she was determined to enjoy it. Life had been far too serious recently.

* * *

She was on her second glass of wine and seated next to Jenny who worked in HR when Nick said, 'So, Jen, got any goss for us?'

Jenny smiled. 'You know I can't tell you anything. I don't know why you keep asking.'

'Because I'm nosey,' Nick said, quite unashamedly.

'Nosey Nick,' Jen said and laughed.

'Well, I did hear on the grapevine that Heather has resigned.'

'Jumped before she was pushed more like,' Brian the bar manager said. Emma suddenly felt sick.

'I hope it's nothing to do with me,' she said.

'I think the way she treated you was certainly a trigger,' Jen said. 'Faye was fit to burst and made a complaint about her.'

'If you ask me, she's been getting away with doing very little of anything for years. It was bound to catch up with her eventually,' Nick added.

Jen smiled. 'Well, Nick, you seem to know all the details already, so you don't need me to fill you in.'

'So, she has resigned, then?'

'I can neither confirm nor deny,' Jen said. 'Now, Nick, I think it's your round, isn't it?'

Nick groaned and got up. Emma declined another drink. She was already feeling light-headed, having not eaten since lunchtime. She had a long day ahead of her tomorrow and she didn't want to wake up with a hangover.

Jen patted her hand. 'Don't look so worried. Nick was right — she'd had it coming for a long time. It's about time she got her comeuppance.'

'All the same, I can't help feeling sorry for her.'

Jen snorted. 'Really? Why? I thought you'd be glad to be rid of her.'

'Oh, I am. Life is so much better at work now that Faye is my line manager. But I can't get my head around why Heather behaved like that and I do feel a bit sorry for her.'

'It's admirable that you feel any sympathy for her, but I wouldn't waste your emotions. Anyway, while Nick's at the bar, I just wanted to say something, between you and me.'

'Sounds ominous.'

'No, not really. It's just that I've seen the way he looks at you and I know you're already in a relationship.'

'Yes, I am.'

'It's just that he can be a little, um . . . how can I put it? Intense at times. Just be on your guard if you're not interested in him.'

Emma nodded. Jen had only summed up what she'd already thought. 'Thanks for the warning, and just for the record, no, I'm not interested.'

'What are you two looking so serious about?' Nick asked as he brought the drinks back to the table. 'It's Friday night, the start of the weekend.'

'It may be the start of the weekend for you,' Emma replied, trying to deflect him. 'But I've got a full shift tomorrow and then in the evening I'm serving at a function for my friend Liz.'

'All work and no play,' Nick said.

'Are you saying I'm dull?' Emma asked in mock horror.

'No, of course not!'

'Well, I hope you've got Sunday off,' Jen said.

'I have.'

'Then you'll have to make sure you do something nice and relaxing, or you'll suffer from complete burnout.'

'Yes, I will,' Emma said.

But Sunday all depended on what Jay was doing. Taking a final sip of her drink, Emma made a decision. If Jay wanted to spend time with her then that would be great, but, if not, she wasn't going to sit around the flat moping on her day off. She'd take herself into town and treat herself to something nice in the shops or go to the cinema. Life was too short to be at the beck and call of Jay Williams, and whether or not he had time for her.

CHAPTER TWENTY-SEVEN

Jay was having a wonderful night. The alcohol, adrenaline and joy of having made it to the banquet was a heady mixture. He did feel a twinge of guilt about Emma — she'd been so supportive of him throughout the competition — but this was the last time he would see the other competitors until the day of the actual banquet. He pushed his guilt aside. He was keen to not let it ruin his evening.

'I'm starving,' Chloe said. 'Anyone fancy going for a meal?'

'Not me,' Rav said. 'I need to get home. My wife will have dinner waiting for me and if I hurry I'll be able to read my girls a bedtime story.'

'Oh, that's lovely. How old are they?' Chloe asked.

'Seven and five,' Rav replied. The grin on his face made it obvious that he adored them.

'And is your wife as good a cook as you?' Chloe continued.

He smiled again. 'She is, yes, even though she doesn't believe it. If I know her she will have been cooking all day, because she knows that I won't have eaten.'

Jay felt another pang of guilt. Emma had offered to cook for him too, but he had turned her down.

'Earth to Jay?' Chloe said, and Jay realised she'd been talking to him.

'Sorry, what?'

'I said, as it's just the two of us, do you fancy eating, or do you want to celebrate with your girlfriend? Emma, isn't it?'

Fleetingly, Jay wondered if he should go home. But then he remembered how he had brushed Emma off when he had been so caught up in the thrill of getting through to the banquet. She probably wouldn't be that pleased to see him, now. And he was hungry.

'I'd love to,' he said.

'What do you fancy, then?'

'Um . . . er — I don't know.'

'All this talk of Rav's banquet has made me fancy an Indian. What about you?'

'Sounds good to me.'

Rav pulled his jacket from the back of the chair. 'I'll leave you two to it then. See you both at the banquet. And again, congratulations. I'm really pleased the three of us will be working together. We make a good team.'

'We do.' Chloe smiled at him. 'And I'm glad you got through too.'

'And me,' Jay said.

When Rav had left, Chloe said, 'So where shall we go then? There's a really good restaurant in Elephant and Castle if that's not too out of your way.'

'I live in Kennington, so that's perfect.'

'Great.'

As they sat together on the Tube, Jay was completely tongue-tied. It suddenly felt strange to be alone with Chloe outside of the competition and he wondered if he'd done the right thing in agreeing to go for a meal with her.

'You've gone quiet,' Chloe said eventually.

'It's just the Tube,' he said, lying.

She chuckled. 'Yes. No one speaks and no one can look anyone in the eye. You wouldn't get that in Manchester. Can't shut people up there.'

Jay laughed. 'I wouldn't know, I've never been.' He considered this for a moment. Apart from the odd holiday to Spain or Greece, he'd never been anywhere outside of London. They hadn't had the money for holidays or weekends away when he was a child, and since training as a chef he just hadn't found the time.

'If you haven't been to Manchester then you haven't lived.' Chloe interrupted his thoughts.

'And yet you live in London?' he said, glad that their conversation was on safe ground.

'It suits me for work at the moment, but I'll always be a northern girl at heart.'

'And I'll always be a London boy.'

Chloe jumped up. 'This is our stop.'

As they emerged into the dusk of the summer evening, Chloe led the way to the Indian restaurant while Jay tried to convince himself he was just going for something to eat with a colleague, and that this wasn't strange at all.

When they'd ordered, Jay asked, 'So once the banquet is over, what are you going to do? Go back to the restaurant you're in already or try something new?'

Chloe took a sip of lager. 'I don't know. I suppose initially I'll go back, but I really fancy doing something different. This competition has been a challenge, but I've loved every minute of it. It's made me realise that I want to keep pushing myself. There's no point in treading water.'

Jay admired her confidence and the fact that, if there was something she wanted, she'd have no hesitation in moving forward. Unlike him. He knew what he wanted yet he was still holding himself back. Working with Liz — was that treading water when his real goal was to set up on his own?

'Honestly, Jay, you're miles away tonight. I asked you what you're going to be doing after the competition,' Chloe said.

Focusing on her, he said, 'My business partner, Liz, is pregnant, so I'll be stepping up while she's on maternity leave.' And in choosing the words 'stepping up' he realised that he too would be moving forward, maybe just slightly slower than Chloe would contemplate. Also, remembering Angela's advice, he knew it was the right thing for him to do at the moment. 'So although I'll be doing the same job, it doesn't feel like a step backwards to me,' he added.

'Sounds interesting.'

'It was Liz's business originally, but when she wanted to expand she asked me to become her partner,' he said, convincing himself that he should be proud of what he'd achieved so far. 'Shortly afterwards we took on a contract to cater for functions at Diva's restaurant in Fitzroy Square, as well as private functions.'

Chloe's eyes widened. 'I didn't know that. Diva's has a fabulous reputation. What are the owners like?'

'There are three of them altogether. Roberto Bianchi is Chef Patron. He's brilliant. I used to work for him at La Emporium. Liz worked there too. Alex Sinclaire, Liz's husband, is pretty hands-off. He's more involved in the property side of things. And then there's Tia McIntyre.'

'Socialite and interior designer?' Chloe asked.

'The very same.'

'Wow!' Chloe said. 'You do move in some fancy circles.'

Jay grinned as their food arrived. They both tucked in with gusto. All day they'd been surrounded by food, but hadn't had the opportunity to eat.

He glanced at Chloe and realised he would miss her company once the competition was over. He remembered his conversation with Liz. It would be fun working with Chloe. She'd bring a new zest to his working environment, if she was interested. He decided to bite the bullet. 'Actually, with Liz on maternity leave, we were thinking of taking on another chef. It might only be on a temporary basis, say six months to a year, if you're interested in something new?'

Chloe stared at him. 'Are you serious?'

'Yes. It wouldn't just be up to me, though. You'd have to meet Liz and she'd be the one to make the decision. But having worked with you, I know you'd be a good fit for the business.'

Chloe beamed. 'That would be amazing and I'd love to work with you after the competition is over.'

'I'll sort something out with Liz then, after the banquet.'

'Oh, God, the banquet!' Chloe said. 'I'm so pleased to have got through, but now that I have I'm rather terrified. Are you?'

'Absolutely,' Jay said. 'I've been having nightmares about apples. And to scale that dish up to feed a hundred people, I'm beginning to wonder if I've taken on too much.'

Chloe put her hand on his arm and smiled at him. 'We're all in this together, Jay. We'll all help each other.'

'We will,' he said, at a loss to know what else to say.

CHAPTER TWENTY-EIGHT

'I bet Jay's over the moon that he's got through to the banquet,' Liz said. It was Saturday night, and she and Emma were preparing for the function that evening.

'He is,' Emma replied, this was the last time she had to have this conversation.

She'd been in bed when Jay had stumbled into the flat last night. In no mood to speak to him, she had feigned sleep, again. This morning he too had been fast asleep as she'd got up to go to work, and she had taken a change of clothes with her so there was no need to go home before coming to the function this evening.

'What did you do to celebrate?'

Emma looked up from the glasses she was polishing over an ice bucket full of steaming water.

'*We* didn't. He celebrated his success with his new besties.'

'Ouch.'

Emma sighed. 'Maybe I'm just being over-sensitive and jealous, but I can't help feeling pushed out. Again.' She set a sparkling glass down, picked up the next one, turned it upside down and held it over the steaming water before she continued to polish it.

'It can't be easy, but once the banquet is over I'm sure things will get back to normal.'

'I hope so,' Emma said. Was she reading too much into Jay's behaviour at the moment? Maybe she was, but it wouldn't hurt to create more of a life for herself, even if it was just a distraction until this blessed competition was over.

* * *

She woke late the next morning to the smell of coffee and bacon sandwiches.

'Morning, sleepyhead,' Jay said. He put a tray down next to her on the empty side of the bed. Gently she pulled herself up so as not to disturb the coffee, and rubbed her eyes. 'What's all this in aid of? It's not my birthday.'

'No, but you had a full-on day working yesterday, so I thought you deserved a treat.'

'Much appreciated,' Emma said as she picked up the mug. Jay sat down on the bed. 'But it's also an apology.'

'Really?'

'Yes. For Friday night.'

'You wanted to celebrate with your new friends,' Emma said. She tried her best not to sound offended.

'I pushed you out again and I promised I wouldn't do that. I just got caught up in the moment.'

'And that didn't include me.' She was unable to keep the hurt out of her voice.

'No. Like I said, I got caught up in the moment, and later I regretted it. Rav had to go home part way through the evening, and Chloe and I were starving so we went for something to eat.'

'Just the two of you?'

'Well, yes. I wanted to talk to her about after the competition. We'll need another chef when Liz goes on maternity leave and Chloe would be perfect for the job.'

'So just a colleague, then? Like me and Nick.'

Jay sighed. 'I suppose so. I haven't exactly bathed myself in glory recently, have I?'

'No, you haven't.'

'I'm sorry, Em, really I am. I know I've been neglecting you, but once this competition is over things will be different.'

'Jay, I'm really pleased you got through to the banquet, but I have to admit I'm looking forward to it all being over.'

'Me too. It's been great in many ways, but it has kind of taken over. Let's not think about it now. We've both got the day off, so why don't we do something?

'Sounds good. I'm really tired, though, so nothing too strenuous. Cinema, maybe?

'Good idea. Followed by a boozy pub lunch?'

'Perfect,' she said. She was glad that she wouldn't be spending the day alone after all and was determined to make the most of having Jay's attention for once.

CHAPTER TWENTY-NINE

Having successfully finished her training programme in the housekeeping department, Emma had moved into working in the office. Although it was always busy, she didn't find the work as stimulating as working front of house during a busy service. But she was still determined to learn as much as she could from the experience.

When her phone rang, she answered it immediately. It was Faye, asking Emma to come and see her in her office. Her heart immediately started to beat a little faster. Why did Faye want to see her? Had she done something wrong? She racked her brains, wondering what it could be.

But when she knocked and walked into Faye's office, she was relieved to see that her line manager was smiling.

'Morning, Emma. Take a seat.'

Emma smoothed her skirt as she sat down. 'You wanted to see me?'

'I did, yes. Now, I know you're supposed to be working in admin, but I've pulled rank and asked for you to work with me for the next few days.'

'Oh! Any particular reason?'

'Yes, we're going to be hosting a very special lunchtime function on Friday. I could use your expertise and your organisational skills.'

Emma blushed at the compliment. 'I'd be honoured to help you. What is it?'

'Well, you probably already know about it. It's the banquet for the London and south-east regional food competition. I believe your partner is one of the finalists.'

'He is, yes. But I thought that was being held at the Guildhall.'

'It was, yes, but they've had a flood in their function room, so the organisers were desperate to relocate. Fortunately, the Clover Suite was free, so we agreed to take it on. It is short notice, but it's a prestigious event and will garner a lot of publicity for the hotel.'

'I'm sure it will.' Emma was struggling to take it all in. If the event had been relocated, then surely Jay had been told. But he hadn't said anything to her. *What a surprise.*

'We have a lot of work to do before Friday,' Faye continued. 'Fortunately we don't have to worry about the food. Although Chef isn't too keen about giving up a large section of his kitchen to people he has no control over, but we'll leave him to worry about that. We need to concentrate on the front of house and make sure that everything runs efficiently. Most importantly, we must have enough servers rostered on so that the food is put in front of the guests as soon as it comes to the pass. The last thing we need is for it to be late and be delivered lukewarm. There will be many prestigious people attending the event, including Michelin chefs, and we want to give them a good impression of the Rosemont.'

'Yes, of course,' Emma replied. She realised she would finally have some involvement in Jay's competition journey, whether he wanted her to be there or not. And she would also get to meet his newfound friends.

'Do you want me to contact the agencies to make sure we have enough staff?'

'Yes, please, Emma. And make sure they know we want their best people. I need this to be perfect.'

'So do I,' Emma whispered.

* * *

'I've got two guest tickets to the banquet. I was going to ask Liz, but I was wondering if you wanted to come with her?' Jay said when Emma got home after her shift.

She smiled, glad that she was included. 'Don't you want to invite your nan and mum?

'Nan doesn't feel up to it. Mum wouldn't want to come on her own, which means she'd invite Steve, and I don't think I could handle that. Don't you want to come?'

'Of course I do, but unfortunately I can't. I have to work.'

'Oh, so you know about the change in venue, then?'

'Yes. I must admit it was a bit of a surprise to find that the function was being held at the Rosemont. How come you didn't tell me?'

'It's all been a bit last minute,' Jay said distractedly. 'I suppose I could invite Alex instead. That way he and Liz can have a nice time out together before the baby is born.'

'That sounds like a lovely idea, Jay. And I'll still be there for you, even though I won't be at one of the tables.'

'Yes, of course. Must say though, now it's only a few days away, I'm incredibly nervous. I just want it all to be over.'

'Me too,' Emma replied, hoping that, when it was, she'd get the old Jay back.

* * *

It was the day of the banquet. The day Jay had been working towards for so long. After today it would be all over and he could settle back into his normal life. Back in February, he'd been yearning for something more, some way to prove himself, but he'd done that now and it had been all-consuming. He didn't regret doing it. He'd learned so much and met many interesting people, not least two of the chefs he'd most admired throughout his career. He'd learned that he didn't need to set himself unrealistic goals. It didn't matter that he'd be thirty next year and there was still no sign of his own restaurant. It would happen when he was ready for it, and not before. In the meantime, he'd throw himself into the business he was already involved in. He'd commit himself to it one hundred per cent and make a success of managing it on his own while Liz was on maternity leave.

His nan's recent health scare had brought home how important family was to him. Time was precious, so he'd be making more time for his nan once this was over. And his mum too. That was definitely a relationship that needed nurturing. And he would need to work on getting to know his half-brothers too and hope that, over time, they could develop some sort of relationship.

And then there was Emma. He turned his head to watch her sleeping beside him. He'd neglected her terribly recently and all she'd given him was love and support. She deserved so much better than that, and he was determined to do better. He was sad that she wouldn't be a guest at the banquet tonight, but he was glad that she would still be there. Hopefully she'd realise that the last few months had all been worth it.

Jay pushed the duvet aside and quietly got out of bed, careful not to wake her. It was only five o'clock and way too early to be getting ready, but he was wide awake now. Lying in bed worrying about the day ahead wouldn't do him any good at all.

In the kitchen, he made himself a cup of coffee and sat down at the table to read through the schedule he'd written out after days of practice. In theory he would have more time than the others as his own dish would go out last. But it was a complex recipe and it only needed one element to go wrong for everything else to be thrown out of sync. He'd found that out during the last heat. Now he had the added complication of scaling the quantity up to accommodate one hundred guests. He wondered if attempting such a complicated dish was a fool's errand, but it was the dish that had got him to the banquet. If he'd chosen something simpler, he might not even be cooking today. He'd just have to find the courage to get on with it and pray that nothing went seriously wrong.

He finished his coffee and rinsed out his mug in the sink. It was still early, but he couldn't just sit around. At least at the hotel he'd be able to familiarise himself with the kitchen.

It would be strange stepping into Emma's working environment, but Jay knew he would just have to put that to the back of his mind and concentrate on the cooking. As he pulled into the staff car park, someone got out of a car and headed towards him. It was Chloe. He opened his door and greeted her warmly. She was pale and visibly shaking.

'I'm not sure I can do this,' she said immediately.

'Yes, you can.' He didn't dare tell her that he'd had similar thoughts himself. 'It's just the waiting that's getting to you. Once you're in and cooking, it will all be okay. And don't forget, although they'll be voting for an overall winner, to get this far we've already won the prize.'

'I suppose so, but I'm absolutely terrified.'

He tried to look as though he too wasn't scared. 'The other week you told me that we're all in this together, and you were right. If you need any help all you have to do is to shout for one of us. The main thing to remember is not to panic.'

She nodded and wrapped her arms around him. 'Thanks, Jay.'

He hugged her back. She felt comfortable and familiar in his arms. *What am I doing?* he asked himself, realising how wrong this was. The hug might be perfectly innocent, but it wouldn't look good if someone saw them.

He moved away from her. 'Come on, let's go in and see if we can start setting up.'

Rav and Alan arrived soon after. From then on, as Jay had predicted, there was little time to think, let alone give in to nerves.

* * *

216

When Emma arrived at work, she met with Faye and they walked to the Clover Suite to organise the positioning of the tables. Then it would be all systems go in getting them laid up and ready for the start of the function at one o'clock. The guest list was impressive — it was full of renowned chefs and businesspeople. Alex and Liz, of course, along with Roberto. Emma smiled when she saw Lord Weatherton's name on the list. He'd be in his element with all the delicious food that was on the menu.

When everyone was organised and busy concentrating on the set-up, Emma paid a quick visit to the kitchen. She wouldn't disturb Jay, because she didn't want to interrupt his flow. She knew how nervous he'd been — his tossing and turning had kept her awake most of the night and, when she had woken at six, he had already left for the hotel. She only hoped that once he got into the rhythm of cooking his nerves would disappear.

'How are things going?' she whispered to the head chef. Since asking him to provide that last-minute vegan requirement at the afternoon-tea birthday party, they had developed a good working relationship. In fact, Emma was one of the few people Chef didn't shout at.

'It's going well so far and they're not disturbing the rest of my kitchen too much.'

'That's good, then.'

'Yes, and they all seem to get along with each other. They certainly help each other out.'

Emma looked across to where Jay was working next to a dark-haired woman who she could only guess was Chloe. As she watched, Chloe called Jay's name and he instantly looked up and rushed to her side. She was stirring something in a large pan with a forlorn expression on her face. Jay stood so close to her that it was almost intimate. Then she moved to one side and Jay began to beat the contents of the pan with vigour. When he finished, he looked at Chloe and smiled, and she put her hand on his arm. Emma felt the blood drain from her face. She could feel her heart beating frantically in her chest and she felt sick.

'Are you okay?' Chef asked.

Emma replied on autopilot. 'Yes, I'm fine. Well, I'm glad everything is going well. Now, I must get back to the function room. Make sure everything is going as planned there too.' And with that she fled from the kitchen.

For the rest of the morning, Emma tried to focus on her work and not the scene she had witnessed. She chivvied the staff into getting everything done on time, while checking and re-checking that once the function started everything would run smoothly.

But no matter how hard she worked, she couldn't forget how Jay and Chloe had looked together. Chloe was incredibly beautiful with shining dark hair that hung down her back in a thick plait, huge green eyes and high cheekbones. Emma would defy any man not to fall in love with her. Jay had been spending so much time with Chloe recently, it was hard not to imagine that he had fallen for her. And the way they had stood so closely together had screamed intimacy. Was there something going on between them, even though he had sworn they were only fellow competitors? Or was she overreacting and jumping to conclusions, just like he had done with Nick? But then when she thought about how distant he had often been with her recently and how much he had kept her away from the competition and the other competitors, it all suddenly made so much more sense. Jay had said he was thinking of employing Chloe while Liz was on maternity leave, and with a sickening dread she couldn't help wondering where that might lead.

* * *

Once Jay had overcome his initial nerves he had got stuck into the cooking, and so far everything was going amazingly well. Even though he'd had to make it in batches, the chocolate tempered correctly each time and the moulds were now resting in the fridge. Even the mousse had come together perfectly. It was light, fluffy and most importantly hadn't split.

'Oh, shit!'

Jay looked up at the sound of Chloe's voice next to him. 'What's wrong?' He was instantly on alert.

'It's this sauce — it's gone lumpy. What is it with sauces at the moment? I just can't seem to get them right. And today of all days.'

'Here, let me have a look.' Jay moved to her side and manoeuvred the pan onto the worktop, peering into it. 'It is a bit lumpy.' He took a whisk out and began to beat the sauce vigorously. 'Let's see if we can't sort that out.'

Chloe stood close to him and peered into the pan. 'I'm not used to working with such big volumes. And I don't have the same strength in my arms that you do.'

For a moment he stopped beating to look down at her. The last thing he needed was for her to panic, so he tried to make light of the situation. 'Who needs to go to the gym when you're catering for a hundred people?'

She smiled back and their gazes locked. Jay was startled for a moment at the way she was looking at him. Confused, he turned his attention back to the sauce.

'Here, it's much better now. But it might be wise to pass it through a sieve before serving, just in case there are any hidden lumps.'

'Thanks, Jay. You're a life saver.'

'No problem,' he replied before quickly moving away.

When he got back to his own workstation, he found that his hands were shaking.

* * *

Liz was impressed by the Rosemont Hotel. She'd never been here before. Although she'd heard a lot about it from Emma, it was a different experience being a guest. She was looking forward to being the one waited on for a change, and was glad that her appetite appeared to be back to normal again.

Emma greeted them by the door with a smile.

'It's lovely to see you both. I'm glad you could make it.'

'I'm only sorry that I'm here with your ticket,' Alex replied. 'It's such a shame you're working.'

'Oh, it doesn't matter. At least I'm here,' Emma said.

'How's it all going?' Liz asked. 'Jay must be a nervous wreck.'

'He certainly was last night. I don't think either of us got much sleep as he was tossing and turning so much. But I popped into the kitchen earlier and everything seemed to be going well.'

'At least after today it will all be over,' Liz said. She was all too aware that Emma's cheerfulness seemed forced.

'Yes, I suspect it will,' Emma replied. 'Anyway, let me show you to your seats. I think you'll be pleased. You're on the same table as Roberto and your old friend, Lord Weatherton.'

'Oh, good, Henry's here. He'll keep us all entertained.' Liz tried to match Emma's enthusiasm, but she was puzzled by her friend's response. She had a horrible feeling that Emma's reply hadn't just been referring to the competition.

The food throughout lunch was divine and the conversation light-hearted. Liz was thoroughly enjoying herself. But the star of the meal was Jay's apple dessert. It looked exquisite and so lifelike, but she knew that what was inside would taste even better.

'Oh, my.' Liz stared at it in awe. 'Jay has outdone himself. It almost looks too good to eat.'

'Oh, I wouldn't go that far,' Lord Weatherton said, cracking the outer shell of chocolate with his spoon and diving inside. He lifted a full spoon to his mouth and closed his eyes in delight as he tasted it. 'My word,' he eventually said. 'That is simply exquisite. You'll have to get Jay to put this on your menu.'

'I definitely will,' Liz replied. 'Although how he's managed to make this for so many people, I don't know. They all look identical.'

'It certainly is a triumph,' Roberto said. 'He's come on leaps and bounds since he left La Emporium and started to work with you, Liz. I'm so proud that both of you started out under my wing.'

Liz smiled back at him. 'Which just goes to show how good a teacher you are.'

'It's a shame that as Jay's friends Liz and I are precluded from voting for the best dish. Because I'd definitely be voting for him.'

'I'm going to vote for him,' Henry said. 'Even though I'm acquainted with him, his dessert is definitely the dish of the day.'

'I completely agree,' Roberto said as he picked up his form.

The forms were collected by the servers, and then coffee was served. Liz poured herself another glass of water. Coffee was still something she couldn't tolerate.

Henry turned to her. 'You're going to have to watch Jay. Everyone's going to want him to cook for them after today.'

'As long as they're willing to pay for us to cater for their functions, that's fine. But he's promised to cover my maternity leave, so he can't go anywhere else just yet. I need him too much.'

They all laughed, but Liz was conflicted. Jay had promised to cover for her, but she didn't want to hold him back if someone offered him something wonderful. On the other hand, she didn't know how the business would survive if he decided he wanted to work elsewhere.

'It certainly won't do the reputation of Diva's functions any harm either,' Roberto said.

Liz and Alex exchanged glances. He and Roberto hadn't managed to sit down with Tia yet as she was away on a buying trip for her interior-design company, and Roberto had no idea that she and Jay were thinking of not renewing their contract when the time came. Fortunately, further conversation was prevented as the competition sponsors stood up to make a speech about the reasoning behind the competition and how successful it had been in showcasing the food that London and the south-east had to offer. After that they handed over to the two judges, Angela and Philip, who explained how the competition had been run and how the final four chefs had been selected. The four chefs were still wearing their chef's whites, which were no longer pristine but clearly showing the toils of the day. Liz felt a presence behind her and turned to see Emma standing behind her chair. She nodded a silent hello as Angela continued.

'I think I can speak for both of us,' Angela said, 'when I say that this has been a very challenging but rewarding process. The level of talent we have witnessed has been incredible. However, today has confirmed to us that our selection of the final four chefs was absolutely the right decision and that all four of them have brilliant futures ahead of them. I'm also absolutely delighted to announce that the final judging, on who the overall winner is, is not down to Philip and me, but to all of you. The votes have been counted and we are now in a position to reveal your decision.'

Philip took over. 'And the winner is . . .'

* * *

Emma fixed her gaze on Jay. She couldn't help noticing that he and Chloe were standing so closely together that she doubted anyone would be able to slide a piece of paper between them. The sight of them made her feel as nauseous as she had earlier that morning and she had to take several deep breaths to calm herself down.

'Jay Williams!' Philip said.

The room burst into spontaneous applause and Emma watched Chloe throw her arms around Jay's neck and bounce up and down as she hugged him. Emma took a step backwards and clutched the back of Liz's chair to stop herself from falling over.

* * *

'Em!' Liz jumped up to support her. She noticed that Emma's gaze didn't leave Jay and the woman beside him. She could understand why Emma suddenly looked so fragile. Even in the heat of the moment of winning, such a public display of affection didn't seem fitting when the man's girlfriend was in the audience. Especially when they were just supposed to be colleagues. The two of them separated, but Jay was surrounded by others wanting to congratulate him. If this was the Chloe that Jay wanted to employ while Liz was on maternity leave, then she had a very bad feeling.

Liz put her arm around Emma. 'Come on, I think you need some fresh air.'

'I can't. I'm working.'

'No one's going to miss you for the next five minutes.'

'No, probably not,' Emma replied. 'Especially not Jay.'

* * *

When they had made their way outside, Emma turned to Liz. 'You must think I'm stupid reacting like that.'

'Actually I don't.'

'I tried to convince myself it was just the competition and, to be fair, he's been very attentive when he's not in actual competition mode. But I got a funny feeling whenever he spoke about her and, now I've seen how they are together, I think I had good reason. I saw them in the kitchen earlier and it was just the same.'

'I hate to say it, but I agree with you,' Liz said quietly. 'They definitely looked like they'd formed a bond, but I can't imagine Jay would have done anything untoward. He's just not like that.'

Emma nodded. 'I know. He's so against cheating.'

Liz squeezed her arm. She didn't know what to say to make her friend feel better. She doubted there were any words that would. 'It'll be over after today.'

'Their friendship won't be, though.'

'No, well . . .'

'He told me that you're thinking of taking her on as a chef.'

'Jay did mention it a while back and initially I said I'd be happy to meet her, but now . . .' She paused.

'That's yours and Jay's decision. Not mine.'

'Oh, Em! Don't give up without a fight. You two are good together.'

Emma turned away and Liz suspected it was because she didn't want Liz to see her cry. 'I'm not sure, Liz. Sometimes I feel he's with me because it's easy for him. He says he loves me, but I find myself wondering if he's trying to convince himself rather than me. I know how much he loved Susie—'

'Susie is history.'

'Yes, I know that. But I don't think he'd be as devastated as he was when Susie left him if the same happened to us, and I wonder if I'm the rebound relationship.'

'If you are, it's lasted for a long time.'

Emma sighed. 'Like I said, I make it easy for him.'

'I think you're underestimating both yourself and your relationship,' Liz tried to reassure her. 'But if that's the way you feel, you need to tell him.'

'I think it might be past that stage. But I know Jay — he'll tell me what he thinks I want to hear and then nothing will change. I don't think I can live like this anymore.'

'What are you going to do?' Liz asked. She was sad that it had come to this. She wanted Emma to fight for her man, but she could see that her friend thought it would be a battle she would lose. Maybe Jay was just caught up in the emotion of the competition, but it was clear that he and Chloe had developed a bond that was more than that between just competitors.

'Nothing just yet. He's worked hard for this and I want him to be able to enjoy his success. But I won't be able to keep up the pretence for long. I've started to think that maybe I should move out.'

Liz gasped. 'Where will you go?'

'I don't know. There is staff accommodation at the hotel. My friend Jen organises it, so I suppose I could ask her if there is any space.'

Liz sighed. 'Oh, Em, that sounds desperate.'

Emma shrugged. 'It couldn't be any worse than living with a man who has feelings for someone else.'

'I think you need to bide your time. See how things develop now that the competition is over.'

'Maybe, but I think I need to be prepared for the worst.'

'Just don't do anything too hasty. You've got too much to lose.'

Emma nodded. 'We'll have to go back in. I've got work to do.'

As they walked back into the room, Liz said, 'We'll have to go and congratulate him. If we can get to him that is. He's surrounded.'

Emma and Liz waited on the edge of Jay's well-wishers until he eventually noticed them.'

'Em! Liz!' He beamed at them.

'Congratulations,' Emma whispered as he reached out to embrace her.

'Thank you. I can't believe I actually won.'

'I can,' Liz said. 'And you absolutely deserve it.'

'I don't know. I was up against some tough competition.'

Emma couldn't help noticing his glance towards Chloe and her reciprocating smile. Anger burned within her and, when Liz squeezed her hand, Emma realised she must have seen it too. At least after today she knew she wasn't imagining it.

The organiser of the competition interrupted them.

'Jay, I'm sorry. Can I just drag you away? There are people I want you to meet.'

Jay glanced apologetically at Emma. She pinned a smile to her face.

'It's okay, I need to finish up here anyway. I'm on till close.'

'I'll try to catch up with you later, then.'

'Yes, that will be nice,' Emma said, trying to keep her voice light.

CHAPTER THIRTY

Jay should be feeling over the moon. Winning the competition was a massive achievement and more than he ever could have expected when he first entered. But something wasn't right, or should he say *someone*. That left him feeling deeply unsettled.

Ever since the day of the competition, Emma had been off with him. On the surface she was bright and cheery. But there was a distance between them that he couldn't breach. Whenever he asked her what was wrong, as he had done several times over the last few days, she denied that anything was the matter. Perhaps he'd pushed her too far over the last few months. He had got so caught up in the competition and the people taking part that he'd neglected the people he cared most about.

'Are you okay, Jay? You seem a bit quiet,' Liz asked as they were preparing for a function.

'I've got a lot on my mind.'

'The aftermath of the competition?'

'Yes, you could say that.' He sighed and decided to ask Liz. She would know what to do. 'Do you know what's wrong with Emma?'

'Emma?'

'Yes. Ever since the banquet she's been very distant with me.'

'Um . . .'

'So you do know.'

'Yes, Jay. I'm afraid I do. It's Chloe.'

'Chloe?' Jay looked puzzled.

'Yes. It was obvious at the banquet that you're very close.'

'There's nothing between us.' He was quick to defend himself, while at the same time realising how stupid he'd been. Yes, he'd seen the way that Chloe sometimes looked at him, and how often she put her hand on his arm, but he'd deluded himself into thinking it was the impact of the competition. But what if there were feelings there? From Chloe's side anyway. And what if the way he had behaved had led her to think there could be something between them? Liz was staring at him silently, waiting for an explanation. 'I admit, we did bond during the competition and I do admire her. We get on really well, and she's an amazing chef, but it's all perfectly innocent.'

'Maybe it is at the moment. But I saw the way you were with each other and Emma saw it too. It wouldn't take much for things to change.'

'Well, that's not going to happen.'

'It might if you're working together. You said you wanted her to provide cover during my maternity leave.'

'I know. And she seemed really keen, but . . .' He paused.

'I'm still happy to meet her if you think she's the right person for the job, but you need to think very seriously about the implications of that. If you have feelings for Chloe, then you'll need to come clean to Emma. There's no way your relationship with her can survive if you're working with Chloe under those circumstances. And if Chloe has feelings for you and they are not reciprocated, you need to set your boundaries.'

'Yes, I can see what you mean.'

'Like I said, I'm happy to interview her, based solely on her skills. The rest you will need to deal with. But please

227

remember that Emma is my friend too, and I don't want her to be hurt any more than she has to be.'

Jay concentrated on chopping onions. He couldn't look Liz in the eye. What a mess he had got himself into. He'd have to speak to Chloe and take it from there.

'Oh, Liz, I've been such a fool. I never meant to hurt Emma, it's her I want to be with, not Chloe. I'm just going to have to convince her of that, but I can't imagine that's going to be easy.'

'No, Jay, I can't imagine it will.'

CHAPTER THIRTY-ONE

'So what do you think, then?' Jenny asked as Emma looked around the staff accommodation later that week.

Since the banquet, she'd tried to keep things light between her and Jay. She hadn't wanted to put a dampener on his success, but she knew she couldn't let it carry on much longer. Being around him when she knew he had feelings for someone else was just too painful. She had to move out soon for the sake of her own sanity. All she could think of when she saw Jay was Chloe, and so she'd asked Jen to show her the staff accommodation.

The room itself was small with a bed, en-suite bathroom and an easy chair, with a shared kitchen and lounge outside. It was very much like the student accommodation she'd lived in before she'd moved in with Jay. But she was qualified now and in a management job she loved. Living here would seem like a step backwards.

'I know it's a bit basic, but most of the staff don't spend a lot of time here. They get most of their food in the hotel and they do socialise a lot together.'

'Well, it's clean and tidy, and it will save me time and money on the commute. It's certainly got that going for it.'

And it's fine, she thought. Even if it wasn't ideal, it was okay as a stop-gap. And at least it would be cheap, so she could save up for something better. It wouldn't be for ever.

'I think it could work, I'm just . . .' She trailed off. She needed some time on her own, away from Jay. This would be fine. 'I'll take it. When can I move in?'

'Well, it's empty now, so whenever you want.'

'Great. I'll sort something out in the next few days.'

* * *

'I hear you're moving in with us,' Nick said in the staffroom the following day. He was always the first to winkle out the gossip, so she wasn't surprised to find that he knew about her move. But what did he mean by 'us'?

'Sorry? What?'

'I hear you're moving into the staff accommodation.'

'I am, yes, but don't you live near Kennington? You told me that when you walked me home.'

'Ah, yes, well. That was a little white lie, I'm afraid. I thought if you knew where I really lived, you wouldn't let me walk you, and I wanted to spend some time together. Just you and me.'

'And you came all the way back again?'

He held his hands up in submission. 'Guilty as charged.'

Emma shook her head. She'd been doing her best to keep her distance from Nick. Living in the same accommodation as him would make that difficult to say the least.

'How about I cook you a meal the night you move in?'

'I don't know. My life's a bit of a mess at the moment.'

'All the more reason to have a home-cooked meal. I make a mean risotto.'

Nick could be very persistent when he wanted something, but she wasn't sure it was a good idea. She had other things to think about. She couldn't put off telling Jay any longer and she suspected her news would come as a shock to him. Especially as she had already made arrangements to move out.

'Have you and your fella split up, then?' Nick asked when she didn't answer.

'It certainly looks that way.'

'And you're the one doing the dumping?'

'It's complicated.'

'It always is. So risotto? Tomorrow night?'

'Nick.' She sighed. 'Jay and I might be over, but I'm not ready to get into anything else.'

'I get that. And I know I've made no secret of the fact that I fancy you, but I can see that you don't feel the same. If you need a friend, though, I'm your man.'

'Thanks, Nick.' He was right — she did need a friend. Just as long as he didn't try to cross any lines.

'So how about it, then?'

'I'm not sure. I came here to give myself space.'

'It's just food.'

She did need to eat and it would be nice to do that in company. 'Risotto it is.'

* * *

Jay concentrated as he kneaded the fresh pasta dough. He needed to start making amends with Emma somehow. The atmosphere between them over the last week had been so tense. Several times he'd attempted to have a proper conversation with her, but each time he'd chickened out, afraid that if he said the wrong thing it would all be over between them. But they couldn't carry on like this any longer, so this morning he'd checked the calendar, seen that Emma would finish her shift at six tonight, and had decided to cook her favourite pasta dish — spinach-and-ricotta ravioli with walnut pesto and a creamed basil sauce. There was wine chilling in the fridge and homemade profiteroles for dessert.

After the conversation with Liz, he'd realised how badly he'd got it wrong with Emma. Of course she felt taken for granted, the way he had treated her recently. He'd been selfish and blind, thinking only of his own needs. No wonder she'd got the wrong idea when she'd seen him with Chloe. That should never have happened. Emma had always been there for him — that was one of the reasons he loved her, because she was so caring and giving, and that was what she needed from him in return. Tonight he would do his best to show her that she was the only girl for him. It was her turn to receive the love she deserved. First though, he needed to have a serious talk with Chloe.

He finished kneading the pasta, wrapped it in cling film and placed it in the fridge. Then he washed his hands, wondering what he was going to say to Chloe. He would just have to wing it and make it up as he went along. He'd been putting off ringing her but tonight, when he sat down with Emma, he wanted to be able to speak to her with a clear conscience. He picked up the phone.

'Jay, hi! It's lovely to hear from you.' Chloe sounded so happy to hear from him. Jay swallowed nervously.

'Chloe, hi, I was ringing about—'

'It must be intuition because I was just about to call you.'

'You were?'

'Yes, I've got some amazing news to tell you. Angela's offered me a job in her restaurant.'

'She has? But I thought you wanted to move away from restaurants.'

'Well, I certainly don't want to work in the restaurant I'm in at the moment, but working for Angela will be completely different. It's her whole ethos of mentoring and treating people with respect and equality. It's going to be like a breath of fresh air and I know I'm going to learn so much from her.'

'Yes, I think you will.' Jay breathed a sigh of relief. Not working with Chloe would make life so much less complicated. And working with Angela would benefit her career, far more than covering Liz's maternity leave with him. 'That's such good news, Chloe. Congratulations.'

'Oh, I'm so glad you're pleased for me. I was a bit worried about telling you, to be honest. I know we'd talked about me coming to work for you and Liz, but this really is an opportunity I couldn't turn down.'

'I completely agree with you. And don't worry, we understand. I can see why this is the right choice for you.'

'Thank you, Jay. And I just want to say that working with you during the competition played an important part in me getting this job.'

'It did?'

'Yes, for the first time in a long time I was working with people who believed in me as a chef. You've no idea how much confidence that gave me.'

'Well, I'm glad I could help.'

'And it's nice to have made such a good friend. You stuck up for me in other things as well and I'll always be grateful for that.'

'I'm just glad it's worked out for you, Chloe. You deserve it.'

As he put the phone down, his hands were shaking with relief. But he still needed to get things back on track with Emma. That would be the hardest part, convincing her that he deserved another chance.

* * *

Emma put her key in the door with something akin to dread. She'd been putting this conversation off all week and now she would just have to rip the plaster off and get it over and done with.

As she opened the door, she heard Jay clattering about in the kitchen and the most delicious smell hit her. Her heart sank. She hoped he wasn't cooking for her.

Emma put her head round the door. 'Hi,' she said quietly. Jay was stirring a sauce and tasting it until he got the flavour he wanted, as she'd watched him do so many times before. 'What are you up to?'

'Emma, hi, you're early.' He looked at his watch.

'It was quiet in the office so they let me go.'

'Well, I'm glad you're here because I've cooked you dinner. We haven't spent much time together recently and I wanted to talk to you.'

'Oh, okay.' This was the last thing she'd been expecting.

'Why don't you get changed out of your suit and then we can relax with a glass of wine before dinner.'

'Sure.'

She made a hasty retreat to their bedroom. She would do as he said and get changed. After months of practically ignoring her, why did he choose tonight, the very night she was going to tell him it was over between them, to cook her dinner?

Her hand shook as he handed her a glass of wine in the living room.

'Jay, look, this is all very nice, but there's something I've got to tell you.'

'Please, can I just say my bit first?'

She sighed and sat down. 'Go on then.'

He sat down next to her and tried to take hold of her hand, but she moved it away before he could touch her. He leaned back, frowning.

'I know the last few months have been really difficult and that's down to me.' When she didn't reply, he carried on. 'I've been completely caught up in the competition and have neglected you. And you haven't deserved it. In fact, you deserve so much better. I'm so sorry I pushed you away and I understand why you're angry with me.'

'I'm not angry with you,' she said softly.

'Well, I would be. But I've realised that, even though I won, the competition wasn't worth it. Not at the risk of losing you.'

Her heart started to beat faster. Was he telling her the truth? Could they actually make it work now the competition was over? But he'd said similar things in the past and nothing had changed. And he still hadn't mentioned Chloe.

'I think it's too late for that.'

'Don't say that.' He reached out for her and managed to hold her hand before she had a chance to pull away from him.

'We love each other. I know I've been a useless boyfriend recently, but I promise you, that's all going to change. Starting now.'

Emma shook her head. 'But that's the problem, Jay. I don't think you do love me, not the way I love you. And I can't bear to be second best.'

'But you're not second best.'

'At the banquet, I saw the way you looked at Chloe. You used to look at me like that, but not anymore.'

'No, Emma, you've got it wrong. That was just the competition. I got caught up in the moment.'

'It wasn't just one moment, though. I saw you in the kitchen together earlier in the day.'

'Oh.'

'I saw the way you looked at her. And it made me realise that it's over between us.'

'No, Em, it can't be over between us. Me and Chloe, that was nothing. Honestly, nothing happened.'

'Even if that's true, I saw the connection between you. And if you and she are working together—'

'We won't be. She's accepted a job at Angela Markham's restaurant.'

'She has?'

'Yes.'

'But that doesn't change the way you've made me feel.' She'd spent all her life feeling like she was on the outside. She couldn't bear to feel like that with the man she loved. Not anymore. 'I'm going to move out, Jay. I can't be around you while I'm feeling like this.'

He stared at her, open-mouthed. 'You're moving out? Without even giving us a chance?'

'I've given us every chance there is. I'm sorry, Jay. I love you, I really do, but I have to put myself first.'

'But Em, I've told you things are going to change.'

'I'm sorry Jay, but you've said that before, and it hasn't.'

'This time it's different.'

'And I don't believe you.' She watched as a look of anguish crossed his face.

'Is there nothing I can say to change your mind?'

She shook her head sadly. 'If there was, believe me I'd give it a go.' He slumped back on the sofa.

'Where are you moving to?'

'I've got a room in staff accommodation at the hotel.'

'You've got it all sorted, haven't you? You must have been planning this for a long time.'

'Not a long time, no. I was just lucky that a room was available when I made my mind up.'

'Lucky?'

'I can understand this has come as a shock, but in time I think you'll see it's for the best.'

'I don't think I will.'

She blinked back tears, not wanting to cry in front of him. How had it got to this? This feeling that there was no way back? She couldn't explain it to him, she couldn't even find the words to explain it to herself. But she knew she needed time and space away from him, to try to get everything clear in her head.

'I'm sorry, Jay, really I am, but I can't live with you at the moment.'

'At the moment?' he asked. 'Does that mean you might change your mind?'

'No, Jay. Oh, I don't know. I just need to get away. I need to be on my own.'

'Okay, I'll give you space if that's want you want, but please, please, Em, don't give up on me just yet, don't give up on us. We don't have to live together to still be together.'

'I don't know, Jay. I can't think straight. I just need to go, so I'm going to pack my things.'

* * *

Back in the kitchen, Jay tried to take in what had just happened. He was torn between so many emotions. Anger that Emma wasn't prepared to give their relationship a fighting chance. Sorrow that his obsession with the competition and his closeness with Chloe had made her believe he didn't love her. Guilt for treating her this way.

He thought about their relationship and how they were together. How they had been together. The way he loved Emma was based on a real connection, built over time. They had common interests and a shared outlook on life, and he'd always thought they were in it for the long haul. Maybe that was why he hadn't made as much effort as he should have done. What he was certain of was that he didn't want to lose her. He began to clear away what would remain their uneaten dinner. He would give her a bit of space and then take her a cup of tea, and hope that they could carry on talking. He wasn't ready to give up yet.

* * *

Emma pulled down her suitcases from the top of the wardrobe and began to throw her clothes into them. She didn't care whether they were folded properly or if she even wanted to take them with her. Her actions were clouded by her tears. Because while this was a rational decision, her heart still belonged to Jay and the grief of losing their relationship was breaking it.

A knock on the door startled her and she hastily scrubbed her tears away before answering it. She just hoped that her mascara hadn't run all down her face.

Jay offered her a steaming mug. 'Thought you might like a cup of tea.'

'Thanks.' Her throat was parched with all the crying.

'Look, I can see you're set on leaving, and maybe some time apart is what you need to have time to think. But I really don't want this to be the end. I do love you, Em, but I have taken you for granted and for that I'm deeply sorry. Maybe we can still sort things out. Perhaps living apart could give us some space to work on our relationship.'

'I don't know, Jay. It might be too late for that.'

'Just think about it. Please?'

She nodded, unable to speak.

'How were you thinking of moving everything?' he asked.

'I don't know.' She realised she hadn't really planned much beyond actually telling him. 'Taxi, probably.'

'There's no need for that. I'll give you a lift.'

'You'd do that.'

'Of course I would.'

* * *

'I didn't realise I had so much stuff.' Emma looked at her belongings dubiously. 'I'm not sure it will all fit into the back of your van.'

Jay began to move her suitcases towards the lift. 'We'll get it in, don't worry.'

'Thanks, Jay. It's so much easier with you helping me out. I'm not sure I could have coped with it on my own. And even now, I'm not sure what I'm going to do with all this stuff. I don't even know if it will fit in the room I've got.'

'You can leave anything you don't need straight away here, if you like. I can always store it for you until you decide what to do with it.'

She nodded. 'That would be good.' She turned her head away so that he wouldn't see the tears that were once more threatening to spill over. Why was he being so nice? It certainly didn't make leaving him any easier.

CHAPTER THIRTY-TWO

The apartment seemed empty without Emma. Jay wandered around aimlessly feeling as though part of him was missing. He'd been alone here so many times, especially when they'd worked separate shifts, but then he'd always known she'd be coming back. Now he was truly on his own, and it was all his fault. If only he had nurtured their relationship more, then maybe he wouldn't have failed so spectacularly.

When he'd gone to bed last night, he'd come into the bedroom to see a beautifully wrapped package lying on the bed. She'd left him a present for his birthday next week. The tears he'd been holding back all evening had finally spilled over. How like her to be so thoughtful, even when she'd known she would be leaving. Right now he didn't even want to acknowledge his birthday, knowing he would be spending it without her.

With no work to attend to today he'd gone to see his nan, looking for comfort. He hadn't found any there, though. Instead she'd admonished him for letting Emma slip though his fingers.

'She's such a lovely girl, Jay. And it was obvious that she loved you very much. You might have been foolish to mess this up now, but give her a bit of time and then you must try to win her back.'

'But what if she won't change her mind? She seemed pretty definite last night.'

'Like I said. Give her time.'

'And if that doesn't work?'

Betty sighed. 'Then at least you'll have tried.'

Of course his nan was right, he thought as he walked into the kitchen to make himself a cup of coffee. The problem was he didn't have the confidence with women that other men seemed to have, but, if he was going to convince her she wasn't second best, he was going to have to go out of his comfort zone.

In the meantime, he had to stop moping around. He needed to concentrate on work right now. While he was waiting for the kettle to boil, he texted Liz to arrange when they could meet up to plan ahead for her maternity leave. And then he took his coffee into the living room, to make some notes on what they needed to talk about. It was then he noticed Emma had left her laptop charger plugged into the wall. Jay looked at his watch. She should be finishing work soon. He would drive over and give it to her. He wouldn't stay or ask to talk, he would just let her have the charger back, thank her for her birthday present and leave. Give her the space she'd asked for. But hopefully she'd see that he was thinking of her.

Jay parked the van at the back of the hotel where they'd unloaded Emma's things yesterday. He was just getting out when he saw her come out of the staff entrance and head towards the accommodation block. Her name was on his lips but he stopped short when he saw another person follow behind her.

'Hey, wait for me.'

Nick. He might have known he'd be around. Jay clenched his fists as his frustration mounted. Nick was the kind of man who had the confidence with women that Jay lacked. He was also the kind that wouldn't take no for an answer until he got what he wanted. Jay moved behind the door of the van so that he could see them, but they might not notice him. He watched as Emma turned towards Nick and waited for him to catch up. He put his arm around her.

'I've been thinking about tonight all day. I've got wine chilling in the fridge and you're going to be blown away with the food!'

They entered the staff accommodation, so Jay didn't catch Emma's reply. But he didn't need to. It was quite obviously they were together. All her talk of needing some space to be on her own was a smokescreen. She just wanted to be with Nick. For a moment he was unable to move. But he couldn't stay here. He looked down to his hand, where he still held her laptop charger. He shut the van door and walked round to the front of the hotel. He would hand the charger in to Reception and ask that they pass it on to her. And then he would leave her to the life she had chosen. He accepted that his behaviour had driven her away. But he hadn't thought she would move on from him so quickly. He didn't stand a chance of making amends now. And that was what hurt the most.

CHAPTER THIRTY-THREE

Agreeing to have dinner with Nick had seemed like a good idea yesterday, but now she wasn't so sure. Despite the fact that she had told him she was only interested in friendship, and he had agreed, he was acting with a possessiveness that implied otherwise. She hadn't liked the way he put his arm around her when he greeted her in the courtyard and had managed to shrug him off as they walked into their accommodation. He had immediately poured her a glass of wine, and kept topping her up as he talked to her while he cooked. She'd been hoping to do some unpacking before they ate, but it was obvious that Nick had other ideas. She didn't want her life here to get off on the wrong foot, so she'd decided to be polite to him for now. But as soon as they had finished eating, she'd make her excuses and escape to her room.

'Right, nearly ready,' he said. 'Let me top up your drink.'

She put her hand over her glass so he couldn't pour any more wine into it. 'No, I'm fine, thanks. I've had quite enough for a school night. Early start in the morning.'

'Oh, that's a shame. I thought we could make an evening of it. Watch a film after we've eaten, maybe?'

'Thanks, but I've still got a lot of unpacking to do. I barely made a dent in it last night.'

'I could help?' He spooned the risotto onto two plates and grated Parmesan cheese over it.

'That's enough cheese for me.' She didn't just mean the dairy variety, but she wasn't sure he'd registered her meaning.

He handed her a plate and she tucked in. She was hungry and she needed to soak up the wine. The risotto was as good as he'd said it would be, but she was uncomfortable throughout the meal. This had been a mistake.

Nick broke the silence after a while. 'How's the food?'

'It's delicious,' she said. 'You were right. You do cook a mean risotto.'

He grinned at her. 'I love cooking. I should have been a chef rather than a bar manager. Though, maybe I wouldn't love it as much if I did it for a living. But there's plenty more I can cook for you.'

'So tell me, who else lives here?' She changed the subject to avoid making any kind of commitment.

'There are ten of us in total.' He listed off the names of the other occupants and what departments they worked for.

'You've met Mike the chef when we've been out for a drink, and there's Holly who works in the restaurant, I don't know if you've met her, but she can be fun. The rest pretty much keep themselves to themselves.'

Emma nodded, deciding she would get to know Mike and Holly better. Maybe she could socialise with them as a group rather than just with Nick.

'We'll all have to go out one night then, so I can get to know everyone else.'

'Sure, although they tend to work late shifts a lot, so they're not around that much.'

Emma nodded, wondering how she was going to avoid Nick. She didn't want him arranging any more intimate meals for two.

When they'd finished eating, Emma insisted on washing up, and as soon as it was done she escaped to her room.

'Sure I can't offer you another drink?' Nick said.

'No, thanks, I need to get on.'

'Coffee, then? I can make it and bring it to your room?'

'No, I'm good, thanks. Better just crack on and then I can get myself organised.'

As Emma shut her bedroom door behind her, she breathed a sigh of relief. From now on, she'd make sure her door was locked at all times.

* * *

'Are you okay, Jay? You seem a bit distracted,' Liz said. They were sitting in her living room to talk about her upcoming maternity leave.

Jay shook his head to chase away his thoughts. He kept remembering how Nick had walked out of the hotel and possessively put his arm around Emma last night.

'Sorry, I promise I'll concentrate. I want to crack on with getting everything arranged.'

'Perhaps it would help if you talked about whatever is bothering you first. Get it off your chest and then you might be able to concentrate a bit better.'

Jay sighed. 'Maybe you're right. Emma's left me.' He paused. 'She's moved into staff accommodation at the hotel.'

'Oh, right.'

Jay looked up suddenly. 'You don't seem that surprised. Did you know?'

Liz shook her head. 'Not as such, no.'

'But you knew something?'

'She mentioned it as a possibility, but I didn't know it had come to anything.'

'Right.'

'Jay, it's difficult. I'm friends with both of you. She told me in confidence, and, to be honest, I was hoping it would all blow over once the competition was over.'

'I see.'

'Don't be like that. I've barely spoken to Emma since the night of the banquet because I don't want to be in the middle of this. I was really hoping it would sort itself out.'

'Well, that didn't work.'

'Look, I'm sorry if you think I should have said something, but I wanted to be a friend to you both. Whatever you say to me is completely in confidence, as is what Emma says to me too. That's the only way this will work, don't you think?'

'Yes, I suppose so.' Despite feeling hurt, he knew Liz was making a good point, and he would probably do the same thing if it was the other way round. 'Sorry, I didn't mean to be off with you. I'm just a bit unsettled at the moment.'

'I can imagine. But I'm here for you, Jay. If ever you need a shoulder to cry on, or even just to talk, I am still your friend.'

'Thanks for that. I appreciate it. But it's over, so all I want to do is concentrate on work.'

'It's a good distraction, yes. But are you sure you can't find a way to work it out? Look at me and Alex. I definitely thought that was over when there was all that business with Nikki, but there can be ways round these things.'

'No, it's definitely over. Emma's made that very clear.'

'Maybe she just needs some time.'

'Nope. She's making herself very busy. And I can't compete with lover boy.'

'Lover boy? What do you mean?'

'So she hasn't spoken to you about Nick, then?'

'Nick? No, I've never heard of him. And I definitely didn't get the impression there was anyone else in her life. She was too gutted about you.'

Jay could tell by the surprise evident both on her face and in her words that Liz was telling the truth. 'Well, she didn't seem very gutted last night.' He told her what he had seen at the hotel.

Liz frowned. 'And you're sure they were together?'

'It looked that way to me.'

'It wasn't just friendly?'

'He met her outside the hotel, put his arm around her and talked about their dinner arrangements. It wasn't the behaviour of someone she's just friendly with. Besides, he's got form.'

'Form?'

'Yes, I've seen them together before. He walked her home after a work night out and, if I hadn't pulled up in the van next to them, I don't know what would have happened. Well, I can hazard a guess.'

'It just doesn't sound like Emma to me.'

'Nor me — that's why I was so shocked.'

'Okay, but just try not to jump to conclusions. You didn't like it when she did the same with you and Chloe.'

'That's true. But she told me she needed time on her own, and the very next night she's with him. I just don't know what to think.' He sighed. 'Look, I'm fed up with talking about this. Let's make some plans for the business.'

'Sure.'

'So, first things first. What are we going to do about Diva's?'

'I don't know. Something weird is going on with Tia. Alex and Roberto have been trying to tie her down to a meeting, but she's being elusive. I'm not sure I want to be involved with someone who's playing games, not when I've got more important things to think about.'

'Okay, well, let's put personalities aside for the moment. When the contract comes up for renewal I think we should negotiate for the terms we want, but be prepared to walk away if we don't get them.'

Liz nodded. 'Good point. What terms do you think we should go for?'

'Well, no rent for the kitchen — that's for certain.'

'She hasn't really got a leg to stand on now that we're only there for the prep of a function.'

'Exactly, but I also think we should go for either an increase in our percentage or an increase in sale prices so that we improve our profit margins.'

'With the cost of everything going up, we do need to keep an eye on the margins. I'll do some costings to prove that it's necessary. But in the meantime, are you sure you want to take on both Diva's and our own work? We still need at least one other chef.'

'Absolutely. And I've had some thoughts about someone else who might fit the bill.'

'Oh, don't you want me to interview Chloe?'

'No, she phoned me the other day. She's been offered a job with Angela Markham and she's already accepted.'

'Lucky girl. Before I started my own business I would have given a lot to work with her.'

'I know what you mean. I'm really happy that she has such a good opportunity.'

'And it will certainly make life for us a lot less complicated. So who else do you have in mind?'

'There was another chef I worked with in the competition. Chen. He didn't get through to the banquet and I think his nerves got the better of him. But he's a good chef and we get along really well. He's Chinese and does a lot of Asian-British fusion food, which I think would be interesting.'

'I agree, and is he interested?'

'I haven't spoken to him directly. I wanted to catch up with you first. But I do know that he's not happy where he is, so it might be the right time to approach him. And I'd certainly feel more confident, working with someone I already know.'

'Give him a ring as soon as possible so we can see if he's interested, otherwise we'll have to start looking elsewhere.'

'Will do.'

'And in the meantime, how do you feel about considering Mia for the front-of-house position.'

'Mia from college who works part-time?'

'Yes. She's just graduated. This might be a good opportunity for her. It would give her more responsibility than she would normally get in a graduate post, but she's very level-headed and organised, and I think she'll do well with a bit of guidance.'

'Yes, I like her.'

'She's also social media savvy, so that could be good for generating business.'

'It will. Why don't you sound her out and we'll see if we can meet up with both of them on the same day? The sooner the better.'

Liz smiled. 'Great. I'd like to have plenty of time to train Mia up and then I can put my feet up for a little while before this one arrives,' she said, touching her bump.

* * *

After Jay left, Liz changed into a hoodie and leggings, made herself a cup of tea and sat down on the sofa with her feet up on several cushions. Her back was aching, so she shifted around to get comfortable as she flicked on the television. She knew she needed to rest more. Her ankles were getting puffier by the day and Alex as usual was worried she was doing too much. She was glad that she and Jay had managed to resolve so much today, and it was good to see he was once more focused on the business. But she found what he'd said about Emma very worrying. She was positive Emma hadn't found someone else that quickly — she'd been far too distressed about Jay. But Jay seemed certain about what he'd seen. It was so sad. She'd always thought they were perfect together, but maybe people needed to go through these difficult patches to make them realise how much they cared about each other. It had worked for her and Alex, and she only hoped it wasn't the end of the road for Jay and Emma.

'Now, that's what I like to see — you with your feet up for a change.'

'Just obeying my lord and master.'

'Glad to hear it. How was your day?' Alex asked.

'Good. I had a meeting with Jay, which was very productive.'

'How is he?'

'Upset, obviously, but he's focusing on work.'

'Always the best distraction. So have you finally made plans for your maternity leave?'

'We're definitely getting there.' She told him about their staffing plans. 'And if we can get new staff in place, Jay is keen to negotiate the contract renewal for Diva's.'

'Oh, that's good. I was thinking we'd have to find another company and that's really a hassle we don't need at the moment. But if Jay is happy to go ahead.'

'Well, there would need to be certain conditions,' Liz said carefully. She didn't want to mention anything about costings yet, not even to Alex. She needed to get the figures together first to back up their proposals.

'You mean Tia.'

Liz nodded. 'I don't know what she's up to, but I think we could all do without her mind games.'

'She is being very elusive but we do need to get this sorted. I'll arrange a meeting date to discuss the contract renewal and if Tia can't commit to it then Roberto and I will go ahead without her.'

Liz sighed. 'I don't mean to sound awful, but if Tia wasn't around it would make things a lot easier.'

'I know, but don't count your chickens.'

'Oh, where Tia's concerned I don't count on anything. How was your day?'

'Not as good as yours, I'm afraid. The estate agent contacted me earlier.'

'Not good news then?' Although a revised offer on the house in Holland Park had been accepted and the survey done, they were still no nearer to exchanging contracts, let alone completing.

'It's not. Apparently there's a delay further down the chain, which is holding everything up. The way everyone is dragging their heels, I can't see us getting in there before the little one is born.'

Liz sighed. 'Well, maybe that's for the best. Maybe we should wait until after the baby arrives and take our time instead of rushing.'

'As long as you're happy with that.'

'Of course I am. It's not as though we're living in a hovel, is it?'

'No. But it's not what you wanted.'

'Well, I have you, and hopefully a healthy baby, so I haven't got much to complain about.'

'No, neither of us have.' He leaned down to kiss her. 'Now, you sit there and relax while I cook you dinner.'

She appreciated how lucky she was. 'Sounds good to me. I'm starving.'

'You're always starving.'

'It's not me, it's the little one.'

'That makes a nice change from the start of your pregnancy.' A frown creased his forehead fleetingly. 'All I want now is a happy and healthy wife and baby.'

'Me too.'

CHAPTER THIRTY-FOUR

Liz shifted on the chair she was sitting on in Diva's restaurant. She had barely slept last night, the baby had been so active. She was twenty-eight weeks pregnant now and felt huge. Her back ached and her ankles were swollen. At least she had an appointment with the midwife next week. She had so many questions, the most important being, was it normal to feel so uncomfortable all of the time? It had taken three weeks to set up the meeting for the contract renewal with Tia and the last thing she needed now was to be waiting around for the woman to bother to show up.

Roberto looked at his watch and tutted. 'If she's not here in five minutes, I suggest we start the meeting without her.'

Alex nodded. 'I completely agree. Are you okay, Liz?'

'Yes, I'm fine.' Liz smiled at him, even though she felt anything but. She was grateful that there were no functions until the weekend.

The door opened and Tia breezed through it.

'Hello, everyone.' She spoke without a hint of an apology in her voice.

Roberto looked pointedly at his watch again. 'We were expecting you twenty minutes ago.'

'Well, I'm here now, so we can get started, can't we?'

'Yes, let's, because I for one have other places I need to be,' Roberto replied.

'I'll make this as quick as possible then. Liz, Jay, we're here to discuss the changes to your contract.' Tia continued unruffled. 'As I have intimated before, you have been using Diva's kitchen to fulfil your own business needs as well as ours.'

Jay tried to defend them. 'That's not true—'

'And as such, we feel that as part of this contract renewal we need to discuss what level of rent we will charge you in order for you to continue working here.' Tia ignored him.

'Where's the "we" in this?' Roberto asked. 'Liz, Jay, I just have to say that this proposal has come from Tia and is not something Alex or I, as her business partners—' he glared at Tia — 'have had any input on.'

'That's correct,' Alex said. 'So, Tia, as we have finally pinned you down today, I think the three of us need to talk when we have finished our meeting with Liz and Jay. Roberto and I are very keen to discuss the future of our own partnership.'

'Well, let's deal with our business here first, shall we?' The look she gave Liz and Jay could only be interpreted as *not in front of the servants*. 'So, let's get back to the subject of rent.'

'I don't agree with the idea of charging rent,' Alex said. 'Liz and Jay are doing an excellent job catering for the functions at Diva's and I know for a fact that they use their own kitchen for their own functions. So for them to incur an extra cost would be counter-productive to the current working relationship.'

'Thanks, Alex.' Liz smiled at her husband. 'But I have been giving this matter some thought. And I'm not completely opposed to the idea of paying rent.'

There were several shocked gasps around the table, especially from Jay.

'I'm sorry, Jay, I haven't had a chance to discuss this with you before as it only occurred to me on the way in this morning.'

Jay nodded at her. She was glad he had her back even though he had no idea what she was about to say. Liz looked to the others. Alex and Roberto both had confused frowns on their faces, while Tia was grinning like the Cheshire Cat.

'Well, Liz, I can only say that I'm glad you've come round to my way of thinking,' she said.

'Actually, Tia, I haven't quite finished,' Liz said. 'If we were to pay rent to you, then we would become your tenants instead of your contractor, and, as such, what we really need to be discussing here are the future lease terms, not contract-renewal terms.'

The smile slipped from Tia's face. 'I don't understand.'

Alex interjected as he caught on. 'What Liz means is that, if we charge rent, they will require a legally binding lease setting out the terms of how, and for how long, they are entitled to occupy their part of the building. As such, we will become their landlords and we will have no say in how they run their business as long as they operate within the terms of the lease.'

'But the deal is they cater exclusively for Diva's customers.'

'That's exactly my point, Tia. You can't charge us rent and then expect to have a say in how we run our business. Of course, we owe a certain amount of *loyalty* to Diva's, and I'm sure we can come to some kind of preferential agreement with yourselves to cater for Diva's clients.' Liz looked to Jay, who nodded in agreement and smiled. 'But effectively we would also be free to cater for our own private clients in the space we occupy and pay for, and charge at our own pricing points.'

Tia looked outraged. 'No, that's not what I was suggesting at all.'

'It's quite clear that you need to decide on one way or the other. You can't have both, Tia.'

Liz smiled inwardly at the way Tia's lips puckered in disapproval. If she hadn't been sitting down, Liz could imagine her stamping her foot in frustration at not getting her own way.

'I suggest that Jay and I leave you to your discussions,' Liz said. 'Although if we could reach a decision quickly, I would be grateful. I'd really like to get everything finalised as soon as possible so that I can then get everything in place before I go on maternity leave.'

Alex reached for his phone. 'I'll book a taxi for you on my account, seeing as I won't be able to drive you back as planned.'

'No need. I'll see Liz back home,' Jay said.

'I'm not a child,' Liz replied, feeling indignant.

'No, but we have plenty of things to discuss along the way.'

* * *

As Jay drove back to Liz and Alex's flat, he said, 'Well, I have to admit it, you played a blinder in there.'

'Certainly wiped the smile off Tia's face, didn't it?'

Jay chuckled. 'Oh, it did. I could hardly contain myself. Although I couldn't have been more shocked when you agreed to paying rent.'

'I know. I'm sorry. Normally I'd have discussed it with you first, but the I didn't get a chance before the meeting. Something Alex said about leases on the way in struck a chord and I realised it might be the perfect way to get Tia to relinquish control.'

'Genius idea if you ask me.'

'The lease on our own kitchen ends in a few months. If we do agree to lease Diva's we could terminate that lease and reduce some of our overheads. I know it won't be as convenient for you though, not having the workspace downstairs from where you live.'

'I don't mind that at all. I actually prefer the kitchen at Diva's.'

'I do too, although I will be sad to say goodbye to that little kitchen. I have lots of good memories there.'

'Yes,' Jay said. 'It's where it all started. But looking to the future, you moving house has made me realise I can't rely on being your tenant for ever.'

'I'm not thinking of selling, Jay. I told you, you're welcome to stay there as long as you want.'

'I know, but after everything that's happened I think I need some stability in my life. I've got some money saved, so I was thinking I might look into buying my own place.'

'But what about your plans for your own restaurant?'

'I've realised it's a long way in the future and maybe a house would be a good investment. Besides, it doesn't feel the same being in the flat without Emma, so maybe a fresh start is just what I need.'

'How are you coping, Jay?'

'I'm just taking it one day at a time and trying to keep busy.'

'Well, you're certainly going to be that for the foreseeable.'

'Yes, and it'll be great to have something else to focus on.'

Liz fell silent as they continued their journey. She felt certain that Emma wasn't seeing someone else, but Jay seemed pretty convinced. She still hadn't got round to meeting up with her friend, but she'd give her a ring later and invite her round. Then she could really get to the bottom of what was actually going on.

* * *

Liz was dozing on the sofa when Alex returned from the meeting later that afternoon.

'Sorry, didn't mean to wake you,' he said as she stirred.

'It's okay, I was cat-napping. It's the only kind of sleep I seem to get at the moment.'

'Must be the little one preparing you for all those night feeds. But it's good to see you're getting some rest. You must need it after this morning.'

She pulled herself up into a sitting position. 'Yes, it was a bit dramatic.'

'Wait until I tell you what happened after you left. It got even worse.'

'Oh, I can't wait to hear about that.'

'Let me get myself a cup of coffee first. Can I get you anything?'

'A peppermint tea would be nice. I've got terrible heart-burn and a thumping head, so some paracetamol wouldn't go amiss either.'

'Consider it done. And when you've caught up with everything, I think you should go for a proper lie-down.'

'Yes, I will. It's really taking it out of me at the moment so I'll be glad to see the midwife next week.'

'Me too. I'd like to make sure that everything's okay.'

'I'm sure it will be, but you can understand why I want to get everything in place as soon as I can.'

He put the tea, a glass of water and two painkillers on the coffee table and sat down opposite her.

'So, come on then, spill,' she said when she'd swallowed the pills.

'Tia wasn't a happy bunny, I can tell you. I must admit the way you handled everything was inspired. I was all set to fight your corner, but I should have realised I didn't need to.'

'Well, it did come from something you said to me this morning, so I'd say it was teamwork.'

He smiled. 'She certainly didn't like being outmanoeu-vred. In fact, she had a complete meltdown.'

Liz frowned. 'That's not like her. She's usually so in con-trol. But she has been acting oddly for a while now.'

'I know, and, when Roberto and I joined forces and insisted that a tenancy agreement was the way forward, she really lost it. Said we were ganging up on her. That the res-taurant and hotel were the only things she had control over in her life and we had no right to take that away from her.'

Liz frowned. 'I don't understand.'

'It turns out Tia wants to meet "the one", settle down and have children but she knows she's running out of time.'

'I can see how that would upset her.'

'It's more than that. I fear she's on the verge of some sort of breakdown.'

'Poor Tia,' Liz said.

'I know. I went into the meeting feeling aggrieved with her, but now . . . Well, I just feel sorry for her.'

'Me too. So what happens now?'

'Eventually Roberto and I managed to calm her down. We persuaded her to take some time to work things out. She's going to book herself into a retreat in Bali.'

'That sounds like just what she needs. But surely that puts more pressure on you, at a time when you need it least.'

'It's not ideal. But Roberto is going to spend more time at the restaurant and the hotel is running relatively smoothly. We've got a good management team, so hopefully I'll only have to step in if there are any problems.

'As long as you don't overdo it yourself.'

'I won't. But at least we can sort out the terms of the lease together.'

'That's something,' Liz said with a sigh of relief. 'I do sympathise with Tia, but sorting out the lease will be a lot easier without her involved.'

'Completely.'

'And managing the business while I'm on maternity leave will be a lot easier for Jay if everything is operating from one place.'

'Leaving us to be able to concentrate on our new addition to the family.'

Liz smiled. She loved her work, but she was more than ready to focus on this new chapter of her life.

CHAPTER THIRTY-FIVE

Emma was running late and struggling to find some clean clothes for work. She wasn't used to living in such a small space and she had far too much stuff. Having to share a washing machine with everyone else in the accommodation didn't make life any easier either. She knew she needed to get organised but she was always so tired when she finished a shift, compounded by the fact that when she did go to bed she would spend hours lying awake thinking about Jay, only falling into the deepest of sleeps when it was nearly time to get up.

She'd finished her training in general admin and finance, and today was her first day in the HR department, which she hoped would be a slightly more interesting role. If nothing else, being in the hotel office area prevented her from bumping into Nick, at least while she was at work. It was a different matter when she was in the accommodation. If he was around she tended to spend most of her time in her room, which she found quite depressing. Despite the number of times she'd told him she wasn't interested in anything romantic, he still didn't seem to be getting the message.

Emma was beginning to regret moving into staff accommodation, and not just because of Nick. She was missing Jay, wondering if she'd acted too hastily in ending their relationship. She hadn't contacted him, but he hadn't been in touch with her either, not even when he'd dropped off her laptop charger. She had been adamant that she wanted her own space, so maybe he was just giving her what she'd told him she wanted. She couldn't really have it both ways. She should just get on with her life and try to find a flatshare somewhere else, although the thought of living with strangers didn't appeal to her either.

Having found some clothes that were just about passable, Emma hastily got ready for work. She promised herself that, if the washing machine wasn't free when she finished her shift, she'd take her clothes to the launderette and have done with it.

In the HR office later that morning, Emma sat with Jenny.

'So whenever we take on a new member of staff, we set up a file for them, both electronically and a hard copy, which goes in the filing cabinets here,' she said. 'They're organised by department and then alphabetically by surname. The first thing we have to do is contact their references and then, if they're suitable, we send out a contract for them to sign, along with a job description and general information, which can be found in the templates folder here.'

'Sounds pretty straightforward,' Emma replied.

'And then we put together an induction and a training package, in conjunction with their line managers.'

Emma frowned.

Jenny noticed her hesitation. 'What's the matter?'

'It's just that I don't remember ever receiving this. I got the original information with the offer letter, but not a training package.'

'It was definitely on the file,' Jenny said. 'When it was flagged up by Faye that you weren't following a programme, we were asked to look at the records.'

'Can I see it?' Emma asked.

'Sure.' Jenny retrieved the document and handed it to her.

Emma read it and then shook her head. 'I didn't receive it.'

'It's up to the managers to send them out, so maybe Heather didn't do it. I can't say that surprises me.'

'I really don't understand what was going on with her. And I do wonder what she's doing now.'

'I wouldn't waste your time. Heather thought she was a cut above the rest. Eventually what she did caught up with her and she paid the price. It's as simple as that. Now we've got a couple of new servers starting in the restaurant soon, so if you wouldn't mind contacting their referees we can get on with sending out their contracts.'

Emma nodded. She was glad to have something to occupy her mind.

But for the rest of the day, try as she might, she couldn't stop thinking about her former manager.

* * *

Liz showed Emma into her living room the following evening. 'How are you? I haven't seen you since the banquet.'

'I know, it's been a bit full on. I suppose Jay told you I moved out.'

'He did, yes. So, how's it going living in staff accommodation?'

Emma grimaced. 'Not great to be honest. I thought it would make life easier, that I was doing the right thing, but now I'm not so sure. I really miss him.'

'I think he misses you too.'

'Does he?' Emma asked hopefully. 'I haven't heard anything from him, not even when he dropped off my laptop charger. He brought it to the hotel, but he just left it with Reception.'

'That's because he saw . . .' The words faded on Liz's lips and she looked stricken.

'That's because he saw what?'

'You and some guy from the hotel together. He thinks you've moved on. In fact, he thinks you moved on before you even left him.'

Emma gasped. 'That's not true.' She cast her mind back to the night they were talking about. The night Nick cooked for her. 'He's got the wrong end of the stick.'

'When he told me I said that it didn't seem likely, but he was convinced. So, you're not seeing someone?'

'No, of course I'm not. I'm not going to get over Jay that quickly.'

There was a pause before Liz answered. 'I told Jay that, but he didn't believe me.'

Emma groaned. 'Nick lives in the accommodation too. We've got friendly, going out in a group, and one night he walked me home. Jay saw us together and jumped to the wrong conclusion. Then Nick offered to cook for me on the night after I moved in. I thought it would save me some time while I unpacked.'

'So why did Jay think you were together? He said this guy had his arm around you.'

'Nick's a bit touchy feely. I think . . . no, I *know* he'd like there to be more between us, but I've told him that's not going to happen.' Emma paused. 'I don't think he's got the message, though, so I'm spending most of my time in my room trying to avoid him.'

'Oh, that's not good.'

'It's not. And now I'm worried that Jay has the wrong impression and thinks I lied to him. I know it shouldn't make any difference, I was the one who ended it, but we were together for a long time and, despite everything, I still have feelings for him.'

'You need to talk to Jay. Tell him he's jumped to the wrong conclusion.'

'I doubt he'd believe me.'

'Maybe not at first, but the only way to sort this out is for the two of you to have a proper conversation.'

'Yes, I know.' Emma shook her head. 'Anyway, let's change the subject. How are things with you?'

Liz told her about her and Jay's plans for the business while she was on maternity leave, and how they were going to interview another chef Jay had met at the competition, Chen. Although Jay had already told her that Chloe had been offered a job elsewhere, she still felt relieved that they wouldn't be working together in the future, even though it made no difference now.

'And what about front of house?'

'We decided to interview Mia for the job.'

'Mia's a good choice. She was in the year below me at uni and she's well respected.'

'Let's hope it all works out then. I'd like to get it settled as soon as I can. But what about you? How are things at the Rosemont now?'

'Good. I started in HR today.' Emma told her about Heather and the training programme that she never received.

'She certainly sounds odd,' Liz said

'The strange thing is, I can't help feeling a bit sorry for her.'

'Sounds like she got what she deserved.'

'That's what everyone else seems to think but I was wondering whether I should go and see her, just to make sure she's okay.'

Liz pulled a face. 'That might do more harm than good. What if she thinks you're rubbing salt into the wound?'

'That did cross my mind. And I wouldn't know what to say to her. Maybe I should just forget about it.'

'I would. She's responsible for what she did, not you. And right now you should be concentrating on yourself.' Liz shifted in her seat and grimaced.

'Are you okay?' Emma asked. 'You haven't looked comfortable all night.'

'It's just backache. I get it all the time now, not surprising really with this bump I'm carrying around.' She put her hand protectively over her stomach as she spoke. 'I'm knackered most of the time and, even though I'm exhausted, I still can't sleep at night. On the one hand I can't wait for the baby to be born, but on the other I'm terrified. What if I'm a rubbish mother?'

Emma laughed. 'The fact that you're worrying about it tells me you're going to be a brilliant mother. And Alex will make a good dad too. Where is he tonight, by the way?'

'He's at a corporate event in the counties. Something to do with Henry Weatherton.'

'Lucky him. He'll be getting the full dining experience, then.'

'He will, and he's staying over, so hopefully he'll get a decent night's sleep without me disturbing him.'

'And what about you? Are you going to be able to sleep?'

'I doubt it, but I guess I'm just going to have to get used to it.' She yawned and Emma took that as her cue to leave.

'Well, I'm going to get going. I have work in the morning.'

'And Jay and I are interviewing tomorrow. Let me walk you out anyway.'

Liz gasped as she stood up and Emma turned around, concerned.

'Are you okay?'

'Yes, the baby must be a bit cramped.'

'Are you sure? I can stay over if you don't want to be on your own.'

Liz laughed. 'Don't be daft. I'm getting used to aches and pains.' But as she reached the door, she almost doubled over in pain.

'Right, that's it. I'm not going anywhere,' Emma said.

Liz's face was pure white as she clutched her stomach. Then all of a sudden water gushed onto her feet.

'Oh, shit, I think my waters have broken. But it's too early — I'm only twenty-eight weeks.'

'Everything's going to be fine.' Emma tried to keep her voice as calm as possible even though she was panicking on the inside. 'I'll call an ambulance.'

'No, let me speak to the maternity ward first.'

Emma nodded, picked up Liz's phone from the coffee table and handed it to her. She waited, listening to the one-sided conversation. After a few moments Liz put the phone down. 'They want me to go straight in. They're sending an ambulance, but said we should phone them back if things progress before it arrives.'

'Really? They think it might happen that fast?'

'It's unlikely,' Liz said, but she didn't look convinced.

The thought of possibly having to deliver a premature baby on her own made Emma panic even more, but she did her best not to let Liz see she was completely freaked out.

'First things first, let's get you into some dry clothes.'

Liz snapped out of her daze. 'Yes, you're right. Can you call Alex?'

'Of course. Are you okay getting changed or do you need me to help?'

'No, I can manage.' Liz bent over as pain gripped her again. 'It may take some time, though.'

'Just do your best and, if you need any help, give me a shout.'

'Just get Alex.'

'Will do.'

While Liz was in the bedroom, Emma grabbed her phone and dialled Alex's number, but it went straight to voicemail.

She put it down and shouted down the hall, 'You okay in there?'

'Yes, I'm fine.' Liz sounded anything but fine. 'Did you get through?'

'Not yet, but I'll keep trying.'

In between trying to phone Alex, Emma mopped up the mess on the carpet, hoping to save it from being completely ruined.

Liz emerged from her bedroom, her face ashen.

'Oh, Em, this isn't right. I'm so scared.'

'It's going to be fine. The ambulance is on its way.'

'I wish it would hurry up.'

'It won't be long.' Emma prayed that what she said was true. 'I'll try Alex again.'

Liz edged into the living room, supporting herself on the back of the sofa, with her other hand holding her stomach.

'Can I get you anything?' Emma asked.

Liz nodded. 'Water would be good. There are some bottles in the fridge.'

Emma handed a bottle to Liz, who accepted it gratefully. 'Do you have a bag packed for the hospital?' she asked.

Liz shook her head. 'No, we hadn't got round to it yet.'

'I'll put together some things that you might need.'

'I'd appreciate that. Don't forget my phone charger — it's plugged in by the side of the bed.'

Emma nodded, grateful for something to do. She hastily found a bag and filled it with underwear, nightclothes, leggings, T-shirts and some basic toiletries. Finally she added Liz's hairbrush and the charger she had asked for. Back in the living room, Liz was doubled over in pain. Emma went over to rub her back and, when the pain had subsided, she tried Alex again. There was still no answer.

'I've packed some things for you, but what about the baby? Have you started to get some things together?'

'No.' Liz shook her head. 'I felt it would be tempting fate to buy anything too soon.'

'Well, never mind,' Emma replied. 'We can sort that out tomorrow.'

She bit her lip as she worried. *Where was that ambulance?* She went over to the window and opened the blinds. Down below she saw a flashing blue light approaching and almost sagged in relief.

'It's okay, Liz. The ambulance is here.'

'Oh, thank God!'

'I'll wait by the door to let them in, unless you want me to wait with you?'

'No, you let them in. The sooner they're here the better,' Liz said before taking another slug of water.

Emma stood by the open door, willing the lift to open. She breathed a sigh of relief when it did and a man and a woman in green paramedic uniforms stepped out.

'She's in here,' Emma said. 'Her waters have broken and she's having contractions, but she's only twenty-eight weeks.' She ushered them inside the flat.

'I'm sure it will be fine. My name's Dave by the way, and this is my colleague, Andrea.'

'Some babies are just in a bit of a hurry,' Andrea said. 'Don't worry, we'll take care of her.'

'Thank you,' Emma said, relieved.

After a quick examination Andrea said, 'Well, Liz, it looks like your baby is keen to say hello to the world, so let's get you to hospital.'

'But it's too early!' Liz said.

'Try not to worry. The maternity staff are very experienced with premature babies. Does the father know what's happening?'

Liz gasped with another contraction, so Emma answered for her. 'He's away at the moment. I've tried calling him, but he's not answering. I'll keep trying.'

'Okay, so do you want to come in the ambulance?'

'Of course. Is that okay with you, Liz?'

Liz nodded. 'I don't want to do this on my own.'

* * *

Emma sat in a corridor in the maternity wing while Liz was assessed by the midwives. Despite her continuously trying to get in touch with Alex, his phone kept going to voicemail.

Not sure what to do next, she phoned Jay. He didn't answer either, so she left a message asking him to call, telling him it was about Liz and urgent. She hoped he'd call back. Even if he didn't want to speak to her, Liz needed him. Within moments her phone rang.

'Emma, what's the matter?'

'It's Liz,' she said, relieved. 'She's gone into early labour. Alex is away and, despite me ringing him constantly, he's not answering. I don't know what to do.'

'Okay. That must be stressful.' He paused. 'You said Alex is away — do you know where is he?'

'No. Liz said he was on some corporate jolly, somewhere in the counties. Golf, I think.'

'Do you know who he's with?'

'No, of course I don't!' Then she remembered. 'Oh, hang on, I think Liz mentioned something about Lord Weatherton.'

'That's good. I have his number. I'll try ringing him. If he's not with Alex, he might know where he is. What hospital are you in so I can let him know?'

'St Thomas's.'

'I'll phone you straight back.'

'Thanks.' As Emma ended the call, the door to the room Liz was in opened, and two nurses guided a trolley out.

Emma jumped to her feet. 'Liz?'

The worried face of her friend looked back at her. 'They're taking me for a Caesarean. Looks like this baby is determined to come early, on top of which, I have pre-eclampsia. Have you managed to get hold of Alex yet?'

'No, but Jay's on the case. Don't worry, we'll get him here.'

Liz nodded. 'Thanks, Em.'

Emma watched as her friend was pushed away, and a wave of loneliness and fear washed through her. Her phone rang, making her jump.

'Jay?'

'Good news. Alex is with Lord W. His driver is bringing Alex back right now.'

'Oh, that's a relief. But ring him back and tell him to put his foot down. Liz is having a C-section and she's got pre-eclampsia.'

'What's that?'

'I've no idea. I haven't had time to look it up it yet, but it sounds pretty serious.'

'Right. I'll let Alex know. Are you okay?'

'Not really. But don't worry, I'll be fine.' For a moment it was as though their break-up had never happened. Then it all came rushing back and she realised that Jay wasn't part of her life anymore. She shouldn't be leaning on him like this.

'I'll come and sit with you, if you like? At least until Alex gets there.'

Emma paused, but she couldn't resist his comforting presence. 'Would you?'

'Of course. Liz needs us.'

'Yes.' A wave of disappointment hit her. He wasn't coming for her. He was coming for Liz. It was a selfish thought because he was right. Liz *did* need them. But at least he was coming.

* * *

Jay grabbed his keys, phone and coat. Too impatient to wait for the lift, he ran down the stairs. He drove on autopilot, thinking of Liz. She must be terrified, going into labour so early and having to undergo surgery without Alex by her side. This was definitely not how she would have imagined her baby coming into the world. Then he thought of Emma, who'd sounded distraught as she hadn't been able to get hold of Alex. She was sitting in the hospital alone, not knowing how she could help her friend. Jay had been in the kitchen when he'd heard his phone ring. He was shocked when Emma's name had flashed up on his screen, but as he hesitated the call went to voicemail. He heard the bleep that a message had been left, and listened to it straight away. And he was glad he had, because Liz needed him. There was a little voice in his head telling him that Emma needed him too, but he pushed that to one side. He was doing this for Liz. Emma was with someone else now and the sooner he got used to the idea, the better.

* * *

The minutes ticked by increasingly slowly as Emma waited. Hospital staff walked past her, each intent on their own destination. No one seemed to have anything to say to her. She'd looked up pre-eclampsia on her phone and realised how serious it was. Liz had been complaining of her puffy ankles and backache, which were symptoms of the condition, but they were also things that could be associated with pregnancy anyway. But having a baby so early was terrifying. Would he or she be all right? Who knew what complications lay ahead for the poor little mite.

Emma looked up as she once more heard footsteps, but this time they belonged to someone who was much more familiar to her. As Jay approached, she smiled and instinctively stood up, reaching out to hug him. To her dismay he held himself stiffly away from her and she sat down abruptly, her face flaming in embarrassment.

'Any news?' Jay sat down next to her, but kept his distance.

'No, nothing,' she said quietly. 'Any news on Alex?'

'He's about half an hour away.'

'He won't be here in time, then.'

'No, but at least he'll be here when she comes out of surgery.'

'Thanks for coming. I'm sure Liz will appreciate it.'

'Well, I couldn't sit at home just waiting.'

'No, I don't suppose you could.'

They lapsed into silence, but, after a while Emma couldn't stand it any longer. 'Look, Jay, I know this is really awkward for us both, but I think we're going to be seeing a lot more of each other over the next few weeks. We need to get to some point where being together doesn't feel this uncomfortable.'

'I agree,' he said. 'It's just very difficult. I understand why you left and I'm so sorry for making you feel like that was your only option, and I really wish we could have made things work. I accept that you're with someone else, but the speed at which you moved on from me hurts, and it's going to take me a while to get over that.'

'I haven't moved on.'

'I know what I saw.'

'Liz told me, but it's not what you think.'

'Really?'

Emma sighed in exasperation. 'I know you've always thought there was something going on between me and Nick, but I'm not interested in him.'

'So you say.'

'I'm telling you the truth. I was lonely and just wanted to make friends with the people I worked with. Nick was just always there.'

'And he still is.'

'But I don't want to *be* with him.' She hissed, not wanting to make too much noise in the hospital corridor. Why couldn't he just listen and believe that what she was saying was the truth?

'That's not what it looked like.'

'He put his arm around me, but did you see me reciprocate?'

'No, but you looked pretty cosy and you were having dinner together.'

'He lives in the same accommodation and he offered to cook for me while I unpacked.'

'And that's all it was?'

'Yes. Nick has been trying it on, but I've made it very clear that I'm not interested. That I'm not ready for a relationship. That I'm not over you.'

Jay sighed. 'I'd like to believe that, Emma, I really would.'

'Well, if you weren't so stubborn you'd realise it was the truth. I'm not a liar, Jay, and if you think I am then you're not the man I thought you were either.'

They lapsed into silence once more. Fury bubbled away inside Emma. How could Jay think so little of her?

* * *

Jay was genuinely shocked by her words. Was Emma telling the truth? Had he really got it so wrong and there was nothing between her and Nick after all?

But he'd seen them together and he couldn't get that image out of his head. And even if there wasn't anything between them, the fact still remained that Emma had left him, even though he understood why. She might not be over him as she'd said, but she didn't want to be with him either. And now she was angry with him, which was the last thing he wanted. Even if there had been a chance of them fixing things before, he'd definitely blown it tonight. Why had he been, as she'd said, so stubborn? Stubborn and stupid. That was him.

Jay's thoughts were interrupted by the arrival of Alex, running down the corridor.

'Where is she?' He asked, out of breath.

'She's not back from surgery yet,' Emma said. 'We haven't heard anything, but it's been a while since she went down there.'

Alex nodded. The panic on his face was clear. 'I need to find someone, see what's going on, then.' And as swiftly as he'd arrived, he left.

'I have no idea how long it takes to have a Caesarean section, but it does seem to be taking a long time,' Emma said.

'I know what you mean.' Jay instinctively put his arm around her. He expected her to flinch away and he was relieved when she didn't.

'It must be like déjà vu for him.'

Jay nodded. 'Yes, I can't imagine what he's going through.'

They sat in silence for a while before Emma spoke again. 'Obviously this is going to change everything for you. You weren't expecting Liz to go on maternity leave so soon.'

'I know, and we're not nearly prepared enough. We're supposed to be interviewing new staff tomorrow, but now I'll have to make that decision on my own. I'll be making all the decisions on my own for a while.'

'If I can get the day off tomorrow, or should I say, today, would it help if I sat in with you?'

Jay felt a surge of relief. Emma might be angry with him, but she still wanted to make things better. It was one of the things he loved about her. 'You'd do that?'

271

'Of course I would. Look, Jay, we've got a lot of history together and with Liz. This is an extreme circumstance and I want to help you as well as her.'

Jay nodded. He was partly elated that she wanted to help him, but also aware that it wasn't just for him. 'It would be great if you could. Just to have someone sitting next to me would give me a bit more confidence. I've never interviewed anyone before.'

Emma managed a chuckle. 'Neither have I. We are going up in the world.'

'Yes.'

'If Mia agrees to the job, I could always see if I can take some holiday, to give her a helping hand, while she gets used to the role.'

Jay squeezed her shoulder affectionately. 'I'd love that, Em, and it really would be a massive help.'

'My pleasure.'

* * *

The noise of a bed being pushed down the corridor by two porters made them look up. Alex was walking alongside it, but there was no baby. Liz smiled wearily at them and asked the porters to stop as they approached.

'I can't believe the two of you are still here.'

'We couldn't just leave,' Emma replied. 'Is everything okay?'

'There were some complications with the operation, but we have a beautiful baby girl. She's so small, though, so they've whisked her off to the special care unit. We hope she's going to be okay, but only time will tell.'

'We'll keep our fingers crossed. But at least she was delivered safely. And you're okay?'

Liz nodded. 'Bit tired.'

A nurse came from behind two double doors. 'Sorry to interrupt, but we need to get you onto the ward and settled in.'

'Of course. We'll come and see you tomorrow, or rather later today,' Emma said as Liz was pushed away.

Alex hung back. 'I want to thank you two so much. Without you, especially you, Emma, I don't know what would have happened. You really are true friends. I switched my phone onto silent during the speeches after dinner, and forgot to change it back. I can't believe I made such a stupid mistake. So thanks, Jay, for getting hold of Henry. I may have missed the birth, but at least I got here to be with Liz in these first few hours.'

'We're just glad that so far everything is all right. That little girl gave us all a bit of a fright.'

'She certainly created some drama. Although as long as she's okay — as long as they're both okay — I really don't mind.'

'You just concentrate on your two girls and try not to worry,' Jay said. 'If she asks, tell Liz that between us Emma and I have the business under control.'

'Oh, you know Liz. She will be worrying about it.'

'Tell her there's no need. We'll keep her fully up to date to put her mind at rest, but she won't need to lift a finger.'

'Thanks. Now, I'm going to make sure she's settled and then hopefully I'll be able to see my daughter.'

* * *

After barely any sleep, Emma phoned Faye at work. She explained the situation and asked if she could take the day as holiday to help out with the business.

'Of course you can,' Faye replied without hesitation. 'And if you need more time off, just let me know what's happening so I can sort out the rota. But don't worry, we'll just extend your time in HR and you can pick up where you left off when things calm down.'

Relief flooded through her. Emma thanked Faye and put the phone down. She never would have had that response if Heather had still been her line manager.

273

CHAPTER THIRTY-SIX

'So what's been going on in your life, then?' Betty asked Jay when he called round to see her the following afternoon.

He and Emma had spent a productive morning interviewing Mia and Chen. Thankfully they'd both been happy to come and work for him. Chen had to give notice on his current job, but as Mia had been enjoying some time off after graduating she was happy to start the following week. Emma had agreed to help out with the first functions, although considering Mia's experience he doubted she would need help for long. Still, it was good to know that someone was around to support her while she was getting used to running the front of house without Liz. That meant that Jay could concentrate on the food.

Emma. His thoughts kept slipping back to her. It had been great being with her today. It had been just like when they'd used to work together. They'd always made a good team, but he'd had to keep reminding himself that they were just friends and that Emma had been there to help Liz out as much as she'd been helping him.

'Hello, earth to Jay.' His nan's voice brought him out of his reverie.

'Sorry, Nan. Well, actually there's been a bit of a drama at my end. Liz had her baby last night.'

'*What?*' Betty banged the cup of tea she'd made for Jay down on the kitchen table and some of the liquid slopped over the top and into the saucer. 'But she's not due for ages yet.'

'I know, but the baby obviously thought otherwise.'

She sat down beside him. 'And are they both okay?'

Jay explained what had happened and Betty's eyebrows almost rose into her hairline. 'Flipping heck, that was a drama.'

'It was scary. I'm going to the hospital in a bit. I don't know if I'll get to see the baby, but I'm hoping I'll be able to take a quick peek. I just wanted to see how you were doing before I went.'

'And as you can see, I'm fighting fit. I don't much like taking these tablets, but they seem to be doing the trick. Now, as it happens, I've just finished knitting a matinee jacket this morning. I don't suppose it will be any use to the poor little mite just yet, but I've got some pink wool in my bag, so I can get cracking on a smaller version straight away.'

Jay laughed. 'It's nice to see you back to your normal self.'

'Can't keep me down for long, Jay, love. Now tell me, how's young Emma?'

The smile slipped from his face. 'Well, I was with her at the hospital last night and she's been helping me out today, but I think she's only doing it for Liz. I can't say I blame her.'

'Oh, Jay!' Betty leaned over and gave him a hug. 'If you're still in love with her you have to fight for her. You'll need to do something big to convince her that you made a mistake, but she really is the one for you.'

'What kind of something big?'

Betty shook her head. 'Now, that, son, is up to you.'

* * *

'Oh, my word, Liz, she's so tiny!'

When Emma had arrived on the ward, Liz had asked if she'd wheel her down to the baby unit so they could visit the baby together.

'I know, but she's a fighter. The nurses say she's doing really well considering how prem she was.'

'And she's going to be all right?'

Liz shrugged, suddenly looking downcast. 'I don't know. It's just a question of taking it one day at a time and hoping for the best. She could have problems further down the line, but we won't know until they do tests and see how she develops.'

Emma's heart went out to her friend and she tried to find the words to console her. 'As you say, though, she's a little fighter and we'll all keep our fingers crossed for her. How's Alex?'

Emma could see that Liz was welling up. 'To be honest, I don't think it's really hit him yet. He's still in shock. But he was dog-tired so I sent him home for a few hours' sleep. I just hope he gets some.'

'And what about you?'

'I'm okay. Sore, but that's inevitable. If all is well they're going to send me home tomorrow. I'll still be here most of the time until this little one is well enough to come home, but that won't be for weeks.'

'Like you say, all you can do is take it one day at a time.'

Liz smiled as she gazed at her baby. 'Yes. I can't tell you how much love I feel for her already. The mum hormones have really kicked in.'

'You're going to be a great mum. And Alex will be a great dad too.'

'I hope so. It's only what baby Isabel deserves.'

'Oh, what a lovely name!' Emma peered into the crib.

'Yes, I think it suits her.' She saw Liz yawn. 'Shall we go back to the ward?'

Liz nodded. 'I'll come back later when Alex is here.'

When they were back on the ward, Emma handed over the bag of goodies she'd bought this afternoon, after she and Jay had finished their interviews. 'Here's a few bits for you and the baby.' She'd had a lovely time shopping for Babygros, bibs and cardigans, as well as some luxury items for Liz and a big box of chocolates.

'Oh, Emma, thank you. There's no need for that.'

'It's only a few bits. I bought the smallest Babygros I could find, but even they probably won't fit her yet.'

'No, but they are adorable, Emma, and hopefully she'll soon grow into them. Thank you.'

'My pleasure,' Emma said.

'So tell me, then, how are you and Jay?'

'Good,' Emma said. 'We interviewed Chen and Mia this morning. Chen is happy to start as soon as he's worked his notice and Mia can start next week. I've spoken to my manager and she's agreed for me to take some leave so I can help her out in her early days.'

'Oh, Em, that's so good of you. Thank you. I know Jay was getting ready to take over, but not quite as soon as this. And I'm so glad you've made it up with each other.'

'We're not back together,' Emma said hurriedly. She didn't want Liz to get the wrong idea. 'We had a good talk last night and he understands that I'm not with Nick, or at least I think he does. But we've agreed that we're only going to be friends from now on. Especially while I help out with the business until everyone's up to speed.'

'But you still love each other, don't you?'

'It's not as simple as that,' Emma said.

Liz sighed. 'I just wish you could see how perfect you are for each other.'

'Really? Liz, I know you must have lots of hormones swimming around at the moment, but perfect? I don't think so.' She looked up as she saw Jay walking into the ward. 'Talk of the devil.'

Emma waited until Jay had settled himself down in a plastic chair on the other side of the bed before getting up herself.

'I'll go now, if you don't mind, Liz. It's been a long day and I didn't get much sleep last night.'

'Oh, must you go so soon?' Liz asked. Emma knew she was engineering for her and Jay to spend some more time together.

But the truth was, being with Jay was painful. It would be easy for them to slip back into a relationship, but she knew in the long term it would only cause her more pain.

* * *

'Well, she couldn't get away fast enough,' Jay said when Emma was out of earshot.

'Maybe that's because she still has feelings for you,' Liz replied.

'She's firmly put me in the friendship zone and that's where she wants me to stay. Still, I suppose it's about as much as I deserve.'

'Don't give up on her, Jay. You two will work it out, I'm sure you will.'

'Don't give up your day job. Relationship counselling's not for you,' Jay replied grimly. 'Anyway, I've been to see Nan. She's finished her first matinee jacket, but obviously it's going to be too big so she's starting on a miniature version today, in pink. I hope you don't mind gender colour stereotyping.'

'Not at all and I can't wait to be able to dress her myself.'

'I'm sure it won't be long. Have you got a name yet?'

'Isabel.'

Jay grinned. 'That's a beautiful name.'

'It is, isn't it?' Liz said, unable to keep the answering smile off her face.

They chatted for a while, and Jay assured her that all she needed to do now was concentrate on her family and he'd take care of the rest.

'Thanks, Jay. I'm so glad you're my business partner, I don't know what I'd do without you, especially at the moment.'

'Well, that's what partnership is all about, isn't it?'

'It is,' Liz said. She grinned as she spotted Alex arriving with a large bag in his hand. 'And talking about partnerships, don't give up on Emma.'

Jay got up to leave. 'I won't. But I rather think she's given up on me.'

* * *

Emma was hoping that she could sneak into her room unobserved when she got back to the hotel. She was so tired, she'd almost fallen asleep on the Tube on the way home. All she wanted was her bed and the oblivion of sleep. But as she walked into the living room, Nick accosted her.

'Emma! There you are. Where have you been all day?'

She sighed as he cut off her escape route.

'My friend had her baby last night. She was only twenty-eight weeks so it was all a bit frantic.'

'Oh, I'm sorry to hear that. They're okay now?'

'Hopefully, yes.' She moved to one side, hoping he would let her pass, but he moved with her.

'So, do you fancy wetting the baby's head, then? I've got a bottle of wine in the fridge.'

'No, I'm fine, thanks. I just want to go to bed. It was a long night last night and I'm shattered.'

He still didn't move. 'Are you sure? A glass of wine might help you sleep.'

'I don't think I'll need any help, thanks.'

'Oh, go on, just to be sociable.'

'I really don't feel like being sociable at the moment.' She took a deep breath. Knowing that she couldn't keep avoiding him, and seeing as he didn't seem to be taking no for an answer, it looked like she would have to spell it out to him. 'And as I've told you before, I'm not interested in any kind of relationship.'

'I was just asking you for a drink, not a relationship.' A hard note had entered his voice.

'And I said I didn't want one, so if you don't mind I'd like you to let me pass so that I can go to my room.'

'I was only being friendly.'

'And if you are my friend, Nick, you'll respect what I say when I tell you that I don't want to be bombarded every time I step through the door.'

'There's no need to be like that.' But he finally stepped aside and she was able to get to her room.

She locked the door firmly behind her. As she tried to slow her heartbeat back to its normal level, she thought that she would have welcomed a glass of wine. But she'd have to make do with the rather warm bottle of water in her bag.

She just hoped that her words to Nick had hit home and he'd finally leave her alone.

CHAPTER THIRTY-SEVEN

Two weeks later, Emma was back in the HR office at the hotel. All the staff were welcoming and she particularly enjoyed working with Jenny, but she'd quickly come to realise that office work was not for her. Helping Jay last week had reminded her of what she liked most about the hospitality industry. The preparation of a function and then bringing it all together at the last minute. Watching as people enjoyed the food that had been prepared for them and ensuring that their whole experience was enjoyable. Working in HR was a good insight into what was required to make sure the workforce operated like a well-oiled machine, but she wouldn't be disappointed when her time here ended and she was back out on the 'frontline'.

Last week had been difficult, though. Working so closely with Jay, and not being able to be with him as she was used to, had been hard. She'd lost count of the number of times she'd wanted to reach out and touch him, to be able to share the closeness that she'd taken for granted in the past. Sometimes she'd spotted him looking at her and had wondered if he'd been thinking the same as her, but she'd quickly pushed that thought to the back of her mind.

Emma stifled the urge to yawn as she continued to fill in the payroll spreadsheet that would mean all the staff received their correct payments at the end of the month. She needed to concentrate or she would get it wrong, which would cause a lot of unhappiness, something she didn't want to be responsible for. Unhappy staff. Her thoughts drifted back to her former line manager as they often did these days. She wondered what Heather was doing, now that she was no longer at the Rosemont. The way Heather had left still niggled at Emma. It felt like unfinished business, something she needed to resolve before she could move on. Making sure that no one was watching, Emma pulled up Heather's file, found her address and quickly wrote it down. She decided to pay her a visit, soon. Although she knew it might end in disaster, it was something that she instinctively knew she had to do.

* * *

Emma stood across the road from the block of flats where Heather lived. The area was down-at-heel — the kind of place where gangs of teenagers congregated. She was glad she'd decided to come on her day off, in daylight, rather than after finishing a shift.

For the umpteenth time, Emma wondered why she was doing this. But she was here now and, she decided, she was just going to get on with it. Heather probably wouldn't even want to speak to her and she'd be back on the Tube within half an hour, but at least she could say she'd tried.

She received a few jeers from a group of teenagers as she walked past. She kept her head straight and ignored them, but her hands were clenched in her pockets with fear. Inside, the building smelled of stale beer and urine, and Emma immediately wanted to turn round and walk back the way she'd come. Instead she contemplated the stairs and the lift. Bearing in mind that Heather lived on the sixteenth floor, Emma decided to take the lift, even though she feared it might break down on the way up. She stepped inside and quickly pressed the button to floor sixteen. As the doors closed, she breathed a sigh of relief that she was alone and no one had followed her inside.

The door to Heather's flat had once been painted red, but that had largely peeled off, revealing a grey undercoat. Before she could chicken out, Emma pressed the buzzer and waited. Nothing happened so she pressed it again, half hoping that she'd had a wasted journey. But then she heard footsteps, bolts slipping back and eventually the sound of a key turning in the lock.

When Heather opened the door, Emma tried her best not to reveal her shock. Even though it was the early afternoon, Heather was wearing a dressing gown that had seen better days and bore the stains of many meals. Her hair was lank and greasy, and looked as though it hadn't been brushed in a long time. Her face was pasty and blotchy.

Emma stared. She didn't know what to say.

'What are *you* doing here?' Heather asked.

'I, um, wanted to come and see how you were.'

'Come to gloat, have you?'

'No! I was worried about you. I wanted to see if there was anything I could do to help.'

'Help!' Heather laughed harshly. 'Don't you think you've *helped* me enough? You certainly *helped* me out of my job.'

Emma tried to defend herself. 'I'm sorry if you feel like that, but it wasn't down to me.'

'Started the ball rolling though, didn't you? By snitching on me to management. That's why I had to go off sick and that's when they got me.'

'I didn't speak to management. I was going to. I was angry, but then I thought better of it and went to calm down. Then I heard you'd gone home and I was busy with the functions, so I never said anything.'

Heather frowned at her.

Emma was conscious of being on the landing. 'Can we talk about this inside?'

Heather eventually spoke. 'I suppose so,' She turned and led the way into the living room. Emma followed her, shutting the door behind her.

Inside, the air smelled stuffy and, when Emma walked into the living room, she could see the reason why. The table and floors were littered with old takeaway cartons, dirty plates, mugs and glasses that looked like they'd been there for weeks.

'You'd better sit down.' Heather pointed to a sofa, which was littered with clothes and old newspapers. 'Just push everything to one side.'

Emma cautiously did as she was told — she didn't know what she would find beneath — and gingerly sat down on the edge of the sofa.

Heather plonked herself down into a battered armchair. 'So come on, out with it, what are they saying about me?'

Emma paused. It was obvious that Heather wasn't taking care of herself and she was reluctant to tell her the truth. She wasn't here for revenge.

'That you jumped before you were pushed.'

Heather laughed scornfully. 'That's very true. Largely thanks to you.'

This was the Heather of old. Twisting things so that everything was Emma's fault.

'No, actually, Heather, it's largely down to *you*. Like I said, I never made a complaint about your bullying, but when I was asked questions I answered them honestly.'

'What questions?'

'Like where I was up to on my training programme. The training programme I didn't know existed. You were supposed to be my line manager, there to support me, yet all you did was bully me. I wanted to learn, but all you wanted was to shove me into menial jobs and do the paperwork you were supposed to do but couldn't be bothered.'

'That was all for your own good.'

'How was that for my good?'

Emma flinched as Heather jumped up, but thankfully she just began to pace the cluttered room.

'Because you came in, little Miss Perfect, thinking you knew everything. You needed to be brought down a peg or two.'

'I didn't think I knew everything.'

Heather turned towards Emma and laughed. 'Oh, yes, you did. *Why do you do it this way? Why don't you do it like this?* She mimicked Emma's voice.

'I wanted to learn why things were done a certain way, that's all.'

'No, you didn't. You wanted to criticise. Because you were so perfect, with your perfect looks, your perfect boyfriend and your rich friends.'

'You were jealous.'

'Damn right I was jealous.' Heather was almost screaming at her. 'You've never experienced half of what I have, never had to deal with the shit that life throws at you, and there you were thinking you were better than me.' She began to cry and slumped back down in the armchair with her head in her hands.

Emma was so shocked it was all she could do not to stare at her. Liz had been right all along — the bullying came from Heather's own insecurities. But no matter what Heather had gone through, it didn't give her the right to treat other people the way she had, even if it did explain it.

'That's not true. I wanted us to be friends. How many times did I ask you to come out for a drink with me? And how many times did you turn me down?'

Heather mumbled, 'You only asked me out of pity.'

'No, I didn't.' And while Emma didn't want to tell Heather the real reason she had asked her, the truth was she had wanted to try to understand her. 'I wanted to get to know you.'

'Why?'

'Because I thought that maybe you were lonely.'

'So you did pity me?'

'No, I didn't pity you, because I was lonely too.'

Heather laughed. 'You? Lonely? How could you possibly be lonely with your perfect friends?'

'They're not perfect. But they are ambitious and sometimes that means they get caught up in their own lives. I wanted a friend in the place that I worked. Someone who understood my day-to-day life.'

'Didn't take you long to find some, though, did it, and what did you do when you did? You ridiculed me!'

'I didn't, Heather. It's true, I didn't defend you. It was very difficult to do that, the way you were behaving towards me. But it didn't come from me.'

'And I'm supposed to believe you?'

'That's up to you. I promise you it's the truth, though.' Emma got up, preparing to leave. She was fighting a losing battle here, but at least she had done what she had come here to do. 'I'm going now, but just remember, I took the trouble to come and see you. Why would I do that if I hated you so much?'

'I . . .' Heather faltered. 'I don't know.'

Emma picked up her bag and slung it over her shoulder.

'Please don't go,' Heather said. 'I do believe you and, if it means anything to you, I'm sorry for what I did. I couldn't help myself. I was just eaten up with jealousy.'

Slowly Emma sat back down. 'You have nothing to be jealous of.'

Heather laughed. 'Says you. With your youth, your looks and your slim figure.'

'Looks aren't everything.'

'They are when you haven't got them.'

'So what are you going to do? Wallow in self-pity for the rest of your life?'

Heather sighed. 'What choice do I have?'

Emma stood up again. 'You have the choice not to be bitter and twisted. You have the choice to concentrate on what you do have and make the best of it. Make a real go of your life, rather than sitting here in your own mess, thinking how badly everyone has treated you and taking it out on everyone else.'

'Hah, you make it sound so easy.'

'No, it's not easy.'

'And how would you know?'

'Because, Heather, I don't have the perfect life you've imagined. No one does. I'm on my own too. My parents live abroad and don't give a stuff about me. My ex-boyfriend was obsessed with his career so now I'm living in staff accommodation in one tiny room, that most of the time I daren't leave in case I get pounced on by someone who won't take no for an answer. But it's not always going to be like this. I'm going to make the most of every opportunity and do something with my life.'

'Good for you. But I don't have your opportunities.'

'Opportunities don't just come along,' Emma replied. 'You have to make them happen.'

'There you go again, thinking you know everything. Sit down and I'll tell you about opportunities or lack of them.'

Emma sat down and Heather continued.

'You say your parents don't have time for you, but at least you have parents. I didn't know my father. In fact, I don't think my mother even knew him. He was just someone she slept with when she was blotto with drink. She loved a drink, did my mother. In fact, she loved the drink more than anything else, including me. Even when I was little she'd leave me on my own for hours, often days at a time, when she was on a bender. And when she came back, it was me who looked after her rather than the other way around. She died of liver failure when I was twelve. Looking back, it was amazing she even lasted that long.

'After that I went from one foster home to another. No one loved me enough to keep me and then I went into a children's home with all the other kids that no one wanted. And if you think *I* was a bully, you don't know how bad bullying can be. Most days, I just didn't want to live. But then I met someone. He was called Billy. We fell in love and I thought that was it, that we'd be together for ever, just like in the films. But he left the home before me and got into a bad crowd.' She paused and Emma could see she was struggling with her emotions. 'One night, I was waiting for him at the precinct after school, but he didn't turn up. I was devastated. I thought he'd gone off me. Like everyone else, I wasn't good enough for him. Later I found out he'd been in a fight. The other boy had a knife and that was the end of my Billy.'

'Oh, Heather, I'm so sorry.' Emma wanted to hug her, but didn't think Heather would welcome it.

'And that was that. I realised then that the only person I could ever rely on was myself. And so I did. I got myself a job and I worked my way up. But I never made friends. I couldn't trust anyone to stick around and I've been lonely all my life. I admit I took my unhappiness out on the staff I was supposed to be managing because I was jealous. Not very attractive I know, but I can't help the way I am. And you. I was more jealous of you than anyone else. With your fancy friends and your connections. I couldn't figure out why you'd want a job as a trainee manager at the Rosemont when you had all those endless opportunities. And then you tried to befriend me and that made me even angrier. I didn't want your pity and I'd never trust someone like you. I went out of my way to make your life miserable.' She paused. 'So there you have it. I'm not a nice person and I deserve everything that's happened to me.'

'No, you don't,' Emma said quietly. Heather looked up. 'Yes, you've done some nasty things. In fact, I used to dread coming in to work, not knowing what was in store for me each day. But at the back of my mind I always knew there must be a reason for it. And now I know.'

'Good for you. You've salved your conscience, so you can go now.'

'And what about you?'

'What about me?'

'Are you going to sit here wallowing in self-pity or are you going to clean yourself up, get out there, get yourself a job, and make something of your life? Maybe even find yourself some friends.'

Heather laughed. 'Who would want to be friends with me?'

'Me for a start,' Emma said. 'Now, get yourself in the shower, wash your hair and put on some fresh clothes while I start cleaning up this place. It stinks.'

Heather stared at her open-mouthed for a moment, then turned on her heel and walked into her bedroom.

Smiling, Emma went into the kitchen. But her smile quickly slipped as she took in the devastation. It was far worse than the living room. She found some bin bags tucked away in a drawer and started by tipping all the rubbish into them.

Three big bags were stacked by the back door by the time Heather emerged from the shower. Her hair was wet and she was wearing clean clothes and smelling much fresher.

'Better?' Emma asked.

'Much,' Heather replied. 'Why are you doing this?'

'Because everyone needs some help from time to time. And I'm not doing it out of pity before you say anything. I'm doing it because I think that you deserve a second chance. You've had it tough.'

Heather shook her head in disbelief. 'I don't get why you want to help me.'

'Well, I do,' Emma said. 'But don't think I'm doing all this clearing up on my own.' She threw a clean tea towel at Heather. 'You're on drying-up duty.'

Together they cleared up the flat and an hour later it was looking — and smelling — much better.

'Thanks for this, Emma,' Heather said when they decided to call it a day. 'I got myself into a rut and I didn't know how to get out of it.'

'I'm glad I came. You've helped me too, you know. I was carrying around so much guilt about the way you left, but now I understand what was going on.'

'That I was being a complete bitch.'

Emma smiled. 'You were, but at least I know why. Now, I don't know about you but I need a cup of tea.'

'You'll be lucky,' Heather replied. 'There's no milk or much of anything to be honest.'

'Then we'll go to the shops?' Emma asked.

'Let's go to the pub first. There's one down the road that isn't too bad and does okay food. I'll get you a meal and a drink, and then I'll get some stuff to tide me over until I do a proper shop tomorrow.'

'Okay, then,' Emma said. She felt pleased that Heather seemed keen to get out of her rut. 'But you don't have to pay for me.'

'Yes, I do. If only to thank you for everything you've done for me today.'

* * *

Emma sat back, full after eating an enormous plate of pie and chips, and drinking two glasses of wine from the bottle she and Heather were sharing.

She smiled. 'You know, you're surprisingly good company when you make the effort.'

'You aren't so bad yourself,' Heather replied. 'Maybe I should have taken you up on your invitation before.'

'Maybe you should. But let's not dwell on the past.'

'Well, that's a thought. Might be a hard habit to break. But you're right, I do need to focus on the future.' She paused and then almost whispered, 'Emma, you won't tell the others about my past, will you.'

'Others? You mean the staff at the Rosemont.'

Heather nodded and Emma put her hand over hers. 'I know you must find it difficult, but you can trust me. And, no, I'm not going to go tittle-tattling back to the staff at the hotel. I wouldn't even if I had anyone to tittle-tattle back to.'

'But you're great friends with the crowd, aren't you?'

'Not really. I've been out with them a few times. And I really like Jenny in HR. But apart from that, they're really only work colleagues. I wouldn't call them friends.'

'And what about Nick? He was always drooling over you like a little lost puppy dog.'

'Ah, yes, Nick. He's the one who won't take no for an answer, even though I've made it perfectly clear that nothing is ever going to happen between us.'

'I thought you liked him.'

'I was lonely and I wanted some friends. Jay was always far too busy, especially when he got involved with the competition. And, yes, I admit, like you, I was jealous. He shut me out of his life, celebrated his successes with his fellow competitors and made me feel like I didn't count. So I ended it and that's why I'm living at the Rosemont.'

'But you're still in love with him?'

Emma nodded and felt herself well up.

'And are you sure it really is over between you? From what you've said, it sounds as though there might still be a chance for you two.'

'I don't know. His work will always come first.'

'And you're pretty work-driven from what I can see.'

'I am, but it's not just that.'

'What is it, then?'

Emma stared into the depths of her wine glass. 'Okay, this is going to sound silly, but I felt like he didn't love me enough. He made me feel like I didn't matter, and I loved him so much that I couldn't cope with that.'

'We all need to feel as though we matter,' Heather said.

'He kept saying he'd change, that he'd try harder, but he never did. And besides, if he had really loved me he wouldn't have had to try so hard. That's why I can't go back to him. I can't risk getting hurt like that again.'

To Emma's surprise, Heather burst out laughing. 'We're more similar than I ever expected.'

Emma smiled back. 'Maybe you're right.'

'And yet, you're prepared to give me a second chance, someone you don't even like, but you're not prepared to do that for the man you love.'

'That's because I have too much to lose if I do give him another chance.'

'Looks to me like you've lost everything already. So in that respect you don't have anything to lose.'

'It's not that simple.'

'Then make it simple. Give him a chance to talk to you. You might find that he loves you more than you think he does.'

'That does make sense, I suppose. I still value him as a friend.'

'There you go, then. Practise what you preach and take the opportunity.'

Emma nodded. 'Maybe.'

'Good.'

'And what about you? What are you going to do?'

'I'm going to get myself a job. Maybe not in management.' Heather laughed. 'I don't think I'm very good at that. And something that doesn't involve a lot of paperwork. I hate that.'

'I had noticed.'

Heather's smile faltered. 'I know you think it was because I was lazy. But it's actually because I'm dyslexic.'

'Oh! Why didn't you say something? I could have helped.'

'I didn't want your help, remember?'

'Yes, okay, but I'm here to help now if you need me.'

'Thanks,' Heather said. 'I'll bear that in mind. But I need to get back on my feet through my own efforts.'

'But you'll stay in touch?'

'Of course I will. I want to hear what happens with you and Jay.'

CHAPTER THIRTY-EIGHT

Jay couldn't stop thinking about Emma. He didn't want it to be over between them. Couldn't stand the loneliness of only having her in his life as a friend.

These last weeks had made him realise just how much she had supported him and how much he'd taken that for granted. She had every right to walk away from him. But this had been a massive wake-up call and he wanted to do something to convince her that her actions had made a difference. That he had changed. Nan was right, he needed to fight for her. And if he tried to win her back and it failed, then he would accept that he had done his best and walk away, if that was what she wanted. The only problem was that he was no good at big romantic gestures. The only thing he knew how to do was to cook. Not that that had worked for him the last time he had tried it, he thought, remembering the night that Emma had moved out. What if he cooked for her at Diva's, somewhere on more neutral ground than inviting her round to the flat. Maybe he could ask her as a thank you for all the help she had given him recently? At least then he might have a chance to tell her what was in his heart. Before he could change his mind, he rang her.

* * *

Emma was pondering what to wear after her shift. Jay had asked her to come over to Diva's, and she had happily accepted. They needed to talk. Who knew what the outcome of this evening would be, but everyone was telling her that they needed to listen to each other. And maybe they were right. In their previous conversations, both she and Jay had been too busy trying to get across their own points of view to actually understand what the other was saying. So tonight she was going to listen and, if she did walk away at the end of it, then it would be for the right reasons.

She checked her watch and realised she'd spent far too long faffing over what she was going to wear. If she didn't hurry up, she was going to be very late.

* * *

Jay straightened the knives and forks on the table for the umpteenth time and stood back. He knew he was fussing, but he couldn't help it. Tonight was so very important to him and the outcome could change the rest of his life. He checked his watch. Emma would be here soon. He went back into the kitchen to make sure that everything was ready, even though he'd planned tonight's meal meticulously and knew that he'd done everything he needed to. At least for now. The toughest part would actually be when he was in front of Emma, speaking his truth. If she'd give him a second chance, he would prove to her that he truly loved her. That since she'd left him, his life had only been half worth living.

Jay checked his watch again. She was late. Emma was rarely late for anything.

A knot of fear tightened in his stomach. What if she wasn't coming after all?

* * *

Emma locked her bedroom door behind her, conscious that she was going to be late. As she rushed through the kitchen,

Nick stood up from one of the dining chairs and blocked her way. She had successfully managed to avoid him over the last few weeks, but it looked as though her luck had run out.

'Hi, Emma. Long time no see.' He smiled down at her and took a step towards her.

She took a step back.

'Um, yes, Nick, hi. I've been very busy recently.'

'So I've been hearing. Helping out your ex, I believe.'

'And his business partner who's my friend,' she said defensively. Although why she felt the need to justify herself to him, she didn't know. 'I'm sorry, Nick, I'm just on my way out and I'm already late.'

'Are you avoiding me, Emma?'

There was a sinister note in his voice that she'd never heard before and Emma suddenly felt afraid. She became uncomfortably aware of how empty the accommodation was. 'I'm not avoiding you, Nick. But perhaps we could catch up another time. Like I said, I'm on my way out and I'm late, so if you could just let me pass?'

He ignored her request. 'You look very nice. Going somewhere special?'

'I'm just meeting someone.'

'Meeting Jay?' he asked.

'Well, yes, I am as a matter of fact.'

'He's a very lucky man.' Nick stepped forward. 'But he doesn't deserve you. If you were my girlfriend, I would never neglect you the way he has.' Again she stepped backwards, and realised her mistake as she found her back against the wall with only inches between her and Nick. She could smell beer on his breath and caught a whiff of stale sweat. She stepped to the side, but he blocked her once more.

'Nick, please let me pass.' She cringed as she heard the fear in her voice.

'But I haven't seen you for ages. Can't you at least spare me five minutes?'

'Tomorrow,' she said, trying to pacify him. 'Let's arrange a time tomorrow. Like I said, I need to go.'

'But I don't want to wait until tomorrow. I'm here now and you've been avoiding me for long enough.'

She was about to push him out of her way and make a run for it when her phone rang in her pocket. She quickly grabbed it and glanced at the screen. Jay. She tried to swipe the screen to answer his call, but didn't get a chance as Nick knocked the phone out of her hand. It crashed to the floor.

'Nick! What are you doing?'

She began to tremble.

'Don't fight this, Emma. You know you've wanted me since the moment we met.'

'And you know that's not true.' She tried to remain calm even though now she was very scared. He didn't look or sound like a man who could be reasoned with.

He pushed her against the wall, leaving no room for escape, and then his hands were all over her. She was repulsed by his touch.

'Get off me!'

She attempted to push him away, but he just laughed and leaned in to kiss her.

* * *

Emma was really late now. Jay was torn between convincing himself she wasn't coming and thinking it unlike her to not turn up without letting him know. Even if it was just a text message. He decided to call her. If she told him she wasn't coming he'd be disappointed — more than disappointed — but at least he'd have an answer. His throat went dry as he listened to the number ring out. Then it went dead. Had she rejected his call? It wasn't at all like Emma to ignore him, especially as she had agreed to come, and knew he would be waiting for her. He was hit with a terrible suspicion that something was very wrong. Without thinking, Jay grabbed his keys and rushed out to his van. Instinct told him he needed to get to Emma as soon as he could.

Jay was in a state of near panic by the time he reached the hotel, his eyes scanning the pavements as he drove. And then he spotted her dashing down the road towards the Tube station, glancing over her shoulder from time to time as she ran. There was a look of sheer terror on her face. He pulled in towards the pavement and called to her through the open window. Emma turned at the sound of her name. Fear was written all over her face, but it was quickly replaced by relief as she realised who it was.

'Jay!' She rushed over to the van, wrenched the door open and threw herself inside, slamming the door behind her. 'Can you just drive, please? As quickly as possible and lock the doors too?'

Although he was desperate to know what was wrong, Jay did as he was asked.

'Where do you want me to drive to?'

'Anywhere as long as it's far away from here.'

He glanced at her. She was breathing heavily and her blouse was in a state of disarray. She normally looked so neat. When her breathing had slowed down, he asked. 'Are you okay?'

'Yes, I think so.' But her voice was wobbly. 'At least I am now.'

'Did someone hurt you?' He tried to keep his eyes on the road and not on her.

She nodded. 'Nick.'

Rage flared inside him.

'Do you need to go to hospital?'

'No, I'm fine. He scared me more than anything. Although . . .' She paused. 'I bit his lip, which was enough to make my escape. He's the one who's injured.'

'So he attacked you?'

'He wouldn't let me past, pinned me against the wall, put his hands where I didn't want them to go.' He glanced over and saw her shudder. 'If I hadn't managed to fight back, I don't like to think about what might have happened.'

Neither did he.

'So, tell me what you want to do?'

In almost a whisper she said. 'I want to report him to the police. I suspect this isn't the first time he's tried something like this and I doubt it will be the last.'

'Okay, that's fine. And if I'm being honest, I think that's the right thing to do. I'll drive you.'

'Thank you.'

'Do you want me to come in with you, or would you rather do this on your own?'

'I'd like you to come with me, Jay, if you don't mind?'

'Of course I don't mind, and I'll wait for you until it's all over.'

'Thanks, Jay.'

* * *

An hour later, Jay's backside was numb from sitting on the hard plastic chair while he waited for Emma. He wished he could have been by her side during her interview. She'd been through enough tonight. He was so angry with Nick that he wanted to go round and smash his face in. But he knew he had to leave it to the police and hope that they would be able to do their job properly.

The sound of a door opening and footsteps approaching alerted him to Emma's return. His instinct was to hug her, but he stopped himself just in time as he realised she might not welcome physical contact right now. Instead he smiled at her.

'You okay?'

She nodded, but her face was pale. 'They're going to bring him in for questioning. Oh, Jay!' She slumped into one of the plastic chairs and he sat down next to her, resisting the urge to put his arm around her. 'I don't know what to do. I can't go back there and I've nowhere else to go.'

'Of course you do. You can stay with me. In the spare bedroom, of course, or if you're not comfortable with that I'm sure my nan will put you up. She thinks the world of you, you know.'

'No, I'd rather stay with you.'

'Then you shall. Are you okay to leave?'

Emma stood up. 'Yes. Let's get out of here before they bring him in.'

* * *

Emma sat on the sofa, her legs curled up to the side of her, the gas-flame fire flickering and lulling her into sleepiness. She knew she would have to get up and go to bed soon, but the thought of sleeping and possibly reliving tonight in her dreams put her off.

'Do you want another cup of tea?'

Emma shook her head. 'No, thanks. I suppose I should try to get some sleep. If I can sleep that is.' She paused. 'I'm supposed to be in the office tomorrow, but I'm not sure if I can face it.'

'I doubt they'll expect you to come in when they find out what's happened.'

She nodded. 'All my stuff's there. I've got nothing with me. Not even my phone. He swiped it from my hand when I tried to answer your call, and I didn't get a chance to pick it up. I just ran.'

'Speak to work in the morning and, if they can make sure he isn't around, I'll go and get your things. Hopefully I'll find your phone, too.'

'You'd do that?'

'Of course I will. But I'd prefer it if he wasn't there. I don't think I could be responsible for my actions if he was.'

'Thank you, Jay. I really appreciate everything you're doing for me.'

'There's no need for thanks. I just wish it hadn't happened in the first place.'

'Me too.' She yawned. 'I think I'll try to get some sleep.'

'The spare bed is all made up for you. Sleep is probably the best thing.'

'Yes, I just hope I don't have nightmares.'

299

'Well, if you need anything at all, whatever the time, just give me a shout and I'll be there.'

'Thanks, Jay.' She paused. 'There's one thing I don't get about tonight.'

'What's that?'

'Why did you come looking for me?'

He shrugged. 'Instinct, I suppose. I knew it wasn't like you not to answer my call when you knew I was expecting you. So I just assumed that something was wrong and that you might need my help.'

'And so you dropped everything to come for me.'

'Well, yes.'

'I'm glad you did, Jay. That means so much.'

* * *

Despite waking with a jolt several times throughout the night and having strange dreams, Emma woke the next morning with a sense of relief. She was safe and lying in the spare bedroom of her former home. Not the staff accommodation, where Nick could be waiting for her.

There was a knock on the door and Jay walked in with a tray of coffee and toast.

'Oh, Jay, you didn't have to do that. But thank you.'

'I've got my phone here too in case you want to call work.'

'Oh, yes, I'll need to phone in before my shift starts.'

'I'll leave you to it, then. I've got to pop out for a little while, so you've got the place to yourself to shower and what-not, but I'm around later if you want to arrange a time for me to pick up your stuff. I'm sure you'll feel a lot better when you're wearing different clothes.'

'That would be great. Thanks.'

Emma's hand trembled as she dialled the number for the hotel and asked to be put through to Faye. It took a while for her to explain what had happened, but Faye was appalled at what she'd been through at the hands of Nick.

'Rest assured, Emma, we will conduct a thorough investigation into this. I won't stand for my staff being assaulted, especially by other members of staff. He'll be suspended while we investigate and told to make other living arrangements.'

'Thank you.'

Emma was relieved when she put the phone down. She'd been given a week off work while Nick was being investigated and she would ask Jay if he could pick up her things later that afternoon.

Jay. She sighed as she thought about him. She would always be grateful for how considerate he'd been last night, and that he'd cared enough to come and find her.

Later that afternoon, Jay returned with her belongings and she changed into fresh clothes, then she went back into the living room and sat down on the sofa opposite to where Jay was sitting.

'Feeling better?' he asked.

'Much.' Emma paused. 'I'm really sorry if I'm a burden to you, Jay. I'll find somewhere else to live as soon as I can. Even if Nick isn't around anymore, I can't face going back to the staff accommodation.'

'I don't blame you, Em. And you're not a burden. There's no need to find somewhere else as you're always welcome here.'

'I'm not sure, Jay. It's very kind of you, but we're not together now so it will probably just confuse things.'

'That's what I wanted to talk to you about last night.'

'It is?' Hope flared within her.

'Yes, but after what happened it wasn't the right time for a conversation about the state of our relationship.'

'Maybe it wasn't then.' Emma could feel her heart pounding, hoping that Jay would tell her what she wanted to hear.

'I know you feel I took you for granted throughout our relationship,' he began, 'especially during the competition. It's something I bitterly regret. I wish I could turn the clock back and change the way that I acted. And I want you to know that I do love you. Very much. And I don't want to be without you. Life without you has been utterly miserable.'

301

Emma nearly cheered at his words, but she couldn't push her own feelings under the carpet. She needed to explain too.

'It's been miserable for me too. But I realise now that I rather acted in haste. I was hurt and my instinct was to protect myself, so I ran away.'

'I made you feel that you weren't good enough for me. But if anything, it's the other way round. I've always felt so at ease with you. You really get me and you've always understood that my ambition is a big part of me. You made me feel safe and I thought you'd always be around, so I neglected your needs. I realise now that I needed to put the work into our relationship to make sure you always knew how much you mean to me.'

Emma felt the tears well up in her eyes and blinked them back. This wasn't the time for tears — it was time to be brave. 'Well, you certainly proved that last night. But it takes two to make a relationship work, Jay. And I'm prepared to put the work in too, that's if you're willing to give us another go.'

Jay sprang up from the sofa, sat down beside her and cupped her face with his hands.

'Oh, Em! Of course I'm willing. That's what last night was all about. I said it was a meal to thank you for all the help you'd given me, but really I just wanted the opportunity to talk to you, to tell you how I really feel.'

Her eyes widened. 'Diva's? I'd forgotten all about that. What will Tia say about your abandoned meal?'

Jay laughed. 'Tia's gone away, so she won't be saying anything. Besides, Liz and I are now officially tenants, so we can do what we like. Although I left in such a rush that I had to go there first thing this morning to tidy everything away.'

'I wondered where you'd gone.' She leaned in and kissed him gently. Their kiss deepened and she felt her whole body tingling. Before they got carried away, she pulled back. 'So we're back on, then?'

He smiled. 'If you'll have me.'

'Oh, I'll have you, all right.'

EPILOGUE

'Will I do?'

Betty walked into the kitchen wearing a cream blouse and lilac two-piece suit.

'You look lovely, Betty,' Emma said.

'Well, I wouldn't want to show Jay up.'

'You could never do that,' Emma replied. 'Besides, it's your eightieth birthday party so you can wear whatever you want. And say whatever you want, too.'

'I don't know about that, going to a posh place like Diva's.'

'It's the function room, Betty. It's been hired for you and Jay is making all your favourite foods. Everyone is going to be there to celebrate you.'

Betty pulled at the sleeves of her jacket. 'Can't say I much like being the centre of attention.'

'You'll be all right once you get there and you're surrounded by all your friends and family. And until you're comfortable, I'll be right by your side.'

Betty smiled. 'You're a good girl. Our Jay's lucky to have you.'

'That's what I keep telling him.' Emma grinned back and took Betty's arm. 'Now come on, that's our taxi outside bibbing its horn.'

As they moved through the London traffic, Emma contemplated the last six months. Her and Jay's relationship had gone from strength to strength, now that they understood each other better. And while he was still very much focused on work, thriving at running the business alone, they made sure they spent their time off together doing fun things. Shortly after the competition, Jay had been approached by Lord Weatherton.

'I'm not going to beat around the bush and I know that you're busy holding the fort for Liz at the moment, but my contacts tell me you have a hankering to have your own restaurant.'

'That's the dream, yes, but it won't be for a while yet.'

'Well, that's okay, I'm prepared to wait.'

Jay frowned. 'What do you mean?'

Lord Weatherton grinned at him. 'Well, I'm sure you know how much I like my food.'

'Your feedback is always much appreciated.' Jay tried to be diplomatic.

'Well, then. I took a shine to Liz and her catering, and since then I've taken a shine to you too. Especially since you won the regional competition.'

'Well, thanks, but I still don't understand.'

'I want to back you. Your talent and my money and business experience. I don't see how we could fail.'

'But I . . .' Jay was at a loss for words.

'I won't pressure you, though. I know you've got your hands full at the moment, and you will have until Liz can come back to work and you can get things in order for her to take over again. But when you're ready, come and see me, and we'll talk about what can be done.'

'Thank you,' was all Jay could say.

Emma smiled to herself. Jay had been astounded by the offer and hardly able to take it all in, but it had given him the confidence he'd needed to start planning his future. The best bit, though, as far as Emma was concerned, was that he talked his ideas through with her and valued her opinion. No longer was she on the outside looking in.

Another massive change to Emma's life was her friendship with Heather. After dusting herself off, Heather had found a job in an elderly persons' care home. Despite how she had been at the hotel, it turned out that she loved caring for the elderly, and she had soon developed a rapport with the residents. And when Betty had announced she was going to look for a lodger and someone who could also help around the house, Emma had thought she knew the perfect person. She'd introduced Heather to Betty, and the pair of them had become instant friends, as she'd known they would.

Heather was a different person to the one Emma had first met at the Rosemont, and she had blossomed under Betty's care. Likewise, Betty had told Emma that she couldn't imagine living on her own again.

The taxi arrived at Diva's and Emma helped Betty out of the car. Betty looked at the front of the restaurant nervously.

'Lovely. It looks posh, though.'

'Fit for the queen you are.' Emma smiled and took Betty's arm. 'Come on now. Time to meet your fans.'

Although it wasn't a surprise party, Jay had asked everyone to arrive early so that Betty could make a proper entrance with her guests already in situ.

Heather was the first to greet her at the doors to the function room and, as she led them inside, cheers rang out for Betty. And then Jay was standing in front of them with a big grin on his face and Betty visibly relaxed. As Emma had predicted, it wasn't long before she found her stride and revelled in being the centre of attention.

Smiling, Emma left her to it. Jay's mum stopped to talk to her.

'I know I've said it to you before,' Mary said warmly. 'But I'm really glad you're in Jay's life.'

'I'm glad I am too.'

'Everything's changed so much since you got back together. He's the happiest I've ever seen him and I can't tell you what it means to have him back in my life too.'

'There was always something missing when you were estranged,' Emma said. 'And it's so good to be part of your family.'

'If you can stand our noisy lot.'

'Oh, that's not a problem at all,' Emma replied, thinking of how quiet her own childhood had been and how she had always longed for the chaos of a happy family. Even if they weren't blood-related, she was part of that now and they couldn't have made her feel more welcome.

Over the last six months, Jay's family had started to regularly drop round at Betty's, and she and Jay cooked Sunday dinner for them all, which was a lot less stressful than that first time. Even Jay was more relaxed around them. His relationship with his stepfather was never going to be easy, but at least they could bear to be in each other's company, and the bond between Jay and his half-brothers was slowly developing.

'And look at Heather,' Mary continued. 'Hovering over Mum like a mother hen.'

'They've certainly hit it off,' Emma said, pleased with herself for introducing them.

'And I'm grateful that Mum isn't living on her own anymore. It's a real weight off my mind.'

'I think everyone's happy with the arrangement,' Emma said. 'And she's good for Heather too, which makes it more of an equal relationship, while giving Betty her independence.'

Mary laughed. 'And goodness knows, my mother needs her independence.'

'It looks as though everything is coming right,' Emma said, although she couldn't help thinking about the fly in the ointment. Nick.

Although the police had charged him with assault, he'd pleaded not guilty and in the next few weeks she was going to have to give evidence against him. She was dreading it, but she knew she'd have the courage to do it because Jay would be by her side. Her management-trainee contract at the Rosemont was almost at an end and while she had thoroughly enjoyed working at the hotel, and had learned so much, the spirit of Nick still remained and often made her uneasy. After the investigation he'd been sacked and, although he was officially not allowed to come anywhere near her, she was constantly looking over her shoulder, wondering if he might show up. Recently she'd begun to contemplate whether she should change jobs at the end of her contract so she wasn't living in fear of him.

Liz joined Emma and Mary, carrying baby Isabel on her hip. Isabel had grown so much over these last few months and Emma absolutely adored her. Both she and Jay had been thrilled when Liz and Alex had asked them to be godparents.

'It's a lovely party,' Liz said. 'And Betty's in her element.'

'She is now, yes.' Emma smiled. 'Looking at her, you wouldn't believe how nervous she was earlier. She thought that Diva's was far too posh for her and told me she didn't like being the centre of attention.'

Liz burst out laughing. 'Well, I think she's got over her fears.'

'Looks that way. She puts on a big front about how nothing fazes her, but she took quite a knock when she found out about her illness. Underneath she's a lot more vulnerable than she makes out.'

'She's lucky though, she's got all her family supporting her. As well as Heather.'

Liz had been shocked when Emma had told her about her growing friendship with her former boss, and even more surprised when Emma had suggested that Heather move in with Betty.

'You were spot on that day at Lord Weatherton's when you told me the key to understanding her behaviour was finding out what her insecurity was.'

'And it's down to your perseverance that her life has changed.'

'She deserves some happiness,' Emma said. 'She's had it really tough.'

Liz nodded. 'And what about you? Are you happy? You and Jay?'

'We are,' Emma said. 'Couldn't be happier.'

'I'm pleased for you,' Liz said and smiled.

'What?' Emma asked. 'You're hiding something, Elizabeth Sinclaire. I can always tell.'

Liz laughed. 'Purely your imagination. I'm not hiding anything. Listen, Alex and I can't stay long as we need to get this little one to bed or life won't be worth living tomorrow. But I know that Alex wanted to have a word with you before we leave.'

'Oh, yes, what about?'

'I'll let him explain,' Liz said as Alex joined them.

Emma smiled at Alex. 'Sounds mysterious.'

'I'll just go and say my goodbyes to everyone,' Liz said.

When she'd gone, Alex said, 'I know your contract at the Rosemont is coming to an end shortly.'

'Yes, it is.'

'And Liz told me you've felt a little bit uncomfortable since Nick.'

'I have, yes. I've loved working there, but I'm still nervous around the place.'

'I can see why you'd feel like that. The thing is, we've got a management position coming up at the Grange and we were wondering if you'd be interested in it.'

Emma was speechless. 'Really?'

'Yes, I know when we've spoken about working with us before, you said you preferred to go your own way, but I think you've learned so much at the Rosemont that we'd be offering you the job based on your skills and experience, rather than because we know you.'

'Oh, I see. And what makes you say I've learned a lot at the Rosemont?'

'Ah, well.' Alex couldn't quite look her in the eye. 'I had a word with Faye — and she couldn't sing your praises highly enough.'

'You spoke to Faye?'

'Yes.'

'And she wants to get rid of me, does she?'

'Quite the contrary. In fact, she was miffed about me headhunting you. But she thinks a fresh start might be good for you.'

'Oh, right.' Emma was once more lost for words at Faye's thoughtfulness.

'In fact, if you do agree to work for us I think I'll have to watch out for her poaching you back further down the line. So what do you think?'

'I'm a bit shocked, to be honest,' Emma said. 'But I am interested.'

'Great.' Alex grinned. 'Why don't you give me a ring next week and we can fix a date for you to come and have a look around the hotel, and meet some of the staff? We can take it from there.'

'Sounds like a plan,' Emma said.

Liz came back over to them. 'Well, you're both smiling, so that must be a good sign.'

'Let's just say we're working on it.' Alex gave Emma a wink.

'That's good timing because I think Betty is about to give a speech.'

Betty stood up from the chair she'd been sitting in, while Jay tapped the side of a wine glass with a fork.

'So much for the woman who didn't want to be the centre of attention,' Emma whispered as the room hushed. Liz chuckled.

Betty thanked everyone for coming and said that she was delighted so many people had turned up to share her eightieth birthday with her.

'My family and friends mean everything to me, so it's wonderful that you're all here tonight. And while this may be my eightieth birthday, I still feel like I'm in my twenties and I have plenty of things to do before I pop my clogs, so I'm planning on sticking around for a good while yet.'

Everyone laughed, and then began to sing as a birthday cake was brought into the room. Betty blew out the candles and as the cake was taken away she looked towards Jay, who called once more for hush. 'Over to you, Jay.'

The colour rose in Jay's cheeks as he cleared his throat. 'As you all know, I'd much rather be hiding back in the kitchen than taking centre stage, but tonight is a very special night and I'm hoping to make it even more special.' He looked over to Emma.

'Em? Could you come and join me, please?'

Puzzled, Emma looked to Liz and Alex, who were both smiling.

'You knew about this, didn't you?'

Liz said nothing, but pushed her gently forward. Hesitantly Emma made her way towards Jay, and felt her face flush with embarrassment as everyone's eyes landed on her. Jay held out his hand and drew her to him.

'Emma, you know I'm not big on romantic gestures, but tonight I wanted to show you how much you I love you.' He reached into his jacket pocket, pulled out a small box and went down on one knee before opening the box. 'Emma Taylor, will you marry me?'

Emma looked at Jay in disbelief and saw love shining in his eyes.

All her life she'd felt second best, but not tonight. Tonight she knew she was truly loved, and knew exactly where she belonged. She wanted to hang on to this feeling for ever.

Without hesitation she answered with a smile that lit up her face.

'Yes, Jay, I'd be absolutely honoured to become your wife.'

THE END

ACKNOWLEDGEMENTS

I would like to thank the Choc Lit team for their support, encouragement and belief in me as a writer. I am so lucky to have you as my publisher.

Thank you to my editors, Becky Slorach and Jasmine Callaghan, who have worked with me to strengthen this book.

Thank you also to the Choc Lit family, who are such a support.

Finally, thanks to The Lightfooters, a writing group based in Southport, and named in honour of Freda Lightfoot. You a such a lovely bunch of people and I finally feel like I have found my tribe.

THANK YOU

I hope you enjoyed Jay and Emma's story and also catching up with Liz and Alex following their wedding in *Things They Never Said*.

If you enjoyed *Things We Need to Say* then please do leave a review on the website where you bought the book. Every review really does help a new author like me.

You can find me on Twitter, Facebook and Instagram:

Facebook: linda.middleton.735

Instagram: @middletonwrites

X (Twitter): @middletonwrites

Please do get in touch for all the latest news. I look forward to chatting with you.

Much love
Linda x

THE CHOC LIT STORY

Established in 2009, Choc Lit is an independent, award-winning publisher dedicated to creating a delicious selection of quality women's fiction.

We have won 18 awards, including Publisher of the Year and the Romantic Novel of the Year, and have been shortlisted for countless others. In 2023, we were shortlisted for Publisher of the Year by the Romantic Novelists' Association.

All our novels are selected by genuine readers. We are proud to publish talented first-time authors, as well as established writers whose books we love introducing to a new generation of readers.

In 2023, we became a Joffe Books company. Best known for publishing a wide range of commercial fiction, Joffe Books has its roots in women's fiction. Today it is one of the largest independent publishers in the UK.

We love to hear from you, so please email us about absolutely anything bookish at choc-lit@joffebooks.com.

If you want to receive free books every Friday and hear about all our new releases, join our mailing list here: www.joffebooks.com/freebooks.